An Obedient Father

KT-171-463

Praise for *An Obedient Father*

'Sharma's style is direct . . . His triumph is that he makes his crowded urban canvas not only vivid but memorable as well. In Karan, in particular, Sharma has created an iconic character in South Asian literature: a cross between Jabba the Hutt and Uriah Heep, an evil, ingratiating man festering in a society that refuses to acknowledge the rot at its core.'
Daily Telegraph

'"Weeper of handsome tears": it perfectly sums up Akhil Sharmer's cunning, dismaying and beautifully conceived portrait of a corrupt man in a corrupt society. . . . Our tradition says more or less: A person is evil and is or is not punished, at some point internalising the evil in the person. Mr. Sharma's message is subtly different – *An Obedient Father* is hard, as well as rich and enthralling.'
Richard Eder, *New York Times*

'An almost demonic energy is locked up in Akhil Sharma's debut novel . . . This is an uncompromising novel, a portrait of a country ravaged by vendetta and graft, its public spaces loud with the complaints of religious bigots and its private spaces cradling unspeakable pain. There is no forgiveness for Ram. He is only one monster among many, but he is the monster we know; we have heard him run the gamut of his excuses, and we excuse nothing. But the compassion and energy of Sharma's fine novel alerts us to this: a man his more than his crime.'
Hilary Mantel, *New York Review of Books*

'*An Obedient Father* is a harsh and elegant novel. . . . The triumph of the book is not to make this character appealing or defensible – how could it do that and why would it want to? – but to make him such an intelligent witness of his own disarray.'
The London Review of Books

'The themes of crime and punishment that Sharma explores so tellingly make the parallels with Dostoyevsky's masterpiece compelling and instructive. To the ever-growing list of Indian-American writers lighting up the American sky . . . we must now add the name of Akhil Sharma. That this novel is a début is an astonishment.'
Newsday

'Brilliant . . . Sharma's central achievement in this compelling novel is the subtlety and stealth with which he reveals the extent of Ram Karan's moral decay . . . This is a book that grips with its realism, the language is direct and uncomplicated, the characters' thoughts simply and clearly stated, the descriptions sharp and hard. Yet there is no lack of compassion . . . Sharma writes without judgment, the possibility of redemption always present. Vile though his creation is, Ram Karan is real and totally alive, even after this extraordinary book is closed.'
The Scotsman

'A supernova in the galaxy of young, talented Indian writers, Sharma débuts with a bold and shocking novel that casts a mesmerising spell.'
Publishers Weekly

'Akhil Sharma must be quaking in his boots. How can he follow up such an incredible first novel? . . . Sharma's characters are larger than life. He shows people as they are, with their mixtures of absurdity and moral ambiguity, and paints what he sees, no matter how disturbing the sight. The result is a gripping novel which cannot fail to shock'
Punch

'Sharma adopts a dogged realism of the type once described as gritty or dirty . . . (his) prose is clear, dry and short on obvious felicities . . . For those who like their realism hardboiled, Sharma's the man.'
Literary Review

'It is strong testament to Akhil Sharma's skill as a writer then, that as the novel progresses and more of Mr Karan's despicable actions are revealed, you feel pity rather than contempt for him. Sharma has a great understanding of human weaknesses, and his technique of relating the incidents from the viewpoint of both father and daughter makes the reader party to this understanding . . . It may not be the most enjoyable book you'll read this year, but it'll be one of the most compelling.'
The List

'The subject matter may be grim, but the book is full of fascination and even charm, thanks to its vivid descriptions of contemporary Indian life and deftly drawn characters.' *Sunday Express*

'Akhil Sharma's smoothly startling, highly accomplished début novel . . . Its great strength is the unflinching tragi-comic portrayal of emotional negotiations in families anywhere. A good global read.' *Hampstead and Highgate Express*

'Beautifully conceived . . . *An Obedient Father* is hard as well as rich and enthralling.' *New York Times*

'A powerful début novel that establishes Sharma as a supreme story-teller with a gift for the macabre . . . Emotions run at feverish levels throughout the novel and Sharma's direct prose helps maintain a remarkably even keel . . . In Karan, Sharma has created one of the most distasteful protagonists in recent memory.' *Philadelphia Inquirer*

'Squalid and compelling: the tale of a corrupt civil servant in Delhi who ruins lives, his own included, by having seduced his own daughter . . . The story is almost Aeschylean in the tumult of its misery – deaths, heart attacks, widowings, suicides, even murder – yet the plain, unstoried quality of life itself is never neglected by Sharma. The daily life of poverty-stricken Delhi is ever made real and even the monstrously ruinous Karan consistently makes evident his intelligence, depth and sensitivity . . . a début that's pathetic, remorseless and wrenching.' *Kirkus Review*

'Sharma's writing is calm and precise, partaking more of Raymond Carver's compressed rhythms than Salman Rushdie's winding indulgences . . . Sharma does more than map a terrain of despair. By withholding judgment of his characters he allows them to fully engage with considerable flaws – but also with desperate humour and struggling hopefulness Sharma cannily offers redemption as a possibility, without allowing his characters to embrace it. This strategy pays off in a novel that is astonishingly rich and vivid yet unremittingly realistic.' *Philadelphia Weekly*

'Sharma's talent lies in bringing alive his characters and the dark world they inhabit.' *Seattle Times*

an *OBEDIENT* *father*

AKHIL SHARMA

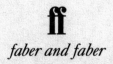

faber and faber

For my brother, Anup,

and for my parents, Jai and Pritam

I wish to thank Carolyn Helene Wilsker Green,
my high school English teacher; also Naeem Murr,
Nancy Packer, Lisa Swanson, and Chris Wiman.

———————————

First published in the United States by
Farrar, Straus and Giroux Inc., New York in 2000
First published in the United Kingdom in 2001
by Faber and Faber Limited
3 Queen Square London WC1N 3AU
This open market edition first published in 2001
This paperback edition published in 2002

Printed in England by Mackays of Chatham Ltd, Chatham, Kent

A CIP record for this book is available from the British Library

ISBN 0-571-20678-6

10 9 8 7 6 5 4 3 2 1

AN OBEDIENT FATHER

ONE

I needed to force money from Father Joseph, and it made me nervous. He had bribed me once before, for a building permit, soon after he became principal of Rosary School. Also, he had admitted my granddaughter, Asha, into his school without our having to make the enormous donation usually required. But Father Joseph was strange and unpredictable.

Several months ago, his school, in a posh part of Old Delhi, had given a dinner party to introduce him. Because of my work for the Delhi municipal education department, I was invited. During the party Father Joseph demonstrated his expertise in karate. The party was in the school's front field. A steel pole had been cemented upright several meters from the buffet tables. Father Joseph, short, and heavy with muscle, wearing the white robe of a karate teacher, beat at the pole for half an hour with his bare feet and fists while

3

forty or fifty people watched and ate. Sometimes he would step a few feet from the pole and groan at it. Near the end of his demonstration, he became so tired that there were pauses as long as a minute between blows. Because this was so odd, and because Father Joseph had spoken to me in English when the party started, at first I thought the display might be an example of a foreign affectation. After he was done, still dressed in the robe, Father Joseph spent the rest of the night meeting his guests. He kept clenching and unclenching his hands from soreness.

It was morning. The sky was a single blue from edge to edge. I had just bathed and was on my balcony hanging a towel over the ledge. The May heat was so intense that as soon as I stepped out of the flat, worms of sweat appeared on my bald scalp. In the squatter colony behind our compound several women crouched before their huts, cooking breakfast on kerosene stoves. Two men wearing only shorts and rubber slippers stood next to a hand pump, soaping their bodies. On the roof of a nearby building, a woman was bathing her daughter with a tin bucket and a bowl. The naked girl, perhaps seven or eight years old, kept slipping out of her mother's grasp and running about the roof.

I had been Mr. Gupta's moneyman for a little less than a year and was no good. It did not take me long to realize this, and once I did, unwilling to give up the increased pay, I tried to delight in having achieved a position that exceeded my ability. I enjoyed believing that I had tricked Mr. Gupta into giving me a place near all the illegal money that poured through the education department. This pleased me so much that I pictured myself weeping in the middle of negotiations with some school principal and calling myself a "whore" while I kept a hand over my heart. But on the mornings before bribe collections, these fantasies came involuntarily. Now, instead of making me laugh, they made me feel threatened, as if I were crazy and out of control.

The principals I extorted were better educated than I was and generally far more competent and responsible. I had never graduated from higher secondary, and my job as a junior officer in the physical education department officially involved little more than counting cricket bats and badminton rackets and making sure that 4 percent of a school's land was used for physical education.

My panic in negotiations was so apparent that even people who were eager to bribe me became resentful. At the meals they were custom-bound to serve with the bribe, they joked about my weight. "You're as good as two men," they might say as I piled food on my plate, or would remark, "Have you been fasting?" With principals who appeared even more uncertain than I was, I sometimes grew angry to the point of incoherence. Occasionally—because of my heart attack seven months earlier and the medicines I now took—as I talked with them, I got tired, confused, and sleepy.

My general incompetence and laziness at work had been apparent for so long that I now think it was arrogant of Mr. Gupta to pick me as his moneyman. I am the type of person who does not make sure that a file includes all the pages it must have or that the pages are in the right order. I refuse to accept even properly placed blame, lying outright that somebody else had misplaced the completed forms or spilled tea on them, even though I was the last one to sign them out or had the soggy papers still on my desk. All this is common for a certain type of civil servant who knows that he is viewed with disdain by his superiors and that he cannot lose his job. My predecessor as moneyman, Mr. Bajwa, used to lie even about what he had brought for lunch. He would rather eat on the office roof than not lie. Mr. Bajwa, however, had incredible energy. He also had a compulsion to court everyone who came near him. Many times he had told me that I was one of his best friends, even though it was apparent that he did not like me.

He had to be replaced because, when V. P. Singh defeated Rajiv Gandhi and became Prime Minister in the last elections, the Central Bureau of Investigation wanted to show its loyalty to the new rulers by attacking the Congress Party and its supporters. They brought corruption charges against Mr. Bajwa. Since then, Rajiv Gandhi had forced out V. P. Singh and put Rajiv's pawn Chandrashekar in power. And the upcoming elections might make Rajiv Gandhi Prime Minister again.

When the mother finished bathing her daughter, I went inside.

The last twelve months had been long and sorrowful. They began with my wife, Radha, finally dying of cancer. A few months later, I had a heart attack that woke me in the middle of the night screeching, "My heart is breaking," so loudly that my neighbors kicked open the door of the flat to see what was happening. More recently, my son-in-law Rajinder had died when his scooter slipped from beneath him on an oil slick. And then Anita, my daughter, and eight-year-old Asha had come to live with me, bringing with them a sadness so apparent that sometimes I had to look away.

Asha was asleep on my cot with one knee pulled up to her stomach. My room is a windowless narrow rectangle, and the little light from the balcony and kitchen, funneled through the common room behind me, was a handkerchief on her face. Asha sometimes fell asleep on my cot while she waited for me to leave the bathroom. I knelt beside the cot to wake her gently. Her eyelids were trembling.

When Rajinder was alive and Anita used to bring Asha with her on visits, I would ask Asha how school was and offer her round orange-flavored toffees that, despite her laughing denials, I claimed grew on a small tree in a cupboard. Nothing else was expected from me. Since they had moved in two months ago, misery as intense as terror had drained all the fat from Asha's body, making her teeth appear larger than they were and her fingers impossibly long. This made me try to say more, but when I asked her about herself, I felt false and intrusive.

As I kept looking at Asha, I noticed it was possible to see her as pretty. Her face was almost square and her hair chopped short like a boy's, but there was something both strong and vulnerable about her. She had long eyelashes and a mouth that was too large for her face and hinted at an adult personality. I wondered whether I was finding beauty in Asha because her youth was a distraction from my own worries, like turning to a happy memory during distress. I put a hand on Asha's knee. It was the size of an egg and its delicacy made me conscious of her lighter-than-air youth and of my enormous body pressing down on my scarred heart.

In the squatter colony a hand pump creaked and someone made clucking sounds as a horse stomped. I heard Anita's sari sighing as she moved about the kitchen. The municipality gave our neighborhood water in the morning for only three hours. "Wake up," I said. "The water will go soon."

Asha stepped out of the bathroom into the common room. She wore her school uniform, a blue shirt and a maroon skirt. The common room is nearly empty and has pink walls and a gray concrete floor. In a corner a fridge hums, because the kitchen is too small to hold it. Along a wall crouch a pair of low wooden chairs. On the bathroom's outside wall are a sink and a mirror. Asha looked in the mirror and combed her hair. The prettiness she had had while sleeping was still there. I could take care of Asha, as I had by arranging her admission to Rosary School. The idea of purpose soothed me.

Father Joseph was going to be difficult and disorderly. I had no subsidized land or loan to offer in immediate return for the money I needed to collect. The funds were for the Congress Party's parliamentary campaign, and the favors earned by donating would have to be cashed in later. Also, this was the second time in twelve months that Parliament had been dissolved and elections called. Most of the principals I handled for Mr. Gupta, the supervisor of Delhi municipality's physical education program, were resisting a second donation. Besides, I had to collect enough to impress the Congress Party officials who reviewed Mr. Gupta's efforts, but I could not take so much that Father Joseph would later resist giving when the money was for those of us who worked in the education department.

Asha went onto the balcony and hung her towel beside mine on the ledge. In comparison, hers looked little bigger than a washcloth. When she returned, I asked, "Do you want some yogurt?" The only time Asha ate anything eagerly was when she thought that the food was in some way special. Asha normally got yogurt only with dinner. I ate yogurt twice a day because the doctor had suggested it.

For a moment she looked surprised. Then she said, "Absolutely."

"Get two bowls and spoons and the yogurt."

Asha brought these. I was too fat to fold my legs and so usually sat with them open in a V. She knelt before me and, placing the bowls between my legs, began spooning yogurt into them. I was wearing just an undershirt and undershorts, as I normally do around the flat. But that morning, because I had seen Asha as pretty for the first time, I felt shy and tried pulling in my legs. I couldn't, and a bright blossom of humiliation opened in my chest.

Anita stepped to the kitchen door. "What are you doing?" she asked. Anita was wearing a widow's white sari. For a moment I thought she was asking me.

"Nanaji said I could have some yogurt," Asha answered.

Anita considered us. Her forehead furrowed into lines as straight as sentences in a book. She was short, with an oval face and curly hair that reached her shoulder blades. Anita turned back into the kitchen. I believed she felt her presence was a burden on me. When I offered to pay for Asha's schoolbooks, Anita refused, even though Rajinder had not left her much. She also gave me detailed accounts of what she bought with my money.

Anita came out of the kitchen with our breakfasts. She and Asha sat across from me. We all had a glass of milk and a salty paratha. Asha ate her yogurt first and quickly. When she could no longer gather anything from the inside of the bowl with the spoon, she licked it.

"We should buy more milk so you can make more yogurt for her," I told Anita. I was carefully scraping my bowl to get the last drops. I held the bowl at chest level and dipped my mouth down to suck on the spoon, because bringing my hand up to my neck caused it to tremble. The yogurt's sourness made my shoulder muscles loosen and made even this indignity bearable.

"She wouldn't eat it."

"I would," Asha said.

"She'd eat it two days, Pitaji, and then stop."

Asha stared into her lap.

After a moment Anita contemptuously added, "Milk is going up every day. I ask why and the milkman says, 'Tell America not to fight Iraq.' "

"His cows drive cars?" My voice came out loud and Anita's face froze. "Let's try it for two days, then," I added softly, feeling sorry that Anita thought I could turn on her.

Anita gathered our plates and stood. She went into the kitchen and squatted beneath the stone counter that runs around the kitchen at waist level. She turned on a tap. It gave a hiss, but only a few drops fell out. Anita sat down and looked at the plates for a moment. Beneath the counter were several tin buckets full of water.

"Thank God we had water this long," I said.

Anita turned to me, and she appeared so intent I thought she might be angry. "We should thank God for so little?" She did not wait for me to answer. Anita began washing the dishes with ashes and cupfuls of water from a bucket.

Often I felt Anita was acting. She wore only white and always kept her head covered as if she were a widow in a movie. These details, like many others about her, appeared so exactly right, they felt planned.

"We should buy a water tank," I said. "Ever since I became Mr. Gupta's man, I make so much money I don't even know how to hide it." Anita did not respond. My guilt thickened. The kitchen is tiny, yet Anita spent most of her days there, even reading the paper while crouched on the floor. I think Anita did this because she filled the kitchen completely and this comforted her.

I asked Asha to get me a glass of water from one of the clay pots in the corner of the room. When she brought it, I held up the pills I must take every morning and asked, "Do you know what these are?"

"Medicine, Nanaji."

"Yes, but they are of three different kinds. This one is a diuretic," I said, lifting the orange one with my thumb and forefinger. "It makes me get rid of a lot of water so that my heart doesn't have so much to move. This one"—I pointed to the aspirin—"thins my blood, and that also means my heart works less. And this one," I said, referring to the blue one with a cross etched on it, "is called a beta blocker." I said beta blocker twice because it sounded dramatic. "This keeps my heart from getting excited."

I had not meant to start the explanation, but the quick self-pity and anger it evoked made me realize guilt was irritating me. I continued talking and the feelings eased. I was glad I had found an opportunity to reveal some part of my life, because it would make my asking Asha questions feel more natural. I held the pills out for a moment and then swept them into my mouth.

Asha wandered to the living room and turned on the television. Before leaving for school, she would move more and more slowly, so that it took her ten minutes to put her books in their bag. Asha was taking classes in May, even though most schools were closed, because she had missed many days when her father died. Rosary was one of the few schools that had government approval for a summer program and that was why I had had her admitted there. I went into the living room to watch the television news. Eventually Asha shuffled into the bedroom she and Anita shared. Through the doorway I saw her putting on white ankle-length socks and small black shoes. At a quarter past eight, she slung a satchel full of books around one shoulder and came to her mother in the kitchen to say goodbye. Anita kissed both of Asha's hands and her forehead. I saw this from my room, where I was dressing, and felt sad and guilty again. The first anniversary of Radha's death was in two days.

Half an hour later, when I left for the office, Anita was on her knees mopping the floor of their bedroom. She had a fold of her sari over her head and held it in place by biting it. The bed she and Asha sleep on almost completely fills the room. Flies were switching about. The sight of Anita kneeling and the formality and shyness of the covered head made me think of how badly I had used my life.

"Talk to the pundit," Anita said, looking up at me. I had yet to arrange the pundit for Radha's prayers. Although Anita had told me to do this several times over the week, there was nothing accusatory in her voice. Suddenly I was angry. I glared at her, until she turned her head down. Then I said, "Why are you always covering your head? You aren't at your in-laws.' People will think you're afraid of me."

M y office is in a low white building that used to be a school. A dirt field circles it and a wall surrounds all this. Lately the wall had been lathered with political posters and painted with the giant lotuses of the fundamentalist Hindu BJP and the open hand of Rajiv Gandhi's Congress Party. For those of us who were involved in raising money and votes, the appearance of these signs of the coming election had created a sense of nervous festivity.

The building itself is dark and musty. When I entered that morning, the sounds of typewriters and of voices came from departments like Hindi or science, where people were already planning for next year. In the physical education department no one even makes a pretense of working during the summer. We were almost proud of our laziness. We joked, "What can be done today can certainly be done tomorrow."

The department's four assistant education officers shared one large room with four desks, four iron armoires behind the desks, and four ceiling fans. Mr. Gupta had his own room down the hall from us.

Mr. Mishra was in the office, and he was asleep, bare feet on his desk and a handkerchief over his eyes to block the light.

"Mr. Mishra," I said, assuming Mr. Gupta's husky voice, "the public expects so little from its servants."

"It's finally learning." He tugged the handkerchief off and smiled. There was a graciousness to his round pockmarked face that reminded me of a silver teapot. "Mr. Karan! I only arrived this morning from Bihar," he said. "Pritam and I were planning to come by the afternoon train yesterday, but we wanted to spend more time with our son. I haven't even bathed." He brought his feet down and sat up.

"How was your grandson's naming?" I asked, taking the chair from him. Mr. Mishra was very proud of his son, an Indian Administrative Service officer, and took every opportunity to talk of his successes.

"Amazing! You always think IAS officers are powerful, but it's hard to understand what it means for one man to be head of justice, the police, and the civil service. Two hundred people came. Every person who has any business of importance with the government tried to get invited. And those who didn't, probably worried that my son might be unhappy with them."

"I assume your son didn't have to pay for the whole celebration."

Mr. Mishra continued smiling, but his voice became irritated at the suggestion of bribery. "It was expensive," he said.

I felt embarrassed. Mr. Mishra and I had worked together for many years but became friends only when he visited me in the hospital while I recovered from my heart attack. Because Mr. Mishra did not accept bribes, I had thought he looked down on those of us who did. I also believed he was smarter and more generous than I was, and this made him especially irritating. During the conversations we had in the hospital, I realized that he was one of those people who love to gossip but are too well mannered to initiate such chatter. Our friendship was built on this insight, upon my leading conversations where I sensed he wanted to go but was too polite to go on his own.

Mr. Mishra asked, "What news?"

"Inspections, files, giving grants. Last week a young man, maybe twenty-six, came to me and said he wanted to open a school and needed a thousand square meters of land. I said you have to go to a different department and deposit a hundred forms before you'll get one meter on government discount. So he pushes two ten-thousand-rupee packets toward me." I slid my hands slowly across the surface of the desk toward Mr. Mishra. To delight him, I sometimes exaggerated my crimes. "I had to say, 'Put it away or I'll call the police.' I've never seen him before and he's giving money like that. For a day or two, I was so certain the corruption people were after me, I could hardly eat."

Mr. Mishra snorted and shook his head.

"Oh! Last week a monkey went into the women's latrines," I said. "The ones down the hall. There were three typists inside. They see the monkey and begin screaming. The monkey begins screaming, too." I made the sounds of the women and the monkey screeching. "One woman runs out of the bathroom. And she shuts the door behind her. Shuts it and holds on to the doorknob. By now everyone has come to see what's happening. The screams are still going on." I started laughing. "The monkey has begun flushing the toilets." I pretended I was jerking the toilet chain. Mr. Mishra joined my laughter. "I have to pull the first woman's hands off the doorknob. One of the other women runs out. And she shuts the door and holds on. I tell her to open it and she says, 'If I do, the monkey will bite me.' Now the woman left inside is weeping. I open the door. The woman runs out. She's been bitten on her arm, her leg, her stomach. The monkey didn't leave till the hall was empty."

"Human nature," Mr. Mishra said. As he laughed, he leaned over one side of his chair.

"The needle for the rabies injection is a foot long." In my anxiety to please him, I had been talking faster than normal.

When our chortling stopped, Mr. Mishra asked, "Is there an inspection today? My stomach says, 'Feed me.'" Every school we were responsible for had to be inspected twice a year to see if government regulations were being followed. For us, these occasions were something close to a party. The home economics department of the school would spend all day cooking an elaborate lunch for us. Everywhere we went in the school, we would be met with obsequiousness.

Mr. Mishra's gentle corruption renewed my confidence in our

friendship. "Father Joseph's school," I said, and rubbed my hands for him to see. "And tonight is the wedding reception for Mr. Gupta's son. We can fill up for the next three days."

Narayan, the driver I always used, was sitting on the building's front steps drinking tea from a glass and reading a Spider-Man comic book. He was a short Brahmin in his late thirties who shaved his head and wore a blue uniform every day, even though drivers aren't required to wear a uniform.

"Narayanji, we are ready to go," Mr. Mishra said.

"Is the thief coming?" Narayan asked, glancing up at me standing beside Mr. Mishra.

Neither of us answered for fear it would encourage his insults. Mr. Mishra bent and adjusted the rubber bands that held up his socks. Narayan finally stood and walked ahead of us to the jeep.

Narayan and I had been friendly till I became Mr. Gupta's man. We still shared a small business of renting out the education department's jeeps at night and on holidays. Our friendship ended because Narayan had expected to grow rich from my new position, but since nearly all the benefits the position bestowed flowed directly to me, he felt cheated. He relieved this disappointment by insulting me whenever he could. Lately he had begun to claim falsely that I owed him fourteen hundred rupees from some complex embezzlement of the education department's diesel.

Our office is near Delhi University, and on our way to the inspection, we went through Revolution Square, where last winter several college students had set themselves on fire to protest V. P. Singh's increase in caste quotas.

As we entered the square, Narayan snorted and said, "Rajiv Gandhi's sons." The outrage over their deaths had led to Rajiv Gandhi's overthrow of V. P. Singh and Chandrashekar becoming Prime Minister. This was the first thing he had said since we got in the jeep, and I think he said it because he knew how much I had been moved by the actions of those foolish boys.

"Be kinder," I said, leaning over the front seat. "They didn't know better."

"How smart do you have to be? Even I know a few thousand government jobs don't matter."

"Don't be an animal," I said. "Laughing at young boys dying."

"Call me an animal, and I'll make you walk."

In the way that some people get religious with old age, over the last few years I had become sentimentally political. The young men's actions reminded me of the days when I cut telegraph wires to slow the British.

"They sacrificed themselves like Mahatma Gandhi, like the Independence leaders who went to jail." My throat began tightening with emotion.

"Mahatma Gandhi was crazy, too," Narayan answered, waving a hand near his ear where my mouth had been. "He thought sleeping naked but chaste with young girls gave him special powers. These boys probably thought dying would create new jobs out of nowhere, like magic, like my son thinks being bitten by a spider will let him climb walls."

Mr. Mishra leaned forward also and said, "Still, Narayanji, respect the dead."

"Now Rajiv Gandhi wants to take control directly, so Parliament has to be dissolved."

"Narayanji, we should at least do what we can," Mr. Mishra replied.

"You and I both eat Rajiv Gandhi's salt," I said.

"I am too far from power to eat anyone's salt," Narayan said.

Mr. Mishra opened a newspaper. I looked out at the colonial-style university buildings that we passed. They were white turning yellow, with verandas and broad lawns. Perhaps the thought of the boys who immolated themselves shamed me into trying to be better than myself. "Narayanji, I will give you the money you were speaking of."

Narayan honked his horn and reached over his shoulder to take my hand. I had bribed him and now, I hoped, Father Joseph would bribe me.

. . .

Two or three rows of students in blue shorts and white shirts were lined up doing jumping jacks in front of Rosary School's main building. The steel pole that had defeated Father Joseph was gone.

Narayan stopped the jeep before the steps of the main entrance. We got out and stood beside the jeep and waited for our presence to be recognized. A peon came, greeted us, and went to tell Father Joseph. After a few minutes, the head physical education teacher, Mrs. Singla, a heavy woman with hennaed hair and a widow's white sari, came down the front steps smiling. "You should come see us even if there isn't any work reason," she said, pressing her hands together in namaste.

Mrs. Singla led us along a gallery that had classrooms on one side and was open to the sun on the other. A peon in khaki shorts and shirt sat on the floor outside Father Joseph's office. Mrs. Singla said, "I'm sure we meet all your requirements." The peon stood and opened the door.

Father Joseph was behind his desk reading a man's palms. Father Joseph looked up, said, "One minute," in English, and motioned Mr. Mishra and me to a sofa along the wall. We sat down. There were rugs on the floor, and the walls were lined with bookcases made of glass and curved steel. An air conditioner chilled the room with barely a hum. This school is rich, I thought.

"You have to fight your selfishness," Father Joseph said.

"I try," the man said. He was in his early twenties and might have been a teacher.

"The palm you were born with shows that you have a small heart. But the palm you have made shows that you can change."

Mrs. Singla stood near the sofa. "Sir, one day, will you read my hands?"

"Someday," he answered with his eyes on the man's palms. Father Joseph twisted his lips. "I won't tell you everything now," he said, and released the hands. "Some things only suffering can teach."

"Thank you, sir," the man said, and stood.

Father Joseph got up from behind his desk. He had on black pants and a white short-sleeved shirt which revealed thick arms with veins like garter snakes. Mrs. Singla and the man left.

Father Joseph moved to a chair across from us and crossed his legs. There was a mannered quality to his gestures. Like some other Christian priests I've met, Father Joseph had an air of condescension, as though we were still in the Raj and Christianity were still the religion of the powerful. He leaned forward and pointed at some papers on the table between us. "I've looked at your forms and I've personally made sure everything is right."

"Much of the inspection report depends on our impressions," I said, also in English. Mr. Mishra giggled at seeing the jousting start. Father Joseph glanced at him. "We have to see how the teachers teach," I said. To have to lie and justify myself without any introductory chatter made the conversation feel out of control. Also, for me, speaking in English was like wearing too-tight clothes. I had to plan all my motions or a seam might give.

Father Joseph shifted back in his chair. "Will you have something cold to drink or something warm?"

"Why don't we have something cold while the tea is being made," Mr. Mishra said. He was grinning.

After the peon had been sent to bring drinks, it was hard to start a conversation. Father Joseph appeared both aloof and firm. He took a pack of cigarettes from a pants pocket.

I moved forward on the sofa and knitted my fingers together. Normally, whoever had come with me would leave to examine the school after we had our drinks and I would be able to talk to the principal alone. But I had the feeling that Mr. Mishra wanted to push our new friendship and stay as long as possible.

I watched Father Joseph smoke for a moment and then asked if he thought Rajiv Gandhi would be a better leader for having lost the prime ministership. He knew I was raising money for the Congress Party and politeness should have made him say that Rajiv Gandhi had benefited from losing his title.

"Does a lion's nature improve from fasting?" Father Joseph asked, arching an eyebrow.

I became flustered. The peon entered with three Campa Colas and three teas on one tray. "Still," I said, immediately feeling the need to defend Congress and through it my authority, "the Congress Party is the only party that can rule India. What other party has ever been able to hold power for long. They are the only ones who have appeal all over the country. They are the only ones who have people in the villages."

"Would Congress say something else?" Father Joseph smiled at me. "We'll see how many seats they get in the new elections." I don't think he had any strong political affiliations.

I accepted the tea with one hand and the Campa Cola with the other, and having both hands full simultaneously made me feel greedy and crass. Mr. Gupta raised money for Congress because Congress had controlled Delhi when he started in education. Currently the BJP was very strong. To keep Mr. Gupta from defecting, Congress had given him more and more freedom. Mr. Gupta was able to grant favors to principals by carefully bribing whoever might oppose him in the BJP.

Mr. Mishra slurped his Campa Cola loudly. Father Joseph glanced toward him, and Mr. Mishra smiled, revealing his teeth.

"Rajiv Gandhi thinks that India is his family estate. The Nehru family has controlled the Congress Party for too long. Jawaharlal Nehru, then Indira Gandhi, then Rajiv. How much longer?" Father Joseph spoke too quickly for a conversation, but not quickly enough to be obviously argumentative.

"And before Independence and Jawaharlal there was Motilal Nehru," Mr. Mishra said. "And every night on TV now, you see Rajiv Gandhi's daughter handing out blankets to the poor, as though she's already started campaigning for her seat." Father Joseph and Mr. Mishra both looked at me as if waiting for an answer. My helplessness began churning into anger.

"The Nehrus gave birth to India."

"And they've been taking advantage of their child for a hundred years," Mr. Mishra responded.

"This is Jawaharlal's centennial anniversary," Father Joseph confirmed. "At least for one hundred years, the Nehrus have run Indian politics."

I felt surrounded. "Would you rather have the BJP win?" I asked, putting my empty Campa bottle on the table. I had accepted the fact that these negotiations were going to be more about force than about delicacy. "They are the only party other than the Congress that can win the central government, and the BJP is full of Hindu fanatics. If they had their way, they would make every non-Hindu leave the country."

Father Joseph shrugged and took a sip of tea. "That's not going to happen. There are too many non-Hindus in India." He paused, thought for a moment, and, as if ending the conversation, added, "What do I know about politics. I am just an ordinary headmaster."

We finished our tea in silence. I did not know what to do or say to show my strength.

"Shall I send for more tea?" Father Joseph asked. I thought his English sentence was hiding the Hindi slang for bribe. I became outraged. He smiled broadly and I knew that he had mocked my bumbling delicacy. I cleared my throat and casually spat a clot of phlegm on the bit of rug beside my foot.

Father Joseph looked at me in shock. I glanced at him and said in Hindi, "I know how much you charge students to get in here. I know the land we give you for one rupee a meter you then draw loans on for one hundred rupees a meter. You are a priest. What kind of religion do you follow?" I settled back on the sofa. Mr. Mishra had stopped smiling. "Why be greedy when there is so much."

"At last," Father Joseph said, now in English.

"At last what? Are you still a baby after all you've done?" I asked from where I was on the sofa. "We don't sell toys."

Father Joseph said nothing. He put his teacup on the table.

Father Joseph had not drunk his Campa. To highlight my greed I asked, "Can I drink yours?" He nodded and I gulped it down. "At last, little baby," I said, and stood. "Take some time and think while we go look at your school."

Mrs. Singla led us around the school. I noticed as I walked through the halls that I was holding my shoulders back and letting my arms swing free. Mr. Mishra had never seen me behave this way, and I kept catching him looking at me. I began to feel contemptuous of him. I imagined myself as ruthless and powerful. I thought of finding Asha's classroom and in front of her letting Asha's teacher know our relationship. Mrs. Singla took us to a storeroom where cricket bats and field hockey sticks lay in mounds. I asked Mrs. Singla if there were any extra badminton rackets, because I wanted to give Asha a gift. I picked up a leather cricket ball there and kept flipping it from hand to hand for the rest of the afternoon.

Eventually Mr. Mishra and I were left to wander by ourselves. The school has a lift, and I like lifts very much. We rode it up and down several times. Mr. Mishra went into various classrooms and asked children random questions. "What is a binary star?" or "What does D.C. mean in Washington, D.C.?" When someone answered, he might say, "Is that what you think?" I found this hilarious.

Early in the afternoon Mr. Mishra was walking down a hall about thirty or forty meters ahead of me. I called out to him. When he turned around, I held up the cricket ball and mimed bowling it. He crouched and brought his hands together as though he were a wicket keeper. I don't know what made me stop miming, but I sent the ball shooting toward him. The ball hit the ground with a loud clap and Mr. Mishra was too surprised to catch it. Each time the ball hit the ground, there was the same loud clap. The classes all along the hall became quiet. The pride which had filled me evaporated. The surprise let me feel my ridiculousness.

We roamed the halls till a bell dismissed the classes. Because it was summer, the school day was shorter than normal. The children lined up in the front field for their buses and we went to have lunch with Father Joseph.

Mrs. Singla joined us for the meal. I remained quiet. Girls from the home economics department had remained after class to serve us. There was chole bature, malai kofta, nan, rice, kheer, gajar-ka-halva. Once the food was in front of us, conversation ended. Father Joseph ate with knife and fork, but everyone else used bare hands. Mr. Mishra chewed so loudly it sounded as though he might be trying to say something. Mrs. Singla ate steadily, with her head bowed. Every now and then she looked up at the ceiling, shook her head, and moaned. I yearned to stuff myself, to eat until all my blood went to my stomach and getting up would make me dizzy, but my doctor had warned me against rich foods and I barely touched the various dishes.

When we were ready to leave, Mrs. Singla gave me two badminton rackets and a tube of shuttlecocks. She offered Mr. Mishra a similar set, but he said no. Mr. Mishra stood as he refused her. Then he and she moved out into the hall. I moved back to the sofa I had sat on earlier.

Father Joseph went to his desk and took out two small newspaper-wrapped bundles. "Forty thousand," he said, putting them at the edge of the desk. I had only expected him to pay twenty-five or thirty. Father Joseph, I thought, was one of those people for whom money is not real, and once he had surrendered in the bargaining, he gave up completely. I picked up the packages. I pretended to weigh the money. The heft of it and the feeling of victory removed the embarrassment I had been feeling. I asked for a plastic bag.

"Do I need to bring a gift to Mr. Gupta's party?" Father Joseph asked and laughed as I left.

On our way back, I fell asleep. I dreamed of Radha and Anita, and when I woke I was grinding my teeth, though I could not remember the details of my dream. The back of my shirt was sticking to the seat and I had a slight headache from the sun.

Mr. Mishra was looking out the window. He had finished the inspection report without my asking and it was on his lap. We were nearing my home. We had passed the Old Clock Tower and were beside the Old Vegetable Market's layers of stalls. The jeep was moving in slow shudders. Pollution had created a blue haze on the road.

"You don't notice it till you're away, but Delhi is so polluted it's like living inside an oil tanker," Mr. Mishra said.

The dream and the money in my lap made me feel unworthy of his friendship. "Why do you think your son is so successful?" I asked him.

"I don't know," he said, continuing to look out the window. "Children are born with personalities. He was born determined to be successful. And he's smart."

"I have a daughter who is a scientist in America. I have a son who has a Ph.D. in history. The fact that Anita never studied wasn't my fault." Saying this made me feel as though I was pleading. "My daughter Kusum has met the American President." Mentioning Kusum's achievements made me feel that perhaps she had accomplished them because she had stayed mostly outside my influence.

Mr. Mishra turned toward me. "Of course not," he said.

I think I was still dazed from my dream, for I kept going. "The things I do for Mr. Gupta . . . I do them only because I never had a wife who works, like yours." Mr. Mishra didn't respond. "Mr. Bajwa deserved to be caught. He had a wife who worked, but he was still Mr. Gupta's moneyman. As the Gita tells, possessions possess you. To achieve peace, let go of desire and seek only to fulfill your duties." When Mr. Mishra still did not say anything, I became angry at him. "You were lucky. Your first child was a boy and you could stop right there. I had two girls and only then a boy. How could I have supported five people on my salary?"

Mr. Mishra shrugged and kept quiet. We neared the temple where I was going to get the pundit for Radha's prayers. I told Narayan to stop in front. As I climbed out of the jeep with my badminton rackets and shuttlecocks, the plastic bag full of money dangling from a wrist, Mr. Mishra said, "Once we get this old, Mr.

Karan, there is no longer time to make up for our mistakes. We must try to forget them."

There are four or five steps up to the temple gates. To one side of the doors is a little space where a fat unshaven Brahmin with a little ponytail sits most days selling prayer pamphlets, flowers, and coconuts. When I entered the temple, he was asleep on his back, with a brick wrapped in sackcloth under his head as a pillow.

The temple is set at the end of a long, narrow hallway: an open courtyard with a marble floor and walls painted saffron. There is a tulsi bush in the center. Alcoves with statues of God Ram, Hanuman, and Krishna line the wall. There was no one in the courtyard. I bowed before each of the idols and asked them to take care of Radha's soul and guard Anita and Asha. I tried asking forgiveness from God Ram, but when I attempted to name specific sins, my mind would not form the words. I put a rupee in the collection box and the silliness of this offering made me feel a sudden keen grief for Radha.

After I finished praying, I knocked at a narrow blue door in a corner of the courtyard. After a moment or two, the pundit's wife, a thin seventeen-year-old named Shilpa, unchained the door. Shilpa, like the pundit, was from my village, and I had known her all her life. "Namaste, Ram Karanji," she said.

"Is Punditji in?"

"He's gone to the village. He'll be back tomorrow night, probably."

"Wednesday is the first anniversary of Radha's death and I would like Punditji to pray at my home in the morning," I said. Shilpa didn't answer, and I wondered whether she thought I was neglectful for coming this late to her husband and whether she would gossip about this. "Tomorrow night he'll be back?" I asked. If the pundit turned out to be busy, I would have only Wednesday morning to find a priest.

Shilpa stared at me and then, half smiling, said, "An ice-cream factory is starting in Beri and he's gone to pray for it." As she spoke, her smile opened fully. It was as though she was bragging that the pundit had moved up from blessing new scooters and new rooms in houses to blessing whole factories.

"I'd like him to pray at my house Wednesday morning."

"I'll tell him."

As I walked to our alley, I considered hiring some other pundit to pray for Radha, but Radha had believed that the prayers of a pundit who did not know the person on whose behalf he was appealing were ineffective. The idea of letting some stranger pray for her made me sad. Then I felt disgusted with my sentimentality. When she was alive, I visited prostitutes two or three times a month. It was only the trauma of the heart attack and Radha's slow death from cancer that had sapped my desire for sex.

Going up our alley, I held the badminton rackets upright in one hand like a bouquet of flowers. I passed the flour mill with its roar and smell of grain burning. I passed the booth of the watch repairman, who was asleep on his stool, his head resting on the plank where he performs the repairs. Entering the dark archway that leads into our compound, I thought that all these details were part of Asha's life as well as mine, and this gave everything a purpose.

Asha squinted when she opened the door. "I woke you?" I asked, stepping into Asha and Anita's bedroom. The bedsheet was wrinkled on one side. She could have been home only an hour.

"What do you have?" Asha said, closing the door to keep out the heat. The only light now came through the living room.

"For you," I said, giving Asha the rackets and shuttlecocks.

"Thank you. Thank you," Asha said in Urdu as she took the gift. Asha's choice of switching to a formal language surprised me. It suggested an inner life of which I knew nothing and made me aware that all day I had been imagining her only as a witness.

I sat down on their bed and took off my shoes. Asha stood before me and began swinging a racket.

"Maybe you can play with some of the compound children," I said. Asha laughed and nodded. "Get me some water."

Asha went to the common room carrying a racket in each hand. Anita came into the bedroom doorway. She was wearing her black rectangular eyeglasses, which meant that she had been unable to nap and had been reading the paper in the kitchen. "Couldn't sleep?" I asked as I unbuttoned my shirt. When I reached the top two buttons, my hands trembled.

Anita shook her head no.

"I went to the temple." I paused and tried thinking of a way to hide my mistake of going this late to the pundit. "Punditji's gone to Beri."

"What happens now?" she said with panic in her voice.

"He'll be back tomorrow night."

"He could stay in Beri. People might come and there'd be no pundit." Anita's body had become stiff and the lines on her forehead were sharp and deep. "Think of the shame." Although Anita had most of the responsibility for the ceremony, the strength of her response made it appear affected.

"I can get someone else," I said softly. "Don't worry." It took a moment for Anita's body to loosen. When the lines on her forehead had eased, I said in a light joking voice, "You're like me. Under pressure we stop thinking." Anita didn't reply.

Asha came back with the glass of water. "How was school?" I asked.

"Good."

She looked at me as I drank and I could tell that already our morning conversation and this gift had shifted our relationship. I put the glass on the ground and asked, "Your teachers don't bother you, do they?"

"No. I have good teachers."

"It's bad to hit children." I felt silly for saying something this obvious, so I tried hiding my inanity with more words. "When I was in higher secondary, the untouchables sat in the back of the class.

The teachers couldn't slap the untouchables because then they would be touching them. The untouchables knew this and would always be talking. Sometimes the teachers became very angry, and to shut up the untouchables they threw pieces of chalk at them. And the untouchables, because all the students sat on the floor, would race around on their hands and knees, dodging the chalk."

When I churned my arms to show how swiftly the untouchables crawled, Asha laughed and said, "My teachers only hit with rulers." She was quiet for a moment and then spoke eagerly: "I had something happen. There's a girl in school who last week got one of those soft papers you blow your nose on. Those papers that rich people use instead of handkerchiefs in advertisements. She's been using it all week. She doesn't have a cold, but she keeps putting it in her nose. I told her today the paper was ugly. She said, 'If I throw it away, you'll take it.' I said I wouldn't, so she threw it onto the floor and waited. Two girls tried grabbing it. The one who got it blew her nose in it all day."

I laughed at Asha's attention to detail and tried tickling her stomach. Asha jumped away, smiling. "Do you want to come with me to a wedding reception tonight? Since I can't eat much, I should bring someone who can." I said the last sentence because I felt I had to wheedle Anita's permission to do this. The possibility of taking Asha out of the sadness of her life and showing her all the people who knew me had come to me as I left Rosary School with the bag of money.

"This is Mr. Gupta's?" Anita asked.

"I can show her off to everybody I know."

"Will there be ice cream and Campa Cola?" Asha said.

"You can just eat ice cream if you want."

Asha giggled at the idea.

"How is Mr. Gupta?" Anita inquired.

Mr. Gupta's son had eloped with a Sikh and this wedding party was coming after many tears and curses. "He keeps wanting to know what he did wrong." Anita sat down on a chair across from me. "I tell him it's all written in the stars."

"It'll be late when you come home. Asha has school tomorrow."

"We'll take an autorickshaw."

Anita looked at Asha beating the air with a badminton racket. Asha was moving from side to side and talking to herself as she played an imaginary opponent. "You can't beat me."

The sun had set forty minutes earlier, and the sidewalks and road were soaked in the same even gray light. I had been so afraid of having nothing to say to Asha that ever since we got in the autorickshaw I had been unable to stop talking. "Mr. Gupta's son had gone with a friend to look at a used car and the man selling it had a daughter who gave them water. Ajay fell in love immediately," I shouted over the beating of the engine. The boy driving the three-wheeler ground gears as he sought the narrow channels of movement which kept appearing and disappearing in the traffic. "I've never seen her, but Sikh women are either very beautiful or very ugly." Asha was looking out of the autorickshaw and I wanted her to listen to me. "I actually predicted this. Long ago, when he was about to go off to college, I read his horoscope and predicted it. And then one day Mr. Gupta comes crying to me: 'Oh, Mr. Karan! I have gone bankrupt.'" Asha held her folded hands between her legs and stared at the traffic. She appeared stunned to have left the flat and to be on the way to a party. Asha wore olive shorts and a white shirt. I saw again how small her kneecaps were. I wore a blue shirt that stretched so tight across my stomach that the spaces between the buttons were puckered open like small hungry mouths. I was using cologne and wondered if Asha had noticed. "I told him, 'What use is it to cry.' Pretend everything happened with your permission and that way your nose won't be cut off before everyone. People always say bad things anyway." As I spoke, I actually began feeling as though I were Mr. Gupta's friend. We passed through the Old Vegetable Market. The vendors were lighting the kerosene lamps, which look like iron-stemmed tulips. "I am only a junior officer," I said, "but Mr. Gupta always turns to me for advice. I spend as much time in his room as I do behind my own desk. If only Mrs. Chauduri would retire, I could be senior junior officer. She's had cancer for six years. She's worked hard. She deserves her rest. She doesn't even come into the office much. Sometimes she sends her son to pick up her files."

I tried thinking of something that might interest Asha. Making cheese had become illegal a few weeks ago when the heat started and cows began giving less milk. "There are going to be cheese dishes, I'm sure. Mr. Gupta has only one son and he's a rich man. He's not going to wait for the rains to come so he can have cheese at his son's wedding reception. You want to bet how many cheese dishes there are going to be? Three? Five?"

After a pause, Asha unenthusiastically guessed, "Four."

"I'll bet five." When the conversation didn't move from there, I said, "There's going to be so much ice cream. Did your father buy you ice cream often?"

Asha didn't answer for a moment. Then she said, "No, but I like to think he did. I like to think he would come to me from his office during recess and take me with him to drink Campa Cola."

This answer struck me not as just pitiful but as frightening. To slip into fantasy like this seemed the first step into madness. Looking at Asha at that moment I felt as if I had entered my bedroom late at night and found a strange man sitting quietly on my cot. "You're imaginative," I murmured. I was silent for several minutes. We had passed Kamla Nagar and were speeding down a straight road. Lights shone from the houses and shops on either side. "Thinking these things might hurt you in some way," I told her and, putting one arm around her shoulders, pulled her to me.

Strings of red and green lightbulbs fell three stories from the roof and covered the front of Mr. Gupta's house. There were cars parked on both sides of the street. There was a large fenced green across from his home. Because it is so dirty in the Old Vegetable Market that your spit always holds black grains, this park is what I always associated with Mr. Gupta's wealth and power.

When Mr. Gupta joined the education department twelve years

ago, each education subject had collected its own political donations. The physical education program had always had more influence than other departments because the physical education
teachers, like the captains of Calcutta's athletic clubs, have access to
large pools of hooligans. Only when Rajiv Gandhi lost the prime
ministership was Mr. Gupta able to consolidate fund-raising under
himself in return for continued loyalty to the Congress Party.

Mr. Gupta was standing at his gate, receiving visitors. The
veranda behind him was crowded with guests. Waiters in red turbans and white jackets and pants moved among them carrying trays.
I took Asha's hand in mine and walked up to Mr. Gupta. He was
wearing a handsome blue suit and a tie flecked with yellow and blue.
"This is my granddaughter, Asha," I said after he had thanked me
for coming.

He bowed and shook Asha's hand. "You do my house honor," he
said. Asha was so surprised by his formality she moved behind me.
Mr. Gupta is tall and muscular, with delicate features and hair that
is just turning gray. "We have all this ice cream and cold drinks and
so few children," he said seriously. "Children are the only ones who
can really appreciate ice cream. Don't you think so, Mr. Karan?"

"I'll eat a lot," Asha promised.

"I know you will," Mr. Gupta said, and prodded Asha's stomach
with a finger. "You're so thin you look as though you could die right
here." He looked at me. "If you could, you'd bring your entire family to eat." Mr. Gupta laughed.

Sisterfucker! I thought. He reached around me to shake someone's hand. Without knowing it, I put my hand on Mr. Gupta's
shoulder and shouted, "Happy?" He appeared surprised. "Happy?"
I bellowed again to fluster him. Mr. Gupta looked embarrassed and I
felt powerful. "A gift," I said, and from my pants pocket pulled out
an envelope with a hundred and one rupees.

"Very kind." He smiled and wrote my name on the envelope with
a small pencil.

"Any booze tonight, Mr. Gupta? We should celebrate. Guess

what Father Joseph gave. I will only drink foreign whiskey, though."
I let my voice ring with a village accent to remind him that we were
both small corrupt bureaucrats.

Mr. Gupta looked confused but kept smiling. He tried leaning
around me and shaking a hand. I moved into his way to tell him how
much Father Joseph had given. But Mr. Gupta stopped smiling and
snapped, "Just ask the waiters and they'll get it from the back."

I moved onto the veranda. I stopped a waiter and asked for a
whiskey and a Pepsi Lahar for Asha. Asha peered around. Her hand
was so small in mine that I felt enormous.

More men than usual were wearing traditional kurta pajamas
instead of suits in anticipation of a BJP victory. There were perhaps
a dozen Sikh men with their beards tied beneath their chin. All the
Sikhs wore suits. After the thousands of Sikhs who had been set on
fire and macheted to death in the riots following Indira Gandhi's
assassination, some of these men must carry a constant sense of
physical danger with them. What did they feel, I wondered, at seeing all these Hindus so adaptable to the possibility of BJP power?

My whiskey came and I drank it in two gulps. The force of it
made me shake. "Acid," I said, grinning at Asha. She was sucking her
Pepsi Lahar through a straw. After she finished, she asked if she
could save the straw and take it home. I felt embarrassed for her. "I'll
buy you a box of straws tomorrow." I ordered another whiskey and a
cold drink. "A full glass of whiskey," I said.

"Of course, sahib," the waiter said, and I knew he would want
a tip.

I saw Mrs. Chauduri moving around the veranda. She was talking
and eating a samosa from a little plate and looking as if she could
live forever. "Hello! Mrs. Chauduri," I shouted at her. I towed Asha
behind me as I moved through the crowd. Mrs. Chauduri was
wearing a purple sari that made her look like an eggplant. "What
a nice sari," I said, feeling the slight anger of sycophancy and the
sly joy of lying. "I hope you are better." She had had her second
breast removed recently and I wondered whether her husband was

unhappy about this or whether he found some strange pleasure at seeing a scarred woman beneath him.

"It is as God wills," she answered, shrugging. "I have to live for my husband and sons." Whenever she talked of her illness, her voice became soft and slightly vain. The voice made me think of how when Mrs. Chauduri was a school principal she nearly ended up in jail for secretly selling ten thousand rupees' worth of her science department's mercury.

"God is only testing you, Mrs. Chauduri. I am sure you will be fine." She nodded and sipped her cold drink. I noticed that I was slightly aroused at the idea of what her chest, creased by the surgery, must look like. This was the first time in several months that I had had such feelings.

The waiter came with my whiskey. "Reward, sir, reward," he said. "You are rich. I am poor."

I avoided his eyes and praised Mrs. Chauduri for her bravery. Then I introduced Asha and asked, "Have you seen Mr. Mishra?" She hadn't. Mr. Mishra didn't like Mr. Gupta and I was glad to know that he had been brave enough not to come.

Mrs. Chauduri moved closer to me. "Mr. Gupta's son is passed out drunk. That's why he isn't out shaking hands. And they can't show the girl without him." Noticing my surprise at her bitter voice, she added, "The girl's family is here. Why should their friends not get to see their daughter?" After Mr. Bajwa was charged with corruption, Mrs. Chauduri should have become Mr. Gupta's representative, but she had been passed over because she was a woman. Now she was always presenting examples of injustice against women.

Asha looked bored, so we left Mrs. Chauduri and wandered through the crowd. I have no resistance to alcohol and the second drink pushed me into drunkenness. The world and my mind appeared to move at two different speeds. When I turned my head, the people before me also shifted. I introduced Asha to several people. "Isn't she beautiful?" I would challenge them. Asha smiled when

I demanded praise for her. I felt as if I could do anything and it wouldn't matter.

I ordered another drink and moved with Asha into the room where the buffet was laid out. "Oh!" she said. The walls were lined with tables covered by trays laden with food. On one side of the room there were ice chests full of ice cream. As we moved around the tables, we counted the cheese dishes. Nine, not including desserts. Asha filled her plate so high, food overflowed it and dripped down her wrist. At first I felt embarrassed by her greed; then I saw a fat woman with a ring on every finger and a heavy gold necklace picking cubes of cheese out of a tray.

Asha and I stood in a corner of the room and ate. It was very hot and sweat kept slipping into my eyes. But the food was so good that neither of us wanted to leave the room. I ate only a little bit, but chewed every mouthful for a long time. "Don't eat so much that you have no space for ice cream," I said to Asha.

She laughed and said, "Don't worry." Asha went back for a second plate. Her blouse was tucked in and I noticed how tiny her waist was. I put my plate down. I wanted to live a long time.

In the middle of the second plate, Asha suddenly turned pale. I took her to the bathroom to vomit. Then I got her a bottle of Campa Cola to rinse her mouth with. "Spit it out," I said, cupping the back of her head in my hand, "you're rich tonight."

I ordered another whiskey and drank it standing beside Asha while she ate plate after plate of ice cream. There were colored sprinkles for the ice cream. "Clown dandruff," Asha called them at some point. The strength of her imagination made her appear even more valuable. I put one hand on her shoulder and pulled her next to my leg. I was so drunk I expected to feel nauseous.

At some point Mr. Gupta entered the room, leading Mr. Maurya behind him. Mr. Maurya wore a plain white kurta pajama that made his black skin appear shiny. I noticed that he kept pulling up his left sleeve to better display a heavy gold watch. "Then just make your mouth sweet before going," Mr. Gupta was saying. I smiled in preparation for shaking Mr. Maurya's hand and felt myself getting nervous. I had known Mr. Maurya long before Mr. Gupta met him, when Mr. Maurya's only business was collecting used paper and turning it into bags.

"No, no," Mr. Maurya said, his voice loud and easy. "My doctor says I have to eat very simple things. No salt or sugar." When Mr. Maurya's eyes swept the room, they snagged on mine. He smiled and turned his attention back to Mr. Gupta. I felt myself swelling with rage. I had been the one who got Mr. Maurya appointments with school principals so that he could convince them to sell him their paper.

"One gulab jamun, then," Mr. Gupta said.

"It's only just, Mr. Maurya," I called out, "that after eating so much all our lives, our bodies stop letting us eat." My words were slurred and I couldn't even tell if they all left my mouth. Mr. Gupta glanced coldly at me. Sisterfucker! I thought, I'm the one who can go to jail. "Mr. Maurya, I hear you're the biggest textbook publisher in Delhi now."

"I didn't see you, Mr. Karan," Mr. Maurya said.

I walked up to him and shook his hand. "As long as one of us sees the other." Mr. Maurya was a small man. I put my hand on his shoulder and left it there. "Why don't you call me anymore?"

"You're drunk, Mr. Karan," Mr. Maurya said. For some reason I had expected Mr. Maurya to pretend I wasn't drunk. His words made me realize that I was unimportant.

Mr. Maurya took my hand off his shoulder and held it between his two hands. He looked into my eyes. I knew he thought me a buffoon, and I knew then that the decision to have me murdered would involve for him all the emotion of changing banks. "What I meant, sir," I immediately said, "is that you should honor me with more work." I backed away, nodding my head. "It was so nice to meet you again, sir." I pulled Asha after me.

I walked out of the room and out of the house. My fright had made me almost sober. I stood at the edge of the road and tried to empty my head so that I could think. Asha was leaning quietly against me. I caressed her hair and taut neck to let her know that everything was all right, but her face remained pulled in. I knelt and kissed her cheeks and neck. Her body slowly relaxed. I hugged her and looked up. The moon was full, yellow, and so low it looked as if it were wedged between two roofs. It appeared helpless and mournful. I shivered with fright.

By the time we found an autorickshaw, the drunkenness had crawled back into me. Now it made me sad, not giddy. The recent embarrassment bobbed in and out of my consciousness and my stomach began turning. I wished I had drunk another whiskey.

There was little traffic on the road and soon we were out of Model Town and on the main road back to the Old Vegetable Market. It was nine-thirty, but already homeless people had placed their cots along the edges of the road. The grassy swaths of land which divide the road were spotted with the stoves and dung fires of more homeless people. I pulled Asha next to me. "Did you enjoy yourself?" I asked.

"Yes," she said softly.

"Sit on my lap," I said. I put my arm around her waist. I blew softly on her neck. "Tomorrow I'll buy you some ice cream," I said. Then I was quiet for a little while. "Our house is so sad. We should be happy. I don't know why your mother wants to be so unhappy, but you and I can be happy." I kissed her neck. "I love you, my little sweet mango, and I want you to have a happy childhood. Making your childhood happy is the last thing I want to do before I die." Thinking of the nearness of my death, I felt my eyes tearing. "I wish I could watch you grow into a woman. You will be a beautiful woman."

We got out of the autorickshaw and walked up our alley holding hands. There were no lights and we had to be careful not to step on dogs sleeping in the middle of the alley. "Do you love me?" I asked.

"Yes," she said.

"I am such a sad bad man. Other than you no one loves me." I began sobbing gently. I picked her up and held her for a moment.

"You're my little mango." Asha also began crying. "I've tried to do the best I can, but I am a weak man."

"I love you," Asha said.

"But I am such a sad bad man."

I put her down and entered the courtyard of our compound. People were sitting on cots playing cards. The English news was playing on televisions. Crying all the way, we climbed the narrow stairs to the second-story gallery.

When Anita opened the door and saw us, her face flattened with alarm. "What happened?"

"Nothing," I said. Asha stood crying softly beside me. "I began thinking of Radha and that made me sad. Asha is such a good girl she began crying with me."

I left them and brushed my teeth and washed my face. I wished I had drunk more. I took off my pants and shirt, and wearing just my undershirt and undershorts, I went and sat on my cot and waited.

When Asha walked past my room, I told her to get me some water. She came into my room with a glass. She was wearing a purple nightgown that went to her ankles. Her eyes were red. I was excited and even happy, but the alcohol kept me slightly removed from the moment. I took Asha's wrist in one hand as she handed me the water. "Such a good girl you are," I said. I took a sip and put the glass on the floor and pulled her toward me. I turned her to face away from me and made her stand between my legs. I kissed her neck lightly and placed my erection against the small of her back. Asha's body was relaxed, as if she didn't sense anything wrong. "I love you," I said. I brushed my penis lightly against her. Nervousness and excitement rubbed with each other. I took an earlobe between my lips. "You're my little sun-ripened mango."

Suddenly Anita was in the doorway with her toothbrush clenched in one hand. For a second I panicked. I felt as if I had been kicked in the chest, and there was a rushing in my ears. But then I thought, Anita couldn't see anything. I wasn't doing anything wrong. I was not naked. Asha didn't know what I was doing. All I was doing was touching her, and without Asha knowing, I couldn't be doing something wrong. Anita couldn't see. I continued leaning over Asha's shoulder. "What a nice daughter you have," I said to Anita.

There was no emotion on Anita's face as she stared at me. "What are you doing?" she asked me.

"Giving Nanaji water," Asha said.

She stared at us a moment and then motioned for Asha to come to her. "Brush your teeth." Asha left me and went past her mother into the common room. Anita stayed in the doorway. I wondered whether she remembered. How could she remember after decades of silence? She kept looking at me. "I'm drunk," I said in case she remembered.

Anita stepped out of the doorway and out of my sight.

TWO

Pitaji is dead. Asha and I are on the roof. The sky is ashy from the city's trapped lights. It is three in the morning, or later. Moisture is finally collecting on the sheets. I am sitting on my cot. I have not slept at all since I saw Pitaji dead. I am staring at my daughter, because otherwise Pitaji appears before me. Asha's hands are on her hips above the white sheet that reaches her waist.

On a nearby roof a woman coughs and spits. Asha rolls onto her side so her back is to me. A few months ago, Pitaji's ankles turned black for lack of blood. Before, I had seen this as a sign of death and been happy. Since he died, I've been thinking of the ankles, like a child's socks, and wanting to wrap my head in my arms.

Pitaji appears against the night. He is on his stomach, lit by the summer sun coming through the common room. His eyes are turned toward where I stood in the doorway; blood covers his chin from biting his tongue; one arm is buried beneath him; the other is draped over the edge of the cot. I try peering through this. The image does not fade. I close my eyes. He is inside my lids.

I wish Rajinder were here to say, "Don't think too much." Once Rajinder decided to put something out of his mind he did it. If I had loved him or even let him hold my attention, perhaps I would have become more like him. Then the last year and a half might have been completely different. If I had been more like Rajinder, I would have been able to maintain the agreement between Pitaji and me. Instead, when he broke it, I took revenge.

I move to Asha's cot. She does not wake. I try to lie beside her. Half my body is on the cot's wood frame. Rajinder was necessary for Asha to be born. Even when I am angry with her, I always think there is a reason for her to be in the world, and for me. I may be stupid, but Asha was born from me.

I did love Rajinder once, through an afternoon's end, the whole of an evening, into a night. I was only twenty-two when I fell in love. It was easy then to think that even love was within my power. Six months married, suddenly awake from a short deep sleep in love with my husband for the first time, I lay in bed that June afternoon, looking out the window at the swiftly advancing gray clouds, believing anything is possible.

We were living in a small flat on the roof of a three-story house in Defense Colony. Rajinder signed the lease a week before our wedding. Two days after we married, he brought me to the flat. Although it was cold, I wore no sweater over my pink sari. I knew that, with my thick eyebrows and broad nose, I must try especially hard to be appealing.

The sun filled the living room through a window that took up half a wall. Rajinder went in first. In the center of the room was a low plywood table with a thistle broom on top. Three plastic folding chairs lay collapsed in the corner. I followed a few steps behind. The room was a white rectangle.

"We can put the TV there," Rajinder said softly, pointing to the right corner of the living room. He stood before the window. Rajinder was slightly overweight. I knew he wore sweaters that were large for him, to hide his stomach. But they suggested humbleness. The thick black frames of his glasses, his old-fashioned mustache thin as a scratch, the hairline giving way, all created an impression of thoughtfulness. "The sofa in front of the window."

I followed Rajinder into the bedroom. The two rooms were exactly alike. "There, the bed," Rajinder said, placing it with a wave against the wall across from the window. He spoke as though he were describing what was already there. "The fridge we can put right next to it," at the foot of the bed. Both were part of my dowry. Whenever he looked at me, I said yes and nodded my head.

From the roof, a little after eleven, I watched Rajinder drive away on his scooter. He was going to my parents' flat in the Old Vegetable Market. My dowry was stored there. There was nothing for me to do while he was gone. I wandered around the roof. Defense Colony is composed of rows of pale three- and four-storied buildings. There was a small park edged with eucalyptus trees behind our house.

Rajinder returned two hours later with his older brother, Ashok. They had borrowed a yellow van to carry the dowry. It took three trips to bring the TV, the sofa, the fridge, the mixer, the stainless-steel dishes. Each time they left, I wanted them never to return. Whenever they pulled up outside, Ashok pressed the horn, which played "Jingle Bells." With his muscular forearms, Ashok reminded me of Pitaji's brothers, who, Ma claimed, beat their wives.

On the first trip they brought back two VIP suitcases that my mother had packed with my clothes. I was cold, so when they left, I went into the bedroom to put on something warmer. My hands were trembling by then. When I swallowed, my throat felt scraped. Standing there naked in the room gray with dust and the light like cold clear water, I felt sad, lonely, excited to be in a place where no one knew me. In the cold, I touched my stomach, my breasts, the inside of my thighs. Afterward I felt lonelier. I put on a salwar kameez.

Rajinder did not notice I had changed. I swept the rooms while they were gone. I stacked the kitchen shelves with the stainless-steel dishes, saucers, spoons that had come as gifts. Rajinder brought all the gifts except the bed, which was too big to carry. It was raised to the roof by pulleys the next day. They were able to bring up the mattress, though. I was glad to see it. Sadness made me sleepy.

We did not eat lunch. In the evening I made rotis on a kerosene stove. The gas canisters had not come yet. There was no lightbulb in the kitchen. I had only the stove's blue flame to see by. The icy wind swirled around my feet. Nearly thirteen years later I can still remember that wind. We ate in the living room. Rajinder and Ashok spoke loudly of the farm, gasoline prices, politics in Haryana, Indira Gandhi's government. I spoke once, saying that I liked Indira Gandhi. Ashok said that was because I was a Delhi woman who wanted to see women in power.

Ashok left after dinner. For the first time since the wedding there wasn't anyone else nearby. Our voices were so respectful we might have been in mourning. Rajinder took me silently in the bedroom. Our mattress was before the window. A full moon peered in. I had hoped that this third time together my body might not be frightened. But when he got on top of me, my arms automatically crossed themselves over my chest. Rajinder had to push them aside. Then I lay looking at the heavyhearted tulips in the window grille. Once Rajinder was asleep, my body slowly loosened.

Three months earlier, when our parents had introduced us, I did not think we would marry. Rajinder's ambiguous features across the restaurant table held nothing significant. Ashok on one side of him, his mother on the other were more distinctive. I sat between my parents. I did not expect to marry someone particularly handsome. I was neither pretty nor talented. But I had believed I would recognize the person I would marry.

Twice before, my parents had introduced me to men, contacted through the matrimonial section of the *Sunday Times* of India. One received a job offer in Bombay. Ma did not want to send me that far away with someone we did not yet know. The other, who drove a Honda motorcycle, was handsome, but he had lied about his income.

Those introductions, like this one, were held in Vikrant, a two-story dosa restaurant across from the Amba cinema. I liked Vikrant, for I thought the obvious cheapness of the place would be held against us. The evening that I met Rajinder, Vikrant was crowded with people waiting for the six-to-nine show. We sat down. An adolescent waiter swept bits of dosa from the table onto the floor. Footsteps upstairs caused flecks of blue paint to drift down.

The dinner began with Rajinder's mother, a small round woman with a pockmarked face, speaking of her sorrow that Rajinder's father had not lived to witness his two sons reach manhood. There was a moment of silence. Pitaji tilted slightly forward to speak. "It's all in the stars. What can a man do?" he said. The roughness of his voice, the danger that his enormous body always projected, sharpened my anxiety. I shifted toward Ma.

The waiter returned with six glasses of water, four in one hand, with his fingers dipped into each. Rajinder and I did not open our mouths until ordering our dosas. At one point, after a long silence, Pitaji tried to start a conversation by asking Rajinder, "Other than work, how do you like to use your time?" Then he added in English, "What hobbies do you have?" The door to the kitchen in the back was open. I saw two boys near a skillet, trying to shove away a cow which must have wandered off the street into the kitchen.

"I like to read the newspaper. In college I played badminton," Rajinder answered in English. He smoothed each word with his tongue before letting go.

"Anita sometimes reads the newspapers," Ma said.

The food came. We ate quickly.

Rajinder's mother talked the most during the meal. She told us about how Rajinder had always been favored over his older brother—a beautiful, hardworking boy who obeyed his mother like God Ram. Rajinder had shown gratitude by passing the exams to become a bank officer. Getting from Bursa to Delhi was three hours in the bus every day. That was very strenuous, she said; besides, Rajinder had long ago reached the age for marriage, so he wished to set up a household in the city. "We want a city girl. With an education but a strong respect for tradition."

"Kusum, Anita's younger sister, is finishing her Ph.D. in molecular biology. She might be going to America in a year, for further studies," Ma said slowly, almost accidentally. "Two of my brothers are engineers. One is a doctor." I loved Ma very much in those days. I thought of her as the one who had protected me all my life. I believed that she had stayed with Pitaji for my sake. Therefore, whenever I heard her make these incredible exaggerations—the engineers were pole climbers for the electricity company while the doctor was the owner of an herbal medicine shop—to people who might find out the truth, I worried for her. Ma did not believe her stories, so she was not crazy. Ma just had no control over her anger. I looked down at the table.

Back then I felt Ma believed that I had partially seduced Pitaji. I thought Ma's aimless anger came from having to sacrifice herself for someone like me.

I put my hand on the back of Ma's neck. I liked to touch her. She was the person I loved most in the world.

Dinner ended. I still had not spoken. When Rajinder said he did not want any ice cream for dessert, I knew I had to say something. "Do you like movies?" It was the only question that came to me.

"A little," Rajinder answered seriously. After a pause he added, "I like Amitabh Bachchan most."

"Me too," I said.

Two days later, Ma asked if I minded marrying Rajinder. We were in the living room. Ma was sitting on the sofa across from me. I thought, What is the hurry, after all? I'm just twenty-one. But I believed that Ma was worried for my safety at home.

I did not think my marriage would occur. Something was sure to come up. Rajinder's family might decide my B.A. was not enough. Rajinder might suddenly announce he was in love with his typist.

The engagement took place a month later. Although I was not allowed to attend the ceremony, Kusum was. She laughed as she described Pitaji, the way his blue jacket rode up when he lifted his arms, revealing that the shirt he wore underneath was short-sleeved. Rajinder sat cross-legged before the pundit on the floor. He was surrounded by relatives. The room was light pink. Rajinder's uncles, Kusum said, pinching her nostrils, smelled of manure.

Only then did I understand that Rajinder was to be my husband. I was shocked. It was as if I were standing outside myself, a stranger, looking at two women sitting on a brown sofa in a wide bright room. Two women. Both cried if slapped, laughed if tickled, but one had finished her higher secondary when she was fifteen, was already doing her Ph.D., with the possibility of going to America; the other, her older sister, who was slow in school, was now going to marry, have children, grow old. Why was it that when Pitaji took us out of school saying that we were all moving to Beri, Kusum, then only in third grade, reenrolled herself, while I waited for Pitaji to change his mind?

As the days till the wedding evaporated, I slept all the time. Sometimes I woke thinking the engagement was a dream. At home the marriage was mentioned only in connection with the shopping involved. Once Kusum said, "I've read you shouldn't have sex the first night. Just tell him, 'No loving tonight.' "

The wedding occurred in the alley outside the compound where we had a flat. The pundit recited Sanskrit verses. Rajinder and I circled the holy fire seven times. When told, we put necklaces of marigolds around each other's necks to seal the marriage. I was wearing a bright red silk sari which had the sour smell of new cloth. There were many people surrounding us. Movie songs blared over the loudspeakers. On the ground was a red dhurri with black stripes. The tent above us had the same stripes. The night traffic passing outside the alley caused the ground to rumble.

The celebration lasted another six hours, ending about one in the morning. I did not remember most of it till many years later. The two red thrones on which we sat to receive congratulations are only in the photographs, not in my memories. There are photos showing steam coming from people's mouths, so it must have been especially cold. For nearly eight years I did not remember how Ashok and his mother, Ma, Pitaji, Kusum, Rajesh got into the car with us to go to the dharamshala, where the people from Rajinder's side were spending the night. Nor did I remember walking through the dharamshala's halls, passing rooms where people were asleep on cots, mattresses without frames, blankets folded twice before being laid down.

I did not remember any of this until recently. I was wandering through Kamla Nagar market in search of a dress for Kusum's daughter and suddenly felt the shock of my shopping while Pitaji was in his room waiting to die. The waste. My life was a waste. I was standing on the sidewalk looking at a display of hairbands. I thought of Kusum's husband, a tall yellow-haired American with a kind face, who I believed had taught Kusum kindness. Standing there, I thought of the time I loved Rajinder. I started to cry. People brushed past. I wanted to sit down on the sidewalk so that someone might notice and ask whether anything was wrong.

I did remember Rajinder opening the blue door to the room where we spent our first night. Before we entered, we separated for a moment. Rajinder touched his mother's feet. His mother embraced him. I touched my parents' feet. As Ma held me, she whispered, "Earlier your father got drunk like the pig he is."

Then Pitaji put his arms around me. "I love you," he said in English.

The English was what brought the tears. The words reminded me of how Pitaji came home drunk after work once or twice a month. Ma, thin arms folded across her chest, stood in his bedroom doorway watching him fumbling with his clothes. I tried to be behind Ma. This was after Pitaji was caught with me. I had to watch. To leave was the same as saying I had nothing to do with all this.

Usually Pitaji was silent. But if he was very drunk, Pitaji might call out to me, "No one loves me. You love me, don't you, my little sun-ripened mango? I try to be good. I work all day, but no one loves me." He spoke in English then, as if to prove he was sober. The "little sun-ripened mango" was something he used to call me before we were caught. Eventually Pitaji began crying softly. After a while, he appeared to forget that he was being watched. Sometimes he turned out the lights and wept in the dark.

Those nights Ma served dinner without speaking. When Rajesh saw what was going to happen, he might take his food to the roof. Sometimes Kusum was there. Mostly it was just me.

There were beautiful lines in the story Ma told to explain everything. Lines like "In higher secondary, a teacher said, in seven years all the cells in our body change. So when Baby died I thought, it will be all right. In seven years none of me will have touched Baby." Ma did not eat dinner. She might stand still as she talked, or she might walk in circles around me. "I loved him once," she usually said many times before she began talking of Baby's getting sick, the telegrams to Beri for Pitaji to come, his not doing so, her not telegramming about Baby's death. "What could he do?" she might conclude, while looking at the floor, "although he always cries so handsomely." I knew, of course, that everything was about me.

When Pitaji woke from his drunken sleeps, he asked for water to dissolve the powders he took to purge himself by vomiting. On my wedding night, while Pitaji spoke of love in English, it was the soft wet vowels of his vomiting that I remembered.

Rajinder bolted the door of the room where we spent our first night together. There was a double bed in the center of the room. Near it was a small table with a jug of water and two glasses. The room had yellow walls. The mattress smelled faintly of mildew. I stopped crying. I was suddenly calm. I stood near the bed, a fold of the sari covering my eyes. I thought, I will just say our marriage has been a terrible mistake. Rajinder lifted the sari's fold. He looked into my eyes. *I am lucky*, he said. He was wearing a white silk kurta with tiny flowers embroidered around the neck. With a light squeeze of my elbow, he let me know I was to sit. He took off his kurta, folded it like a shirt, put it on the table. *No, wait. I must tell you*, I said. The tie of his pajamas was hidden under his drooping stomach. Hair rose in a cord up his belly. At his chest it spread into a stain. What an ugly man, I thought. *No. Wait*, I said. He did not hear or I did not say. Louder. *You are a very nice man, I am sure.* He took off his pajamas. His penis looked like a slug resting on lichen-covered rocks. He laid me down on the bed, which had a white sheet dotted with rose petals. I put my hands on his chest to push him away. He took both wrists in one hand. *No loving tonight*, I said, but he might not have heard, or I might not have said. I wondered whether it would hurt as much as it had with Pitaji. My breath quickened from fear. Rajinder's other hand undid my blouse. I felt its disappointment with my small breasts. The ceiling was so far away. The moisture between my legs was like breath on glass.

Rajinder put on his kurta, poured himself some water. After drinking he offered me some.

Sleep was there as soon as I closed my eyes. But around eight in the morning, when Rajinder woke me, I was exhausted. The door to our room was open. One of Rajinder's cousins, a fat hairy man with a towel around his waist, walked past to the bathroom. Seeing me, he leered.

I had breakfast with Rajinder's family in our room. We sat around a small table eating parathas with yogurt. I wanted to sleep. Again Rajinder's mother talked the most. Her words were indistinct. I would blink and my eyes would remain closed. "You eat like a bird," she said, smiling.

After breakfast we visited a widowed aunt of Rajinder's who had been unable to attend the wedding because of arthritis. She lived in a two-room flat whose walls, floor to ceiling, were covered with posters of gods. The flat smelled of mothballs. As she spoke of carpenters and cobblers moving in from the villages to pass themselves off as upper castes, the corners of her mouth became white with spit. I was silent, except for when she asked me what dishes I liked to cook. As we left, she pressed fifty-one rupees into Rajinder's hands. "A thousand years. A thousand children," she said.

Then there was the bus ride to Rajinder's village. The roads were so bad I kept being jolted awake. My sleep became fractured till I dreamed of the bus ride. In the village there were the grimy hens peering into the well and the women for whom I posed demurely in the courtyard. They sat in a circle around me, murmuring compliments. My eyes were covered with my sari. As I stared at the ground, I fell asleep. I woke an hour later to their praise of my modesty. That night in the dark room at the rear of the house, I was awakened by Rajinder digging between my legs. Although he tried to be gentle, I just wished it over. There was the face, distorted above me, the hands which raised my nipples so cruelly, resentful of being cheated, even though there was never any anger in Rajinder's voice. He was always polite. Even in bed he used the formal you. "Could you get on all fours, please?"

Winter turned into spring. The trees in the park beside our home swelled green. Rajinder was kind. When he traveled for conferences to Baroda, Madras, Jaipur, Bangalore, he always brought back saris or other gifts. The week I had malaria, he came home every lunch hour. On my twenty-second birthday he took me to the Taj Mahal. When we returned in the evening, he had arranged for my family to hide in the flat.

Rajinder did not make me do anything I did not want to, except for sex. Even that was sometimes like a knot being kneaded out. I did not mind his being in the flat. The loneliness I felt, however, when Rajinder was away on his trips was not based on missing him. It was only the loneliness of being a person in the world. I do not think Rajinder missed me on his trips, for he never mentioned it.

Despite my not thinking of Rajinder when he wasn't there, he was good for me. He was ambitious, and watching his efforts gave me confidence. He was always trying for a degree or certificate in something. Anything can be done if you are intelligent, hardworking, open-minded, he would boast. Before Rajinder, I had not actually believed one event pushes into another. I took a class in English. Because I studied it two hours a day, I progressed quickly. Rajinder told me there was nothing whorish in wearing lipstick. Wearing lipstick and perfume began making me feel attractive. Along with teaching me to try, Rajinder took me to restaurants where foreign food was served, to plays, to English movies. He was so modern he even said "Oh Jesus" instead of "Oh Ram." The world seemed slightly larger than it had been before.

Summer came. Every few days, the luu swept up from Rajasthani deserts, killing one or two of the cows left wandering unattended on Delhi's streets. The corpses lay untouched for a week sometimes, till their swelling tongues cracked open their jaws and stuck out absurdly.

For me, the heat was like a constant buzzing. It separated flesh from bone and my skin felt rubbery. I began to wake earlier and earlier. By five, the eastern edge of the sky was too bright to look at. I bathed early in the morning, then after breakfast. I did so again after doing laundry, before lunch. As June progressed, the very air seemed to whine under the heat's stress. I stopped eating lunch. Around two, before taking my nap, I poured a few mugs of water on my head. I liked to lie on the bed imagining the monsoon had come.

So the summer passed, slowly and vengefully, till the last week of June, when I woke one afternoon in love.

I had returned home that day after spending two weeks with my parents. Pitaji had been sick. I had helped take care of him in Safdarjung Hospital. For months a bubble had been growing at the base of his neck. We noticed it when it looked like a pencil rubber. Over two months it became a small translucent ball. If examined in the right light, it was cloudy from blood. We told Pitaji to have it examined. He only went to a herbal doctor for poultices. So when I opened the door late one night to find Kusum, I did not have to be told that Pitaji had wakened screaming that his pillow was sodden with blood.

While I hurried clothes into a plastic bag, Kusum leaned against a wall of our bedroom drinking water. It was three. Rajinder sat on the edge of the bed in a blue kurta pajama. I felt no fear. The rushing, the banging on doors seemed to be only melodrama.

As I stepped into the autorickshaw which had been waiting for us downstairs, I looked up. Rajinder was leaning against the railing. The moon behind him was yellow and uneven like a scrap of old newspaper. I waved. He waved back. Then we were off, racing through dark, abandoned streets.

"Ma's fine," Kusum said. "He screamed so loud." She sat slightly turned on the seat so that she faced me. Kusum wore shirt pants. "A thousand times we told him, Get it checked. Don't be cheap. Where's all that black money going?" She shook her head.

I felt lonely talking of our father without concern. "He wants to die," I said. "That's why he eats and drinks like that. He's ashamed of his life, of his bribes, all that." This was one of the interpretations Pitaji had been suggesting for years, so it came unbidden to my tongue.

"If he was really ashamed, he'd change. He's just crazy."

I had not meant to defend Pitaji, for I did not think he needed defending. I viewed Pitaji impersonally, like a historical event.

"The way he treats Ma. Or the way he treated you. I remember when he'd stamp his foot next to you to see how high you'd jump. If he wants to die, he should do it quietly. You and Ma are cowards."

"Ma hates him," I murmured. The night air was still bitter from the evening traffic. I wondered if Kusum's capacity to expect things from people was due to her not being raised at home. I said, "We have to live with him. Why be angry?"

"That's what he's relying on. Be angry. It's a big world. There are a lot of people worth loving. Why waste time on somebody mediocre?"

In the hospital there was broken glass in the hallways. Someone had urinated in the lift. When we came into the yellow room that

Pitaji shared with five other men, he was asleep. His face looked like a shiny brown stone. He was on the bed nearest the window. Rajesh stood at the head of the bed. Ma sat at its foot, her back to us, looking out at the bleaching night.

"He will be all right," I said.

Turning toward us, Ma said, "When he goes, he wants to make sure we all hurt." She was crying. "I thought I didn't love him, but you can't live this long with a person and not love just a bit. He knew that. When they were bringing him here, he said, 'See what you've done, demoness.'"

The world slipped from under me. Ma had often said she hated Pitaji. I became dizzy. One second Ma was herself and then, the next second, there was no one in the world who loved me.

Rajesh took her away. Kusum also left, so that she would not be tired for her laboratory in the morning. I spent the rest of the night awake in a chair next to Pitaji's bed.

Around eight, Ma returned. While we were there, I kept looking away from her, because it made me too sad to see her face. I went to the flat. In the days that followed, it was I who replaced Ma in the morning. Kusum lived at home while Pitaji was sick, but she came to the hospital only once.

At night, Kusum, Rajesh, and I slept on adjacent cots on the flat's roof. I sometimes played cards with Rajesh before going to bed. Kusum did not join us. Instead, every night, in preparation for going abroad, she read five pages of an English dictionary. She would write down the words she did not know. Kusum did not brag about her work as I might have.

I had thought I would be anxious alone with Pitaji. After Ma caught Pitaji and me, he and I were rarely together. When we were, it was either in public or with Ma in a nearby room from which she would periodically appear. Her surveillance made me feel that she had no faith in me. Now, despite the other patients in the room with Pitaji, I worried that since only Ma knew how dangerous he was, he might be able to hurt me. Even asleep, Pitaji looked threatening. But the medicines kept him unconscious. When he woke, it was only to ask for water or food, then he fell asleep again. If I did not respond quickly enough to his demands, Pitaji screamed and I cringed.

Two or three days after I began staying with Pitaji, I was looking out the window at the autorickshaws lined up across the street when Pitaji shouted something at me. I turned to him, saw his mouth opening and closing like a digging machine or a dog, and I thought, I can leave right now. I can be home in twenty minutes in one of the autorickshaws. Suddenly I could see only Pitaji. Everything else vanished in a white rage. I felt as if I were tipping forward.

In a few hours the anger was gone. Once it stopped, I doubted its intensity.

When I replaced Ma the next morning, she greeted me by nodding toward Pitaji. "He won't die a natural death," she said with a strange pride.

The anger came back momentarily. I nearly said, "Let's kill him, then."

That afternoon Pitaji wasn't able to sleep. He told me again the story of how an exorcist had been called to beat his mother sane. Pitaji had been unable to watch. But he could not leave, for he felt he would be abandoning her. He stood in the doorway of their one-room mud house, looking out as she was beaten behind him. A crowd of children had gathered beyond the front yard. Whenever his mother screamed, the crowd whispered. Pitaji told the story calmly, as if it were someone else he was talking about. When he finished, he changed the topic. But Pitaji had told the story before, so the desire to create a reaction was obvious. I was looking out the window at the groundskeeper. He was walking around the compound sprinkling the dust with water from a bag the size of a man's body that was slung over one shoulder. When I did not turn around at the story's end, Pitaji said, "I'm sorry. I'm an old man. I shouldn't always be trying to get pity." This self-awareness made me feel for the first time that Pitaji need not have raped me. I had been raped because for Pitaji no one was as real as he was, so nothing he did to others had substance. My anger kept me from moving. When I did begin turning to him, I was frightened I might stab him with the scissors on the stool near his bed.

This rage did not evaporate. I now hated Pitaji constantly. It was like a steady buzz in the background. Once, he screamed at me for not giving him his food on time, and I took his lunch and scraped it into the trash canister. "What will you eat now?" I said. I stopped giving him his lunch till he asked. If he forgot to take his medicines, I did not remind him.

I also imagined Ma getting pneumonia that caused her lungs to collapse. I liked to think of her struggling to breathe. But to neither one did I show my feelings directly. I might show disrespect or challenge Ma over every petty thing, but to say something directly about what Pitaji had done felt like the end of the world.

I did not see Rajinder for the two weeks I was with my parents. But thinking of Rajinder was a comfort, like the reality of the bed during malarial dreams.

My hatred was so constant that it was as if gravity had increased. It exhausted me. But when I slept, as soon as I gained a certain minimum relief, I woke. My eyelids sometimes twitched for a minute at a time. My temper was wild. Kusum suggested I should go to a doctor; I answered, "My eyelids twitch, Kusum, because I work all day while you read in your air-conditioned laboratory."

Around eleven the day Pitaji was released, an ambulance carried him home to the Old Vegetable Market. Two orderlies, muscular men in white uniforms, carried his bulk on a stretcher up the stairs into the flat. Fourteen or fifteen people came out into the courtyard to watch. Some of the very old women, sitting on cots in the courtyard, kept asking who Pitaji was, although he had lived there six years. A few children climbed into the ambulance. They played with the horn till somebody chased them out.

The orderlies laid Pitaji on the cot in his bedroom before leaving. It was a small dark room, smelling faintly of the kerosene with which the bookshelves were treated every other week to prevent termites. Traveling had tired him. He fell asleep quickly. Pitaji woke as I was about to leave. I was whispering to Ma outside his bedroom.

"I don't know when I'm coming back. I have my own family."

"How much I suffer, only God knows."

"You should have made him go to a doctor right in the beginning."

"What could I do? I can't make him do anything."

"Are you talking about me?" Pitaji tried to call out, but his voice was like wind on dry grass.

"You want something?" Ma asked.

"Water."

As I started toward the fridge, Ma said, "You can't give him anything cold."

I got water from the clay pot. Kneeling beside the cot, I helped Pitaji rise to a forty-five-degree angle. Ma had undressed him. He was wearing only his undershorts. His heaviness, the weakness of his body made me feel as if I were embracing an enormous larva. Pitaji held the glass with both hands. He made sucking noises as he drank. I lowered him when his shoulder muscles slackened. His eyes moved about the room slowly.

"More?" he asked.

"There's no more," I said, even though there was. Ma was clattering in the kitchen. "I'm going home."

"Rajinder is good?" He looked at the ceiling while speaking.

"Yes," I said. "The results for his exam came. He'll be promoted. He came second in all Delhi." Telling him this felt like a taunt, as if I was suggesting he was a failure.

Pitaji closed his eyes. "I feel tired."

"All you've been doing is lying in bed. Go to sleep."

"I don't want to," he answered loudly.

Remembering that in a few minutes I would leave, I said, "You'll get better."

"Sometimes I dream that the heaviness I feel is dirt. What an awful thing to be buried, like a Muslim or a Christian." He spoke slowly. "Once I dreamed of Baby's ghost."

"Oh." I was interested, because Baby's importance was confusing.

"He was eight or nine. He didn't recognize me. Baby didn't look at all like me. I was surprised, because I had always expected him to look like me."

There was something polished about the story, which indicated deceit. My hatred increased. "God will forgive you," I said, wanting him to begin his excuses and disgust me further.

"Your mother has not."

Had she forgiven Pitaji for what he had done to me but not forgiven him for making her unhappy? "Shhh." Now there was so much unhappiness that even anger was overwhelmed.

"At your birthday, when she sang, I said, 'If you sing like that for me every day, I will love you forever.' "

I was on my way home. "She worries about you."

"That's not the same. When I tell Kusum this, she tells me I'm sentimental. Radha loved me once. But she cannot forgive. What happened so long ago she cannot forgive." He was blinking rapidly, preparing to cry. "But that is a lie. She does not love me because I—" he began crying without making a sound—"I did not love her for so long. Radha could have loved me a little. She should have loved me twenty for my eleven."

Ma came to the doorway. "What are you crying about now? Nobody loves you? Aw, sad baby." Holding the sides of the doorway, she leaned forward. She appeared eager.

"You think it's so easy being sick?" he said.

"Easier than working."

"I wish you were sick."

I watched them. For a moment I didn't have the strength to stand. Then I remembered, I can go to my home.

.   .   .

My sleep when I returned to my flat was like falling. I lay down, closed my eyes, plummeted. I woke as suddenly, without any half-memories of dreams, into a silence which meant the electricity was gone, the ceiling fan still, the fridge slowly warming.

It was cool. But I was unsurprised by the monsoon's approach, for I was in love. The window curtains stirred, revealing TV antennas. Sparrows wheeled in front of distant gray clouds. The sheet lay bunched at my feet. I felt gigantic, infinite. But I was also small, compact, distilled. I had everything in me to make Rajinder silly with tenderness. I imagined him softening completely at seeing me. I am in love, I thought. A raspy voice echoed the words in my head, causing me to lose my confidence for a moment. I will love him slowly, carefully, cunningly. I suddenly felt peaceful again, as if I were a lake and the world could only form ripples on my surface while the calm beneath continued in solitude.

I stood. I was surprised that my love was not disturbed by my physical movements. I walked out onto the roof. The wind ruffled treetops. Small gray clouds slid across the pale sky. On the street, eight or nine young boys were playing cricket.

Tell me your stories, I will ask him. Pour them into me, so that I know everything you have ever loved or been scared of or laughed at. But thinking this, I became uneasy that when I actually saw him, my love might fade. My tongue became thick. What shall I say? I woke this afternoon in love with you. I love you, too, he will answer. No, no, you see, I really love you. I love you so much that I think anything is possible, that I will live forever. Oh, he will say. My love will abandon me in a rush. I must say nothing at first, I decided. Slowly I will win his love. I will spoil him till he falls in love with me. As long as Rajinder loves me, I will be able to love him. I will love him like a camera lens that closes at too much light and opens at too little, so his blemishes will never mar my love.

I watched the cricket game to the end. Again, I felt enormous. When the children dispersed, it was around five. Rajinder should have left his office.

I bathed. I stood before the small mirror in the armoire as I dressed. Uneven brown areolae, a flat stomach, the veins in my feet like pen marks. Will this be enough? I wondered. Once he loves me, I told myself. I lifted my arms to smell the plantlike odor of my perspiration. I wore a bright red cotton sari. What will I say first? Namaste, how was your day? With the informal you. How was your day? The words felt strange, for I had never before used the informal with him. I had, as a show of modesty, never even used his name, except for the night before my wedding, when I said it hundreds of times to myself to see how it sounded—like nothing. Now, standing before the mirror, when I said Rajinder, the three syllables had too many edges. Rajinder, Rajinder, I said rapidly several times, till it no longer felt strange. He will love me because it is too lonely otherwise, because I will love him so. I heard a scooter stopping outside the building, the metal door to the courtyard swinging open.

My stomach clenched as I walked onto the roof. The dark clouds had turned late evening into early night. I saw Rajinder roll the scooter into the courtyard. He parked the scooter, took off his gray helmet. He combed his hair carefully to hide the emerging bald spot. The deliberate way he tucked the comb into his back pocket overwhelmed me with tenderness. We will love each other carefully.

I waited for him to rise out of the stairwell. My petticoat drying on the clothesline went clap, clap in the wind. How was your day? How was your day? Was your day good? I told myself, Don't be so afraid. What does it matter how you say hello? There will be tomorrow, the day after, the day after that.

His steps sounded like a shuffle. Leather rubbing against stone. There was something forlorn to the sound. Rajinder, Rajinder, Rajinder, how are you?

First the head: oval, high forehead, handsome eyebrows. Then the not so broad but not so narrow shoulders. The top two buttons of the cream shirt were opened, revealing some hair, a white undershirt. The two weeks since I last saw him had not changed Rajinder, yet he felt different, somehow denser.

"How was your day?" I asked, while he was still in the stairwell.

"All right," he said, stepping onto the roof. He smiled. His helmet was in his left hand. In his right was a plastic bag full of mangoes. "When did you get home?" The you was informal. I felt a surge of relief. He will not resist, I thought.

"A little after three."

I followed him into the bedroom. He placed the helmet on the windowsill. The mangoes went in the refrigerator. I remained silent.

Rajinder walked onto the roof to the sink on the outside bathroom wall. He began washing his hands, face, neck with soap. "Your father is fine?" he asked. Before putting the chunk of soap down, he rinsed it of foam. Only then did he pour water on himself. He used a thin washcloth hanging on a nearby hook for drying. When I am with him, I promised myself, I will not think of Pitaji. It's much more than seven years since Pitaji touched me.

"Yes."

"What did the doctor say?" he asked, turning toward me. He was like a black diamond.

"Nothing."

I watched Rajinder hang his shirt by the collar tips on the clothesline. I suddenly became sad at the rigorous attention to details necessary to preserve love. Perhaps it is easier for other women, I thought, women who are braver, who have less to be afraid of, who have more trust. That must be a different type of love, I thought, in which one can be careless.

"It will rain tonight," he said, looking at the sky.

The eucalyptus trees shook their heads from side to side. "The rain always makes me feel as if I am waiting for someone," I said. Immediately I regretted saying it, for Rajinder was not paying attention. Perhaps it might have been said better. "Why don't you sit on the balcony." The balcony was what we called the area near the stairwell. "I'll make sherbet."

He took the newspaper with him. The fridge water was warm. This slight disappointment was enough to start melancholy pooling. I gave him the drink. I placed mine on the floor near his chair, then went to get a chair for myself. A fruit seller passed by, calling out in a reedy voice, "Sweet, sweet mangoes. Sweeter than first love." On the roof directly across, a seven- or eight-year-old boy was trying to fly a large purple kite. I sat down beside Rajinder. I waited for him to look up, because I did not want to interrupt his reading. When he looked away from the paper to take a sip of sherbet, I asked, "Did you fly kites?"

"A little," he answered, looking at the boy. "Ashok bought some with the money he earned. He'd let me fly them sometimes." The fact that his father had died when he was young was encouraging. I believed one must be lonely before being able to love.

"Do you like Ashok?"

"He is my brother," he answered, shrugging. With a sip of the sherbet he returned to the newspaper. I felt Rajinder had reprimanded me.

I sat beside Rajinder and waited for the electricity to return. I was happy, excited, frightened being beside him. We spoke about Kusum going to America, though Rajinder did not want to talk about this. Rajinder was the most educated member of our combined family. After Kusum received her Ph.D. she would be.

The electricity didn't come back. I started cooking in the dark. Rajinder sat on the balcony with the radio playing. "This is Akashwani," the announcer said, then the music like horses racing which plays whenever a new program is about to start. It was very hot in the kitchen. Periodically I stepped onto the roof to look at the curve of Rajinder's neck. This confirmed the tenderness in me.

Rajinder ate slowly. Once, he complimented me on my cooking, but he was mostly silent.

"What are you thinking?" I asked. He appeared not to have heard. Tell me! Tell me! Tell me! I thought, shocking myself by the urgency I felt.

A candle on the television made pillars of shadows rise and collapse on the walls. I searched for something to start a conversation with. "Pitaji began crying when I left."

"You could have stayed a few more days," he said, chewing.

"I did not want to." I thought of adding, "I missed you," but that was not true. Also, he had not indicated he missed me.

Rajinder mixed black pepper with his yogurt. "Did you tell him you'll visit soon?"

"No. I think he was crying because he was lonely."

"He should have more courage." Rajinder did not like Pitaji, thought him weak-willed. "He is old. Shadows creep into one's heart at his age." I felt as if he were telling me not to be hindered by my doubts. The shutter of a bedroom window began slamming. I stood to latch it.

I washed the dishes while Rajinder bathed. When he came out, dressed in his white kurta pajama with his hair combed back, I was standing near the railing at the edge of the roof. I was looking out beyond the darkness of our neighborhood at a distant ribbon of electric light. I was tired from the nervousness I had been feeling all evening. Rajinder came up behind me. "Won't you bathe?" he asked. I suddenly became exhausted. Bathe so we can make love. The deliberately unsaid felt obscene. I wondered if I had the courage to say no. I realized I didn't. What kind of love can we have? I thought.

I said, "In a little while. Comedy hour is starting." We sat down on our chairs with Gopi Ram's whiny voice between us. This week he had gotten involved with criminals who wanted to go to jail to collect the reward on themselves. The canned laughter gusted from several flats. When the music of the racing horses marked the close of the show, I felt hopeful again. Rajinder looked very handsome in his kurta pajama.

I bathed carefully, pouring mug after mug of cold water over myself till my fingertips were wrinkled. The candlelight turned the bathroom orange. My skin appeared copper. I washed my pubis carefully so no smell remained from urinating. Rubbing myself dry, I became aroused. I thought how abject all this was. I put on the red sari again. I wore no bra so my nipples showed through the blouse. As I dressed, a strange emotion began filling me. I was clenching and unclenching my hands. As I noticed I was doing this, I started shaking. The feeling was close to panic, but not exactly that. I wanted to run toward instead of away. It was not some form of love either. Even one afternoon of loving let me know that. The emotion was like anger.

After a few minutes, I went out. I stood beside Rajinder. My arm brushed against his kurta sleeve. Periodically a raindrop fell, but these were so intermittent I might have been imagining them. On the roofs all around us, on the street, were the dim figures of men, women, and children waiting for the first rain. "You look pretty," he said. Somewhere Lata Mangeshkar sang with a static-induced huskiness. The street was silent. Even the children were hushed. As the wind picked up, Rajinder said, "Let's close the windows."

The wind coursed along the floor, upsetting newspapers, climbing the walls to swing on curtains. There was a candle on the refrigerator. As I leaned over to pull a window shut, Rajinder pressed against me. He cupped my right breast. I felt a shock of desire pass through me. As I walked around the rooms shutting windows, he followed behind, touching my buttocks, pubis, stomach.

When the last window was closed, I waited for a moment before turning around, because I knew he wanted me to turn around quickly. He pulled me close, with his hands on my buttocks. I took his tongue in my mouth. We kissed like this for a long time.

The rain began falling. There was a roar from the people on the roofs nearby. "The clothes," Rajinder said. He pulled away.

We ran out. It was hard to see each other. Lightning bursts illuminated an eye, an arm, some teeth. Then there was darkness again. We jerked the clothes off, letting the pins fall to the ground. We deliberately brushed roughly against each other. The raindrops were like thorns. We began laughing. Rajinder's shirt had wrapped itself around and around the clothesline. Wiping his face, he knocked his glasses off. As I saw him crouched and fumbling around helplessly for them, I felt such tenderness that I knew I would never love him as much as I did at that moment. "The wind in the trees," I said, "it sounds like the sea."

We slowly moved back inside, kissing all the while. When he entered me, it was like a sigh. He suckled on me and moved back and forth and side to side, and I felt myself growing warm and loose. He held my waist with both hands. We made love gently at first, but as we both neared climax, Rajinder began stabbing me with his penis. I came in waves so strong that I wanted to say, Make me invisible; make me the sky. When Rajinder sank on top of me, I said, "I love you."

"I love you, too," he answered.

The candle had gone out. Rajinder got up to light it. He drank some water, then lay down beside me. I wanted some water, too, but did not want to say anything to suggest thoughtlessness. "I'll be getting promoted soon. Minaji loves me," Rajinder said. I rolled onto my side to look at him. He had his arms folded across his chest. "Yesterday he said, 'Come, Rajinderji, let us write your confidential report.' " I put my hand on his stomach. Rajinder said, "Don't." He pushed my hand away. "I said, 'Oh, I don't know whether that's good, sir.' He laughed. What a nincompoop. If it weren't for the quotas he'd never be manager." Rajinder chuckled. "I'll be the youngest bank manager in Delhi." I tugged a sheet over our legs. "In college I had a schedule for where I wanted to be by the time I was thirty. By twenty-two I became an officer, soon I'll be a manager. I wanted a car. We'll have that in a year. I wanted a wife. I have that."

"You are so smart."

"There were smarter people than I in college. But I knew exactly what I wanted. A life is like a house. One has to plan carefully where all the furniture will go."

"Did you plan me as your wife?" I asked, smiling.

"No, I had wanted at least an M.A. and someone who worked, but Mummy didn't approve of a daughter-in-law who worked. I was willing to change my requirements. It's because I believe in moderation that I am successful. Everything in its place. Also, pay for everything. Other people got caught up in love and friendship. I've always thought that these things only became important because of the movies."

After a moment I asked, "You love me and your mother, don't you?"

Rajinder considered how to answer me. "There are so many people in the world that it is hard not to think that there are others you can love more." Seeing the shock on my face, he quickly added, "Of course I love you. I just try not to be too emotional about it." The candle's shadows on the wall were like the wavy bands formed by light reflected off water. "We might even be able to get a foreign car."

The second time he took me that night, it was from behind. He pressed down heavily on my back and grabbed my breasts.

I woke at four or five. The rain scratched against the windows and there was a light like blue milk along the edges of the door. I was cold and tried wrapping myself in the sheet, but it was not large enough.

THREE

Sleep was there immediately. The fear was so great, I could not stay conscious. I closed my eyes and was gone. The sleep lasted only minutes. I roused when Anita snapped off the common-room light on her way to bed, but I kept my eyes closed and hoped to faint again.

Asha moving past Anita into the common room and Anita staying in the doorway; Asha moving past Anita into the common room and Anita staying in the doorway. I dreamed this all night, and each time I did, my heart started wildly and I woke. Then the alcohol and fear dragged me into sleep again. I woke and passed out so many times that I grew confused and began doubting whether Anita had stood in my doorway and called Asha away from me.

Around three that morning, the alcohol thinned to the point that I no longer passed out automatically. My bladder started to ache, but I did not want to get up. Walking to the bathroom would make it harder to believe that I had imagined everything. I stayed on the cot with the sheet pulled over my face and thought, Anita couldn't remember; what happened with her was so long ago. If she couldn't remember, why would she be suspicious? Besides, from where she stood, how could she see I had my penis against Asha's back? When she told Asha to brush her teeth, there was nothing on Anita's face to show that she knew.

As my certainties kept changing, there were moments of complete calm and moments of overwhelming terror. I tried to imagine my life if Anita confronted me over her childhood. I could not. Not only would the future end, but everything I had been would also be erased.

A little before five, the pain in my bladder forced me up. My room had become packed with fears, and leaving it for the common room felt like stepping off a crowded bus into wind. The balcony door and the kitchen shutters were closed, but enough light slipped through them to tint the darkness blue. I could hear the whoosh of my own blood. My fears were joined by horror.

As I urinated in the dank darkness of the latrine, I thought that my fifty-seven years had not only not taught me decency, they had not even taught me caution. The recklessness of caressing Asha while Anita was in the common room was the same as when I had fondled Anita in the storage room on the roof while Radha and the other children could be heard moving about downstairs. My penis's smoothness reminded me of when it was slick with blood and sperm. I began crying. There was something fatal in repeating my crime so exactly. The preciseness had the same inevitability as death. I sobbed so strongly I had to put a hand against the wall for support.

Weeping was comforting. A part of me reasoned that because I was crying and penitent, God could not have let Anita see what I was doing. Besides, if God allowed the discovery, who would be helped? Whatever happened, Anita needed to stay with me because she had no money. Her poverty should keep her from confronting me. Then I noticed how my mind was working, and shame filled me.

I thought of Asha speaking in Urdu when she thanked me for the badminton rackets, and I cringed at what I had done with someone so small.

From the shame came the idea of going to my village and finding the pundit to make sure he was in Delhi tomorrow. This way Radha would be prayed for by someone who knew her. I would be doing something good and God would protect me because of this. Going to Beri also meant one day of not having to see Anita.

Misery often makes me want to look away from the present and leads me to nostalgia. As I swallowed my heart medicine in the blue dark of the common room, I imagined walking through Beri's sugarcane fields and sitting beneath a mango tree. I wanted to be a child again, with the future a wide, still river in the afternoon.

When I passed through Anita and Asha's bedroom on my way out of the flat, I heard one of them roll over. The room was completely dark and I could not see who had turned and whether either was awake. The door chain clacked as I unhooked it, but no one spoke.

The dark sky was beginning to fade in streaks, and night's mildness was still in the air. I found a bicycle rickshaw where the Malka Ganj and Ghanta Ghar roads meet in a V. The streets to the Inter-State Bus Terminal were mostly empty. A few old men were out for strolls, and there was an occasional mysterious person: a woman dressed for a party talking with herself on the sidewalk: "Don't worry about me. I'm a queen. I'm a governor"; or a teenage boy with a suitcase, barefoot and walking with his head tilted up and a rag to his nose to stanch a nosebleed. But mostly there was just the creak of the rickshaw as the driver's feet slowly rose and fell on the pedals.

When I settled back in the seat, memories of my childhood came to me. I remembered that when my mother and I waited by the side of the road for a bus, I would tell my mother to move back, not because I was worried about her safety, but because this was one of the few ways I had to show my love. The sense of loss for the boy I once was made shame settle in my chest like a clot. Asha was so small that if one looked at only her hand or foot, it seemed unreal.

The bus terminal was roaring with the enormous noise of thousands of people arriving and departing and of the buses which brought them and took them away. There were villagers; there were men and women dressed in pants and shirts; there were foreigners. There were carts selling everything from pieces of fresh coconut, to water and lemonade, to hot food, to plastic toys. There was such a sense of energy that everything appeared possible. All this confirmed the rightness of my decision to go in search of the pundit.

Beneath the heaviness in my chest, I felt a pulse of excitement.

I found the Haryana Roadways ticket booth and bought a ticket to Beri. The bus was parked in a corner of the compound that surrounds the ISBT. I stepped over suitcases and small bundles to move down the aisle toward a window seat in the back. The seat was torn, and straw showed through the rips in the green plastic. My belly almost touched the seat in front of me. The bus smelled of manure and sweat and rang with the quick dialects of the villagers who filled it. A wedding party of red-turbaned men sat singing in the front.

My mind hurtled from one thought to the other. There was my shame, my eagerness for the trip, and now that I was in the bus, a worry that in Beri I would meet one of my brothers or their children, whom I had not seen for five years, since we quarreled over a piece of land my father left us. But I would not have a problem remaining unrecognized. I began planning what I would do once I got to the village. I would find the ice-cream factory the pundit's wife had told me he was blessing; then I would walk along the river which I had liked so much as a child; and then, while waiting for the next bus to Delhi, I might have lunch at a dhaba. Thinking of food made me drool.

I was disgusted with myself.

I looked out the window. Buses and people crowded the ISBT compound. Along a wall I saw three old women, their faces covered with folds of their saris, squatting and urinating. I imagined the darkening dust beneath them and I felt again the inevitability of my nature. My mind was attracted to what is loathsome and humiliating. Although I was not sexually attracted to men, I sometimes imagined sucking the penises of the rich and powerful, like Mr. Gupta or Mr. Maurya, and I would feel humiliation and delight at currying favor.

I turned away from the women. On top of the wall next to which they crouched was a billboard with Nehru's handsome smiling face and some quotation about the nature of generosity.

The bus started and we rattled onto the road. We went past the Red Fort and Chandni Chowk and into New Delhi. The crowded roads eased into bright boulevards. No one remembers, I thought, that Nehru had wanted to show how modern he had made India and decided to expand New Delhi while thousands were starving in Calcutta and there were no sewers in Old Delhi.

By the time I woke, the buildings bordering the road had shrunk to one and two stories and the spaces between them had begun expanding. So much dust was coming in through the open windows and the loose metal floorboards that there was a haze inside the bus.

Sleep had clarified my emotions, and the horror and shame were stronger than fear. I remembered twelve-year-old Anita beneath me, far beneath me, as if I were looking down from a great height, and me enormous and sweating and snorting above her. In order to diminish the pressure in my chest, I took shallow breaths. Money would make everything negotiable. The crime against Anita was decades old. Since then I had not repeated the crime with any other child. Asha did not count, because I was drunk and had been caught before anything occurred.

We shot through the ring of small towns which surround Delhi. The white markers that look like gravestones appeared, calling the road a highway even though it was still barely able to contain two buses passing each other. Farms lined the road. Most were only an acre or two, unadorned even by a well or a waterwheel, and separated by well-worn paths. Occasionally we passed large fields, divided by irrigation ditches and edged with neem trees for green fertilizer. I wondered whether, if someone else had lived my life, he would have committed the same sins that I had. The weight in my chest got heavier and I began to worry I might have another heart attack. I clenched and unclenched my hands to see if my fingers tingled. I lifted my arms up to the seat before me to see if they ached. As the pressure increased, I grew restless. My mouth opened on its own, although my mind was not forming any words.

There were times when the highway became the main street of small towns and I could have reached out and pulled drying laundry off people's balconies. We passed women in veils and bright clothes walking down the side of the highway with bundles of wood, which nearly doubled their height, rocking gently on their heads.

In my childhood, when a man and a woman wanted a ride from a passing bus or truck, they simply sat by the side of the road and waited. The men had long, curled mustaches and some held a sword over their knees. They might stand up as the bus or truck approached, but not attempt to hail it, to avoid the shame of rejection. The women wore long, loose shirts and skirts of red, gold, and purple. As the bus or truck neared, they veiled themselves with a scarf and looked away. These women had always made me think of flowers that turn their heads and track the sun across the sky.

Before Independence and before the five-year plans brought irrigation and electricity, Beri was a village of a hundred, mostly Brahmin families living in one-room mud homes that were scattered over several small hills. The only shops were either far away or in the trunk of some entrepreneur who went to town regularly and brought back everything from rose syrup to needles.

My father was the village teacher. I had two older brothers who were, even then, so exactly as they are now—inward, always planning, ready to hate—that I believe some people are born nearly complete and life provides just the details of their personalities.

My mother was the only person I loved, and I think she loved only me. Because she believed peas were very good for you, Ma would take them out of my brothers' food and put them in mine. Ma was short and fat and, as if she were a child, always walked around barefoot. At some point when I was very young, she began to claim that there were ghosts in the dark corners of our house. Later, she was possessed by them. She might claim to be a Brahmin from a hundred years ago or a princess who had taken poison to protect her honor. Several times she buried all our plates and pots in different parts of the farm, claiming that they were treasure. When she went crazy, we tied her hands and feet to a cot or the millstone. One moonless summer night she escaped from the binds and my father, my brothers, and I chased her till dawn over Beri's hills. We could not see her, but we followed her high, giddy laughter. Her laughter was like smoke, filling the night and taking away my breath.

Though I was lonely enough that in my dreams I sometimes fell in love and woke up with my heart aching, I was aggressive and talkative. No matter what games we children organized, I was the captain of one of the teams. I had a gang of five or six boys who called me "Grandfather" and with whom I terrorized the other children. As an assertion of power, if I ran into a younger boy who didn't act properly obsequious before me, I made him run a useless errand, such as going to a particular tree and getting a specific leaf. If the boy refused to do this, or if he did it but I did not like him, I beat him.

No adult minded the small violences I perpetrated. Violence was common. Grown men used to rub kerosene on a bitch's nipples and watch it bite itself to death. For a while, the men had a hobby of lashing together the tails of two cats with a cord and hanging the cats over a branch and betting on who would scratch whom to death. When the father of a friend of mine clubbed his wife's head with a piece of wood, her speech became slurred and she started having fits but not even the village women, friends of my friend's mother, found this to be an unspeakable evil. Their lives were so sorrowful that they treated what had happened to her not as a crime committed by an individual but as an impersonal misfortune like a badly set bone that warps as it heals.

All the things that might mark me as unusual and explain what I did to Anita were present in other people. I was almost always lonely. Though I had friends, no friendship offered comfort. Walking alone through a field, I could set myself crying by imagining Ma's death. But I knew several other boys who were lonely like me, and many shared my longing.

People raised during the 1930s and early 1940s share this sentimentality. Every one of us felt as if he or she was part of a select group because we would live to see Independence. Even in our village, two kilometers from a paved road, one of the men who had nothing better to do was training us boys to manage the country by making us spend our afternoons marching up and down single file through the hills. One of my earliest memories is of my mother discussing with some women how many new sets of clothes the government would give each woman every year after Independence. Miracles were common. A man had cursed Mahatma Gandhi and had immediately fallen down dead. A few villages over, women washing their clothes in the river had seen the goddess Durga ride her tiger across the water.

When I was fifteen my father joined the Arya Samaj, a forerunner of the BJP, and sent me to an Arya Samaj school. The principal told us students to think of ourselves as being in God Ram's army. We were to live a life of simplicity, deprived, as much as possible, of the objects of vanity which might keep us from ourselves and our responsibilities. The lives of all eighty or so students were to be contained by the row of four perfectly square classrooms at the center of the school compound and, behind it, the enormous barracks-style room where we slept. Each student's bed had to be made before breakfast, and no bed could be unmade before nine at night. All personal belongings had to be kept beneath your cot or on the single small table which stood by the bed. In the back of the compound, the part farthest from the town's only road, was a series of latrines. On Sundays the students had to clean each building with ammonia.

I soon realized that all the discipline was to cover uncertainty and I lost interest. I found what I thought was my destiny in the town's wrestling school. I knew instinctively when an opponent's foot was unsteady, where to push and where to hold. More than this, though, I was one of those athletes who need to win and so are capable of intense concentration and surprising recklessness. By the end of the first school year, I was the best wrestler in town and one of the best in the district. Like the pious men and women who rise early each morning to sweep their local temple, I woke before sunrise to rake the dirt of the wrestling yard so that it would be smooth under my feet. I became district champion in my second year and went to the All-Punjab Tournament. I lost there, but I didn't mind, because I knew that the date for Independence was upon us and I would change with the rest of the world.

The first of the corpses was in an alley, curled on its side in the shade of a mud wall. It was late afternoon. Classes were over and I was going down a dirt path between some houses to the wrestling yard. I saw the man in the shade and thought he had passed out drunk. Alcoholism was common. He had an arm tucked under his head as a pillow and the other lay on his thigh. I walked up to him to get a better look. From a few meters away I saw a Muslim's skullcap in the dust. This surprised me, because I knew that none of the dozen or so Muslim families in the town touched alcohol. Then I understood that the darkness on the ground beside him was blood. The path was on a slope and the body was below me. The blood frightened me so much I thought the road's slope would drag me toward him. One of the man's legs stretched out of the shadow as if to trip me.

For a week after the first murdered man, Muslim corpses began appearing everywhere. At the edge of town I found a young woman and a boy of about eight lying a few feet apart next to a thorn fence. Both were naked and slashed all over. One of the blows had parted the skin and meat on the boy's shoulder and I could see white, clean bone beneath. The woman's pubic hair woke me periodically for years, because I imagined ants feeding on her. Scattered along the side of the only road which led out of town I saw the bodies of several men and one very old woman. The corpse of the midget who ran the town's general store showed up in the back yard of an acquaintance. The yard was surrounded by a high wall, its top studded with nails and broken bottles.

That week made me think of a winter afternoon in my childhood when thousands of small, shiny, black-and-green birds suddenly appeared and settled in Beri's trees. As evening drifted in over the hills and lingered into night, the birds began dying. They fell to the ground all night long. Those birds, these corpses, felt wondrous, as if from a fairy tale.

Every Hindu in the school and town, the only people I might have had a conversation with, must have known that the murders were occurring, because we hardly discussed them. India's partition into Muslim Pakistan and Hindu India was only months away and most days the newspapers carried stories of massacres.

When we did speak of the murders, it was usually with one or at most two people. I think this was because, although the partition turned even reasonable people into fanatics, nearly all of us were horrified by the details of death, like the clean bone of the boy's shoulder. Rumors identified a few people as having taken part in the killings, a few students, a few teachers, a man who delivered milk to the school in large tin tanks, but even these people did not talk about what they had done.

Because we did not talk, the horror became intolerable. Each morning we woke with the day before us like some frightening and hopeless task. At night, we boys yelled in our dreams. There was one teacher who cried in class for two days in a row, till the principal scolded him in front of us.

Not a single member of the Muslim families survived. One Hindu lost a hand in an attack on a Muslim home.

The principal decided to shut the school and send all the students home, "in case of more violence." But we knew that he sent us away because he did not know how else to release the pressure under which we lived.

When I returned home, my mother had pneumonia. She had been sick for several weeks and had even broken two of her ribs because of a cough which could lift her upright in a single violent exhalation.

She died one night not long after I came back to Beri. I had gone to a farm a kilometer away to buy her biscuits, which she had asked for in her fever. The sky was bright, even though the sun had set and a bit of the moon showed. In the air there was the dry, almost sweet smell of dung burning. As I walked back from the farm, I wondered whether Ma had died while I was gone. I thought this whenever I was away from her for longer than ten minutes. Ever since the week of the corpses, my mind had fixed on the idea that God was going to punish me in some way. I did not know whether he would be punishing me for seeing the corpses, or for not doing anything to help the Muslims, or because the world had passed into Kali Yug and everyone must suffer for being born in this era. I was seventeen and there was no possibility of happiness in the future. My imagination kept conjuring terrible things that might happen. I could lose my sight; my father and brothers might drink poisonous water; Ma could die.

From the recently plowed field outside our yard I heard women crying. In my head I immediately saw my mother dead, with the village women crouched around her on the floor. But I did not really believe this until I entered the house and saw my mother's body. Then I gasped.

I gasped and, still gasping, started doing the things which must be done when someone dies. I brought the jeweler, who pried the stud out of my mother's nose with tweezers and clipped the silver ring off her toe. I helped carry my mother to the crematorium. Nothing made me cry. Not even the unbearably foul smell of hair and flesh on fire, and the way my mother twitched in the flames when her muscles contracted. In fact, everything caused my grief to burrow inward. Collecting her ashes and bones to pour into the Ganges only made the gasp more solid. I became so quiet that I could not even answer people's questions.

The madness came later. I welcomed it because it brought relief from the bang I kept hearing, which was my mother's stomach exploding in the funeral pyre, and from the image of my father shattering my mother's skull with a staff and chunks of sizzling flesh heaving out of the fire and onto the ground. For months after Ma's death, I woke at sunrise and immediately felt the hole her absence had created in the world and began to cry. The more I cried, the more I needed to cry. The first tears of the day would be from sorrow and despair, but these excavated a greater anguish. By wishing for my punishment to occur, by thinking on my way home that Ma had died, I had incited God to kill my mother. I could not say these words, even though I knew them, because saying them would make the guilt ridiculous and so end it, and therefore perhaps end the hole which kept my mother with me. I wept and wept. It was as if the tears were my flesh's attempt to grow and cover the neat, round hole my mother's death had punched in me. But every time the hole was camouflaged, the skin twitched and broke and the hole revealed itself. Sometimes my brothers grew tired of my weeping. "Go cry in the fields and scare away some crows with your noise," one said. The indifference they had shown to our mother's death (neither had wept) made my unhappiness denser and made me think sometimes that I was the one good person in the world. I would walk crying through the fields and hills until I passed into hysteria. Then I became so exhausted that I lay down wherever I was, next to a well, in the middle of some farmer's crops, and slept.

During this period, India became independent. One afternoon everyone in Beri was gathered on a flat field by the local Congress worker. Someone from a nearby town was there and gave a speech. Then the children lined up and the Congress worker passed out balloons and copper coins with Mahatma Gandhi's face stamped on them. People began to eat. The village women had prepared sweets and filled large clay pots with sweet drinks. After a little while, the larger children tried to steal the smaller children's coins and balloons. As the balloons were knocked out of hands and went floating up, I thought of my mother not seeing this day and not receiving the saris that she had imagined the government would give. I wandered away sobbing.

When I returned to higher secondary, the town was nearly as it had been before the violence. Hindu families were living in the houses the Muslims had owned. Classes started and I took up wrestling once more. But it was as if I had been sick a long time and had become easy to confuse. I had also developed a fear of pain. The idea of being slammed into the ground and maybe cracking my head panicked me, and so, when I was in a difficult position, I found myself giving in, hoping to make my fall easier.

The only thing that took me out of myself was my first woman. Two friends and I hired a prostitute. I paid fifty paisas and they paid ten each to watch through a window. The idea of being watched did not bother me, since my entire family had lived in one room and I had often seen my parents having sex. We didn't tell the woman about the watching, because then she might have wanted to charge extra. I met her outside the school one Sunday afternoon and led her around the back to a hut used by the groundskeeper. The prostitute wore a sari, which I had asked her to wear, and men's thick rubber slippers. I found their inappropriateness erotic, but her feet were cracked and yellow. I was anxious and sad as I led her to the hut. Whatever excitement I had felt in arranging for the woman had been replaced by the sense that I was being forced to admit some deep wrongness in myself. I began to apologize to the prostitute.

Once she was in the hut, I told the woman to remove her clothes. I took off mine and sat on a cot. After she finished stripping, she stood before me. The only light was from the small barred window. She was short and deep brown, with long black hair and large breasts. Her waist and thighs were in the dark. I made her walk back and forth in the narrow aisle between the cot and the sacks of cement which were leaning against the wall. I weighed her breasts in my hands. My shame vanished. No matter what I felt about myself, this was the actual world. We were only bodies and I had more power than this woman. I put my fingers inside her.

"Do you like this?" I asked, wanting to know the range of my strength.

"Whatever you like," she answered. To have power after so much unhappiness and confusion made me feel as if the world could be mine.

I laid her on the cot and got on top. As I started moving, I saw my friends standing outside at the window beneath which they had been hiding. Their watching excited me.

The orgasm didn't feel like much right then. My penis trembled and spurted and that was it. But for the next few days, I was crazy with happiness. I would run and slide down the shaded gallery outside the classrooms. I kept finding myself talking loudly or humming. I had discovered a way to happiness which sidestepped all the demands life made of me.

I went to the prostitute several times after this, paying with a five-rupee wrestling award. Soon I couldn't feel my guilt. I think my mother's death had distended the elastic cord which ties our actions to our conscience and the cord hung slack. The prostitute was eighteen and named Rohini. After I gave the money to her husband, he would sit outside their cottage smoking bidis while I visited. As we had sex, I could hear their children in the courtyard. But I soon began to love Rohini in secret. She had a slow walk that made me think she was heavy with sweetness. Once, Rohini told me I had very handsome eyes, and when I looked in a mirror I noticed that indeed my eyes were quite large. Rohini's husband thought I came from a well-off family and I went along with this. But when he began asking me for cigarettes, I realized that his demands might increase and I stopped going. Once after this, I saw her on a path outside town, but I hid myself in a cane field before she could notice me. My falling in love and then quickly abandoning her felt like a working-out of my destiny.

I failed eleventh standard. Nearly half the students with whom I had entered higher secondary had failed at least one year by then. There would have been no shame in repeating the year. But failing eliminated what little confidence I had remaining, and I decided to leave school.

We were at war with Pakistan and I wanted to fight for my country. I also thought joining the army would provide me with the opportunity to rise quickly in the world. I began imagining myself a general and grew a thick mustache such as I imagined a general might wear. But I had flat feet and ended up in the navy. As soon as I learned I was going to be in the navy, I became happy with the choice that had been forced on me. I saw myself traveling all around the world. I shaved my mustache.

Compared to farm work, the three years in the navy were like a long holiday. This is because a farm is yours, and since it is the only thing that is yours, you are always worried. I did not mind the constant work in the navy, because it was just work. Locks had to be greased regularly, chains and cables carefully examined and repaired or replaced. Equipment, radios, generators, parts of the engines often all of a sudden stopped working. In return for doing this, I saw the ocean for the first time. I visited cities where people spoke strange languages. More than these things, though, leaving Punjab freed me from the sadness I had been feeling for the last year and a half. I again began to believe that my life could be lived purposefully.

If we had ever gone into battle, I might not have considered myself lucky. But my years in the navy were a series of marvels. Once, while we were far from land, enormous dark clouds began pacing back and forth several miles away on one side of the ship. On the other side, also several miles away, were similar clouds, which looked like gigantic jellyfish dragging their million rain legs beneath them.

But directly above us was the sun, a clear sky, bored gulls. It was like being in one of those zoos where the people travel in buses while the animals roam free.

I visited Calcutta, which in my memory is only boxy jute mills and the wonderful green stretch of the Maidan. Madras had strange intricate temples which were so different from any I had ever seen that I doubted whether their Ram and Vishnu could be the same as mine.

The navy was also a time of debauchery. There was so little shame about prostitution that at brothels sailors got lower prices than any but the most frequent customers.

In Bombay I slept with a child. An acquaintance told me about the girl, that she was thirteen. I went looking for her the evening of the same day I heard of her. I imagine this means something. But at that point I was not actually interested in children. What I found exciting was the idea of doing something altogether different from what had become banal to me. When I heard about the girl, my heart began to flutter in a way it had not since several months earlier, when I had had sex with a vastly pregnant prostitute.

The red-light district was several blocks along a narrow road. The brothels were old two- and three-story houses pressed together on either side of the street. I cannot recall whether I went to the girl on a holiday night, but the road was crowded and noisy with voices and radios playing. There were no streetlights, and the only illumination was what spilled out of windows and doors. People came right up to each other before they stepped aside. Most of the houses did not have numbers written out front, and as I walked around looking for the one I had been told about, I kept patting my breast pocket to see if my purse was still there.

Many of the brothels had long balconies, galleries almost, attached to the front of each story. That night I noticed for the first time that some of the men, women, and children on the balconies wore village clothes and some wore city clothes. This made me realize that neither customers nor prostitutes would sit around chatting or listening to music on the radio. The people on the balconies were probably visiting someone who worked there. I had never before thought of brothels as places where people lived for years at a time.

I overcame my embarrassment and asked a man working at a betel-leaf stall for directions.

I walked down the street. A fat woman with an enormous bindi painted on her forehead was sitting sideways on a bicycle before the brothel's narrow door. I asked her if she had a "young girl," because I could not say child.

She immediately said, "Twenty rupees."

I was so shocked by the price that I thought the woman had mis-understood me. "I don't want a virgin," I said.

The woman eyed me. "For twenty rupees you get firewood, not a forest." Probably because I did not say anything, she added, "You'll get your own room and can enjoy yourself with respect. With respect." I gave her the money and she tied it inside a handkerchief and tucked it between her breasts.

Usually I became hard as soon as I entered a brothel, but as I fol-lowed the woman up a dimly lighted stairway and down a narrow hall, I stayed soft. We were on the second story. Small waist-high windows lined one side of the wall. Voices from the street rose to us. I looked down and could tell where people were, because they were even darker than the streets. I wondered whether I would actually have sex with the girl. I believed that if she looked truly young, something at the last moment would deflect me. I did not think I, myself, could do much about what would happen.

The fat woman brought me to a small blue room, where a girl was sitting on a cot reading a comic. The girl looked up at me. I had not remembered that thirteen was so young. She had an oval face, a broad hooked nose, and round bulging eyes which, because she appeared to blink only rarely, gave her an unchanging, startled expression. Her legs were no thicker than her arms, and her breasts were just beginning to grow. She looked so young in her pale green salwar kameez that I felt the enormity of her helplessness. "Half an hour," the woman said as she left the room. She did not close the door but drew a curtain with a weighted bottom across the doorway.

The girl continued staring at me. I sat down beside her. I wondered if she thought the same things each time a man was brought to her room. I told myself I should leave, that twenty rupees was not so much and maybe the woman would let me have another prostitute for the money. "What's your name?" I asked. She did not answer and her eyes did not change. I wondered if she was drugged.

"Chandni," she suddenly said, as if I had only just asked my question.

I knew that prostitutes renamed themselves when they joined the trade, often using the name of a flower or a precious stone, and I felt rebuffed by the pseudonym she had given. "Is that your real name?"

"Stop asking questions," she said.

The girl stood, in the same sudden way that she had given her name. She pulled her shirt over her head and unhooked her skirt. Her pubic hair was sparse. Her waist was no wider than my thigh. She looked almost sexless. I was still not hard. But I stood also and gathered a breast in one hand. That breast was the softest thing I have ever touched. It was like water. I kissed her nipples and laid her on the bed. Her nipples had wide areolae and, like her eyes, appeared astonished. As I took off my clothes, the girl spat into her hands and rubbed the spit into her vagina. This disgusted and excited me simultaneously. I finished becoming hard.

"How long have you been doing this?"

"For twenty rupees you only get to fuck."

I was embarrassed, for the questions were a way to own her more completely. The embarrassment made me protest, "Twenty rupees is a lot of money."

She grimaced, as if she was disgusted by my poverty. "All you get is fucking."

Sex with her was not much different from that with an older woman, except the vagina was shallower.

"Do you like this?" I asked when I was in her. I often asked this.

"No," she said, and then a little later added, "I hate men like you, sweating and talking, talking. Wanting things for free."

"Is it ever good?"

"Never with men who pay."

I had been insulted by prostitutes before, but never this much. As I rode a rickshaw back to the ship, I felt shame. Thirteen was so young that she and I might as well have been different species. I swore out loud: "I will never go to a whore again. For the next three months I will give a tenth of my salary to charity." But there was no solace in words. After a while memories of my mother began coming to me, the way she always walked around barefoot, her taste for sweets, how I moved my cot next to hers when she was sick and dying. I began to cry, because it seemed to me then that being good was, for me, one of those impossible tasks which are given to the heroes of fairy tales.

After I had sex with the girl, I began discovering so many brothels with children that I thought it was a new fad, in the same way that Raj Kapoor's Charlie Chaplin walk would become popular. When I went to a brothel and learned I could have a child, I was always tempted. Occasionally while masturbating, I conjured the little girl spitting into her hands and rubbing the spit into her vagina. But I never again went to a child prostitute.

I left the navy when I was twenty-two. After the first year and a half, all the problems of being trapped on a ship with people I disliked had become unbearable. Thievery was so common that even my undershirts and socks were stolen. A man who slept in the bunk above me masturbated every night by mounting his pillow and rubbing against it until he came.

I left the navy in late June and immediately took a job as a physical education teacher in a boys-only school in Delhi. Teaching exercise did not take much time or effort. Most of any day I could be found drinking tea on a cot near the gate at the school compound. Five months after I started my new job, I married Radha.

A year or two after our marriage, Radha told me that she and her sisters were so frightened of their father that since he did not like to see dry laundry still hanging on the clothesline, they took down the laundry while it was moist.

Radha was nineteen when we married. She was thin, with slightly jutting teeth which kept her mouth open and brittle hair that could never grow beyond shoulder length no matter how she took care of it. But Radha soon became beautiful to me.

Despite everything I had done in the navy, I believed that once I married I would be a faithful husband. Since marriage is so important a part of anyone's life, I thought I would be desolate if I was faithless.

And Radha had a capacity to watch and pay attention which made me feel safe. We spent the first week of our marriage in Beri. Radha had brought a bag of toffees to hand out to the children of all her new relatives. I asked her if her mother had suggested the sweets as a way to charm the relatives.

"No," she said, and then paused. It was night and summer, but because we had just gotten married, we were in the house instead of outside in the wind. Radha was sitting on our cot as I undressed. She was looking away from me. We had not made love yet because Radha was still anxious with me. "When I was a child, a neighbor got married and his wife gave out candies. I thought she was smart."

I was amazed Radha had carried this fact for years. I felt glad to be with someone this intelligent, because it meant she could take care of me. "You're smart, too."

"Not smart. I am understanding," Radha said, and became silent as if she had revealed too much.

Getting Radha to tell me a joke was as thrilling as teaching a wild rabbit to lick sugar from my palm. I took great pleasure in serving her and in furnishing our future together. The ritual of purchasing bedsheets and stainless-steel pots, a poster of a fat pink baby, a clock with hands that glowed in the dark soothed whatever concerns I had about the shape of my life, which seemed increasingly dominated by the silliness of my job, supervising children while they did jumping jacks or making them turn out their pockets after they finished playing table tennis so that no balls were stolen. Buying mangoes for Radha on my way home from work and telling her that she was my mango tree, my wish-granting tree, was a way of replacing the rest of my day. Once, early on, I saw her with her fingertips wrinkled from bathing and I felt lucky to be able to age with her.

Later, Radha would say that even at the beginning of our life together, I took advantage of her pliability and innocence. As an example of this, she pointed to my returning home late after drinking with my friends and expecting her to be smiling and ready with food. Another example she used was our summer trips to Beri. Living in Delhi had made me miss village life, and when I told Radha I wanted to spend the summers in Beri, she acquiesced hesitantly. Radha had never lived outside Old Delhi, but she felt obligated to come with me. Village life is especially hard on women. All day Radha was running to the well or collecting firewood and cow dung to burn. My sisters-in-law hated Radha, perhaps because they kept thinking that I might claim some of the land that they wanted their husbands to inherit, and they tormented her. They would hide the laundry soap from her and give her the hardest work. Radha could not get used to the water and was often sick. Yet she kept accompanying me to Beri until Baby was born.

But I do not think Radha was referring to my selfishness and indifference when she said I took advantage of her. After all, at the beginning of our marriage she was mostly happy. I think Radha meant I should have known that my love would not last. I had misled her, she believed, by treating her as if she were my heart walking unprotected in the world.

Our love wore out after three years, I think. There are always problems between two people, even when one is willing to give in on nearly everything. Despite Radha's demureness and traditionalism, which kept her from challenging me, she had a practical and calm intelligence that saw through all my illusions. When I fantasized out loud that I could move from being a teacher to being involved in citywide education administration and that from there it would be only a few steps to advising politicians and then finally running for election, Radha looked at me with such dismay that I invariably grew angry. Once I began believing that she saw through me, all her mannerisms of innocence, the way she covered her mouth when laughing, struck me as deceptive. Also, of course, there was the eroding power of familiarity.

Radha located the end of our love with Baby's death. Baby was our first child. If he had lived to six months we would have named him Dil, because he was our heart. For many years I accepted this explanation. Now I think there must have been a hidden romantic in Radha for her not to have admitted that our love simply got used up. Instead, she chose a dramatic boundary. Baby was born in February 1955 and died four months later of some water sickness. I was in Beri and Radha was in Delhi, because she thought she could take better care of Baby there. Once he became ill, Radha sent me telegrams telling me to come home. She told me he had a fever that had made him wrinkled and dry, that there was blood in his stool, that he no longer even cried. But I thought she was exaggerating as a way to punish me for leaving her in Delhi. She sent me six telegrams. After the fourth, angry at the money she was wasting, I stopped responding, and when Baby died, Radha did not send a message.

The evening I returned to Delhi, Radha told me she had put the torch to Baby's funeral pyre herself. I sat on a cot in our single narrow room as Radha described the cremation arrangements: the pyre the size of a bush, the kindness of the pundit, the way the people in her family scolded her for going to a crematorium. Radha stood stiffly before me with her arms hanging straight down beside her and her fingers stretched apart. She looked like a student making a presentation. The room opened directly onto a busy road, and the noise of the evening traffic was so loud that Radha's words sometimes got lost under horns and people calling out. I cried as she spoke. After Radha stopped talking, she stood and watched me cry. Then she went and made dinner. Night came. Traffic trailed off. When dinner was ready, Radha came to me and said, "Don't cry, even though you cry such handsome tears." I did stop, but it was because the contemptuous words made me think that perhaps not only was she angry at me but she hated me.

For months after Baby died, Radha would begin to weep without any apparent reason. She could be doing the laundry or cooking dinner and suddenly she would have to wash her eyes. This reminded me of myself at my mother's death, and made me realize that although I had thought I loved Baby, because I was not crying as I had before, I obviously did not have deep feelings for him. Sometimes I went up to Radha and held her. Other times I got angry and left the flat.

I was so unhappy myself that I could not have taken care of anyone. I must have been at least partially unhappy about Radha and Baby, but also because I believed I was heartless, I thought I was just unhappy about being blamed.

Baby's death exhausted me. I used to sleep twelve or fourteen hours a day. About this time, by providing crates of mangoes from Beri to my principal and his supervisors, I was able to switch from teaching to administration. The new job had longer days. Soon after I got home, I would eat and go to bed.

I began drinking regularly for the first time. Until then, I had drunk only with friends. Even in company, drinking depressed me. Now, once or twice a month, I went to a saloon and sat in the back with fried peanuts and a liter of beer. When I first started drinking by myself, I cried loudly, hoping to attract attention. After a young boy who was a waiter there whispered in my ear, "Shut up, fatso," I began holding my tears till I got home. When I returned to the flat and Radha became angry at my drunkenness, I would shout, "Do you think you're the only one with a heart?"

Radha lost interest in my foolishness and I, embarrassed by her clear-sightedness, avoided her.

Radha found a guru and began to pray three times a day, an hour each time. I returned to visiting prostitutes. After a while I thought of Radha only when I wanted something. Even then, she left few traces in my thoughts. Still, Anita came a year after Baby. Kusum followed two years later, and Rajesh after another two years. I remember how Radha would stare up at me expressionlessly as I struggled to climax and to make myself come I would say, "Mine, you are mine. What do you think of that?" I only went to her when I had not had time to go to the brothels on GB Road and my lust had begun nagging at me so much that I could not sleep. By the time she was thirty, Radha had stopped oiling her hair and changing her clothes regularly. Also, when Rajesh was born, Radha clenched her teeth so tightly they all shifted, and within a few years they had splayed out. Radha became, like my children, only a reminder of all the things I had done wrong.

Sometimes, as if seeing my children for the first time, I noticed their tiny hands and mouths and I would feel the responsibility of protecting them. Then I would want to be a good husband to Radha and might try for a few days to look at her when we talked.

I justified my resentment toward the children by saying that at least I took care of them. After seven years in administration, I knew enough people in education and was well known enough that I could nearly double my five hundred rupees a month by arranging admission for children into particular schools or meetings between businessmen and bureaucrats. This was during the second of Nehru's five-year plans, when it was common knowledge that since corporate donations to political parties were illegal, the Congress Party was selling monopolies to raise campaign money. There had always been corruption, but it was so much in the open now that people began viewing it as natural that they could offer me money for favors. My family did not live well, but we drank milk each day.

I never felt any guilt for accepting bribes. And the tremors of remorse I felt for going to the prostitutes on GB Road were so slight that I brushed them aside like cobweb strands.

The prostitutes I went to ranged from sixteen- or seventeen-year-olds to some in their mid-thirties. I preferred the younger ones because, even though I used a condom, I thought they would be less likely to have diseases than older whores. I also found their bodies, so firm that they seemed superhuman, attractive, and I liked the unevenness of our strengths.

I visited the brothels only during the afternoon, when the wide GB Road is crowded. People buy light switches, generators, bathroom fixtures, and such things from the narrow shops on the ground floor of the three- and four-story buildings in which the brothels, sometimes stacked on top of each other, are located. No matter how often you have been to a particular brothel on GB Road, there is always a sense of physical danger when you are in one. In the GB Road brothels, you have sex in wooden closets. They are arranged in a row against one wall of the long room that is the brothel. These closets are so narrow you have to climb onto the plank bed, making sure not to step on the whore, before closing the door. Adding to the claustrophobia is the distraction of the brothel's life going a few inches from you. Women and children are sitting on the floor. "I'm hungry. Anybody want food?" "Dev Anand is much better than Rajesh Khanna. If I was in a movie and had the songs from Anand, my movie would be a hit, too." Sometimes pimps get into loud arguments a meter from where you are in the closet about how much of a commission they should get for bringing in a customer. Outside the room, in the doorway to the hall or stairwell that connects the brothel to the sidewalk, whores sit shouting at a possible customer who stops on the sidewalk to peer at them. "Come, my dream!" they yell, flashing their breasts. The seediness and the fear usually make the sex sad, difficult, abject. Occasionally these very qualities will make the orgasm astonishing.

So the years passed, far more quickly than I could have imagined. My father died and Nehru died, and I cried for both, surprising myself with the earnestness of my tears. India fought Pakistan, China, Pakistan. I used some of my new wealth to start a small restaurant, but there was little money in it and my workers cheated me. I bought two rickshaws with a cousin and leased them out. I did this for a year and a half, till my cousin was murdered, stabbed in the throat by a rickshaw driver over a dispute involving less than forty rupees. Once, Radha developed a habit of eating very little, and after a few months she had to be hospitalized because she was waking up at night screaming from stomach pains. When she got out of the hospital, she told her guru that she wanted to leave worldly things and take sanyas, and travel from pilgrimage site to pilgrimage site. Her guru then came to our home for the first time and berated

Radha in front of me. "You have three little children, faithless woman. Your home is your temple." To guarantee his help in the future I went to him for several weeks to learn yoga for my back pain. To strengthen my spine he recommended I drink water while lying flat. Anita, Rajesh, and Kusum grew into odd children who played only with each other and who were so quiet that strangers at first thought they were slightly retarded. Even when no one was around, they spoke quietly. When I heard the children murmuring to each other, I often wondered whether they were speaking of me.

All those years gone so quickly that even describing them does not take long. Big things do not happen to you and so you think time is not passing. You jiggle the years in your pocket, thinking you are a rich man, and suddenly you have spent everything. I was thirty-eight and an old man overnight, and Anita was twelve and so young that seeing her was like looking down from some great height into a misty valley and wondering what will be revealed when the sun arrives.

O ne afternoon, Anita fell asleep beside me while we listened to the radio announce that Indira Gandhi had become Prime Minister for the first time. The room was dark and the quilt that covered us heavy and warm. I was dozing off as well. In her sleep, Anita rolled over and put her hand on my penis. I woke immediately. I started to remove Anita's hand, but stopped. There was something mysterious and erotic about lying beneath the warm quilt with Anita's light touch, listening to her breath and feeling her weight against my side. I became hard. After a few minutes, Anita rolled over once more and removed her hand.

Later that day I told myself that I had been slightly dazed from sleep and that this was why I had left her hand on my crotch. But my mind was adept at reducing its presence when my body did something shameful. I do not remember whether, before this, I had seen Anita in a sexual way. Probably I had, because I wondered what it would be like to have sex with nearly everyone, even children I saw in the schools I went to. But I am sure that, before the afternoon when Anita touched me while the election results were announced, she had held no special attraction for me. Anita was not a pretty girl. Her hair was dry and short, and she had a round, thick face and a large nose.

One afternoon, a day or two after Anita's hand first fell on my crotch, I played a game of tag with her in the courtyard of the house where we then lived. We laughed and bounced about as I dodged Anita's lunges. But as I swayed in front of her, I kept positioning myself so that when I did let Anita touch me, her hand might brush my penis. One of her dives to tag me finally pressed her open hand against my penis. I felt such a shock of pleasure that I became perfectly still. The mineral flavor of lust filled my mouth. Anita also stopped. She looked frightened. I immediately realized that I must not let Anita associate anything bad with touching me, so I laughed. Our game continued for a little while after that. Then I went off and masturbated.

The pleasure and relief of masturbation was so strong, I knew right away that I would repeat this game. My conscience did not bother me. I reasoned that Anita was not being physically harmed. I was also not damaging her emotionally, because the games hid my intentions. Nor did I wonder when or where the games might end. They would continue till they came to some quiet and natural conclusion.

Games of tag or hide-and-seek, during which I tried getting Anita to touch me, became common. We usually played these games on the roof of our house after I had returned from work. The sky might be fluttering among shades of purple, and the nearby roofs were always crowded. Sometimes people watched us play: Anita trying to tag me and me hopping, swaying, shouting challenges, just out of reach. I would become giddy from the excitement of waiting, and after a while became so distracted that I sometimes got tagged by mistake. Anita and I played till we lost our breath from laughing and running. Then, because I wouldn't let it be any other way, we stood a foot or so apart, trying to pat each other and jump away before being tagged back. Occasionally Kusum, Rajesh, and Radha came upstairs and read or talked or played games, pausing every now and then to watch us. I was so confident of the game's camouflage that before all these people I touched Anita's thighs, the backs of her legs, and sometimes, rarely, her chest. The fact that I was able to do this before so many people confirmed that I was not doing anything wrong.

To win Anita's love, I bought her coloring books and taught her magic tricks. To make sure nobody wanted to examine the oddity of a grown man playing these children's games with such intensity, I tried winning over the rest of the family. I began taking everyone to dinner and a film once a week.

In the beginning I felt no shame for what I was doing, because I was not harming anyone. As time passed and the games continued and the touching became more and more obvious, shame entered me and, settling, strengthened. Every night I had dreams of humiliation, of people catching me with Anita. When I saw a rooster picking at a pile of dung, I wondered what he was eating. Around this time I also began imagining sucking the penises of powerful men.

But I understood the connection between what I did with Anita and my shame the way a lake understands the connection between the cloud above it and the reversed image bobbing on its waters. In my imagination I saw our games as discrete and static, events which occurred once and separately, not as part of a developing pattern. This sense of things meant excuses came after I had already started on something. For example, if Radha and the other children were downstairs, Anita and I would begin on the open roof and then move to the storage shed. Then the shed door would open, as if on its own, and we would walk in; then it closed by itself. There was no difference between being in open sight and being inside the shed.

I remember the first time I put my hand between Anita's legs. We had moved into the shed and were standing less than a foot apart, tagging each other with our fingertips to try and make the other "it." I pretended to reach for Anita's chin and dropped my hand to her crotch. Anita's underwear was moist with sweat. The surge of excitement was so great that instead of touching her and removing my hand, I just stopped. Anita stared into my stomach, and I looked at the thin rectangle of light surrounding the closed door of the shed. For years after all this, anything, a bathroom's moist door-knob, could suddenly make me feel her underwear almost soaked through and the smooth boniness beneath.

I had at one time promised myself that if Anita ever appeared to understand what I was doing, I would stop. Now she reached out and put her hand on my penis in the shed. When we were together, she thrust out her chest. But I reasoned that since I was not harming her physically, the only danger I posed was to her mind. And this was not my responsibility. How could I be held accountable for the way she interpreted what I was doing? There was not that much dif-ference between what I did and a father who makes his children sing before guests at a party.

Instead of worrying about Anita, I tried to seal her mouth. I told her that I often thought about killing myself and that she was the only happiness in my life. I often complained with an air of fatigue about Radha's indifference and the dreary hard work I did to support us.

In all this, Anita seemed increasingly cheerful and outgoing. She no longer hid when strangers came to the house. Her schoolteachers remarked that she was showing more interest in her work. I taught her the basics of palm reading and she would offer to read any guest's hand. Anita now argued with her mother. Radha's and my neglect must have stunted Anita to such an extent that even my tainted attention was relatively benign.

I have no doubt that Anita loved me during this time. When I returned home from work, she came immediately to me and took away my shoes and asked if I wanted water. We always ate dinner sit-ting side by side. Sometimes I found myself feeling a strange, potent combination of fatherly and amorous affection for her. Occasionally we had dinner alone on the roof, and then, if this odd love was with me, the moon felt like a private light.

The whole family was happier than ever. A stranger would have been charmed by the ease with which we bantered, the rituals of picnics, movies, and contests of joke-telling and singing. Radha, who had withdrawn into religion, began to involve herself again in the children's lives and in our plans as a family. Radha had a beautiful voice and she sang to us nearly every night.

Whatever was allowing this happiness stopped working once Anita began spending the night in my room. For a long time I had wanted this so that I could fondle her without the fear and hurry which I always felt in the shed. One evening I said to Anita, "Why don't you sleep in my room?" I said this during dinner, with the whole family around us. We had been joking and laughing and I wanted my idea to appear as if it had occurred spontaneously and was a product of the affection we were all showing each other at the moment. Anita looked surprised, but no one else appeared to notice.

During the two months Anita slept in my room, the first night was the only one she stayed on her cot the whole night. I placed her cot next to mine. That first night she came into my room and sat down at the edge of her cot. I shut the door. I would have locked it, but it could be bolted only from the outside. I was excited and nervous. When I turned around from the door, Anita was leaning forward with her shoulders curved in, looking like a bird in winter. My eagerness, which had been laced with doubt, turned to self-disgust. I gave Anita my little transistor radio and left the light on through the night.

In the morning, though, I did not carry Anita's cot back up to the first story. All day I thought about doing this, but my guilt was not enough. Probably I knew that my guilt would lift on its own. The second night Anita's sad face only made me resentful. I switched off the lights before turning around from closing the door. I got into my cot and told Anita to lie next to me.

She lay stiff and straight. With a single fingertip under her wrist,

I moved her hand onto my penis. Even through the underwear and pajamas I wore, I could feel each finger. I imagined I could even feel the roughness of her fingerprints. But I did not do anything more than lie there with her limp hand on me. There was no pretense behind which to hide my actions, as there had been when we "played." I could not look around her fright or the fact that I was responsible for it. For an hour or two I lay paralyzed. Finally, I sent Anita to her cot.

This pattern was repeated over several nights. Anita's body became less stiff. My shame diminished. I discovered the disguise I needed: pretend sleep. I did not care that it was obvious I was shamming. What mattered was having some excuse.

One night I loosened the cords of my pajamas and, while snoring, took Anita's hand and slipped it beneath my pajamas and underwear. I remember how Anita's fingers were startled to discover my pubic hair. I kept my eyes closed and continued breathing deeply. When her fingers touched the base of my penis, they would have jerked away except for my heavy hand on top of hers. I covered her hand with mine and showed her how to hold me. I made her masturbate me.

The first time, I came suddenly and with such enormous force that my whole body vanished in silver pleasure. I even stayed hard after coming. When Anita pulled her hand away, I sleepily kissed her on the forehead. I didn't want her to associate anything bad with masturbating, and for some reason I thought that if I appeared grateful, she would see herself as less taken advantage of. "Thank you," I murmured from my sleep. "Wipe your hand on the cot leg."

I had Anita masturbate me once or twice a night. I pretended to sleep as I guided her hand. The only sound was my mad, wheezing snore. After she finished, Anita would slip quietly to her cot.

The masturbation made me certain that I would be caught. I had always felt that each of my crimes drew me closer and closer to punishment. Now that I was onto something directly sexual, the likely had become the inevitable.

It might happen at any time. The latrine was on the ground floor, and Radha sometimes came down at night to urinate. A moment's curiosity would be enough. Many times I thought I heard footsteps and literally shoved Anita out of my cot and onto the floor. As I did this, I kept snoring.

But the possibility that Anita might betray me to Radha frightened me even more than the risk of being caught. I decided to make Anita afraid. Once, while Anita masturbated me, I rolled over and looked at her. She was on her back. Her eyes were wide and her face still. I stared at Anita till she began to be frightened. "What are you doing?" I finally asked. She didn't answer. I lifted myself on an elbow and continued staring. I suddenly lifted a hand as if to slap her. Anita flinched so hard she almost fell off the cot. "This is what you do while I'm asleep," I hissed. I didn't say anything then for several minutes. I kept looking at her lying on the edge of the cot. "Never tell anyone about this. If you tell, people will think you're an animal. They will kill you with stones." I sank onto my back and stared at the ceiling. Anita went to her cot.

Nothing would ease my fear, though. I began growing desperate. One night, while the children were asleep and the tube light in the family room was crawling with bugs, I made Radha sit beside me on a sofa and started telling her that I had acted shamefully with her and the children for many years. "I drink. I curse. If I only ate meat and started whoring, I would have done everything. But this is because I have been so unhappy. I was sad with what life has given me." I took her hands in mine and cried.

"Don't cry," Radha murmured. She forced her hands free. I wept for nearly an hour. Radha did not know what to say and kept rubbing the sofa's rough blue cloth. After a while, my tears moved her so much that she started crying as well. From then on, I went to temple two nights a week.

Anita became ill. She had a fever and a prolonged dry cough so deep it made her vomit. Her illness lasted a week and a half. During that time, each cough felt to me like an accusation, as if I had caused her sickness. I felt so guilty that I told her to sleep upstairs.

I think Radha also felt guilty, because she paid more attention to this than she had to other illnesses the children had had. She teased, "The neighbors are going to think you have TB if you keep coughing like that."

The cough had been gone two days when I brought Anita back to my bed. Anita was in the courtyard brushing her teeth before going up to her cot to sleep. I stood in my doorway and watched her. Anita had curly hair as a child, and seeing it, I thought of my own collapsing hairline. I had not masturbated for several days in anticipation of what her small hand would feel like around my penis. "You can sleep with me tonight," I said to her. "Your coughing won't keep me awake." Anita did not say anything. Once more, I carried her cot down to my room.

My guilt about her sickness still lingered and I had doubts whether that night I would have her masturbate me. But when I closed the door to my room and turned around to see Anita lying on her cot, I felt my throat close with desire. "Get into my cot," I said. My voice came out rough and angry. Anita scrambled onto my cot; her fearfulness aroused me. She was wearing a large loose gown that came to just above her ankles. I turned off the light and removed my pajamas. My penis pointed straight ahead. I had never before lain naked next to Anita. I got into the cot and immediately bunched up her nightdress and put one finger in her vagina. She yelped. I wiggled my finger in her to let her know she had to be quiet. Then I sucked on my finger and tried to see how deeply I could sink it. Half an inch. "Ohh!" she said in pain. Shh, I went. Shh. Anita was having trouble breathing. She sounded as if there were sand in her lungs. I took my finger out of her and parted her legs. Then I rolled on top of her and brought my penis to her vagina. Putting my hand over her mouth, I stubbed my penis outside her vagina for a moment. But finding my place, I rammed, once, twice, three times, and gushed sperm. Anita had her lips pressed tightly together and I could feel her face twitching with pain.

As I remembered this on the bus going to Beri, I whimpered. The man sitting beside me glanced in my direction. I looked out the window. The bus was climbing an unpaved road along the side of a bare hill. I touched my face. It was covered with dust and felt swollen from the heat and wind. I've changed since then, I thought. Asha was an accident after decades of being good. It was alcohol. Nothing happened with Asha. Anita was angry because of my thoughts.

Almost immediately after ejaculating, I had felt as if I were swallowing my own tongue. Anita continued breathing loudly. She started crying. The noise frightened me, but I was too ashamed to hush her. I got up and went to the courtyard. The moon was nearly complete. Everything I had done appeared to me clearly. Even outside, I thought I could hear Anita breathing. My stomach was roiling. I squatted to put my head between my knees, but lost my balance and fell stretched out on my face. I wondered as I fell whether Radha could hear me.

I went and washed my penis. There was blood on it. I rubbed Anita clean with a towel. The insides of her thighs were gooey with sperm and blood. Neither of us said anything as I did this. Anita kept crying.

In the morning Anita's face looked as though the bones had given way. When Radha saw her, she was shocked. "Sick all night," I hurried to explain.

"Vomiting?"

"Twice." Anita did not contradict me. How could she have?

For a week and a half I did not go near Anita. I told her she still sounded sick and sent her to sleep by herself. Anita began speaking again and her eyes started moving to follow what was in front of her. The fact that Radha did not ask questions to discover what had happened appeared to me complete proof that she was almost consciously choosing not to know. I think this, but I know that Radha was honorable and would not have shunned her duties.

I believed at that time that it was my unavoidable doom as much as lust which made me tell Anita to come sleep in my room again. But it was probably simply that I did not actually believe that I would ever be discovered, for I could not imagine the world after I had been caught.

When again Anita entered the room, I closed the door and turned off the lights. Anita found her way to my cot. I lay down beside her and lowered my pajamas.

O n the bus I moaned again. The man sitting beside me prodded me in the arm and asked, "Are you going to throw up?" I shook my head no. He shifted to the edge of the seat anyway. "Move away from the window," he said. "You lose all your water from the wind." I hugged myself. I was cold.

The memories of the following days are so morbid—the newspapers under Anita to keep the sheets clean, the painful penetration each night, an ejaculation which I would try catching in my hand because I was afraid of pregnancy, Anita going to wash the blood from her vagina—that in later years I tried blotting them from memory.

It was obvious that something was very wrong with Anita. When she walked, she looked pained. She almost stopped talking completely, and only when I scolded her would she eat. Radha was watching all this, I knew. Watching perhaps in confusion or in growing certainty.

But for four or five nights there was the same horror. The details of what we did, Anita holding her cries in and breathing as though there were sand in her lungs, were so terrible that whenever I finished I felt as if I were swallowing my tongue. Yet each night Anita sat on the edge of her cot and I closed the door and switched off the light before turning around.

M aybe Radha came down to the courtyard to pee and then heard something. Or maybe Anita's condition over the last few weeks had finally forced her to admit the obvious. Or Radha might have just wanted to see if we were sleeping all right.

And there I was, arching on top, Anita flat and still far below me. Radha was silhouetted in the doorway before I had even turned my head. The rolling off Anita and pulling up pajamas and sheet seemed incredibly slow and clumsy even as I did them. Radha stood unmoving long after I was on my back, my pajamas at my knees, the sheet reaching my waist, and Anita beside me.

Radha moaned. Then she grabbed Anita by the arm and swung her onto the floor. "Go upstairs," Radha shouted. For a moment Anita stood there. Then she hobbled out.

I sat up.

"What's this?" she said, noticing the newspapers. Radha slapped me, and the heel of her hand struck my nose. I tasted the iron flavor of blood. She hit me again. "Dog. Disease," she shouted. She kept slapping and cursing. "If people knew about you, they would kill you like a mad dog. They would break your head with bricks. If I told my brothers, they would cut you to pieces with a machete. Do you know what you've done?" I had so much adrenaline in me that I felt no emotion. Radha's blows did not get weaker. I said nothing and did not try to protect myself. "Your own daughter, animal. What is going to happen to her now? Have you done this many times? Have you been doing this long?"

Her questions cut through my befuddlement and made me wail, "I don't know why. I'm a leper." Now that the worst had happened, I felt none of the relief I had expected would come when things ended. I could imagine Radha telling everyone and me being driven from my home and becoming a beggar on the street. "I swear I haven't been doing it long. God is good and let me be caught the first time. I deserve to die."

"Kill yourself, then," she yelled.

"I should. I should." I nodded and wept. A part of me was interested only in escaping blame. Another part would actually have liked to die.

"Do it, then. Use a knife. Use rope. Drown yourself in a spoonful of water."

"I should." As I said it again, I think we both simultaneously realized that this would not happen.

Radha became quiet. "Who will marry her?" she asked. I think she said this only because this is the type of question they ask in movies after a rape. Suddenly Radha took off her rubber slipper and swung it hard at my cheek. The sound was like a wet cloth whipping against a rock. I felt as if my cheek had peeled off. I howled and then became abruptly quiet. Radha grabbed my face and, holding me by my lips and chin, slapped me again with the rubber slipper. I howled and stopped as soon as I could. Radha punishing me herself made me think that she would not tell anyone of her discovery. Immediately following this came grief at what I had done. I tried to speak, to beg pardon, but no words were right. My crime stood out terrible and solitary in my mind. It was sick.

All night I sat there as Radha cursed and hit. By dawn my face was purple and Radha was staggering from exhaustion. When she spoke, her sentences sometimes made no sense. Sometimes she wept. "I should kill myself and the children," she said at one point. "I should pour kerosene over all of us and set us on fire." Part of me wondered if this would not solve my problem.

After Rajesh and Kusum left for school that morning, Radha, Anita, and I went to Hanuman temple. My face was still purple and I could hardly open my lips. Radha and Anita sat in a corner all day and prayed. Most of the morning I crouched on my knees before an idol of God Ram, with my forehead pressed to the floor. Over and over I asked God to take away my evil and madness. I cried and stopped, cried and stopped. I knelt till cramps caused me to fall on the floor. Then I lay there praying, with my face to the floor and my arms stretched out before me. This was a Tuesday, God Hanuman's day, and so the temple was especially full. I was praying in the main chamber, and by early afternoon even this was so crowded that people could no longer go around me and had to step over me.

That night we sent Rajesh and Kusum to bed early and talked with Anita in the living room. Radha and I sat on the sofa. Anita sat across from us on a chair so high that her feet did not touch the ground. We had agreed that Radha would be the one to do most of the talking.

"We don't want you to have any confusion about last night," Radha began. Radha had accepted my story that I had entered Anita only once. Anita pushed herself as far back in the chair as possible and sat still. "Your Pitaji did something bad. It is a shameful thing that he did and God will one day punish him." Since Anita's face was expressionless, Radha stopped and said, "Yes?" Anita nodded, and Radha continued from where she had stopped. "You can't tell anyone about what he did. He is ashamed. He will never do anything again." Radha looked at me and, as if overcome with emotion, slapped me. "But you have to forget what happened. From now on, you empty your head of everything that has happened. What happened wasn't anything." There was a long silence when it was difficult to know if Radha was looking for more words to say or whether it was time for Anita to speak. "You understand? Empty your head." Anita nodded again. The day of praying had made me so remorseful that I felt outraged on Anita's behalf. But I was glad for what Radha was doing anyway. I wondered whether it was in fact possible for Anita to forget. All three of us understood, though, that what actually mattered was Anita's silence. The conversation had lasted not even an hour when we kissed Anita's forehead and sent her to bed.

Radha and Anita started sleeping in the same room. A few weeks after she discovered me, Radha sent Kusum to live with her mother, saying to her mother that she did not feel capable of taking care of three children. Radha offered no excuse to me.

I stopped drinking. For a long time I did not fight with Radha or even raise my voice in anger. If I started to speak loudly, my voice grew hushed on its own. For a while I went to temple every day.

Radha never again mentioned what had happened with Anita. But in the first few years after I was caught, every time she became angry at me I felt shame and fear shoot through my blood. Anita behaved as if she had completely forgotten what I did. I was glad when we moved out of the house where everything had occurred, because I thought it would hasten the process of erasure.

In two or three years I was going to saloons again. I would drink and cry as always, but I tried not to seek anyone's pity when I got home. Radha and I fought, though not as much. I returned to the brothels. I went to them until my heart attack, but I never had sex with someone younger than sixteen, and I never touched Anita again.

We drove past a large whitewashed rock which read 5 BERI KM in black paint. Fields stretched into the distance on either side. Some of the land had been tilled in preparation for planting, and the overturned soil was black. Other fields were a crumbling brown. The sun was directly overhead. I could feel the heat, but it was as if I were generating cold.

After Radha caught me, twenty years passed, and in her forties, she lost her faith in God. Becoming an atheist made her bitter. She grew so thin that the skin on her arms and face hung in folds. My weight increased till the width of my shirts matched the width of my cot. The more years Indira Gandhi spent in office, the more my income grew, for more and more things fell under the government's aegis and we civil servants were the gatekeepers. I bought a toaster, a blender, a refrigerator, and a television. Anita went through higher secondary and into college. She grew up shy and easily panicked, but there was nothing that marked her as damaged. Rajesh completed a Ph.D. in Hindi and then could not find any position as a teacher. Kusum won a government award for her Ph.D. on peanut plants and went to Canada, then America.

The bus stopped at the edge of Beri, in front of a large dirt yard which had an unpainted cinder-block restaurant and automobile repair shop at its back. "We'll be here half an hour," the driver called, and hurried off the bus. He went to a wall and urinated against it. A short young man in a red raw-silk shirt tucked carefully into creased black pants came out of the restaurant toward the bus. "Time to worship your stomach!" he shouted. "Samosas, roti-subji, sweets! Come eat! Come eat!" The bus emptied.

The young man told me where the ice-cream factory was. It had been five years since I was last in Beri, and the water pump and ration store he described on the way had not been there when I was last in town. I had hoped for nostalgia, but being in Beri made me feel nothing special.

Even several streets from the ice-cream factory I could hear the beat of a drum. The factory was on a cracked and pitted dirt road, with tilled fields on one side and single- and double-story houses along the other. In front of the factory, a man had a bear with a rope around his neck. A boy stood nearby playing a drum strapped to his chest. The bear was on his feet and walked swaying, like a drunk.

The factory was squeezed between two houses, and because its façade was no wider than an ordinary shop's, the only indication that it was a factory was the TOYOTA ICE CREAM painted in blue above the entrance and the whirring and splashing sounds coming from inside. As I came up the road, I saw a crowd of forty or fifty people, mostly dark peasant women with heavy silver bands around their ankles and children with bone-thin legs, standing in a ragged line in the fields just beyond the edge of the road. These were the poor of Beri. A smaller and better-dressed crowd stood on the road in front of the factory, eating ice cream off leaf plates with small flat spoon-shaped paddles of wood. In the shade of the factory a table held leaf plates of dissolving ice cream. To keep the crowd from raiding the ice cream, the road was patrolled by three men with bamboo staffs.

I was about forty feet from the factory when the pundit stepped out of its doorway. I immediately recognized his thick wrestler's body and buck teeth. He was holding a leaf plate so heavy with food that he had to keep both hands beneath it. Right behind him, talking, and also carrying a plate of food, came my brother Krishna. I was so startled I stopped in the middle of the road. Krishna was still thin and wrinkled, with a thin mustache. I moved into the fields, hoping to hide in the crowd until I found a way to speak to the pundit alone. I wondered what the pundit would think of my coming to Beri and not attempting to see my brothers.

Perhaps a third of the children in the crowd had the swollen bellies of starvation. Most seemed to be seven or eight years old, although they may have been older. Some of them were naked except for shirts or blouses held closed by one or two buttons. As I left the road and entered the crowd, a starving boy with a shaved head and ringworm scars on his scalp burst toward the ice-cream table. He kept a hand on his belly while running, as if he were balancing a pot of water. He traveled two or three meters before one of the patrolmen took a half step toward him and swung his staff. It was as if the dry whir of the swing, not the blow, sent the boy rolling along the dirt road. People from the crowd along the road cursed the patrolman. The drum was beaten faster and the bear shuffled faster. The patrolman turned his back on the crowd and walked away.

The boy lay on the ground for several minutes. He must have been there without his mother or family, because nobody tried to help him. He got up and, hunched almost in half, went through the crowd and several meters into the field. He lay down on his back in the dirt. I went up to him. His eyes were shut. He was so thin and gray with dust that he looked like a squirrel. My heart was racing and my hands felt icy. Perhaps because of all the remembering and Asha and seeing my brother among the guarded, I felt as if I had hit the boy. I wanted to cry at what I had done. "Take this," I said, crouching down and pressing twenty rupees into one of his hands. He opened his eyes, saw the money, but did not appear to recognize it.

As I stood, I suddenly became dizzy. I lurched to one side and, while moving, vomited. The vomit felt cold in my mouth and was almost clear. I leaned down and stood with my legs apart and my hands on my knees. Some of the vomit splattered my shoes. The ground rose and fell as if it were breathing. My heart was racing so fast that I became frightened of another heart attack. I shivered and threw up once more. From the noises around me, I realized that the crowd had begun to notice me. After several minutes I began to make my way back to the road, but my knees gave and I fell. I was looking at two lumps of dirt with hay and dried leaves embedded in them, then I drifted into a bright haze.

A man gripped my underarms and another grabbed my ankles. "Heatstroke," I heard, and then as I was slowly lifted: "He's worth two men," someone said, grunting, and people laughed. We entered the crowd along the road. A woman said, "Feed him ice cream." There was more laughter, but before it had time to die, another woman suggested, "Take him into the factory. It's cold there." "Into the factory," repeated a man. Suddenly several pairs of hands were pulling me up. "Ice cream. Ice cream," I heard.

As the five or six men, women, and children who were carrying me passed the dancing bear, it jerked forward and nudged a young boy who was pretending to buoy me with one hand. The boy jumped back, screaming. The people carrying me stopped to watch him hop in place and howl. I laughed, but no sound came out.

"This is no cartoon," I heard Krishna say. He stuck his head between the shoulders of the people carrying me and looked down into my face. For a moment he appeared surprised, and then his face resumed its normal irritated expression. He resembled both my mother and my father. Krishna ordered the people to bring me into the factory.

I was laid on a cot in a small office with green walls. A table fan was placed on the floor next to me. Krishna stood by my head and told the people who had carried me, "You can have some ice cream." It occurred to me that Krishna probably owned the factory.

When they left, Krishna turned to me and said, "This is how you return home. To cut my nose in front of everyone. Hiding in some crowd. Hiding and watching and then surprising. People love to talk evil." I didn't say anything. Krishna put his hand on my forehead. He kept it there for a while. "Sleep. You have a fever." He left, and I only had time to wonder whether I should ask for the pundit before I fell asleep.

I was woken several hours later by two of Krishna's sons. One of them, Raju, I liked very much. He was just under five feet tall and had an odd, almost triangular jaw. Because of a heart problem which required him to go to Delhi hospitals, Raju had stayed with me many times. Seeing him relieved some of my anxiety. "Namaste, Chachaji," he said, helping me up from the cot. His brother, Munna, who was almost six feet tall, slipped one of my arms around his shoulder. "We're looking for a girl for Munna," Raju said, "and we don't want people to gossip. That's why Pitaji is so angry." Munna had been married twice. His first wife had been run over by a bus. Munna appeared solemn and sad, and I wondered whether the second one was also dead. Even as a child he had been quiet. I used to joke with him that his seriousness was because, even though he was six feet tall, his father made everyone call him Munna, little one. Raju propped me up on one side. We moved out of the room and down a hall.

"It's for your good, mostly," Munna added. "We don't care what people say." He said this so angrily that I became defensive.

"Would I be hiding in front of your factory if I wanted to avoid you?" My voice was a hiss. "I came to ask your father to Radha's death anniversary."

Munna continued talking without noticing me. "They might start saying you are some opium addict and that's why you passed out." We left the factory by a back entrance and came out onto a dirt yard where a white Ambassador sedan was parked. As Munna slid me onto the back seat, he said, "This factory is ours. The ration store is ours. The restaurant-garage where your bus must have stopped, that's ours also."

I slept in the car and woke briefly as they laid me on a cot against a wall in their house.

I woke in the evening when the sky held by the doorway had turned red. Krishna was sitting on a chair next to me, reading a magazine by the light of a small lamp. I was saddened by the confusion of the day. Nothing had happened in any order I could even have imagined. Krishna looked up and said, "You had a fever, but it's gone now." He stared at me as if he were waiting for me to speak. He closed the magazine, but kept a finger between the pages he had been reading.

I felt no kinship with Krishna. Yet he had my mother's perfectly round nostrils and my father's small mottled teeth. The whole useless, shapeless day was present in my head, and my heart started to break. "You can never stop being brothers. Raju told me." For a moment I wondered what he was talking about. Then I realized that Raju must have told him I had come to ask him to tomorrow's ceremony and therefore make amends. "Both Vinod and I talk about you often. We are still your brothers."

After a moment I asked, "Will you come?"

"I will. Vinod is away on a pilgrimage. Last year he had a brain thing and he promised God if he got well he would pray twice every day and go to Vaishnodevi. He's become so religious now anyone can sell him a statue if they claim the river threw it up."

A short plump woman entered the room with two plates of rotis and subji. I sat up. She put the plates on a stool and placed this next to the bed. "Did anyone tell you to bring food?" Krishna said calmly. The woman became perfectly still. "Does my brother look like he can eat?" Krishna's voice was louder now. She took a step back. "Your parents didn't warn me you were retarded." She picked up one plate. "I'm going to eat while my brother can't?" Krishna stared at her as she took his plate and hurried out. Then he turned to me and smiled. "That's Raju's wife. When she came here, she was so proud of being high school–pass, she would read the newspaper in front of me. Now she barely talks."

At least I am better than Krishna, I thought. I pushed myself up and sat leaning against the wall. Raju appeared in the doorway, drinking a cup of tea. He asked how I was and left. Krishna began telling me what had happened over the last five years, some of which I already knew from mutual acquaintances. Vinod's son Sanjay and Krishna's son Pankaj had smuggled in seventeen thousand dollars from working in the United Arab Emirates. With this capital Vinod and Krishna had seized control of the most profitable businesses in Beri. Their latest acquisitions were the ice-cream factory and a license to sell liquor. Pankaj had recently written to Kusum telling her they were planning to sneak into America and could she help them. She had promptly written back saying her husband wouldn't let her.

I had a hard time concentrating. The odd shape of the day was making me want to cry in frustration. What could I do if things happened unpredictably and I was too weak-willed or stupid to handle anything but the simplest situations? I managed to ask if the pundit was still in Beri, but he had returned to Delhi. Krishna spoke so long and had such a good time talking that when he asked if I was going to spend the night, I felt he would genuinely have liked me to remain.

Raju drove me to the bus stop on a motorcycle. I was so weak that I kept sliding about and throwing him off balance. He got me a seat on the bus, and once I was in it, he bought me oranges for the trip back. He stood in the aisle beside me waiting for the bus to start. I asked what had happened to Munna's wife.

There was such a long pause after my question that I thought Raju meant to ignore me. "She hanged herself," he said finally. It was too dark to see his face. "It isn't Munna's fault. Everybody thinks it is. She used to cry a lot. She couldn't adjust to Pitaji. My wife, she's fine." He touched my shoulder.

"This was Munna's second."

"Yes, that's why it appears so bad. People now say the first one threw herself before the bus." He looked away and sighed. "It's because of her death that Munna's angry all the time." After a moment he shrugged and said, "She was crazy. The fact that she killed herself is proof."

Once the bus left Beri, I leaned my head against the window and fell into a stupor. I dreamed of the bear dancing and the squirrel boy and the cold vomit. The bus moved shaking and rattling down the highway. There was a full moon, but the fields along the side of the road looked as dark as the sea at night. I kept slipping into sleep and being jolted out of it.

I woke from one such sleep when the bus stopped in the middle of the highway. There was a hill on one side and fields on the other. The bus had stopped because a road was being cut up the hill and the engineers had placed their equipment in two tents in the center of the highway. There was a traffic jam as trucks and buses edged off the highway and tried to go around the encampment. I was so dazed that I stared at the hill for a while without fully realizing what was being built.

There were a hundred or so men digging the road, and the only light they had was the moon. They were working in teams, on separate patches ten or fifteen meters long. As they dug, women came behind them, scattering gravel in the spaces which had just been emptied. Some of the men and women looked like shadows, and others I could locate only by the sound of their voices or their shovels hitting dirt. I could not tell how far up the hill the teams were working, whether there was one at the very top.

Perhaps my unhappiness began to ease, because I started to appreciate how lucky I was to have reconciled with my brothers so easily. Or perhaps my mood changed simply because of the strange beauty of what I was seeing. But it took nearly an hour to pass the construction site, and during that hour, as I waited and watched the road being dragged up the hill, I began to believe that my life could be changed in inches, even by accident, the way my brother and I had been reconciled.

The bus shuddered as it went off the highway and onto the slope edging it. When it tried clambering back onto the road, the wheels kept sliding and suitcases and boxes raced down the aisles. I covered my ears against the engine's noise. With a lurch, the bus pushed itself back on the highway. It stood shivering for a moment with the incomplete road on one side and the dark fields on the other. And then again the engine's roar pushed the silence of the night ahead of us.

FOUR

I woke to a knock at my door. The room was dark, the air warm and overused. As I rose, I was afraid. Yet I now believed that Anita suspected nothing. This certainty had arrived in the middle of the night. Perhaps it came simply from the fact that thirty-some hours had passed since Mr. Gupta's party. Also, when I returned home, the door of the flat was unchained, as I had left it, and Anita was lying beside Asha. My feeling that time had not passed also made my reason for fleeing Delhi dreamlike. Nonetheless, I was afraid. There was another volley of raps, then Anita asked, "What about the pundit?"

To have her speak of something other than Asha was comforting. The squatter colony was silent, so I wondered what time it was. "I'll go find him," I said. Anita did not respond. I sat at the edge of my cot. Only a little light was slipping beneath the door, which meant the sun had not yet risen. I thought of the road being dragged up the hill. It made me feel determined.

"Rajiv Gandhi was murdered," Anita said. At first I thought she was speaking metaphorically, that there had been some scandal which had destroyed his chances for reelection. "The city is closed. The radio says there might be riots." The news must not have spread by the time I reached home, otherwise getting to Delhi would have been more difficult.

I got up and opened the door. Anita held out a folded newspaper to me. Her lips drooped in a child's caricature of sadness, but her eyes were expressionless. The white sari and lugubrious face made her look like a symbol of woe. The common room was dark. The door to the balcony and the kitchen windows were shut and bolted in preparation for riots. The light pressing through them revealed that it was early morning.

"Show me." I still could not believe her words. Unlike the time before his mother's death, when the military invaded the Sikhs' Golden Temple and every week terrorists were pulling buses off the road and shooting the passengers, or bombs were going off almost once a day, there had been no violence lately. I took the paper from her. I saw the headline RAJIV GANDHI KILLED and still thought it was a mistake.

Beneath the headline were two large photographs. One was a videotape image of a woman surrounded by a crowd and taken from some distance. The image had been blown up so many times that it would have been difficult to guess the woman's gender without the caption. The other photo was a publicity picture of Rajiv Gandhi facing slightly away from the camera and looking up. The front page was devoted to the assassination. Gandhi's speech in Tamil Nadu was the same as any of the dozens of speeches he had given in preparation for the election. The only difference was that a woman just five feet tall and strapped with dynamite had come up to him as he walked toward the stage. She put a garland around his neck and detonated herself. No group had taken credit yet, and everyone—

the Sikhs, the Pakistanis, the CIA, the Tamil Tigers—was under suspicion.

During the minutes it took me to glance through the articles, Anita stared at me from a meter away. I wondered if she needed to be comforted. Her lips continued to sag. "The world is not what it was yesterday," I said, wanting to let her know her experience was shared. For the first time in nearly a hundred years, a Nehru was not at the center of power. Rajiv Gandhi's wife was Italian and his children were too young to assume control. The sense of strangeness at no longer having a Nehru ready to rule was the same as approaching a familiar place through an alley I had never used before. Was this also the world? "Don't worry. There won't be riots. People didn't like Rajiv Gandhi the way they did his mother." Then I noticed I was holding a newspaper which should not have been delivered on such a day and asked, "Did you go out?"

"To get milk." Before I could respond to the oddity of this, Anita said, "Mr. Gupta's party," and paused. Mr. Gupta belonged to the Congress Party, I thought. The moment between the surge of fear and my heartbeat leaping was like car gears grinding when the speeds are switched too quickly. The fear made everything on either side of me vanish. All I could see was Anita. "You were drunk," she said, and halted again. Her lips stayed curved down. "I don't want . . ." she said.

When she stopped this time, my fear set me babbling. "I was drunk. Everybody at the party was drunk. I was so drunk I was stepping on my own feet. You get old and a little bit of liquor makes you crazy." I kept talking so that Anita would not have time to say something which could not be taken back. "I won't drink again. It was the first time I'd drunk in a year and a half." As I spoke, I willed Anita to think, If I say any more, where will I sleep, who will feed me?

"I would kill Asha . . ." she said, interrupting me. Her voice was thin and shaking.

"Even as a joke . . ." I said.

"I'm not joking," Anita answered. She raised her hand and pointed a finger at me. She shook it. "I would kill you."

"Don't worry. Don't worry. Don't worry." My voice stayed low and calm as I repeated this.

"I can't go anywhere. I have no other home."

"Don't worry." Anita tried saying more, but I kept interrupting. "I'll take care of you. You're my daughter."

Asha stepped out of the bathroom. She noticed the way Anita and I were looking at each other and halted just before the bathroom door. Draped over an arm was a freshly washed shirt and underpants. Anita watched Asha and me for a moment. Then she took the laundry from Asha and hung it over a clothesline she had strung along one side of the common room. Anita returned to the kitchen.

Asha tried catching my eye, and the possibility of Anita seeing this scared me. "I'll go to the temple," I said. I thought, I can take all my money and all the money I've collected for Congress and vanish.

The sky was bright and cool. For May the weather was mild. The entrance to the squatter colony was blocked by a pile of sandbags. The doors were guarded by a neighbor, a young man with an enormous and ancient gun. "My grandfather killed a lion with this," he said. He shut the doors behind me as soon as I stepped into the alley. The piece of road I could see from the alleyway was empty of traffic. Shops had their grilles pulled down over their fronts. Rajiv Gandhi's death would have closed the banks, too, I realized. The ordinariness of this detail reminded me of my nature. I did not have the stamina to disappear.

A rickshaw driver sat in his vehicle at the mouth of the alley, smoking a bidi and regarding the thoroughfare. I came up to him and stopped. The roofs on both sides of the street were completely lined with men, women, and children waiting to see what would happen. I thought of floods I have seen during which everyone in a town is forced to live on a roof. But the road was empty. I did not know whether a curfew had been declared, but even without one, few people would take the risk of going out. I wondered at Anita's having left the flat.

Seven or eight men in their twenties stood bunched together several meters to the right of me on the sidewalk. The top buttons of their shirts were open, and as if this were how they recognized each other, most wore canvas shoes with clumsily copied foreign emblems sewn on. The hoodlums were staring at a Bata shoe shop directly opposite the alleyway. Behind an iron grille fixed to the ground by heavy locks was a large window displaying Bata shoes. The shop was owned by a Sikh, and I knew it was symbolically important that the first shop looted belong to a Sikh or a Muslim. If I died in a riot, it occurred to me, I would never have to speak with Anita again.

The hoodlums talked and joked among themselves, but kept looking at the shoe shop. Their bodies were tensed and, when not moving, tilted automatically toward the shop. I wondered if what had happened after Indira Gandhi's assassination would be repeated. For several days after her murder, the roofs of most of the houses in the Old Vegetable Market remained crowded and bunches of looting men roamed the streets. Periodically people spilled from their homes and a riot started. Then, after a while, a tank or some military jeeps appeared and the roads were abandoned once more. The butchering of Sikhs and Muslims—shooting them, knifing them, hanging them, setting them on fire—continued for weeks after they had been chased out of mixed neighborhoods. I stared at the shop, the hoodlums, the people on the roof. I felt as if the blue sky had become solid and the whole country was now under a lid. Not wanting to return home, I stayed where I was.

A half hour passed. I watched the blue sky and the silent, full roofs. The world felt impossible, like a door larger than the building it belonged to. But this impossibility was strangely comforting. The world had changed, and I must have been changed with it.

The Sikh's wife stepped out of a narrow, dark staircase next to the shop. She was fat and wore a green salwar kameez. I had never spoken with her but had seen her working in the shop and buying milk from the same milkman I used. She stood in front of the steps for a moment and looked up and down the road. She avoided meeting any of the eyes that were focused on her. When she stepped aside, two young boys, about six and ten, came out from the staircase. They were dressed in blue-and-maroon school uniforms and their hair was neatly bunned in small white handkerchiefs. They looked as if they had just bathed. The boys' wet cleanness made me think of newborn rabbits. Making them look young was smart, but I doubted it would help. A moment after the boys, a fat white-haired woman dressed in a widow-white salwar kameez emerged. This was the Sikh's mother. I began to feel sad.

The Sikh's wife stepped to the edge of the sidewalk and waved to the rickshaw driver. He looked at her coolly and continued to smoke. He was eighteen or nineteen and had short bristly hair. To be out on such a day signified the rickshaw driver's predatoriness. One of the hoodlums said, "Bitch." Everyone else remained silent and the word expanded in the air. I sensed the attention of people on the roof. The older boy took the younger one's hand. The woman kept motioning for the rickshaw driver long after it was obvious that he was not going to move. Perhaps she thought that if she stopped motioning, the next part of something preordained would happen.

I wondered how much time it would take to murder the Sikhs. The men would probably make a game of getting them away from the stairs. They might be threatened till the women and children started crying and pleading to be allowed to leave. After the hoodlums had let themselves be bribed, the rickshaw would be ordered forward. The Sikhs would get in. The rickshaw driver would pedal in the exact center of the road and be leaning as far away from his passengers as possible. Then the hoodlums might start running alongside the rickshaw, laughing and talking among themselves, or completely silently. They would begin punching and tugging the women and children. After a block or two, they might grab one of the boys and drag him into the street. Then the rickshaw driver would jump off and run away. I remembered the dead naked Muslim boy of forty years ago, whose shoulder had been opened so that white bone showed.

"Go, friend," I said to the rickshaw driver. I was surprised at having spoken. Once the words were uttered, I felt complete confidence. The rickshaw driver looked at me. He was small, with thin arms. I smiled and cocked my head in the Sikhs' direction. "They are women and children," I said in a loud, casual voice. "The Sikh, he's still up there." The hoodlums must have been surprised as well, for when the rickshaw driver glanced toward them, no one made a gesture. I felt the authority of being incongruous, an old very fat man, dressed in the white shirt and dark pants of a bureaucrat, standing in the open when a riot might start. I was glad that Delhi did not have the fanatics of Bombay, that confusion alone might stop people.

The rickshaw driver pedaled across the street. When he got to the Sikhs, he pulled the rickshaw parallel to the sidewalk and asked, "Where to?" as if they were any other passengers.

"Morris Nagar," the Sikh's wife said.

"Fifty rupees," he responded loudly. The hoodlums rustled at the outrageous sum.

The family got on. The women sat on the sides and the children in between. The hoodlums looked at each other in confusion.

I started walking in the middle of the road toward the temple. The rickshaw driver passed me. He was leaning almost halfway over the handlebars. The rickshaw got farther and farther ahead of me, until I was alone on the road. The Sikh must be watching his family from behind a curtain, I thought. In my head I saw his door being smashed open and him being clubbed and stabbed. Then my scalp prickled as I imagined a brick curving in flight toward me from one of the rooftops.

The temple doors were closed and the alcove next to them where a man usually sits was empty. I tried the doors and they opened. I was impressed that the pundit had been courageous enough not to lock them.

In the temple's marble courtyard I smelled lentils cooking and heard film songs playing in the back, where the pundit lived. "Punditji," I called out, and waited. I went around and bowed to each of the gods. My helping the Sikhs had confirmed my sense that the world was changed. I asked God to give me the strength to behave well. While praying, I realized I would have to admit all my crimes to Anita and beg her forgiveness. I had not confronted this before, but that was the only way I could imagine any future.

When the pundit did not appear, I called again. At the third try, he peered from a side door.

Seeing it was only me, he shouted, "What!" He held the door half open so that only his head and part of his shoulders showed. He had a small mustache and teeth so widely separated you could put your fingers in the gaps.

"Forgive me," I said. "I came to request that you perform services for my wife's death anniversary today." I had known the pundit when he was a boy named Rajan who failed every civil service exam he took, and I resented the politeness tradition forced on me.

"This morning you come?"

"My wife wished to be prayed for by someone who knew her," I said. An excuse came unbidden to my mind about how Anita was supposed to talk to him but that she was slightly crazy and had claimed until this morning that she had done so.

The pundit sighed. "Only a fool like me would leave his door open when a riot can occur at any moment, and only a fool like me would say yes to you," he said. "What time?" Just his head was sticking out of the partially opened door.

The money from blessing the ice-cream factory must have dulled his desire for work, I thought. "Ten."

"Ten-thirty." Without another word, he closed the door.

When I stepped back onto the road, the roofs were still crowded, but a jeep with six or seven khaki-uniformed policemen standing in it was slowly rolling down the road. The hoodlums had disappeared. My scalp crept from all the people gazing down. I wanted to break into a trot, but I made myself keep walking.

As I entered our compound, I smiled with relief and pride. When the world shifts it shifts everything with it, I thought. If I was forthright and admitted my crimes instead of doing something like claiming that Anita's memories were confused, then over the next year or two we might learn to live with what had been acknowledged.

The door to the flat was closed but unchained. Rajesh was reading the newspaper while sitting on Anita and Asha's bed. His shirt was spread beside him on the bed and he was in his undershirt and pajamas. Asha sat on the floor reading a comic book. Seeing her and Rajesh sitting together and wondering if Anita might have told made me so afraid that my confidence instantly vanished.

Rajesh said, "I left Faridabad at three this morning." He toppled onto his side to show his exhaustion and repeated, "Three." He smiled. "Somebody phoned a neighbor, who warned everyone. When I heard, I thought, Better start now, in case there are riots." Across the aisle from the bed were two wooden chairs against a wall. I took off my shirt and draped it over one of these chairs. I sat down on the chair and began unlacing my shoes. Rajesh couldn't possibly be speaking this way if Anita had revealed my secret.

"Water?" Asha inquired.

I nodded and asked, "Where's your mother?"

"Bathing." Asha left.

"No riots. Nobody cares," Rajesh said. He rolled onto his back and stretched. All his limbs were thin, but his stomach was large. He closed his eyes and appeared to fall asleep. Rajesh joined the BJP after Radha died. Before that he had been quiet and somewhat sullen. Hindu nationalism had given him a salesman's buoyancy. This combined strangely with his dislike for me and made his insults strike with greater force. When Asha returned, Rajesh asked, without opening his eyes, "Did you just go to the pundit?"

"Yes," I answered.

"Have you been sleeping for a year that you just went?" Rajesh turned to Asha. "Has he been awake the last six months?"

"I went to Beri yesterday. Before, I was busy with work."

"Busy!" he said doubtfully, and then, after a moment, "You might as well stop raising money for Congress. Without a Nehru, Congress is just another party. The BJP will win for certain."

Anita came into the bedroom with three cups of tea on a tray. Her hair was wet and had left a stain on the back of her white blouse. Looking at her, I understood that I had to admit everything, but I could not imagine the act of doing so. Till then, knowing what I must do had been enough to make me feel as if I would accomplish it, as if, in the knowledge that the moon reflects the sun, I had attempted to warm myself by the moon.

"Muslims will finally be treated like everyone else. In no non-Muslim country other than India can a Muslim marry more than one woman . . . You want to divorce, then you pay alimony, like everyone else . . . Their quota of Parliament seats is more than they should have."

He often spoke about polygamy. "How many wives can you support that you are jealous?" I said without thinking. Because he had a bad job, Rajesh was worried about ever getting a wife. Jabbing him back instead of ignoring him made me realize I was speaking out of my fear of Anita.

As we took our teacups, Rajesh started talking about Pakistan, but I had trouble concentrating and his words ran past me. Both Anita and Asha sat on the bed with Rajesh.

There was a distant explosion and we all jerked in place. Then, after a brief silence, there were two more. Asha began to cry.

Rajesh pulled Asha into his arms. "That was a really fat man farting," he said. Asha laughed. Rajesh made farting noises with his lips and Asha laughed some more. "Fatter even than your grandfather." Rajesh held Asha at arm's length and shook her. "Silly doll," he said. Once Asha was calm, he asked Anita for mathri and mango pickle.

Rajesh rubbed the mango pickle over the wafers, until the oil soaked through the fried dough; then he ate each mathri in a single bite.

Rajesh had an ulcer and was constantly getting sick because he loved the spicy food sold on the streets. I wanted to call for a peace and said, "You should be more careful."

"I can't help eating. I'm your son," he answered with his mouth full. I glanced at Anita to see how Rajesh's insult was received. She drank her tea without any expression.

"I'll take a bath," I said, and stood.

"See how they bribe us," Rajesh exclaimed. "On holidays and days they're afraid of riots, the municipality will let you have water all day. The rest of the year . . ."

"I'd rather be bribed than not get water," I interrupted.

With each mug I poured over my head, I tried to revive my courage. I had done a brave thing with the Sikhs and so should be able to be brave at home. I scrubbed myself. Denial would only make her angry. The bathroom lightbulb was weak. The small room was dark from shadows and mold growing on the walls. To say words which admitted what I had done was like speaking a spell that brought a monster into the world. To admit my crime was to end the world. No possibilities could be imagined after the admission.

Because of the food Anita had begun heating, the common room smelled like a holy day. I heard Rajesh and some man talking eagerly in the living room. It took a moment for me to realize that the other voice was Mr. Mishra's. I had invited him at some point last week and forgotten. I hung my washed underclothing on the balcony ledge, put on pants and shirt, and went into the living room.

Mr. Mishra was on the sofa and Rajesh was on a love seat across from him. Mr. Mishra stood and shook my hand. "I thought I'd come and offer my support," he said. "This is a bad day for many reasons."

I thanked him. His remembering to come seemed proof that there was more to me than my crime against Anita. Just that morning I had saved lives. I sat down on the large bed pressed against the wall between Anita's bedroom and the living room.

The conversation did not resume. Mr. Mishra's presence reminded me I was to be in mourning, and perhaps I reminded Mr. Mishra and Rajesh of the day's seriousness. Rajesh had put on his shirt. I was glad at this politeness, because he could be unpre-

dictably rude. Anita came with tea for us and we drank it in silence.
When I was nearly done with mine, I asked Mr. Mishra if he thought
Rajiv Gandhi's murder would incite much of a pity vote for Congress.

"We were talking about that," Rajesh said.

"Probably not," Mr. Mishra answered, taking charge of summarizing the recent discussion. "He wasn't loved like his mother. His
mother was smart. She wanted people to think she was India."

"The Nehrus may not be gone yet," Rajesh said. "They are like
Ravan's heads. You cut off one and another takes its place. Nehru,
Indira, Sanjay, now Rajiv. Each time we thought, At last the family
is dead."

I could have chosen not to pursue the conversation, but talking
about politics kept me feeling the world had altered. "I didn't think
that," I said.

"Because Congress pays you."

"There's Rajiv's wife. But Sonia Gandhi is Italian," Mr. Mishra
added, ignoring the discord between Rajesh and me by not looking
at either one of us. "Nothing like this has happened before." I liked
hearing of the day's uniqueness.

"Indians are children and they think the Nehrus are their parents. Children must grow up," Rajesh said.

"Who is going to replace Congress?" I said. "The BJP? The BJP
thinks Indians are children. 'God and Bread,' 'God and Bread.'
What sort of platform is that? What does God have to do with the
balance of payments? When the BJP says God, it means India for
Hindus."

"All the BJP wants is for Hindus and Muslims to be treated the
same."

"What do you care about Muslims?" I answered. My voice came
out quivering and slight. "Muslims are a slogan. Let them have their
mosques. Let them have thirty wives."

"No non-Muslim country other than India lets Muslims have
more than one wife," Rajesh told Mr. Mishra.

"Egypt does. Saudi Arabia does," Mr. Mishra said softly. "India has so many worries, why should we care how many times someone gets married?"

Rajesh paused for a moment and then continued, "What kind of a country do we have where one group can do whatever it wants and the other group has to remain silent and get slapped? Can Hindus own land in Kashmir? People are tired of this. That's why the BJP is going to win."

"You know why Congress is doing badly?" I asked Rajesh.

"I know why."

"You know why the BJP is doing well?"

"I know."

"This is the first election where people will choose between completely different ideologies," Mr. Mishra said.

We ignored this commentary.

"It's about Indira Gandhi's Emergency. How many innocent people were jailed during that martial law? Sanjay Gandhi's forced vasectomies of poor villagers," Rajesh said.

"Twenty years later the Emergency matters?"

"Rajiv Gandhi taking bribes. It's about that too. At last people know the Nehrus can't change no matter what the punishment. After twenty years, as if nothing's happened, they're back to their sins. Congress has to be punished for its sins. Congress has to be made an example for all politicians. For the good of the country. So that other politicians know that you can't just do anything."

The idea of punishment sent my heart racing and silenced me.

Radha's elder sister Shakuntala arrived during the silence. Along with her came her husband, two sons, and a daughter. By the time they sat down and the daughter went to make tea, Radha's brother Bittu had arrived with his wife, Sharmila, and his son and daughter. None of them liked me. They all thought I was a drunk and a liar and so did not know how to behave. I moved off the bed onto the love seat next to the one Rajesh was on. By sitting alone I felt as if I were assuming the dignity of a mourning husband.

After some time, conversations started. Most were about the

assassination. Once the older people started talking, some of the children went into Anita and Asha's bedroom and began playing cards.

Shakuntala had heard on the radio that the Tamil Tigers were most likely responsible for the murder. Since no one knew or cared much about the Tamils, the talk quickly moved to the Congress versus the BJP.

Bittu talked the most. He was a superstitious and arrogant man who wore lucky stones on each finger and used to be a pole climber for the electricity company but introduced himself as an engineer. "Good he's dead. When the Muslim moved into Tailor's Alley and started a milk bar," I said to the people there, 'In my life this has always been a Hindu alley. Tomorrow this Muslim will be selling your children milk with cow bones ground in.'" He realized he was merely boasting and brought the conversation back on track. "The Congress Party let the Muslims have Pakistan and then the Muslims stayed here, too." Bittu had become a strong supporter of the BJP over the year and a half since he had retired. Massing the residents of Tailor's Alley to drive out the Muslim shopkeeper was his greatest achievement and he forced it into any conversation he could. He had even written about it to Kusum in America. She had responded with a postcard of a crucifix.

"Every religion in the world is here," Rajesh said. "The only way we can live together is if the government treats us all the same." Rajesh, I thought, was the modern face of the BJP.

"Wonderful," Bittu said. "You come into my home one night, take over one of my rooms, and then I should let you have my room. The Muslims invaded India."

"The Muslims aren't going anywhere. Christians are staying. Buddhists are staying."

"Buddhism started in India," Mr. Mishra volunteered.

"I don't care about them," Bittu said.

Anita groaned. She was sitting on the bed between Shakuntala and Sharmila. As she moaned, she hugged her shoulders and folded into her lap. She stayed bent and we all looked at her. Her face was wet with tears. Shakuntala rubbed Anita's back. Shakuntala had Radha's oval face and crooked teeth. After a moment Anita wiped her face, stood, and left the room. I wanted to follow and comfort her, but knew this was absurd. Instead, I kept leaning toward the talk of politics, like a farmer bowing toward his fire in winter.

A moment or two later Mr. Mishra, who had been sitting at the edge of the sofa, restarted the conversation. "If the BJP comes in, they are going to make some noise about foreigners and make getting World Bank help harder."

"Let the foreigners in," Bittu said, "and they'll eat us. What happened with the British and their tea company?"

Mr. Mishra looked at Bittu and asked, "What is the difference between what the BJP wants and India's economic policy between 1947 and when Rajiv Gandhi came to power?" Mr. Mishra was smiling, as he always did when he knew more about something than the person he was talking with.

"I used to know," Bittu said, smiling slightly, almost like a shy child, "but I've forgotten."

"All right, then tell me, what will the repatriation policy for these companies be? If they have to keep seventy paisas of every rupee they earn here in the country for five years after earning it, what does that mean for the economy?"

"This is difficult," said Shakuntala. Mr. Mishra smiled at her and then turned his attention back to Bittu.

"I don't know," Bittu answered with the same smile.

"What about other countries like India? Taiwan. South Korea. Egypt. Algeria. Turkey. How did they manage their economies? What did they do which would not work here?"

Bittu kept quiet.

I did not know the answers either. I was busy wondering what I would say to Anita later this afternoon.

Mr. Mishra waited a moment before he went on. "If you don't know India's old economic history, if you don't know how India treats foreign companies now, if you don't know what other poor countries have done to save themselves, then why do you talk so loudly?" His voice rose as he spoke, and by the time he had finished, he looked ready to jump up and shake a finger.

"So you know everything and I know nothing," Bittu said.

Mr. Mishra hesitated. "No. I just know a lot more about this thing," he answered hesitantly.

"I know something which you couldn't know in ten years."

Finally Mr. Mishra recognized that this argument was the center of the room's attention. He looked around him. "I don't know that much."

"Om," Bittu shouted. Mr. Mishra, baffled no doubt at this display of religion, nodded and smiled. This enraged Bittu even more. "Om," he shouted again. "The universe begins with om." Mr. Mishra opened his mouth and Bittu boomed, "Om."

At that moment, Krishna arrived. Because my fight with my brothers was common knowledge, his arrival brought the card-playing children back to the living room. The world has changed, I thought.

Anita was the only one who did not come to the living room. Shakuntala went and tried getting her, but Anita said she had too much work.

Krishna sat down beside me. Rajesh moved to a stool near Mr. Mishra. At first, Krishna seemed to want us to ignore him. He was dressed in a white kurta pajama, and this made him look particularly humble. He watched the room with a glass of water balanced on one knee. Despite the small conversations which kept opening and closing, the room's attention was focused on him, and whenever it appeared to drift, Krishna would speak a word or two and draw it back to himself.

One of the children finally broached the subject. "We haven't seen you in a long time."

"Not because I didn't want to see you," he said, looking into the eyes of the boy who had spoken, "but because God chose to keep me apart from my brother." His voice was so soft it sounded as if he was holding back tears. "Have you seen the movie *Time*? It was like that." Shakuntala made approving sighing clicks.

"You were separated by an earthquake?" Rajesh asked.

Krishna ignored him. "Yesterday, like a miracle, my brother appeared at my door and said, 'Brother, let us stop this fighting. What else is there in the world other than family?' And I told him, 'You are right. I have always loved you.'" I began to be stared at. Could I have said these things? Krishna put a hand on my shoulder. After a moment he said, "Learn from us. Don't make the mistakes we have made, losing the many years of brotherly love."

He would have gone on, but the pundit came with his wife. The pundit was garbed in a saffron robe and had a saffron satchel slung over one shoulder. His wife wore an ordinary green sari. Seeing Krishna, she also wanted to hear the story of our reconciliation. I led the pundit to the common room, but everyone else remained in the living room to hear the story again.

From his satchel the pundit pulled out a thermos bottle with the figure of Superman on it. The thermos held Ganges water, and he poured a cupful onto the center of the common-room floor and scrubbed an area several feet wide with a saffron rag. I was not confident of his competence and wondered if the prayer he would perform would be from a Veda, or whether it was a recipe he had concocted on his own. I sat on the ground and watched him as he, on all fours, drew a two-foot-by-two-foot square with flour. Inside the square, along the edges, he drew small rectangles and filled them with oms, swastikas, flowers. He took a large tin box from his satchel and placed it in the center of the square. Then he began bringing out other things from the bag. A coconut, twigs, sugar twisted in a bit of newspaper, clarified butter in a bottle that used to hold hair oil, rose-colored threads, a bunch of bananas, a small paper bag of apples, a purse full of coins. There was no end to what the satchel contained. His efficiency promised the ability to do the impossible. Anita came into the room and I caught her eye by mistake. She looked calm, not crazy. She would not do something reckless that would destroy the world.

When the pundit was ready, Anita gathered everyone. People spread themselves around the room. The pundit lit a fire in the tin box.

The ceremony lasted about forty-five minutes. At first I was concerned only with throwing handfuls of rice into the fire at the proper time and following the pundit's lead when he called out "God be praised" or "God is great." The pundit sat on one side of the fire, and Rajesh and I sat opposite him. Anita was a few feet away, at my side. The sun coming through the balcony and the heat of the fire began to lull me. I knew enough Sanskrit to follow what the pundit was saying if I tried. After a while, the rhythm of the prayer snagged me. I could understand it without effort. "I am the fire and that which is consumed. I am the poison, the cure. The beginning without end and the end without beginning."

I began to pray silently and with steady fervor. I kept asking God to free Radha from being reborn, and that if she was reborn, to let our souls not intersect so that we did not repeat our torments. I asked God to let Radha, Anita, Asha never meet me after this life.

Near the end of the prayer, Rajesh and I began to throw coins into the fire. I was pulling my hand away from the fire when I sensed Radha sitting beside me to my right. I did not turn my head, but I knew exactly how she was seated, with her legs crossed lotus fashion, and I could tell where the veins in her arms and feet stood out. I felt her watch me without emotion, as if she were writing down everything that she saw in my heart and head. I shivered. After two or three minutes, this sense of her abruptly vanished, and when it did, it was as if she had died again.

I wept slowly and quietly. I was not crying for Radha's death but for the tragedy of her life. It took a few minutes for the others even to notice. When they did, there was an appreciative murmur. I tried to stop crying, but the tears kept coming. I pressed my fingertips to my eyes.

The prayer ended and people stood. I heard the pundit's wife say, "I'm so hungry I could eat a dozen puris."

The phone buzzed. Someone picked it up and yelled, "It's Kusum." Anita left the kitchen for the living room. I was unable to look up and saw only her bare feet. The common room emptied except for me.

"Hello," Anita said, and a moment later: "There is no danger here. You are happy, healthy? Carolyn? Ben?"

There was silence for a little while, and then Bittu's son, Rohit, called to me from the living-room doorway and led me through the crowd that surrounded the phone. Anita passed the phone to me. I could not meet her gaze.

The pundit said, "I should talk to her. It will help." He was smiling ingratiatingly, wanting some of the glamour of an international phone call.

"Pitaji, what's happening there?" Kusum asked.

Kusum lived with her grandmother till she went to college. I had last seen her two years ago, when she brought her husband, Ben, to meet us. She phoned a few times a year and sent postcards whenever she went on holiday. The fact that our lives had touched so little over so many years made me feel that my past was heavy and finished.

"It's one year since your mother died."

"I know," she replied, as if I had accused her of indifference. "Are you crying?" she inquired warily.

"Hello, daughter," the pundit called, leaning over my shoulder.

"Who's that?"

"Punditji. He wants to talk on the phone."

"Tell him a minute to America is forty rupees. Are you crying?"

"Yes."

"Give the phone to Anita, then."

I did, and went to my room. The crying had made me feel drunk. I closed the door and lay down.

•   •   •

When I woke in the middle of the afternoon, the flat was quiet. I stayed on my side and fingered my grief as though it were a bruise. I squeezed out a few fresh tears. I knew I must speak the truth or my life would spin out of control.

I got up and went to the latrine. I heard Anita's footsteps as I squatted. She stopped in front of the door. "I'll be in the living room," she said.

"All right," I murmured. A spider had spun a web right above the faucet. The green paint of the door was puffed with moisture and heat. I shat and shat until there was nothing coming out. I washed myself and stood, but my bowels clenched themselves so tightly that I immediately had to squat again. The world had changed, I told myself.

The common room was empty. There were whitish marks on the floor where the pundit had dragged his boxes. I went to the living room.

Anita was sitting on the sofa edge, leaning forward and cupping her knees. When I came in, she looked directly into my eyes, and after that, I could not look at anything but her face. "Asha's away with Shakuntala," she said. Her voice squeaked and she stopped. Anita tried saying something else, but her voice remained unnaturally high and she ceased mid-word. I sat down on the love seat across from her. "I always knew," she began calmly. Her voice continued being high, thin, but she did not stop. "I never didn't know you were cruel, you were merciless. Every time you touched me. Every time you made me touch you, I knew."

I nodded. The sun coming through the living-room window covered her and the sofa with light.

"We have to live together. I can't go anywhere else. I would if . . ." She stopped, and started making rapid gasping sounds, as if the possibility of a different life had overcome her. The gasps sounded like huh-huh.

For several minutes she did not say anything and just tried to control her breathing. I stared at her. Anita must have seen something defiant on my face. She shouted through her gasps, "I knew all the time!"

I nodded again.

"When you'd pretend to sleep and put my hand on your penis." The shrill voice made her sound silly. Anita glared. I could tell that my passivity annoyed her. "When you entered me, it hurt so much I thought I would die, that I had to die. How could I not die? And then I bled. After the first night, I was just waiting to die. Every night there was blood, and I kept thinking, I'm going to die. I won't even have seen the Taj Mahal and I'm going to die. I won't have put on perfume and I'm going to die."

Instead of guilt, I felt anxiety for the lines I must speak. No matter how Anita shouted at me, the world would end only after I spoke.

"And you made it seem as if you would kill yourself if I tried to stop you. I used to think. Think seriously! What's better, you die or me? I wanted you to die, but then I thought, What would happen to everyone else, and I was ashamed."

I imagined how my body must have appeared to her when I was on top.

"I look at twelve-year-olds and think, I was like that. Who could do that to a twelve-year-old? You and Ma! Ma! What kind of a mother was she?" Anita stopped suddenly, as if she had just realized something. I had never known Anita was angry at Radha. "I'd kill myself if anything like that happened to Asha."

Anita turned her palms up as if asking for a response. Was she seeking a promise that I would not go near Asha? I nodded. I waited for her to become less angry so I could make that vow out loud. Once she became quiet, I thought, I should say, What I did was astonishingly evil. But I said nothing.

"Remember when I had just got married and you were sick and went to the hospital? That's when I realized how I hated you. I thought about killing you all the time then . . . Ma with her guru. You with your drunken crying . . . Say something."

Only from her stare did I know I had to open my mouth. I couldn't. "Say something," she repeated. I wanted to turn my head, look toward anything but Anita. I kept gazing at her. "I knew it was your fault but once I started touching you, I was helping you be wrong. I thought I was the worst person in the world."

No, I thought, I am the worst person. I remained silent.

"Say, 'I'm a dog.' Say, 'Forgive me. I am an animal,' and I will forgive you. Say, 'I am a rabid dog that should be beaten to death with bricks.' Admit it and we can go on. Admit it!" I started saying something, but only a hiss came out. "Say, 'I am stinking shit.'" I had never heard Anita curse before and this made her anger mysterious. I kept silent. "Say, 'I know what I did and I should die.'" Anita's pupils were moving wildly. My mouth wouldn't open. She continued speaking this way even after it was obvious I was not able to say anything. When she stopped, she began making the gasping sounds again.

I don't know when Anita started screaming. It might have been two minutes after she stopped speaking or it might have been fifteen minutes. It started as a low note, a stretched sigh. Then it began sharpening, acquiring shape, as it gathered more and more pain to itself. I sat there and watched her sitting across from me. Her palms were facing up on her knees, and her mouth was half open. When the scream could rise no further, Anita began slapping her thighs with the backs of her hands. She slapped them quick and hard.

I thought I had to speak. Instead, I stood. Feeling ashamed, dreamy, caught in the inevitability of what felt like a fresh crime, I went and closed the doors to her bedroom and the common room. Then I came back and sat down. A moment later I rose again and shuttered the windows. Then I returned to the love seat. The light in the room was gray now.

"Ohh!" Anita continued. I still couldn't speak.

FIVE

Several days after Rajiv Gandhi's death, my office reopened. When I arrived, I found Mr. Bajwa, Mr. Gupta's former moneyman, sitting outside my door on the peon's low stool. He was reading a religious novel about the martyrdom of one of the Sikh saints. I had not seen him for nearly a year and at first did not recognize him. He wore a white kurta pajama, a white turban, and, in a brocaded scabbard at his side, a dagger. His beard hung free. When we worked together, except for his turban, Mr. Bajwa had been one of the least reverent Sikhs I knew. Mr. Bajwa came again the next morning because Mr. Gupta had not been at the office during his first visit.

"Sonia Gandhi will have to become Prime Minister," Mr. Bajwa said. He was sitting leaning forward, with his fingertips on my desk, trying to get me to meet his gaze. Mr. Mishra, with whom he was arguing, sat beside him in front of my desk. Mr. Bajwa was at the office because he wanted Mr. Gupta's reassurance that Rajiv Gandhi's assassination would not stop him from protecting Mr. Bajwa against the corruption charges he faced. I was Mr. Gupta's man and so was receiving the attention he would rather have lavished on Mr. Gupta. I tried to avoid his eyes and kept glancing around the room. All four ceiling fans were spinning. "People, when they think of Congress, think Nehrus. There are only two Nehrus of the right age, Sanjay Gandhi's wife and Rajiv Gandhi's. They can't bring in Maneka Gandhi because she's Sikh, and she got pregnant before she married Sanjay Gandhi. Besides, Sanjay Gandhi was never Prime Minister. Sonia Gandhi is left."

"Better Italian than Sikh?" Mr. Mishra asked.

"She held Indira Gandhi's head in her lap as she died." Mr. Bajwa's voice rose at mentioning the assassination. For me it was hard to think of Indira Gandhi's assassination as separate from government-supported massacres of Sikhs. Buses were stopped during bright day with the military a hundred meters away and Sikh passengers were dragged out and murdered.

The abjectness of Mr. Bajwa identifying so completely with those who had power over him stirred my anxieties. Even with the window behind me shut and the thick curtain drawn, the sun outside was a steady pressure on the back of my head. Ever since I had sensed Radha sitting beside me while I prayed for her, I had found myself automatically mouthing prayers, and now one began passing in fragments through my head.

"Congress might have just won if Rajiv Gandhi were alive, but with him dead, half the reason to vote Congress is gone," Mr. Mishra said softly. "I think Sonia Gandhi is going to be Congress president. I am certain of this." He smiled and nodded, as if sweetening unhappy news. "Congress has to pick a Nehru, and Sonia Gandhi could not say no to such an appeal. But there isn't going to be any pity vote."

Mr. Bajwa lifted himself slightly out of his chair in his eagerness to respond, but he continued looking primarily at me. "Congress is still strong in the villages. The villager knows the Nehrus have always been there. He knows the other parties are no better. The villager is most of India, no matter what city people think. I know . . . I know . . . that several village women have hanged themselves in unhappiness over the loss of Rajiv Gandhi." After his claim about the suicides, Mr. Bajwa looked directly at both of us, as if challenging us to doubt him.

"Mr. Bajwa, how many Sikhs did Congress kill after Indira Gandhi's assassination?" Mr. Mishra asked.

"Have I forgotten?" Mr. Bajwa answered, clutching his beard. To me it seemed rude to make the consequences of his position explicit.

Mr. Mishra didn't respond. It appeared as if he finally felt shame at arguing with someone who was nearly crazy.

A peon entered the room with a folded paper in his hand and walked toward me. "Who sent it?" Mr. Bajwa asked.

"For Karanji," the peon said, handing me the note. He was a new man, thin and young, with teeth stained rust from betel leaf.

The note said, "Come see me when he goes." It was unsigned, but the writing was in Mr. Gupta's elegant hand.

"From? From?" said Mr. Bajwa to the peon. The peon left without answering.

"Mr. Gupta?" asked Mr. Bajwa. I could not think of anyone else to name and so nodded yes. He looked above my head and cleared his throat. "What didn't I do for him?"

All this sadness made me think it might be easy to go insane. I wondered if insanity was like being drunk.

"I need kindness," Mr. Bajwa said.

A little later Mr. Mishra stood, announced, "I am going home to sleep," and departed.

Mr. Bajwa's gaze fell back on me. I was too ashamed to look away. After a moment he began singing a movie song: "Oaths, promises, love, loyalty. Words only. What can you do with words? Nobody is anybody's." He did not sing it well, somehow even getting the rhymes slightly off. A cheery laugh started in me. The laugh, along with a need to pray, had begun visiting me in my dark room. I imagined interrupting Mr. Bajwa to tell him that he was pitching his voice incorrectly, and then I would start to sing the song and make him try to copy me. "When everything has turned to dust . . ." Several times Mr. Bajwa forgot the words and just hummed the tune. As I laughed, I also started panicking. I became cold. The chill was a new symptom. I was beginning to find my symptoms comforting.

"Please, Mr. Bajwa," I murmured. "You were not innocent."

Mr. Bajwa, still singing, got up and walked to the window behind me. He pulled the curtain aside slightly and looked out. He finished the song and began it again. This time he remembered more of the lyrics. As he sang, he walked around the room, moving close to the wall. When he reached the door, he opened it and left.

Mr. Gupta's office is at the end of a gallery that is open to the sun on one side. As I went to him, I wondered what would happen to me if the BJP won. There was probably a note in the BJP's files on Mr. Gupta and the money I helped him arrange for Congress. They might try using him to raise money for them. Opposition parties are always hungry for bribes. But the BJP might decide they wanted someone without a complicated history. Any bookkeeper could look at our registers and see that our numbers were gibberish. No matter who won, it was unavoidable that over the next few months several people in our building would face investigations. The sheer activity of a campaign leads to paperwork that, once initiated, takes on its own existence.

Fear stirred in me and it felt like sadness. I stopped and looked out at the dirt courtyard. The wind was sliding sheets of dust back and forth across the yard. My emotions over the last few days had become undifferentiated. Horror could come as chuckling or as grief. Love might be like anger. Above all this was the certainty that I would be punished. A BJP victory could be a way for this to occur.

I knocked on Mr. Gupta's door. He called out that it was unlocked. Mr. Gupta was wearing a deep blue T-shirt and a file was open before him on his desk. His room, more than that of any other officer of his grade, looked as if it belonged in a private house. The walls were lined with bookcases. A light blue carpet with geometric patterns covered the floor, and instead of an enormous air cooler stuck in the window exhaling mildew, he had a small air conditioner. His windows were washed each week, and the light they let in was fresh.

I closed the door. I wondered whether he had summoned me because of how I had behaved at the wedding reception. The relative unimportance of this struck me as amusing. Nervousness made me repeat Ram Ram Ram in my head. Even God's name was amusing.

Mr. Gupta nodded to a chair and, once I sat down, said, "Tell me about the money."

"We have fourteen hundred and eighty-two thousand in twenty-three accounts. I am nearly done with my list of givers. There are one or two big ones left and some small ones." As I spoke, a smile unfurled across Mr. Gupta's face. The smile reached the sides of his cheeks and stiffened so that he appeared dazed. For him to take such personal pleasure was unusual, and I knew that some punishment, vicious and complete, was imminent. "Maybe we'll have a little over twenty-two lakhs by the end."

For a moment after I stopped talking, Mr. Gupta kept smiling and staring at me. "Twenty-two lakhs." I noticed his handsomeness, his exactly curved lips.

"Are you political, Mr. Karan?" he asked.

"No."

"Who will win the election?" The question was presented in an abrupt interrogatory style. Mr. Gupta and I almost never talked politics, and I wondered what he was testing for.

I thought about this for a minute and then said the obvious. "The BJP won't win a majority. Their power is in the Hindu belt. Congress can't win a majority either. They've lost too much ground the last few years. But if they want to rule, they can form a coalition."

"Can't the BJP form a coalition?"

"It's difficult to compromise when you are so extreme." The

BJP's leader, Advani, had recently begun seeking the destruction of the Babri mosque, claiming God Ram had been born there.

"Will the BJP win the cities?"

I wondered at the interrogation. "That's where they are strongest."

"Why?" Mr. Gupta asked, and as I tried reasoning this through, he began laughing. Then he leaned across his desk, and for a moment I thought he was going to take my hands. "Some people from the BJP came to me a few days ago. They asked if I wanted to stand for Parliament from Delhi." He laughed again.

I couldn't believe he would betray Congress, so I felt awe instead of fright. I had always known Mr. Gupta was much more widely and deeply connected than my work for him indicated. He had the type of personality that made people, older and more powerful people than he, ask his advice. But for a major party to ask Mr. Gupta to represent it was like one of my relatives who had bought a medical license discovering the cure for some baffling disease.

"The news isn't that good, though," Mr. Gupta said, leaning back in his chair and putting his hands on his stomach. His smile became wry and self-mocking. "Advani was going to run for Parliament in two districts. One from Delhi. Insurance that if for some reason he lost in one district, he might still win in the other. Now Congress is standing Rajesh Khanna against him in Delhi, and even Advani doesn't want to go against a movie star." Mr. Gupta's smile vanished. He removed his hands from his stomach. "Nobody wants to go against Rajesh Khanna. Also, the BJP wants someone who can bring his own money to the campaign. Anybody who has money already wants easier competition."

At first I didn't understand what money he was talking about. "Your family's money?" I asked, though I was not certain Mr. Gupta came from a rich family. "Congress's money!" The fact that he appeared to be considering cheating Congress filled me with terror. There were men I had met who would come for us with guns if Mr. Gupta went on. A decade ago, a man in our office building who collected for Congress had embezzled some of what he had raised. His body was found in the water tank on the roof of the building he lived in. I knew Mr. Gupta thought he was invulnerable. "You can't win against Rajesh Khanna."

Mr. Gupta raised his hands a few inches into the air, turned them palms up, and brought them down onto the arms of his chair. The injustice of this shrug converted my panic to anger.

"You can't win," I said. I thought of turning him over to Congress, but then the BJP might take revenge.

"If Sonia Gandhi runs, I can't win."

"Think what it means when the president of the BJP doesn't want to run against someone."

"Advani probably would have won. Rajesh Khanna hasn't had a hit movie in ten years."

"Who knows your name? Most of the people in this building don't know you."

"Rajesh Khanna is divorced and his wife sleeps with Sunny Deol. A man like that is not a man. No one will vote for someone like that." Mr. Gupta spoke casually, offering me the details as if he were handing me photographs of places where he had traveled.

"I thought you were smart." I had never before spoken this insultingly to him.

Mr. Gupta raised his hands off the arms of the chair and brought them down. "If the BJP is going to win the cities, even Rajesh Khanna can lose. Besides, I have money." After a moment he said, "Go to Mr. Maurya. Tell him the BJP has asked me to run for Parliament. He must know what the parties are planning to spend." I remembered taunting Mr. Maurya at Mr. Gupta's party. When I did not stand, Mr. Gupta said, "Think about me being in Parliament and you being rich. That will make you feel better."

"It doesn't."

The alley Mr. Maurya lives in is perhaps five feet wide, with a narrow half-meter-deep ditch running along one side. Chickens were wandering about and many of the doors to the houses were open for air. I passed one door, which let into a dark windowless room where an old woman sat on a cot stringing firecrackers. Several years ago Mr. Maurya moved out of Old Delhi to one of the posh colonies, but his wife had found it too lonesome there and forced him to return.

Beside Mr. Maurya's door was a metal plaque that had MAURYA ENTERPRISES etched on it in Hindi, Gujarati, and English. This was the only distinguishing mark on the gray concrete wall behind which he lived. I rang the doorbell. I wondered if Mr. Gupta would be angry at me for how I had acted at the party. A young girl let me in.

The wall facing the alley goes up three stories and has windows with curtains that make it look like the face of an ordinary house. Then I stepped through the wall into a wide courtyard that was open to the sun. The house itself was two stories and painted a pale yellow. It had a broad veranda with large potted money plants. Five or six men were sitting on the veranda reading newspapers and drinking tea. The girl led me to them and I sat at their edge.

Some of the men appeared to know one another and were talking. The others kept to themselves. Tea arrived for me. As I sipped it, I realized that even in the short time since I had left the office, the clear precise fear Mr. Gupta had created had become muddled with the confused unhappy terrors that had been with me for days. I was like a man in the Arctic who is dying of cold and feels any increase in wind only momentarily. I wanted the responsibility of feeling out Mr. Maurya removed from me. I thought of putting my tea on the ground, standing, casually taking off all my clothes, and then sitting down to finish the cup. I smiled at the idea that Mr. Gupta had trusted an almost insane person with an important mission to a gangster. I sang God Hanumanji's song silently.

Occasionally a man came out and one of the men sitting with me followed him into the house. I saw one of Mr. Maurya's sons and waved to him, and he nodded back. Everyone appeared so serious that I wanted to shout, "This is nothing to laugh at."

About forty minutes after I arrived, the man came for me. The rooms close to the veranda were given over to business and everybody in them was typing or working through files. Mr. Maurya could not tolerate laziness. When I was last here, several years ago, it was the middle of a particularly slow afternoon. That time, as I talked to Mr. Maurya, we walked through his offices so he could oversee his employees scrubbing the house clean.

I followed my guide up a white staircase onto the roof. I asked God that Mr. Maurya give me news with which to discourage Mr. Gupta. If Mr. Gupta ran, Congress would want revenge.

The roof had an unpainted brick wall eight or ten feet high running along all sides except the one overlooking the courtyard. As soon as I stepped onto the roof, I began sweating heavily and had to squint.

"Hello, Mr. Karan," Mr. Maurya called out. "Still drunk?" He was sitting on a straw mat against the wall. Above him was an awning made of wire and covered with a printed bedsheet. Mr. Maurya wore only a white kurta and underwear, and his left leg was in a cast which went above his knee.

"What happened, sir?" My guide left as I walked to Mr. Maurya.

"The day Rajiv Gandhi died I rode all over Delhi on my motorcycle to see if everything was fine with my properties. In the evening, when I returned, there was some oil on the ground." Mr. Maurya skimmed his hand through the air to show his motorcycle slipping. He smiled. I stood before him till he patted the mat. Then I sat down at the foot of his unbroken leg. The thinness of his legs surprised me, because he had a large stomach. "So I'm giving my bones sun. I was carrying a gun, and when I fell, the gun went sliding. Some boy, some ten-year-old, grabbed it and ran." Mr. Maurya picked up a bottle of coconut oil that was sitting on top of an iron icebox beside him and passed it to me. "Oil my leg," he said, glancing toward his good one. My chuckling began again at being ordered to do this embarrassing job.

Mr. Maurya closed his eyes and tilted his head back. When I first met him, Mr. Maurya had laughed so easily and so hard his eyes would tear. Because my stomach was so large, I had to get on my knees to oil his legs. I said, "The BJP came to Mr. Gupta and asked him to run for Parliament."

Mr. Maurya did not respond for several minutes. My undershirt and shirt were sticking to me from sweat. In the middle of the silence, he tapped his left thigh and I stood, switched to that side, and began kneading and oiling it. His underwear was bunched, letting me see part of a testicle. I imagined grabbing his crotch. I wanted to hear him yelp.

"Is this the Advani seat?" he asked.

"Yes." I was not surprised at his knowledge. Again Mr. Maurya was quiet. Then he opened the icebox, took out a Campa Cola, and, without offering me one, started sipping. This must also be part of my punishment, I thought.

"Did you know Mr. Gupta's father was in the Indian Administrative Service?"

"No." I was amazed. IAS officers were as rare as lottery winners.

"He was almost a Secretary."

Mr. Gupta had achieved so much, grabbing control of all the education department's money-raising, that I had never imagined he could be a failure relative to his own family. Mr. Gupta's vast connections now made sense.

"He died three, four years ago." Mr. Maurya closed his eyes once more and spoke slowly, thoughtfully. "Mr. Gupta applied but did not get into the IAS. His older brother did but didn't like it and is now the president of British Petroleum–Egypt." Since there was no reason for Mr. Maurya to be giving out free information, I realized he must have some purpose for telling me this. My sense of Mr. Gupta began to shift. "Mr. Gupta is smart, but not too smart. He thinks that because his father and his brother have been part of the world of the great, the worst will not be done to him." Mr. Maurya opened his eyes suddenly, as if to surprise me. I wondered if the people who worked for him were impressed by these mannerisms. "Maybe he's right, but after Rajiv Gandhi nobody can feel confident."

Mr. Maurya adjusted his position and wiped his face with a towel.

"Did the BJP offer him the spot definitely, or do they want to know how much money he can bring?"

I then understood that Mr. Maurya had begun negotiating the price for helping Mr. Gupta. "It was a definite offer," I said, though I did not know.

"If Sonia Gandhi runs he has to spend two hundred, three hundred lakhs. Otherwise, maybe one hundred." The amounts were so enormous I could not imagine them. I started smiling. "You don't want him to run?" Mr. Maurya asked.

"The BJP is very strong," I said, trying to hide my feelings behind words.

"Congress has to form a coalition and win. It has to. None of the possible Congress leaders are famous enough—even Sonia Gandhi—to lead an opposition. They all need to be at the center for a while so that people get used to seeing them as the source of power and gifts."

I was delighted. I swept my hands down Mr. Maurya's leg to his foot and kneaded it. I negotiated automatically. "Congress isn't strong in the cities. They have no advantage, as in the villages."

"Would you rather watch Mr. Gupta sing and dance or Rajesh Khanna?" Mr. Maurya paused and watched me. "The reason Mr. Gupta is going to run is that if he doesn't and Congress loses seats, and the BJP takes over Delhi, which it will, he'll have corruption charges against him. Only if he wins his election is he safe."

To be given evidence that Mr. Gupta would run jolted my fears.

"It all depends on what Sonia Gandhi does."

I did not respond and kept massaging his legs.

Mr. Maurya let me know I was to leave by handing me the empty cold-drink bottles and telling me to take them downstairs. I stood and said namaste. "Ask my cashier for fifty thousand rupees. Tell Mr. Gupta I am happy for him."

After all the confusing talk, the half lakh spun me around some more, because it suggested that Mr. Maurya thought Mr. Gupta was worth betting on.

• • •

Mr. Gupta held the wads of rupees as he sat behind his desk and listened to me. Afterward he said, "Either Mr. Maurya thinks that I might win and that Congress isn't strong enough to be too angry about his support or he thinks that he can buy off Congress's anger by donating to Congress as well as to me." I was pleased to hear Mr. Gupta's caution. "You didn't tell him I have Congress's money?"

"No." I wondered how he could imagine Mr. Maurya would not know where the money was coming from.

"He must guess. He wants the business I can send his way."

Rajiv Gandhi's funeral was the next day, and the city would be closed, making it unlikely for me to find anyplace outside the flat where I could hide from Anita. Once I arrived at the flat I would probably stay in my room till the office opened again. Because of this, after leaving Mr. Gupta, I went to eat.

I ate at a dosa place on a street corner in Kamla Nagar, not far from the Big Circle. It was missing the two walls which should have fronted the street. The restaurant was busy and I had to share a bench and table with two boys who sat with motorcycle helmets at their feet and ate plate after plate of ice cream.

I ordered a masala dosa and, before starting to eat, clasped my hands and asked God to rescue me. I did not know what I meant by rescue. I was not requesting the strength to talk with Anita and cope with whatever came after. I only wished everything to be erased. Nothing else would be sufficient. Even though I was hungry, I found no relief in the greasy, spicy potatoes or the coconut chutney. Usually, as soon as food entered my mouth, something inside me loosened and swelled like a sail. I should have been especially hungry because, between Rajiv Gandhi's death and the office opening, I had eaten little, only the small amounts of food left in the refrigerator overnight. Yesterday morning, as soon as I escaped the flat, I had gone to a dhaba and eaten the equivalent of a lunch and a half of parathas. But since then, even a few bites tamped my appetite. Once the fiercest part of my hunger dulled, I became too restless to continue chewing.

I stopped halfway through the dosa. It was as if my saliva was bitter. I leaned back in the bench and tried to find the humor that had been helping me till now. No absurd images floated up to my consciousness. I prayed again, but no matter how much I invoked God, I would have to go home, where Anita would look at me and not talk and Asha would stay away because she had been warned I was sick and contagious.

From the doorway of the flat, I saw Anita sitting lotus-fashion on a love seat in the living room. She had on her rectangular eyeglasses and was reading a newspaper. When I entered the flat, she looked at me briefly and, turning to an Asha whom I could not see, squeaked "Stay" in the pinched voice which had been with her since she had confronted me.

I crossed their bedroom and entered the living room. I was terror-stricken. I had not spoken a word to Anita since the afternoon of the anniversary of Radha's death. I had tried to avoid even seeing them. The last two days I had bathed and shaved long before either woke, and had left for work quickly, with my head down. Now Asha was on the sofa reading a children's magazine. She wore olive shorts and a white T-shirt. As I left the living room for my room, Asha waved at me as if I were going on a journey. I fluttered a hand. Anita neither glanced in my direction nor spoke, but she watched Asha intently.

I went into my room. I noticed that under my cot was a small clay water pot and the glass I usually drank from. Anita must have put them there. I won't even have to come out for water now, I thought. I closed the door, chained it, took off my clothes, and, wanting to express my anguish somehow, dropped them to the floor instead of hanging them up. I lay down. My fear settled and transformed into despair.

I listened to music on a transistor radio. I slept. The line of sun beneath my door changed colors and receded. I read from old magazines I had collected for photos they contained of places I had been. The Taj Mahal under a full moon, standing out clear and bright as if it had been painted onto the night. It looked more a ghost than those the guards claim to see dancing in the gardens. I heard Asha and Anita eating dinner in the common room. To listen to the sounds of plates and bowls shifting, spoons rubbing against steel, Anita's high-pitched voice meeting Asha's and to lie on my cot in my dark room made me feel buried alive.

In the middle of the night, once Anita and Asha were asleep, I left my room and went onto the balcony. Dust was a lid for the city's lights and made the sky's gradual curve clear. I stood there for nearly an hour. The squatter colony was silent, except when someone got up and creaked the hand pump for a drink of water.

I thought of admitting everything to Anita and begging forgiveness. But I felt no more capable of honesty now than when I had shut the windows to keep the neighbors from hearing her screams. I also believed that Anita was no longer willing to exchange confession for pardon. I thought this because Anita had begun telling Asha numerous lies which appeared unnecessarily extreme, and this implied indifference to the future. Anita had told Asha I was sick and that the sickness had come about because of sinful things I had done. Anita claimed her squeak was caused by my disease and that she did not know if she would ever improve. She also informed the child that I was disgusted with Asha because she was a burden on me. I had heard all these things over the last few days because Anita said them in the common room, intending, I understood, for me to hear.

I stayed on the balcony for hours. At maybe two or three in the morning, far away in the dark, a box kite with a burning candle inside rose and hovered. It was pulled down near dawn, and then I went back to my room.

In the morning I listened to Rajiv Gandhi's funeral on my radio.

There was a biography of the Nehru family and then one of Rajiv Gandhi. Friends of Rajiv Gandhi and important politicians like Nelson Mandela were interviewed. There was a long period when the commentator merely described who was passing through Rajiv Gandhi's residence on Janpath and stopping and praying before the mound of flowers that buried his casket. Anita and Asha listened to something similar on the television. They periodically left the living room, but the television stayed on, as if it were a prayer lamp which, even after the prayer is over, must be allowed to burn itself out.

Rajiv Gandhi had always struck me as sly and somewhat stupid. He had dignity only in relation to his opponents, because they were completely shameless. Yet by eleven, when the body was placed on the back of the army truck and carried to the crematorium at five kilometers an hour, bereavement had overcome me.

When the funeral pyre was lit, I felt such a sense of ending that I opened my door and walked into the living room, where Anita and Asha sat silently together on the two love seats watching television. It was about three-thirty.

"Are you better?" Asha asked.

"I'm still sick," I said immediately and without thinking. I sat down on the bed. When I did not say anything else, Asha concentrated again on the screen. Anita's eyes never left the television.

The pyre shook smoke into the sky. I covered my face with my hands.

"Nanaji," Asha said to me.

She must have touched her mother, for Anita screamed, "Let go."

I removed my hands and saw Anita glaring at me. Asha now faced the television. "When Rajiv Gandhi was collecting his mother's ashes from the pyre, he kept finding bullets," I said, wanting to hide the fact that we were causing each other's misery. "She'd been shot so many times the doctors couldn't remove all the bullets." Asha sobbed. Anita pinched the back of Asha's neck and Asha began crying with her shoulders pulled up.

"What are you crying for? Who is Rajiv Gandhi to you? Would you cry for me if I died?" Asha looked up at her mother. "Lower your shoulders." Anita twisted the skin she gripped. When Asha dropped them, Anita let go. Her actions were so extreme, I wondered if Anita was merely out of control or whether she wanted Asha to be afraid of her so that Asha would obey her and not come near me and my contagion.

I continued to watch television. Asha had to keep wiping her eyes. "Wash your face," Anita said to her, and the child ran from the room. She did not return.

After a while I said to Anita's back, "Forgive me for what I did." My heart was beating so fast I wanted to stand.

Anita turned and looked at me. "What did you do?" she asked slowly, but in a voice so high it sounded like the end of a long, screaming fight.

The words wouldn't come. "I touched you."

"Touched?"

"Raped you."

Anita stared at me expressionlessly. "Is that all you did?"

I did not know what she wanted me to confess, so after a moment I said, "I did everything."

"Yes. Say more."

"I'm a rabid dog that should be beaten with bricks." Anita watched me. "Forgive me."

"How do I do that?" When I gave no answer, she asked, "Do I forget?" She kept looking at me. "Do I think it was just a mistake you made? Or am I a saint and I forgive, knowing you are a devil?"

"I did everything bad that is possible."

"Yes." She again waited for me to speak.

"I will go to hell."

"I forgive you." Anita held up her hand as if endowing a blessing. I knew she was being sarcastic, but her voice was so high it lacked all inflection.

"What I did . . ."

"I forgive you." Perhaps she noticed that she might not be sounding ironic, for she added, "Snake."

The word sounded so awkward in her mouth I wondered if she

had experienced a thrill at breaking the taboo of cursing a parent. "I am a snake."

"What kind of a snake? A cobra?"

Anita watched me for a few minutes and then stood and left.

The phone rang at a little after one in the morning. I heard it immediately because I was awake. The low buzzing *rrrs* must have repeated ten times before Anita picked up. A moment later she knocked on my door.

Mr. Gupta spoke as soon as I said hello. "Mr. Karan, Sonia Gandhi will say no to Congress. Congress has to win the elections by itself now."

I was relieved at being able to talk with someone. "How do you know?" I asked, not believing him. To reject such easy power appeared to go against biological laws. Also, after learning about his family, I could not treat Mr. Gupta as seriously as I had before.

"From someone in Congress," he said.

"A reliable person?"

"Like the sun." I did not say anything. "Come to my home in the morning, by ten. The BJP is having a prayer for me. Bring all the bankbooks."

After he hung up, I sat on the sofa in the dark living room for several minutes. Admitting my sins had brought no relief. Now having to cope with Mr. Gupta began to fill me with self-pity. I had not done anything to Asha, and Anita was twenty years ago. In twenty years a destroyed city can be repaired or buried.

Dressed in a coat and tie, I left half an hour after Asha went to school. The twenty-three bankbooks and Father Joseph's cash were in a cloth bag. I had my wrist through its strap and held the bottom with the other hand.

The Sikh whose family had nearly been killed was washing his sidewalk with a bucket and a broom. He wore shorts and rubber slippers. I wondered what he felt at having things return to normal. I could not imagine him feeling forgiveness for the men who had threatened his children. Seeing him reminded me that criminals who confess are still jailed.

He waved to me and I crossed the road.

"How are you?" I asked. The grille of his shop was down, despite the road having nearly returned to its old busyness.

"Without you my world would have ended," he said. His stomach stuck his red shirt straight out.

"It was nothing."

His voice shook. "More than nothing. My wife, my babies, my mother."

I wished I could have used the credit from here to diminish the damages from other parts of my life. "How is your family?"

An old woman shouted, "Move," at us, and then hurried past.

"My sons don't want to come back. They're in Morris Nagar."

"They'll forget."

"They shouldn't forget."

"Thank God the killers were Tamils."

He looked around and angrily said, "I don't even want to sell them shoes. Watching from the roof. Like a circus."

My guilt made me possessive of this one good deed. I squeezed his shoulder.

"Tea?" he asked.

"Not today."

"You're a hero."

"Hero zero," I said, because I wanted him to protest.

"One hundred percent hero. Gold hero."

As I left, I thought, I've saved lives.

Before going to Model Town, I stopped to eat at a dhaba near the Old Clock Tower. After a few bites it was as if my mouth got bored with chewing.

The radio was playing. Sonia Gandhi had announced that she would in no case accept the Congress Party's presidency. Congress was now discussing who else might be selected. Sonia Gandhi's action appeared inhuman. In the autorickshaw, my thoughts kept turning to her. She was so different from me that I could not enter her thoughts but could only imagine her physically: the long dark hair, the straight-featured face that had lost its beauty over the years and become merely a face.

Mr. Mishra was in front of Mr. Gupta's house, supervising men who were unloading chairs from a truck. He was also wearing a coat and tie. His presence made me feel that the secret of Mr. Gupta's ambition was out and some irrevocable step had been taken.

"When did Guptaji call you?" I asked.

"His son did. This morning."

The fact that Ajay, who had been drunk at his own wedding reception, was involved made me nervous. There were sixty or seventy chairs on the truck, and once these were carried into the house, the men began passing down fans which were bolted onto two-meter-high steel poles. They were working without talking, which made me wonder how much quality labor such as that cost.

"To know a Member of Parliament would be strange, huh?" Mr. Mishra said. A ten- or twelve-year-old boy in blue shorts and a white shirt came and inquired if I wanted tea. "You don't even have to ask for anything," Mr. Mishra said. "Money is being spent."

We began talking about Sonia Gandhi. Mr. Mishra was also amazed, but he thought the explanation was that Sonia Gandhi feared further assassinations in her family. As we spoke, two elephants rounded the corner of the road. They were enormous gray beasts with shaved tusks. Each had a teenage boy sitting on its neck holding a short spear that had a hook just below where the blade began. The boys stopped the elephants across the road from us, next to the iron bars of the park fence, by catching folds along the neck skin with the hooks. The elephants knelt and the boys got off. Mr. Mishra began laughing as soon as he realized they would be part of the ceremony. "Will you give us a ride around the block?" Mr. Mishra called to one of the boys.

The boy looked at us seriously and said, "No." The other one scurried up the fence and hopped onto a eucalyptus tree in the park. He stood on one branch and, grabbing the branch above him, began jumping to break the branch beneath him. The whole tree nodded.

Mr. Mishra hesitantly asked me, "Is it true that Mr. Gupta had to give the BJP twelve lakhs for their support?"

The amount was frightening, because if things changed there wouldn't be anything to use in negotiating with Congress. "I know less than you do," I said. The branch being jumped on broke and fell beside the elephants. They began eating its leaves.

I went into the house to let Mr. Gupta know I had arrived. Servants in blue uniforms were moving about the veranda. A red-and-blue dhurrie, like the ones used at weddings, had been spread across the floor. Thick cables ran beneath the rug and several servants were busy attaching them to fans lined up along the veranda walls. From somewhere inside the house I heard a generator's heavy hum.

Mr. Gupta's son, Ajay, was standing against a wall arguing with a balding man in his forties who wore the white kurta pajama that is the BJP's uniform. Ajay had a thyroid problem that made him alternately fat or very thin. Just then he was fat. Ajay also had on the BJP costume. I was about to pass them when Ajay shouted, "Uncleji," at me. This was surprising, because he usually called me Mr. Karan. I wondered whether it was marriage or his father entering politics that had caused the shift to respectful familiarity. "Daddy is going to sit on the ground for the puja, so I think we shouldn't use chairs," Ajay said, "but he says we have to."

"I don't care whether you have chairs or not," the BJP man replied, only glancing at me. I wondered if he knew we were switching parties. "I was told there had to be chairs." Something about Ajay made people impatient. After a few minutes with him, you sensed something both manipulative and stupid. Ajay changed rings and diets to match his astrological sign. He spoke domineeringly about unimportant things. Up to then, I had thought of Ajay as a shocking disappointment compared to his father. But now that I knew how successful the rest of Mr. Gupta's family was, it seemed reasonable that Mr. Gupta's family was slowly reverting to the average.

"Put the chairs inside," I said to the man. "If we need them, I'll have them brought out."

"Who are you?"

"My name is Ram Karan. I'm Guptaji's man." Maybe the BJP man had heard of me, because he immediately became silent. I felt a rush of pride at this. "Ask me if there are any more questions," I said.

As the BJP man left, Ajay said loudly, "He doesn't listen."

I clapped him on the back and asked how his marriage was. I started thinking that Mr. Gupta would certainly not trust Ajay with much responsibility if he became an M.P., and that power would drift toward me. I imagined arranging water and electricity for whole neighborhoods, exchanging ration cards for votes.

"What's in the bag?"

"Something of your father's." Ajay did not ask what it was, discretion that surprised me.

He took me into the kitchen, where his wife, Pavan, was making sure that the six or seven people cooking did no harm to the room. The kitchen was as large as my living room, and along one wall was a row of brick-colored gas tanks.

"Namaste," Pavan said. She was beautiful. She had wavy hair which reached her waist, a wonderful oval face and rounded, even teeth, and she wore a sleeveless blouse, which meant that she must be daring enough to shave her underarms. Pavan was a Sikh. Seeing her beauty, I was baffled that she had been willing to leave her religion and risk losing her family for Ajay.

"You are doing a lot of work," I said.

"Not so much," Ajay answered for her, and took me farther into the house and up a staircase to meet Mr. Gupta.

Mr. Gupta was sitting on the floor at the center of a wide and brightly lit room. All the furniture had been pushed against its pale green walls. He was wearing only pajamas. He had wide shoulders and distinct muscles on his arms. Around him were five men near my age in white kurta pajamas. One of these was scrubbing Mr. Gupta's face with a mixture of flour, sandalwood paste, and grass while the rest watched. Mr. Gupta's face and chest were streaked with yellow. He was smiling broadly. "I'm marrying again," he said to me when I came in. Then I realized that he was being prepared in the same way a groom is by his sisters before the wedding.

One of the men watching shook my hand and said, "Thank you for coming, Mr. Karan. I am Pankaj Tuli." He was tall and slender, with completely white hair and a young face. I was surprised to be treated with such respect. I wondered whether Mr. Gupta needed to present himself as a leader and so Mr. Mishra and I were to play the role of followers.

A very short man with a slightly hunched back went to a dining-room table that was pressed against one wall and brought back a white plastic bag. From the size of the bag and because of how it felt, I could tell it held cloth. "Naveen Kumar," he said, introducing himself, and, shaking my hand, gave me the bag.

"For you," Mr. Gupta said, as his head bobbed back and forth from the rubbing. I slid the cloth out. It was a shawl made from a reddish brown wool. It was so soft and smooth it felt slippery.

"Pashmina," said Mr. Tuli.

I had never touched pashmina before. To me pashmina shawls had always been something in stories: what the Birlas gave Mahatma Gandhi; what would make you sweat in winter if you wrapped yourself tightly in it. I felt a wonderful wrench of dislocation, of being in my own world and also belonging to a world where gifts of pashmina shawls were given.

Ajay rubbed the cloth between his fingers. "I got a watch and cloth for a suit," he said. I thanked Mr. Tuli and carefully slid the shawl back in the bag.

"Do you have my dowry, Mr. Karan?" Mr. Gupta asked.

I said yes, and he tapped the floor beside him. I put the bankbooks there and went around the room introducing myself to each of the BJP men. I had heard of one of them before, a bald man whose kurta collar bore delicate white embroidery. The others I did not know. I wondered how loyal they would be to Mr. Gupta, knowing he had already betrayed one set of political allegiances.

"Come downstairs," Ajay said, taking my elbow, "and tell me if you think everything is right." I smiled wryly at the BJP men, as if this humoring of a child must be something they were also familiar with.

As soon as we were on the stairs, Ajay said, "They're friendly now, but tomorrow they might not know his name." I sensed that Ajay wanted me to reveal myself, but I merely nodded and let him try to press me. I kept the shawl in one hand. Holding it made me happy. "My father can't show that he knows this, but he does."

"Politics," I said. I felt capable of serving Mr. Gupta.

"You have to be polite." We reached the bottom of the stairs, and Ajay, looking me in the eye, said, "If he wins, we'll have to do the hard things for him, the bad things." I shrugged my shoulders, as if I were a man and knew what men had to do. The more Ajay spoke, the more confident I became that if Mr. Gupta rose in the world, so would I.

On the veranda the servants were stringing garlands of geraniums along the walls in cursive *u*'s. There was no work for us, so we stood in a corner. Ajay nattered on about the BJP. At some point he checked himself, grinned, and asked, "Shall we have a peg?" I had not thought about alcohol for days, but as soon as he said it, I felt desire overcome me. It was as if I had passed a room with the door slightly open and glimpsed a woman lying naked on a bed. "Thinking of these people gets me angry," Ajay said. "A peg of whiskey." There was something so obviously false about him that I knew he had a plan.

We went to a long, rectangular room in the back of the house. It was dark because of the drawn curtains. Excess furniture from all over the house had been placed there. In a corner were chairs arranged in layers of semicircles. Along a wall were two sofas with two more stacked on top, and beside these were several armoires. My stomach had tightened from wondering what Ajay intended.

Ajay took out a bottle of whiskey and two glasses from a cupboard. We said cheers and downed the liquor. To get Ajay to give me more, I said, "Delicious." He smiled and poured. Ajay's solicitousness reminded me of businessmen I had dealt with who had tried to get me drunk.

"Show me the shawl."

I wanted to make him struggle for everything and pretended not to have heard him. I sat down with the shawl in its bag draped over one thigh. "Have some whiskey." I suggested this because I thought he wanted the advantage of being sober in whatever maneuver he was about to try. "Don't give me whiskey if you're not going to drink." Ajay drank a second peg. I extended my glass, and Ajay poured it more than half full. "Delicious." I swallowed the drink quickly, nervous and eager to do this before my good sense intervened. I began feeling drunk and relieved. The muscles along the back of my legs relaxed, and I stretched them.

He sighed with pleasure as I finished the drink. "How much do you think the shawl cost?"

"A lot," I said. I smiled and waited for him to reveal himself.

Ajay smiled back. He was quiet for a little while. "Want more?" he asked finally. I shook my head from side to side and smiled.

"You have some. I've had three," I replied, and stared at him till he drank.

"Pavan would like a shawl like that. How much do you think it was?"

Now I understood that he wanted to buy the shawl at a cheap price from me. "Maybe fifteen thousand."

Ajay's face became serious at hearing the large amount. "Do you want to sell it? Not for fifteen thousand. Three thousand I have right now. I could pay that in five minutes."

"I'm going to give it to my daughter," I answered.

Ajay looked angry.

The bright light of the veranda staggered me. The noise of the servants and the arriving guests was a roar. I had been so unhappy that the relief from the alcohol delighted me. The BJP was not perfect, but I would be so good that over the years my sins would be chipped away.

A fire was lit in the center of the veranda. Mr. Gupta stepped out dressed in a new silk kurta pajama, looked around, shook hands with everyone in reach, and went back into the house. Ajay said we should go to the gateway and greet the guests. Mr. Tuli joined us and we walked out together.

The two elephants were standing on either side of the gate. They were almost completely covered with multicolored chalk drawings of religious and historical events and figures. One entire side of an elephant was taken up by Krishna preaching the Gita to Arjun the morning before battle. Another side had a map of India. Along some of the legs were individual figures. Subhas Chandra Bose, who had been forced out of the Congress presidency by Mahatma Gandhi because he was willing to use violence, wore a yellow turban. Bhagat Singh was slightly blue, and the stick of dynamite he held was very red. Shivaji, who looked very much like the TV actor who portrayed him in the serial, took up another leg. Rana Pratap, atop the leaping Chetak, appeared to be climbing the elephant. Next to and between the elephants stood the boys who had brought them. They now wore shiny gold kurta pajamas and turbans, but still carried their spears. Periodically the elephants would shift and the boys would jab them back into position.

There were already a dozen cars, mostly white Ambassador sedans, pulled up along the park fence, but more kept coming. Ajay was the first person to greet people. He had his hands pressed in a namaste. Then I said namaste and then Mr. Tuli. Ajay's voice was slurred. Afraid that mine might be also, I didn't start conversations.

While we stood in line, Mr. Tuli asked, "You live in the Old Vegetable Market?"

"Yes."

"You should thank me, then."

"Thank you," I said.

Mr. Tuli laughed. Making him laugh, maintaining my deception, imagining being rich and good, all made me feel potent.

"The Old Vegetable Market used to be all Muslim," Mr. Tuli said. "After the partition, I was one of the people sent to punish the Muslims. Pakistan had just sent a train full of Hindu bodies from Islamabad. All along the outside of the compartments they had written *Go to India, Hindu*. We were told to send them a train. We put two thousand bodies in one train. I had to go back to the office to get more bullets. Nehruji knew what we were doing. We would have cleared Chandni Chowk, too, but Nehruji got frightened and said, 'Enough.' After that there were no more trains." I had heard many people make claims like these, and most I had not believed, thinking they were just attempts to impress. Mr. Tuli, perhaps because of the unusualness of his white hair combined with his youthfulness, appeared to be the type of man who might actually have done what he claimed. "We had a parade of naked Muslim girls from the Old Clock Tower to the train station. There was a band." All these stories were familiar. Mr. Tuli read dismay on my face, for he said, "The BJP is about politics and Parliament seats." One of the elephants lurched forward and was prodded back. "You don't believe me."

"I believe you."

Mr. Tuli took out his wallet and showed me what looked like a business card. It was an unevenly scissored rectangle of cardboard. He placed it in my hand. Printed on it in blue ink was a partial list of prices for copper wires. Mr. Tuli turned the card in my hand. The other side had a name and address rubber-stamped on it and a hand-written date: *Gopal Godse. Savarkar Bhavan. 500/2-A, Shaniwar Peth*. My fingers twitched. "I've stayed at his flat in Pune." Gopal Godse had served eighteen years in jail for conspiring to assassinate Mahatma Gandhi. "When I left Pune, he and his wife came to the train station with a bag of guavas. His wife started an engineering company while he was in jail." He put the card in his wallet.

The prayer started, and we went back onto the veranda. The presence of history had given me a sense of scale, and I felt myself shrinking. The ceremony went on for an hour and a half. Sitting behind Mr. Gupta with my drunkenness evaporating, I became colder, and self-disgust began to bead inside me. To have imagined I could use the BJP to make up for my other wrongs was the same as believing that if I did not admit my evils, they would not exist.

The prayers were the same as most others, coins and rice were thrown into the fire, water from the Ganges was carefully spooned out, saffron threads were tied around wrists. At the end came the only unusual thing. The pundit presented Mr. Gupta with a bow and arrow. He then gave me one. I imagined the bows were to identify us with Advani, who was making appearances with bow and arrow in hand because of the BJP's support of tearing down Babri mosque, the supposed birthplace of God Ram. The bows were supple polished wood and their strings were saffron. Later, after the photographs had been taken, when I pulled back my bowstring, I found a black dash in the string, a slight split, which, when stretched, formed an O and rose naturally to my eye. Mr. Tuli told me this was called a peep sight.

During the reception after the prayers, Mr. Gupta wandered about with his bow, having his photo taken with whoever wanted it. Mr. Maurya came for the reception on crutches and I saw him enter the house with several BJP men. Mr. Bajwa also came, but only Ajay greeted him. To have my hands free for eating, I put my bow in a side room, under some sheets that were beneath a table. I ate without hunger. When I was ready to leave, I could not find my bow. I knew immediately that Ajay had stolen it. The foolishness of this made me sad. I was relieved I had never let the shawl out of my reach.

Outside, across the street, the boys were washing down the elephants with brushes and buckets of water. One boy was on top of an elephant and the other was scrubbing India off its side. The other elephant had already been washed and was eating leaves from a pile of branches before him. Chalk had settled into wrinkles. I looked at the elephant's face. A fly sat near one wizened eye. I shivered.

Anita sat on her bedroom floor near the gallery sifting a copper tray of black lentils for pebbles and grit. She did not glance up from her work as I entered the flat.

I had planned to go to my room and take off my shoes, then build up my courage to talk again with Anita. I walked two steps past her and then sat down on her bed. Delay would only make things harder. I stared at Anita's back. She did not turn around, but her back straightened and her fingers flew faster.

I opened my mouth and forced words out. "I promise . . ." Anita's head turned slightly. "I won't hurt you." I thought this was a foolish thing to say, but I could not stop my stupidity. "I won't live long." Anita finally turned around. "I should be dead in a few years. Why hate me when I will be gone soon?" She stared at me. "I can change," I said.

Anita slammed the tray to the floor. The clang was enormous. The lentils rustled across the floor. Anita kept hold of the tray for a moment. Then she set it quietly on the floor and stood. She walked through the bedroom, into the common room.

My mouth tasted of iron. Maybe five minutes later, maybe twenty, I followed her.

Asha was asleep on the sofa, sweating in the sun coming through the window.

Anita sat crouched under the kitchen's stone counter. She had her back to the wall and her knees pulled to her chest. Standing just outside the kitchen, I cringed at this wretchedness.

I squatted in the kitchen doorway. Neither of us spoke for a while. The refrigerator hummed. I thought, Maybe she's desperate to end this, too. "What should we do?" I asked. Anita moaned. "I'll do anything." After a moment or two, I repeated, "What can I do?"

"Die. That's what I want," Anita squeaked. She pointed at her jaw. "Look what you've done to me."

I wanted her to say more, say everything so that some of her anger might be drained. "We have to live together," I said. "I don't want to die this way."

After several minutes Anita said, "I want you to give me money."

This surprised me, but no more than if she had demanded I live in the room on the roof, a possibility I had considered.

"How much money?"

"Two thousand rupees a month."

"All right."

"And I want the flat when you die."

I thought of Rajesh's anger when he heard this but said, "Yes."

"I don't want to pay for any of Asha's schooling, and I want five hundred rupees a month for that."

"Yes."

Anita began crying then, quietly. I waited with her till she said, "Go away."

I returned to her bedroom, where I had left the shawl. I brought it back and, squatting in the kitchen doorway, pulled it slightly out of the bag. I placed it on the floor between us. "It's a pashmina shawl. For you."

She looked at it. "I want cash."

"I'll give you cash also." I then went into my room and took two thousand rupees from what I had collected for Mr. Gupta. Anita had the shawl in her lap. I placed the bundles on top of the shawl.

SIX

When Anita started cooking dinner that evening, I came out of my room. She looked up from the pot of subji she was stirring, and I stopped. I had spent the afternoon on my cot listening to the radio. I left my room because I wanted to act on our agreement right away so there would be no doubt we had struck a bargain. I moved to the center of the common room and sat down on the floor.

I brought with me my transistor radio and a Gita. I did not remember the last time I had opened the Gita. A holy book, I thought, would suggest the solemnity of my commitment to the bargain. Before last week I would have worn just my underpants and undershirt. But I did not want to call attention to my crotch and therefore wore pajamas. The radio played. I sat up straight and tried appearing proper, even though usually if I spent much time on the floor, because of its hardness, I reclined on my side. A distant but distinct satisfaction came through the anxiety of being in open sight, as if I were managing to move through a difficult and dangerous labor. I reread several times Krishna's argument to Arjun that it was acceptable for him to fight his cousins, because he was responsible only for actions, whereas God controlled consequences.

Asha woke from her long nap, and after going to the roof to see whether a kite might have caught on the TV antenna, she sat beside me in silence, switching from station to station on the radio. She kept closing her eyes as though she was ready to slip back into sleep.

"Take a bath," I said. This was the first time I had spoken normally to her in several days, and it felt strange. "You'll be less sleepy." Forming and speaking a sentence was like making something. Anita glanced at me. I continued talking, feeling willful, as if the more words I said, the stronger my hold on the world of the common room would become. "How is school? Do the children talk about Rajiv Gandhi?" I noticed that I sounded as if I had been away.

"No," Asha answered, yawning.

"Strange how somebody so important can just vanish and it makes no difference."

"His family must be unhappy," Asha said, spinning the station dial. Till then I had only thought of Rajiv Gandhi's death as the end of a dynasty. I remembered the swiftness with which Rajinder had died. One side of Asha's hair was matted down and there were hatchmarks on her cheek from the sofa's weave. Her thinness and disheveledness made her look poor.

"Take a bath," Anita said, sounding as if she had already repeated this several times. She poured a glass of water into the subji. We stared at each other. This meeting of gazes felt like something new, one of the benefits of our compact.

"Yes," Asha said, but made no move to stand.

"Has your mother been giving you yogurt for breakfast?"

"No."

"What are you doing?"

"I only asked if she had been eating yogurt." I understood that Anita was drawing the limits of what I had bought.

"Go bathe," Anita said.

"In five minutes," Asha replied.

"This is not a shop that you can bargain with me."

Asha went and got her towel, which was draped over the balcony ledge. I started at the Gita again.

During dinner only Asha and I talked. Asha asked me if I was better, and I found myself replying, "Better than before," even though I had not meant to qualify my answer. When I questioned her, How is school? Why did you sleep so much this afternoon? Did Mr. Gupta's phone wake you last night? she answered in short phrases. Anita was examining us and I think this quieted Asha. Having a home again made me want to talk and talk. In my loneliness, any detail, whether Asha had turned left or right at a street corner, would have been comforting. Even with her short answers, I might have developed a conversation, but I thought that to do so in front of Anita could appear threatening.

Near the end of the meal Asha asked Anita, "Will you play badminton with me?"

"No."

"Why?" Asha said, sounding startled. "You said you would."

"When I tell you to take a bath I want you to do it right then."

I couldn't watch the punishment and looked at the floor. I believed Anita was training Asha to obey her immediately as a way of guarding against me.

"I took a bath."

"I'm not playing with you. You can play with someone else. I don't want to play with you."

"Who?"

"Find someone."

"Will you play with me?" Asha asked me.

"No," I whispered.

Anita stood and went to wash the dishes. A little later Asha climbed the ladder to the roof.

I continued with the Gita on the living-room sofa, unwilling to give up my freedom to be anywhere in the flat.

Nevertheless, when I lay down that night I was happy. Before I fell asleep, I tried to think of innocuous questions I could ask Anita or facts I could chatter about like a beacon pulsing to mark its presence. I had not yet told Anita about Mr. Gupta running for Parliament. That information, if handled well, might last several meals.

I was to meet Mr. Gupta at Safdarjung Hospital. He had gone there to talk with doctors who were striking. After meeting with them, Mr. Gupta decided to donate blood. A doctor who met me outside the hospital told me the sight of his own blood had caused Mr. Gupta to faint.

The hallways were empty, and only the patients who could not be moved were in the hospital. Mr. Gupta was lying on a bed with a wet cloth on his forehead when I arrived. There were two beds in the room. The other one held an unshaven man with a three- or four-year-old boy curled against him. A woman in a frayed cotton sari was leaning against a window and looking at the room. Two young doctors in white coats and a reporter with a camera around his neck stood between the beds.

"We feel bad to be on strike," one doctor was telling Mr. Gupta. "That's why we are all giving blood. But look at this room." The floor had dark mop marks where someone had pretended to clean. "We have machines costing ten lakhs in the hallway because nobody will buy one part that's broken."

"This is because of corruption," Mr. Gupta said. I went and stood near his head, with the bed between me and the doctors. "They are getting my blood," he told me, and tilted his head toward the half of the room with the man and the child. I wondered whether both the father and the child were sick. "My relatives now." The unshaven man smiled.

"Everything gets eaten," said the other doctor, tall and thin, with hair that reached past his collar.

"The machine you were talking about, what do you need for it?"

"It's for imaging, and the part that actually sees is broken. The part costs seventy thousand."

"Give Mr. Karan here your phone number and he'll get it for you," Mr. Gupta said, lifting his eyes to me. The doctor wrote down his number. Mr. Gupta then said, "Photos done?" to the reporter.

"One with the machine, maybe."

Mr. Gupta and the others went to find the machine.

"What are you sick with?" I asked the unshaven man.

"She's sick," he said, and pointed to the woman. "My wife."

"Did you get the blood as well as the bed?" I asked him, and he started laughing. After a moment the woman did as well. "Who will you give the vote to?" I asked him.

"Him."

"You?" I said to the woman. She smiled and did not answer.

"Her also," the husband said. I did not believe him. "I need a job, sahib. I'm fifth-standard pass and can read and write. I used to drive an autorickshaw, but because of diesel prices had to stop."

I promised to help and gave the man my office phone number instead of the address, hoping he would not want to risk wasting a rupee on the phone call.

Mr. Gupta returned and motioned me to join him in the hallway. "This is Anand," he said, introducing the reporter.

Anand nodded as if agreeing that the correct name had been given. "I can put the blood-donating story in one paper and the machine story in another." We spoke in English in case the people in the room could overhear us.

"I'm paying only if they mention the story on TV," Mr. Gupta warned.

"I can't do TV. I told you that before." The reporter looked angry.

"Fine."

"I'll write that the part will come in several months, so nobody checks."

"Good."

They were silent for a minute. I had not been sure whether the gift would actually be made.

Anand said, "I forgot my wallet and need to buy lunch."

Mr. Gupta gave him a fifty-rupee note and he left. "The BJP sent him," Mr. Gupta explained after Anand had turned a corner of the hallway. "He writes for four or five newspapers."

He was about to say something else when I spoke. Even though it was too late, I still wanted to discourage him. "The woman who's getting your blood won't vote for you."

Mr. Gupta looked startled and then laughed. "A voting booth curtain is a license to steal. I give them my blood. My blood! They say they'll vote for me, but then the curtain is drawn and they can do anything." When I did not join in the laughter, he said, "The BJP's votes come from people a little more educated than those two." I still did not smile. "We have money, Mr. Karan. And we have no history, so we can promise anything without them being certain we're lying."

"Where will the money come from?"

He did not answer. The woman in the hospital room said something and a boy's voice answered. Mr. Gupta leaned forward and then tilted back. "Whatever happens to me will happen to you." I nodded. "I am being frank."

"I understand."

"How much is the school system worth? If you sold all the land and money we can grant. If you sold everything. The maps on the classroom walls."

"We can't sell everything. We'd get caught." I knew, of course, what Mr. Gupta wanted, but was trying to resist him.

"Not every school. Not everything literally. The schools that have a hundred students." He was now watching me intently. I wondered what Mr. Bajwa would do in my place. "Some of the small schools sit on good land." Mr. Gupta waited, as if for me to catch up. "How much would people pay? What amount?"

"How many people have connections enough that they can risk buying schools?"

"You tell me." I didn't answer. "If I win, we can put the paper-work in later, saying the property was not useful as a school," he said. "If I don't win, the buyer either loses what he has paid or pays other people."

I did not want to offend him any further, so I said, "I under-stand."

"How much would we get if we sold the school on the Hill?"

The few property developers I knew I did not know well. "I'll find out who has the most contacts."

Seeing I had nothing more to add, Mr. Gupta said, "We have the BJP's support if we don't embarrass them. People think Rajesh Khanna still looks like he did in the movies." Mr. Gupta stopped and appeared to check my response. I shook my head no. "They see him fat and bald now, they'll feel cheated and vote for someone else."

Six or seven schools and stretches of property were out of the way enough that they could be sold without the newspapers discovering what had happened.

Mr. Gaur ran a small school at the base of the Hill. The school was two long yellow rooms in a dirt compound. He and his wife were the only teachers there. It had started out as an experimental year-round school to teach street children basic skills. Instead of regular classes there were supposed to be short repeating units of math, literacy, and government that children could drop in and out of. When Mr. Gaur took over the school, he converted the rooms into a home for his family. Classes were held outside. In the winter, students were discouraged from coming; those who did were accommodated in one of the rooms. The wall behind the school had separated the compound from the brambles and dirt paths of the Hill until four or five years ago, when it collapsed. Bushes now came within a few feet of the school windows.

The Hill, the largest park in Old Delhi, abuts several rich neighborhoods, and I had no doubt the school would sell. I thought Mr. Gaur would agree to the sale because he and his wife were near retirement, his daughters had married, and his son worked outside Delhi. The difficulty was to get Mr. and Mrs. Gaur out without panicking them that the Congress Party would punish them for taking part in the funding of the BJP.

Thirty or so students, from about eight to fourteen or fifteen, were sitting in two clumps under a mango tree in the center of the courtyard. One clump was chanting the alphabet, which was written on a blackboard, and the other was having subtraction explained by Mrs. Gaur. They appeared to be trying to shout each other down. Mrs. Gaur was a tiny woman with a flat face that appeared pressed in. She had a blackboard behind her and was showing how numbers are carried over. The sums were faded, and instead of marking them with chalk as she explained, she only pointed at the figures. I realized she did not write new problems every day.

Mr. Gaur was sitting in a chair on the veranda that ran along the yellow rooms. He was eating rice and lentils with his bare hands. As he saw me, he took a glass of water from beside his foot and, leaning beyond the veranda, rinsed his hands. "How are you?" I asked. Mr. Gaur was under five feet tall and had a face so round you could set instruments by it.

"Your blessings," he answered, smiling and bobbing his head.

He stood and I followed him inside. The stink of shit and heat was so strong I backed out as soon as I stepped through the door. The room was dark. The only windows were high up and narrow. There was a cot against a wall, several cots standing on end, and a table with an enormous radio.

"Oh ho," Mr. Gaur chuckled, and called, "Baby. Baby." He moved into the room and leaned down and scanned the floor. He spotted something beneath the cot and, kneeling, pulled it out. The child was perhaps a year old and wore only a cloth diaper. "My granddaughter," Mr. Gaur said, and carried the child, held beneath its arms and kept as far away from himself as possible, past me. From the veranda he shouted, "Mrs. Gaur! Come take care of this bad girl."

Mrs. Gaur left her class and, after saying namaste to me, took the baby behind the school.

Mr. Gaur and I sat on the veranda.

At first we talked about his children. His oldest daughter had cervical cancer. His son, who worked at a cigarette factory, had been promoted. Mrs. Gaur returned to her classes. After a while the discussion came to the elections. At some point I let a meaningful pause develop to indicate that the serious part of the conversation was about to start.

"Big things are happening," I said.

"What?" he asked, leaning over. There was fear in his voice.

"The government wants to shut down your school."

Mr. Gaur straightened in his chair. He was quiet for a moment. "Can't you save us?" Mr. Gaur asked. "We have rights after living here so long." He said the two things in the same quiet, frightened voice.

Looking at the students, I said, "You have forty students." Most of them were thin and all were barefoot. Mrs. Gaur made them leave their slippers in a pile on the side of the compound entrance because she did not want them bringing their germs into her dirt yard. This detail had, in the past, made me wonder whether she was crazy.

"I can get more, as many as you need."

I did not answer for a while. "That's not what it is. Congress wants to sell your school to raise money for the election." About fifteen years ago a bank robber had phoned the Central Bank and pretended to be speaking on Indira Gandhi's behalf. He had said the Prime Minister needed money and would like it to be ready in a briefcase in two hours. The robber appeared at the bank at the appointed time, showed some identification he had made up, received the money in a bag, and vanished, never to be seen again. When I first heard that, I immediately thought of doing it myself.

"What are we to do? We have to live somewhere."

"Take a flat like everybody else. The government never meant you to live here." I dripped a little anger into my voice so that he would know he was unimportant.

"Don't be angry with me. I am a poor man."

"This is a nation of poor people."

"But what am I to do with my family?"

"Your children are gone." As I was saying this, Mrs. Gaur dismissed one batch of her students and came to the veranda.

Mr. Gaur explained Congress's plans to her.

The thoughtful stare she gave me made me uneasy and I said, "Changes are happening. Changes which if you knew would drive you mad."

"Will we get other jobs?" she asked.

"Yes."

"Will we work in the same school?"

"I give you my finger, you grab my wrist."

"No. No," Mr. Gaur protested.

"What if the BJP wins?" Mrs. Gaur asked.

"That is the good thing about the sale. The BJP and Congress will both share whatever money is made."

"Strange," she said. Women, I think, do not speak as fast as men and this lets them be more reflective.

Mr. Gaur also appeared doubtful.

I said, "Does a lion care what another lion eats as long as its stomach is full?"

Mr. and Mrs. Gaur were quiet. Many of the children that had been reciting the alphabet had stopped and were talking among themselves.

"Can we get government quarters?" Mrs. Gaur asked.

I sighed. No one spoke for a while. "One piece of good news I have. I can offer you one lakh." Mr. Gaur looked at his wife. I had picked this figure by calculating reasonable rent for two years and then doubling it. I was afraid of how long negotiations could take if Mr. Gaur resisted. "But you can't tell anyone what's being done. If anyone asks, and why should they, you say this school is being closed and you are being moved."

"Will you find out about government quarters?" Mrs. Gaur asked.

"One lakh is what you get. You've lived for free all these years."

Again we were quiet. "I can buy stocks," Mr. Gaur said.

"You won't gamble with our money," Mrs. Gaur immediately replied.

"Stocks are not gambling."

"And every type of alcohol is not bad."

I had to begin investigating the property dealers capable of buying the land. The school was about two kilometers from home, and I decided to walk to the flat and make my phone calls from there. The confidence that comes with success made me think I had been superstitious to believe I could not be bad in one part of my life without suffering elsewhere.

Asha opened the door and said, "Every twenty minutes you've had phone calls." She was smiling and excited. I thought the phone calls had to do with Mr. Gupta. I felt a gust of self-importance.

"The same man always," Anita added. She was in the doorway between her bedroom and the living room. "I told him you were at work, and you would be back by three. But he keeps calling." Her squeaky voice made her sound as if she was about to cry.

The phone rang. We became still at the sound. "I'll answer," I said.

"Hello," I murmured. I sat on the edge of the bed and leaned down into the phone, which I held in my lap.

"Ram Karan?" The man had a Haryanvi accent. I didn't answer. "Ram Karan?"

"What's your name?"

"Sisterfucker, you think you're in a toy store. Asking me questions." It was Congress, of course. Immediately I wanted to apologize and claim there had been a mistake, but I couldn't think of anything to say. "We'll kill you. You return the money or they won't find your corpse."

I cut the line and immediately dialed Mr. Gupta at the office. I was so panicked, I started dialing my own number. Anita came and sat on one of the love seats and watched me. She kept her hands on her knees. Once the other end was ringing, I heard a click and the phone became airy. "Who are you calling?" asked the man with the Hariyanvi accent. I didn't answer and the phone stopped ringing. "Who are you calling? Roshan Gupta?"

"Yes."

"Okay. You can dial him now."

I dialed again. The other end rang for a while and then I hung up. I tried Mr. Gupta at home. "Who are you calling now?"

I thought about whether to answer. "I'm phoning his house."

"I have to write down everyone you call. That's why I ask." Now none of the menace that had been in his voice a moment ago was present.

A servant at Mr. Gupta's picked up. Mr. Gupta was out and Ajay was put on.

"Somebody is listening to this," I told him as soon as he spoke.

"Who are you?" Ajay demanded.

"A killer from Bihar," the man answered. "You think you can steal from us?"

"Steal what? From where?" Ajay said.

"Sisterfucker."

"You think this will scare us. Slap you twice and you'll start crying."

"Cut your throat twice. Make your whole family cry."

"I am home," I said softly, fear crushing my voice.

"Don't worry," Ajay said in English, as if his speaking a foreign language would make me more confident.

"Don't worry," the Haryanvi-accented man repeated in English, and laughed.

"This is illegal," Ajay said.

"I am the police."

"You're not the police. The BJP has the police."

When I hung up, Ajay and the man were still arguing.

Now that Congress had confronted me, I knew that Mr. Gupta

had to win or Congress would, if I was lucky, put me in jail for corruption. I couldn't imagine the man being Central Bureau of Investigation, because he would not have revealed himself. I moved the phone from my lap to the stool beside the bed, where it usually sat.

I didn't want to look at Anita, but when I did, she was staring at me. "Mr. Gupta is running for Parliament," I said. My voice quavered. "He's taken the money we'd raised for Congress and is using that."

"Now this," Anita said. She sounded tired, and the fact that her cartoon voice could hold fatigue was surprising.

"I had no say in this."

"Of course you did. You could have said no. You could have said I am not doing any of this."

"It's not like that. I'm Mr. Gupta's man. Everything that happens to him happens to me also. If Mr. Gupta agreed to do this and I went to Congress to warn them, the BJP would come after me. Or he would."

"What's happening?" Asha asked from her bedroom. "Can I come in?" She moved into the doorway. Since neither of us said no, she entered the living room and sat on the love seat beside her mother.

"Mr. Gupta was going to do what he wanted," I said quietly.

"It's never your fault. You can never do anything. Your idiocy will never end." Because of the pride I had been taking in being Mr. Gupta's man her accusations felt deserved. Of course, God was punishing me. The wrinkles on Anita's forehead were ruler-straight. "I'm handcuffed to a crazy man."

"It was wrong," I said. "You were twelve," I started saying. Listening to myself, I wondered why the only response I had to Anita was admitting my crime. "I remember the newspapers under you so that if you bled . . ."

"Go," Anita screamed at Asha, and shoved her off the love seat. Asha fell onto the floor. "This is not for you."

Asha sped from the room.

The shout had shocked me and I didn't know whether to continue. "Anything I could say wouldn't be enough," I said, trying to suggest I could add more if wanted. But I had already said all that needed to be confessed and there was no value in repeating it.

"Stop," she said, and stood and put her hand over her mouth. The space between sofa and love seat was so narrow she was standing over me.

I stopped.

"Don't talk about that with Asha here. What would I do if she knew?" I didn't understand her, and Anita must have seen this, for she said, "She'd be frightened all the time if she knew."

"I don't want to hurt Asha."

"I'm not angry about back then," Anita said. "This is about today." I did not know how to respond. "You think I can't tell the difference between the past and the present? I'm not crazy. You are bringing danger now."

Because I had no answer to this, my jumbled thoughts made me say, "You don't have to be unkind to Asha. I won't ever go near her."

"You want me to rely on your self-control?"

"Anita," I said, and then I had no more words.

"Even by chance, you should sometimes do the right thing."

I wondered if our bargain was going to be broken.

Mr. Maurya, of course, knew the dozen or so property developers with enough contacts to buy large pieces of school property. Instead of phoning, I went to see him. This time I did not have to wait on the veranda with the tea-drinking suppliants.

I had been at a party once with a developer he recommended, Mr. Mittal. One night he and I rode to the school in his car. Other than asking directions, he did not talk. I was glad for this, because I was lost in worries.

We parked along the periphery of Kamla Nagar, a kilometer from the school, because I believed Congress might try to follow us. For extra caution, we climbed the Hill and approached the school from its back. The woods were dark and we had to light our way with flashlights. Birds were scratching and twitching. We walked around a monkey sitting in the center of a path eating its own lice. Because it was out at night we were afraid it might be rabid and made a wide circle around it. We crossed a small pond spanned by a wooden bridge. The air was light and the temperature a few degrees lower than it had been on the road. I wondered how anyone could not want property here.

I called for Mr. Gaur from the veranda. The school was lit with kerosene lanterns because they had no electricity. Mr. Gaur asked us in for tea, but we made excuses, and then he led us around the grounds. He had a hutch full of hares in one corner of the compound, which surprised me, because Mr. Gaur was Brahmin and a vegetarian. "I catch them in the Hill. I let the children play with them and I sell them," he explained. We walked all over the property, sometimes going along its edges and sometimes cutting through it at various angles so that Mr. Mittal could develop a feel for its dimensions. Though the sky above was a city sky, the mild air and the birds nearby made me feel as if I were far from Delhi. Mr. Mittal asked a few questions: where the nearest electrified building was, who had built the school.

We left the same way we had come. Only then did we begin discussing the price. Mr. Mittal was tall and thin, with round glasses. He, along with his brother, ran their family's property business. "I have to wait till I talk with my brother," Mr. Mittal said. He was ahead of me, climbing a series of dirt steps which was kept from turning into a slope by planks. "I think we will offer six lakhs." I had begun liking the school so much that I found the offer rude. I kept following Mr. Mittal. "There is no running water and no electricity, so we have to pay the municipality for that, and for keeping things secret. And, of course, there is this BJP–Congress election."

"This is a fifty- or sixty-lakh property."

"If you were selling counterfeit money, would I even pay a fifth of the face value?"

"This is not paper."

"Paper is easier to hide." He stopped and turned to me. I could not see his face. "I have to be paid for taking this much risk. Land like this is not an easy thing." We climbed the rest of the steps. "It will take at least a day to talk with my brother and get the money. See other developers."

I did not want to show the property to several developers for fear of rumors. All I could do was repeat, "You know how expensive land is here."

"It is," Mr. Mittal admitted. "But even if there were no election, I would still only pay eight, maybe ten lakhs. Jail time makes everything cheaper." We were crossing a grassy field and heard a peacock screech.

"We guarantee that if we win, we'll make sure the papers are done."

Mr. Mittal stopped. "If you didn't guarantee that, we wouldn't bid."

I was selling something that was not mine for enormous money, but I felt cheated. There was not another property like this in Delhi.

We came out of the Hill onto a road lined with tall, expensive houses. We started walking toward Kamla Nagar. Along the sidewalk was a line of parked taxis with their doors open and the legs of sleeping drivers stretching out of them.

"Shall I give the money to Mr. Gupta tomorrow night unless I get a message otherwise?" Mr. Mittal offered.

"If we accept, I'll come by." I knew Mr. Gupta would not want any witnesses to him directly receiving money.

We walked in silence till we neared his car. "This is a good price, Mr. Karan. I say this not to make you sell but because I don't want you to feel cheated." Mr. Mittal opened the Ambassador's trunk and took out a box with a ribbon around it. It was a bottle of Johnnie Walker Blue Label. I had never seen this before. "Thank you for your help," he said, and handed me the present.

Once Mr. Mittal left, I crossed the road to the shops, looking for a place to eat. I felt ashamed for selling something so valuable for so little. The guilt I felt was not that of being corrupt but that of waste. There had always been a corruption discount in the loans and licenses I had arranged, but that had been more indirect than this and not as steep. This is what happens in elections, I told myself. I feel this way only because I already feel guilty about Anita. I found a Pizza King. At first as I ate I kept the Blue Label box standing upright like a trophy. But there was no taste to the food. I laid the bottle on its side.

The guilt only got more intense overnight. What can I do? I thought. God will decide everything. I imagined myself as one of the vandals who pried jewels out of ancient statues and sold them to the British.

In the morning, after avoiding talking to Anita, I went to see Mr. Gupta at his house.

The night before, I had left and returned through the squatter colony in case I was being watched. That day, since I assumed Mr. Gupta's home was under surveillance and I would be spotted anyway, I left through the compound's main door. I did not notice whether I was followed.

Mr. Gupta's house was crowded. There was a foreign woman with yellow hair talking to two men in their twenties. A young boy kept wandering around taking tea orders. I passed a heavy old man in a kurta pajama who was dictating something about India's gold reserves to a typist. Seeing this much energy being expended on things I did not know about made me think I could not be blamed for everything in the campaign.

I was led to a room on the second floor. The curtains were drawn, and on a shadowed sofa, speaking under an air conditioner's hum, were Mr. Bajwa, Mr. Gupta, and Ajay. Mr. Gupta was in the middle, sitting straight, with Ajay draped backward and Mr. Bajwa leaning toward them, smiling. The way they sat made them appear gossipy. I was not surprised at Mr. Bajwa's presence, because I felt that I deserved to lose whatever benefits being Mr. Gupta's moneyman brought.

"We were just talking about you," Ajay said.

I assumed nothing good had been uttered and so replied, "I made at least five lakhs for you last night."

"How is that?" Mr. Gupta asked.

I sat down on a sofa across from them and told him. He listened with attention, and I wondered if he knew how much the school should cost.

After I was done, Ajay asked Mr. Bajwa, "Is that a good price?"

Mr. Bajwa shrugged. This did not make me feel any less cheated. "The price is six, but I have to pay one lakh to Mr. and Mrs. Gaur, who live at the school."

"That's too much," Mr. Bajwa immediately said. "We're not their parents that we have to give them a roof over their heads."

"We needed the money quickly."

Mr. Bajwa glanced at Ajay as if to suggest he could not work with someone as recalcitrant as I was.

"Why is your phone tapped?" Ajay asked.

"Maybe all of ours are," I said.

"We have machines to stop that."

And though I knew nothing about these things, I said, "They have machines for your machines."

"Thank you, Mr. Karan," Mr. Gupta said. "Tell me what you think of this. This is a slogan for vans with loudspeakers. 'If you want to see a movie, go to the hall. If you want to accomplish something, go to the booth and pick Roshan Gupta.'"

"It's too long," Ajay said. "The van will be down the block by the time the slogan finishes." There were other slogans, some based on Rajesh Khanna's movies, such as *My Companion, the Elephant*. The fact that Mr. Gupta was involved in this level of detail made me think the campaign was not being run well, which led me to believe the money raised from the school would be wasted.

"The BJP's Roshan Gupta. God and Bread," Mr. Bajwa suggested.

"What about saying something good about me?" Mr. Gupta asked.

"My uncle is a kind man," Mr. Bajwa answered, "but would you vote for him if you didn't know anything about him except that he was kind?"

I thought surely I would be punished for all this. Then they began babbling about posters, something none of them knew anything about. I sank into the sofa.

Later Mr. Gupta invited me to a speech he was giving, but I told him I had to go see Mr. Mittal.

The flat was hot and still when I returned home that evening. I heard Asha's voice coming from the roof. The kitchen counters were scrubbed clean, which meant that dinner had been cooked, eaten, and the dishes put away. The money Mr. Mittal had given me was in a gray plastic briefcase. Being paid had made me feel worse. I wondered whether I was so confused and unhappy because I was almost not eating. I hid the briefcase beneath some clothes in a trunk in my room and changed into a kurta pajama. After leaving Mr. Mittal, I had gone to Thirty Thousand, where my lawyer has his office, a school desk and two filing cabinets under a tarp next to a wall, and altered my will. Because I knew confession was no way to get Anita to honor her bargain, I had decided to try doing everything she wished.

I killed my hunger with water and went up to join them on the roof.

The sun had set and the sky was stacked with colors. There was a deep red at the base along the horizon, a smoky orange above that, then a yellow, and a blue that faded into white. The roof was gray concrete and had several levels because of the uneven heights of the flat's rooms. Cords of tar ran across its surface from where cracks, over the years, had been sealed. Taller than some, lower than others, our roof merged into the roofs next door, which in turn connected to those near them. Asha was on the roof of my room swinging her arms in circles and rotating in place. She was wearing a blue shirt and red shorts. Anita stood below her, at the level of the common room, arms crossed beneath her breasts, and watched. I had the feeling I had lived this moment before.

Asha stopped turning when she saw me. "I can see America from here," she said. "There are buildings one hundred stories tall, and on the streets all the men wear pants and all the women wear dresses. No woman wears a sari."

"Can you see Kusum?" I asked.

"I'll check," Asha said, and began twirling again.

We watched her for a moment, and then I said, "Here is my new will," and offered Anita the thick manila envelope I had brought with me. "The flat is yours, and everything else is to be divided in half between you and Rajesh."

Anita took it, but there was no expression on her face. "What happens if Kusum challenges it?"

I shrugged. "All daughters have the right to demand an even share of whatever is left when their parents die. But why would she?"

"Kusum Mausiji is driving her car past trees," Asha called out.

Anita took the will out, unfolded it, and, after reading the first page, put it back in the envelope. I wondered if even this was enough to calm her.

"What are you doing for Mr. Gupta?"

"I'm his moneyman."

"What does that mean?"

"I collect money. I arrange cheap loans or property grants for schools. For his election, I am selling property we own."

" 'We' or the municipality?"

When Rajinder was alive, around Diwali, Anita used to give gifts of expensive watches and bolts of cloth which she said Rajinder had received as presents from people who wanted loans from the government. To sell schools was not the same as selling cheap loans; still, the disgust in her voice felt unfair. "Some land is empty. Some schools have maybe forty students. Getting rid of the schools makes the students find better schools."

"It's easy to say that what you are doing is not so bad."

"I am not saying that."

"Do you feel like a thief?"

"I feel like that with these schools because I am selling them so cheaply."

"Not real guilt, then?"

I reached up to touch my lips and Anita grabbed my hand. She must have thought I was going to slap her. She saw from my shock that this was wrong and, laughing sarcastically, said, "After eating a thousand mice, the cat goes on a haj."

Asha must have seen her mother's anger, because she started to cry. Anita noticed it first, and then, through her reaction, I did. Asha's face was completely wet. As soon as Anita saw Asha crying, she went to her and held her from behind. Asha tried pulling out of her embrace. Her sobs sounded like suppressed coughs. "What are you crying for?" Anita asked.

"You. I'm crying because of you."

"What have I done to you?"

"I'm crying because I'm going to die and I'll never have been happy. Sometimes I wake in the middle of the night and I think if I die before morning then nothing good will ever have happened to me." Saying this, Asha wailed and broke from Anita's grip. She ran two steps, then turned around to confront her mother.

"You're not going to die," Anita said. "You're going to live eighty more years."

"You're going to die, too," Asha sobbed.

"I'm not afraid."

Anita hugged Asha again, but she kept crying. After a while Anita began murmuring to her, "What do you want?" This set Asha shrieking.

A boy about Asha's age with a kite came out onto a long roof across the courtyard from us. He put the kite on the ground, jiggled it with the thread in his hand, and then jerked hard. As the kite was flung up, he let the thread flow through his fingers. He gave short, sharp tugs and with each almost immediately released more thread. The kite caught a breeze. I saw Asha focusing on the boy without stopping her crying. After several minutes, when the kite was high and steady, Asha became quiet, though occasional tears leaked from her eyes.

"Why did you cry?" Anita asked.

"We never do anything. We never go anywhere."

"What do you want to do?"

"I want something sweet with dinner."

"All right."

At this Asha gasped and began sobbing again.

"We can do anything you want," I said. Anita did not look at me, and pulled Asha tighter to her.

"I want an adventure," Asha said, looking up at her mother.

Beyond them were roof after roof, like steps which went up for a little while and then dropped. "We could walk across Delhi from roof to roof," I said. "I heard of one man who did that. He used ropes and ladders." I had no idea where the idea came from, but as soon as I said it, the idea's miraculous freedom captured me. Asha's face was startled into calm. I thought of climbing from our balcony to the squatters' roofs and crossing those to a building which faced the approach to the Old Clock Tower. From there, with the help of ladders placed across the narrow alleyways, we could literally walk across roofs to the Old Clock Tower. "We could see how far we can go."

"That's an adventure," Asha said, glancing at me.

"It isn't that dangerous," I said and, of course, realized that it was.

Anita sighed and kissed Asha's cheeks. The sigh was enough to end our fantasies. Asha stared at the boy with the kite. Anita looked at me, but I could not tell what she was thinking.

"There are other things," I said.

"Tomorrow we'll do something," Anita said into Asha's ear. Her voice was thoughtful.

"Let's go out tonight," I offered.

"Yes," Asha said.

After a moment's hesitation Anita said, "All right."

"Let's go to a movie," I suggested.

"Yes. Yes," Asha said, staring up at her mother.

Anita looked at me and then at Asha. "Yes," she repeated.

SEVEN

I started to buy things for Asha. Most nights I purchased a half liter of milk and two Campa Colas and stirred them together with many spoonfuls of sugar. All three of us had contests of eating raisins and almonds. Asha was so thin that when she flexed her hands there was the eeriness of watching individual bones working. Sometimes I brought home coloring books and gave them to Anita to present to Asha. When I discovered that Asha liked stickers, I bought long rolls of them and had Anita hide them in Asha's pocket.

Kindness made me feel competent. When the electricity generators didn't appear at one of Mr. Gupta's rallies, I could imagine feeding Asha canned lychees and this somehow made me less unhappy with the moment. The van driver who blasted Mr. Gupta's slogans from loudspeakers crashed into an autorickshaw. I laughed as I told

Asha this, whereas earlier that day I had felt fear at the inept campaign we were waging.

The first time I met Asha at Rosary School, it was because I was passing near it and thought she might feel protected seeing my familiarity with Father Joseph. Father Joseph sent one peon for Asha and another for Campa Cola.

"Asha is a serious girl. Was she so serious before her father died?" he asked as we waited. I was on the sofa where I had sat and spat onto the carpet when I was extorting money from him. Remembering that made me feel I had power over Father Joseph. I slouched back at ease. Father Joseph was seated on a chair across from me with his legs crossed.

"She was always quiet, I think."

I was surprised that he would know her enough to have an opinion.

"She shouldn't bring her problems to school," he said.

Asha came in as I tried to interpret his words. She wore a blue shirt and a maroon skirt. Her maroon jacket was buttoned over a maroon sweater. When she saw me, her face sagged. She pressed the fingers of both hands over her mouth and keened.

"What happened?" Father Joseph asked.

The slight guilt I felt at being there without Anita's knowledge made me feel as if I had caused the tears. I went and knelt beside Asha. "Everything is all right," I said. She did not remove her hands. I put my arms around her. Asha cried more loudly. Father Joseph stood near us with his arms folded across his chest. "My little mango, you'll get salty crying."

"Mummy is all right?" Asha asked, gasping.

"Yes."

She surged around my neck. I lifted her up. "Mummy came to the school to tell me Daddy died." Asha continued crying and I continued holding her. It took ten or fifteen minutes before she calmed down.

"Have a cold drink," Father Joseph kept muttering. Asha drank the Campa and went back to her classes.

"She cries often in class," he said. "We send her to walk around the grounds. Sometimes she spends the whole day outside. The teacher goes out during recess and finds Asha asleep on the ground. As soon as she wakes, she starts crying again." Father Joseph said this with exasperation. "She has to leave her sadness at home."

I looked at him. He looked back into my eyes. This is his revenge, I thought. The room vanished and all I could see was his round face. Without realizing it, I had moved close to him. Father Joseph tilted back. He had a series of tiny white bubbles growing to the side of one nostril. "Asha's very sensitive," I whispered.

"Yes," he said, and speaking released some fear onto his face.

"Please take care of her."

I took Asha to a restaurant across the road and we ate ice cream. She said almost nothing, except when we were returning to school. "Don't tell Mummy," she asked.

"Why?"

"She'll be angry."

For a moment I wondered if Asha meant that Anita would be angry at me for coming. Then I understood she probably thought Anita would be angry at her. "Why would your mummy be angry?"

Asha only looked ahead at the road we were crossing.

Perhaps we inherit the way we respond to grief the way we inherit height or skin color. The form of Asha's sorrows was so similar to how I had responded to my mother's death that almost instantly I loved her.

When I was young, the first sign of love was fear, the fear of appearing ridiculous or incompetent to some friend I had loved for a week or to the first prostitute or to Radha. The first sign of loving Asha was joy. Instead of climbing onto a bus, I jumped on. The joy explained everything. The dirt field outside my office window existed as something Asha might perhaps see or whose dust might inspire some sentence in a conversation we had. I never believed I could harm her.

If I had told Anita that I was visiting Asha at her school, she would have forbidden it. But I wanted to help Asha and believed it was not possible to do so with Anita nearby. I began going to Rosary School during Asha's lunch hour.

Waiting for Asha in Father Joseph's office, even knowing that I would not touch her or harm her in any way, I still felt ashamed and even criminal. Walking away with her beyond the reach of the school windows, I had the feeling that hundreds of eyes were watching us. But I never asked Asha to keep anything secret from her mother. She must have sensed Anita's hostility toward me and acted on her own.

Usually we went across the road only to eat dosas or chole baturas. I would eat half of mine and Asha would eat her own and what part of mine I did not want. As we talked, Asha drained two or three bottles of cold drinks. Sometimes other students in Asha's class escaped from the school and appeared at the restaurant to spend their change on cold drinks. To win Asha protection and friendship from them, I paid for their drinks or ice cream. Often when I visited Asha, a dozen boys and girls appeared at the restaurant and asked, "Uncleji, will you buy us something?"

My love for Asha made me candid. "Remember when we went to Mr. Gupta's for the wedding reception?" Asha nodded as she chewed. "I asked you if your father used to buy you ice cream and you said no, but that you liked to imagine he did." Asha continued chewing, though now she looked down at her plate. "Why do you like to think that?"

Asha did not answer for a while. "I miss him," she said finally.

It was harder to go from there. "But why do you like imagining that?"

"I don't."

"Were you just saying it, then?" When Asha did not answer, I said, "Your principal says you cry in school." Asha remained quiet.

"I cried all the time when my mother died." The silence continued. "You know why little babies weep?"

Asha shook her head no.

"The little babies are missing their families from their past lives.

The babies have old souls and the old souls have to shrink to become little babies. The tears loosen their memories so they can slide away. They cry at the life they have lost, and then they cry at everything they'll forget."

Asha looked up. Her eyes were shiny. She took a sip of water.

Asha was full of perplexing guilts. Once she said, "Mummy thinks I'm a thief." This was so strange I laughed. We were in the dosa restaurant. "She follows me around." I thought Asha could be referring to how Anita tracked Asha and me when we were in the flat simultaneously. "I've stolen two things only in my life. One was a candy, the other was a pencil."

Making Asha laugh was often my goal. "You are too little to steal the refrigerator. That's the only thing worth robbing. How big are your pockets?" I made her stand and turn out the pockets in her skirt. Then I stood and asked, "Can I fit in them?" I walked around her and lifted one foot toward the pockets. "You can't get a mouse in those." Asha had started laughing loudly. I sat down. "Your mother is strange. She follows around the people she loves. When she was in higher secondary, she loved her home economics teacher. She loved her so much she found out where the teacher lived and walked circles around the block where the woman lived."

Asha also wanted to learn magic spells so that she could bring her father back. But she was so afraid of ghosts that she hated the dark.

"Why would a ghost be here instead of in America?" I asked. "You think a ghost wouldn't get bored watching you in Hindi class?"

The more lunches I had with Asha, the more certain I became that Asha's oddness might have been exaggerated by Rajinder's death but was not created by it.

"If you can see something in your head as clearly as in life, then what's the difference between that and life?" she once asked.

"Close your eyes and imagine being pinched," I said. She did. I kicked her leg.

"Oh," she answered. Asha had not considered this.

Because of her oddities and since I loved her, at first I thought she might be a genius. Helping Asha with her schoolwork, I soon realized she was not. She was slow with math. Her spelling was terrible.

Among the things I hoped to offer Asha was an adult viewpoint of her thoughts. "You're not stupid. Everybody thinks he's stupid. Besides, you don't have to be smart. You only have to be smart enough. How much is seventeen plus thirteen?"

"Thirty."

"That's more than enough brains to be a doctor."

At another time Asha said, "I think I am bad."

"Why?"

"I think if Mummy died, I would be an orphan and everybody would feel sorry for me and I would like that."

"People think anything. That's all right. It's good to think. Even strange thoughts. When I was your age I used to think I would sail a ship alone to England and steal back all the things the British had taken from India. I had never been on a boat in my life. I thought all the jewels and gold they had taken were in one room in a palace and I used to worry how I would be able to carry all these things to the boat by myself. Sometimes I thought I would be caught and killed and become famous."

"But I don't like Mummy. That's why I don't mind being an orphan."

"Did you like me six months ago?" Asha laughed at this, and I felt bad that she had not liked me six months ago.

One week I went to see her four times. I went because I cared for Asha and helping her was an easy task that made me feel good about my generosity. But the idea of wanting to see Asha, remembering that I had rubbed my penis against her back, made me anxious, and the next week I did not go at all.

I also began talking more with Anita. Each night I confessed my political sins. These recountings began because I once returned home and found something intimidating in Anita's sullenness as she mended a sleeve of Asha's school jacket. Sensing her lurking anger I decided to deflect it and told her what crimes I had committed that day on Mr. Gupta's behalf. I thought that providing her with something to rage about openly would be a way to keep us from the topic of what I had done to her.

My confession usually occurred in the living room, after the English news. I would sit alone on the sofa beneath the fluorescent tube light. Anita and Asha sat across from me on the love seats. Sometimes I confessed in the common room with all of us sitting on the floor. And at least twice I did so on the roof, where Anita and Asha slept because it was June and load shedding meant there might be no electricity and no turning ceiling fans for fourteen or twenty hours at a time.

"I went to a hotel this afternoon," I might begin, as if reciting a list of facts. If I started with anything more complicated than a fact, I became nervous. "The Oberoi. A five-star. Mr. Bajwa was already there, waiting in a room."

"How did you know which room?" At the beginning of my confession, Anita was also anxious, and this manifested itself in interrogation which appeared intended to catch me in a lie. I did not mind being questioned, since it allowed me to show I was hiding nothing.

"I asked for the hotel manager's party, because rooms and meals given out free are budgeted under the hotel manager's name." I looked at Anita to see if she had more questions. "The Oberoi doesn't let autorickshaws enter the driveway, only taxis, so I had to get out in front of the hotel and walk up the driveway, which is sloped. The lobby is four or five times bigger than this flat. It's sealed on one side with glass and you can see their swimming pool."

"How big is a swimming pool?" Asha asked.

"As large as our entire compound." I think Asha was allowed to witness these confessions because Anita wanted her to dislike me. But I met Asha often enough during her school lunch hour that I think she saw those nightly confessions as part of a larger conversation.

"It is full to the top with water?"

"Yes."

"Is it as deep as the compound's buildings are tall?"

"No. Maybe three or four meters deep."

"How many people were in it?" Confessions for Asha, despite her mimicking her mother's serious expression, appeared as much travelogue as anything else.

"Two or three."

"See the waste," Anita said to Asha. "Your people," she then accused me. Asha nodded. I wondered how she felt at keeping our lunch meetings secret and whether some part of her enjoyed lying to her mother.

Although I did not mind being questioned, I was afraid of accusations where fair condemnation of my corruption was conflated with something I had never come close to doing. I took bribes, but nearly all went to Mr. Gupta. I could not afford water in bottles, let alone the Oberoi and its swimming pool. "I've seen, I think, seven swimming pools in my life," I said. I waited for this information to be absorbed and then continued.

"The room was no bigger than this living room. It was very cold and it had a sealed smell, perhaps because of the air-conditioning. The curtains were drawn so that the light was dim. There was a view of a road. There was a bathroom to the left, near the door. There were two beds. Mr. Bajwa was lying on one, drinking whiskey and watching TV. He was the only one there. His beard hid his kurta buttons and he had his dagger on, but he was wearing black office shoes. Mr. Bajwa had arranged for property developers to see what we were selling to increase interest." Anita made a noise as if she had caught me at something. "I think he also wanted to show off before the people who had ignored him when he was in trouble. Mr. Bajwa spent a long time arranging the grandest hotel possible for the meeting. A little after I arrived, Mr. Mittal and his brother came. His brother looks just like him. Then Mr. Verma and Mr. Satchu came together. Mr. Poon and Mr. Rajan followed."

"We don't need to know their names," Anita interrupted. "How many people in all?"

"Eleven. Mr. Bajwa kept pouring whiskey for everyone. Johnnie Walker Black."

"That costs how much?"

"Maybe four thousand. After the developers began arriving, Mr. Bajwa stayed on his feet. He had the bottle in his hand all the time and would fill a glass even after only one sip was taken. He wasn't paying for the drinks, so why should he care. Mr. Bajwa started smiling as soon as the first developer came and didn't stop till near the end. As he talked and poured whiskey, Mr. Bajwa kept going to the phone and ordering food, which arrived on carts. Samosas, roasted peanuts and cashews, toast, lamb cutlets. The hotel was paying. When the waiters lingered for their tips, he would say, 'It's all paid for by Manager Sahib. I am a beggar.' He was talking so fast, I remembered how crazy he was even before the corruption investigation. He used to lie about everything. I introduced myself to all the property dealers, but mostly I sat on one bed and watched. This meeting would make my job easier, but I was being presented as less important than Mr. Bajwa."

"You do a bad job, you get replaced."

"Mr. Bajwa is a better moneyman than I am," I agreed. To make sure Anita's anger was actually being consumed, I tried always acknowledging insults and responding as candidly as possible.

"That's like saying he's a better poisoner than you."

"Yes. I am an incompetent poisoner. I give people bad headaches instead of killing them." I waited to see if Anita was going to respond. When she did not, I asked, "Am I less bad now because Mr. Bajwa is taking over?"

"No, because you didn't give up your sins voluntarily."

"I think you are better," Asha said. I ignored this, as I always did compliments from her. Instead of harming me in her eyes, the confessions were making me interesting and, because of my frankness, trustworthy.

"Not much work gets done when there are more than two people in a room," I continued.

"And when you are one of these, not even a little bit," Anita said.

"Normally I am lazy, but I am working hard these days. Still, almost nothing was done at the party. Everybody in the room knew everyone else, but they don't get to meet regularly and so were enjoying themselves. There was food. There was drink. Mr. Bajwa had brought diagrams of the properties, white sheets with black print. He unfolded them on a bed, the one away from the door, and on a table. This meeting was a good idea. It's rare for so much land to become available at once, and someone who might at first think that it isn't possible to build on property obtained this way will think again if he sees another person considering buying."

"Why aren't you smart like Mr. Bajwa?"

"He's bolder," I said. "As people drank, it became something of a party. I didn't even finish one drink." I inserted mention of this restraint because I knew Anita felt threatened by alcohol. "I put it on the night table and left it there. Everyone appeared to actually like Mr. Bajwa. They kept hugging him, grabbing his arms. This surprised me, because it made me realize how unimportant relations are that these people could have dropped him so quickly despite liking him. Mr. Bajwa told a good story about his wife.

" 'My wife is my boss. It's because she never gets excited and she never lies and so I can get excited and lie. When we were first married, she asked me how tall I was. I said five feet six, but that I wasn't sure. I must have known the truth, because I said I wasn't sure. But I liked the number, because you can round up. You can think, I am nearly six feet tall. Rita decides to measure me. She does, and she tells me I am five feet five and a half. I hate this, because now I have to round down. I am a dwarf. I kept waking up the next few nights thinking of this. And I am going to get shorter as I get older. When she told me, I said to her, "If in my twenty-six years I had wanted to know the truth, don't you think I could have found out before this afternoon? Is this the only tape measure in the world?" I sometimes make her lie to me. "Tell me we have ten rooms in the flat." And she will say, "On the ground floor or on the top?"'

"People were getting drunk. People always use the bathroom more when they are drinking, and a line began forming. Finally they began pissing in the tub and sink. Even when something is free, people want more, and when it's free, the only way to get more is to harm it so other people can't use it. After a while Mr. Bajwa decides to order wine. Wines are more expensive than whiskey."

"How much more?" Anita asked.

"I don't know, but Mr. Bajwa placed his order and a few minutes later the phone rang. 'Hello, Manager Sahib,' Mr. Bajwa said. This I knew meant something, because why would we get called back? Mr. Mittal was sitting beside me, asking me about arranging to get his son into a good school. Mr. Bajwa talked for one or two minutes and hung up. I could tell something bad was going to happen. People were drunk. Mr. Bajwa, Mr. Poon, and Mr. Rajan had spent some time looking over the list of wines, which I think meant they had picked very expensive ones. Then this young man came. He was maybe thirty-five and wearing a blue suit. He introduced himself as the assistant manager in charge of client services. I wondered why the manager had not come himself. Mr. Bajwa introduced him to Mr. Poon and Mr. Rajan. Everyone was watching this now, of course, because his introducing the assistant manager to people would make any rejection of his request especially personal.

" 'You ordered wine?' the assistant manager asked, though, of course, he knew we had.

"Mr. Bajwa opened the list of wines. The list was on a desk. He pointed at some and said, 'These three.' Hotels are always willing to let you have empty rooms and order some food and alcohol because it costs them little and later you owe them a favor. But to order expensive things is to make the hotel manager calculate whether you are worth the free things you are getting. The assistant manager asked if Mr. Bajwa would rather not continue with whiskey. Mr. Bajwa looked at him, then slapped him twice, once on each cheek, so loudly it was like a paper bag bursting. The young man stepped back. His eyes began tearing. I realized that the manager had not come himself because he had guessed there might be blows. 'Listen to what I say, son,' Mr. Bajwa said. The assistant manager nodded and left. 'The assistant manager in charge of being hit,' someone said. The wines came. Everybody tasted some. Including me."

"You said you didn't finish one drink."

"It was just a taste."

There was silence, and that's how this confession ended.

I would become nervous as soon as they ended and so I sometimes babbled apologies. "I am ashamed of what we did."

Anita rarely got angry instantly at what I revealed. "I wish I knew more ways to hate you," she might say. Asha would nod, as she often did at enigmatic statements. Then Anita tried working herself from abstraction into specific anger. "The bad schools Asha goes to. The children in her classes who cannot buy schoolbooks and so share with her. We get water five hours a day, and that in drops, and the Oberoi has a pool as large as our compound."

Once the anger was released, it might lunge about for an hour and a half or two, and might include in its ambit everything in the newspaper, from cow-feed prices, which the Iraq war had pushed up, to Nehru's socialism, which had bound us to Russian aid. I never pointed out to her that Rajinder had been corrupt, and that when she was married Anita had been able to live quite easily with the watches and the saris that bribery brought her gift-wrapped every New Year.

Sometimes her anger did not stop, and she and I would be awake until one or two because I did not want to leave her whirling mind alone in such a state. Asha would go to the roof to sleep. Once, during such a rage, after Asha had gone upstairs, I went to the latrine. Almost immediately Anita knocked on the door, and when I asked what she wanted, she said, "Nothing," but I knew she had panicked at the possibility of my following Asha.

Occasionally the open rage lasted into the next day, and if it did, I gave Anita money. I might take a hundred or two hundred rupees, fold them, and put them beside her, and soon her anger would be replaced by exhaustion.

Money always worked. By the end of June I knew Anita was stealing from me. She had stopped giving me accounts for the household expenses. If I left my wallet anywhere other than locked in my closet, I discovered that some of the money was gone. I found these thefts comforting, because they diminished Anita's moral weight.

Perhaps because Anita felt more confident financially or perhaps because she was allowed to confront me, she began challenging other people as well. An electricity repairman came to the flat and before doing any repairs demanded a bribe. Anita refused, and when he persisted, saying, "A little tea money," Anita went out onto the gallery and began shouting "Thief." A crowd gathered in the flat and in front of it; Anita harangued the repairman until he did his job.

There was often an odd jocularity to her hatred. Anita had started calling me a snake, and sometimes she would hiss at me, holding up a hand bent into the shape of a hooded cobra.

It was obvious from Anita's sometimes being too angry to sleep that she could not control her feelings and that, like lightning in the air, her anger required only something standing upright to strike. I realized that if my plan to use up her anger was to work, I must persist. Anita's voice remained a screech, brakes scraping metal.

I never lost faith in the power of confession. Probably this was because I needed to confess.

Also, Anita occasionally gave good advice. Although she hated me, she was the one person in the world whose interests were most parallel to mine. If I went to jail, the government would probably also seize the flat and all my money. Anita, therefore, thought a great deal about what I should do to protect myself.

One night, because I was afraid of becoming unimportant to Mr.

Gupta, I mentioned the possibility of telling newspaper reporters about the corruption charges against Mr. Bajwa.

Anita responded that it wouldn't help. "You think they don't know already? Your problem is you are such a bad moneyman, like when you arranged the tax benefit and miscalculated the value of what you'd given. What a failure you are to spend a whole life being corrupt and still be incompetent at it."

If I wanted advice from Anita I almost had to seek insult. "I know my problem is I'm no good."

"Don't give all the money you collect immediately to Mr. Gupta. Give him a lakh or two at a time. He can't keep the money, or the bankbooks, because of the possibility of a tax raid. Tell him you'll give him the money when he needs it. He won't fight this, because he'll be afraid of angering you. Stupid people are unpredictable and you are stupid. This way, you get some power of your own instead of just being the one everyone can identify to the CBI as the bribe collector."

The boldness of simply not turning over the money was breathtaking, and when I attempted this, it worked so well that it felt as if Mr. Gupta and Mr. Bajwa had been expecting it. Mr. Bajwa only said, "Don't think we don't know every paisa you are getting."

After the confessions started and Anita could be angry with me, the idea of suggesting that we all go to Kamla Nagar and buy Asha her school uniforms did not feel as ridiculous as it would have earlier. Sometimes we went to dinner or a movie, and because I was the one who always proposed these things, Asha would occasionally ask me to recommend such a plan to Anita. I tried not to be alone with Asha in the flat, and the implied confidentiality of Asha requesting something from me made me nervous. The first time she came to me, I told Anita, and she became angry at Asha, accusing her of ingratitude. After this, I always acted as if the suggested venture was solely my idea.

I confessed everything except that I was visiting Asha in her school. When Asha told stories of her schoolday, I would act surprised.

Confessing became as important as sleep for me. If I did not confess for several nights, I grew confused and walked around looking at the ground.

The talking I was doing during Asha's lunch hour and at night became as important as sleep to me. If I did not have an extended conversation with Anita or Asha for several days I began to feel dazed. My talking and explaining gave my world order.

EIGHT

One evening, Anita, Asha, and I went to see Rajesh Khanna speak at the Ram Lila Ground at Red Fort. Seventy or eighty thousand people stretched around the stage and up to the enormous crenellated walls of the fort. The stage was about fifteen meters long and had cords of geraniums dangling from its front. It took almost an hour for us, with Anita and me holding Asha's hands, to push our way near the VIP section so that from where we stood we could actually see the speakers. The section was distinguished by a dhurrie on the ground, plastic folding chairs, and waiters that kept bringing glasses of water. The crowd grew till it appeared unbelievable that this dark mass with its roar and smell was gathering under the thin blue sky only to listen.

I attended from curiosity about Mr. Gupta's competition. The size of the crowd didn't worry me, because over the last month I had given up trying to predict whether Mr. Gupta would win or lose, since all this did was rush me from one emotion to another.

Anita came because Asha had never seen a celebrity and demanded that she must. Anita was trying to compensate for the rage that could still cause her to wake Asha from the middle of a sleep and demand that Asha reveal what she had been dreaming.

There were about twenty people onstage. Some were candidates; each was invited to speak. Their words—"This nation is ours and will remain ours"—spoken about foreign lenders, were similar enough to the BJP speeches I had heard that I could assume the crowd was there for Rajesh Khanna, not to support Congress. Many people appeared so indifferent to the candidates that instead of looking toward the stage, they watched the bell-shaped speakers, tied to bamboo poles along the field, from which the candidates' words echoed out.

Rajesh Khanna's turn to speak came. I lifted Asha onto my shoulders. Even from one hundred meters away he looked heavy and his hair appeared unnaturally dark. This man, at the height of his fame, had married Dimple Kapadia, twenty years younger than he and considered, after she appeared in *Bobby*, the most beautiful woman in India. With his new wife, he retired from movies. After fifteen years of marriage and two children his wife cheated on him, and he had reentered movies only to discover that his films were no longer hits. Now he was running for Parliament.

As Rajesh Khanna moved toward the microphone, dialogue from his movie *Anand* boomed from the loudspeakers. The crowd became so loud in response that my heart raced automatically. Rajesh Khanna stood silently before the microphone a minute as the dialogue concluded. "Namaste," he said then. In the last month and a half I had shaken hands with Advani twice, but there is something thrilling about the familiarity of a movie celebrity's voice which no other type of fame can generate. Rajesh Khanna's voice was immediately drowned by the crowd's roar. "Namaste," he said again, and the crowd's roar absorbed this, too. When he realized the crowd was not about to stop, Rajesh Khanna began a short speech, portions of which he had to keep repeating because of the noise.

Once he was done, the crowd leaked away. I kept Asha on my shoulders and carried her out. Mr. Gupta had never received a response like this, even when he spoke directly after being praised by Advani. But in India even a lip-synching contest in memory of a dead singer can draw thousands.

When things turned bad for Mr. Gupta, I responded with such speed that I must have been expecting disaster. Many other people also acted rapidly, and in the same way, so perhaps our alacrity only revealed a general readiness for betrayal.

One afternoon I came home exhausted and nauseated from a headache. The heat had given me a nosebleed earlier that day, and just before I arrived, the trickle restarted. I lay down on the living-room bed, because when I tried sleeping in the smallness of my room, the ceiling swayed. Anita made me salty lemonade before I fell asleep. I woke an hour later, at about five, with the phone buzzing beside my head. It was late enough in the day that I winced at the idea of a fresh task.

One of Mr. Gupta's servants spoke and in a quick voice requested I come to Model Town.

"Something important?" I asked. From where I lay, I could see a sky so bright that it felt as if day would never end. Beneath it, the roofs, stepped terraces, were abandoned.

"Please come, sir."

"Answer him," said the man who listened to our phone. He liked to enter conversations suddenly and frighten the unsuspecting party.

"Who?" said the servant.

"Your father, baby."

"There was an income tax raid and they found money."

"How much?" asked the phone tapper.

"I don't know. Enough."

I assumed Congress already knew all this information, but I interrupted and said, "I'm coming." The servant hung up.

"I wasn't told about this. That's how I am treated," the man said.

"We are nobodies." I always tried appearing pitiful before him in hope that this might keep him from harming me.

"You are right, Mr. Karan."

When I went to tell Anita about the income tax raid, she was sitting on the common-room floor, wearing glasses and reading the newspaper.

"Of course they had some money hidden away. They couldn't trust you. Also, in case they lose the election, they want to have made something from all this. But to keep undeclared money at home? It's terrible to be both corrupt and stupid."

"This makes me more important," I said, acting stupid. "They can say whatever money found was from family property they recently sold. But that excuse will only work once, so all the money now will have to go through me."

"Life is more complicated than your fantasies," Anita said.

I left for Model Town.

Only two cars were parked in the shade across the road from Mr. Gupta's house. I visited his house several times a week and there were usually ten or more cars and jeeps lined up nearby. My worries about the campaign had been kept in check partially because so many other people were taking part in Mr. Gupta's venture. I had expected even more activity than usual because of the scandal. The silence worried me.

It was now nearly seven, but the sky was unflaggingly blue. As I got out of my autorickshaw, a fat man was climbing into a white Maruti van in front of Mr. Gupta's gate. The fourteen-year-old boy who had brought it for him took his five-rupee tip, and in extravagant obsequiousness backed away, salaaming the man and also stepping on his own feet with little exclamations of pain. The boy, his face terribly streaked by chickenpox, like raindrop marks on a dusty window, had appeared out of nowhere soon after it became obvious that each day there would be a tangle of automobiles outside Mr. Gupta's house. He took charge, parking cars near and far, telling you when he returned the keys that he had had to hunt hard to find shade for your vehicle. In hopes of increasing his tips he had begun behaving clownishly, wearing too-large black shoes and a trained monkey's Muslim outfit of a fez and a vest, and tripping over himself, doing pratfalls and tumbles, when he accepted his reward.

Congress had turned off the electricity on Mr. Gupta's block, and inside the house there was the heavy vibration of a generator but not the overlay of voices to which I had become accustomed during my visits.

Inside, in one of the several living rooms, Mr. Gupta sat on a sofa. Across from him, on another sofa, was Mr. Tuli, the man who had shown me Gopal Godse's business card. The room was very large, and there was a smaller room separated from it by a ceiling-high closet. When I came around the closet into the room, Mr. Tuli was saying, "The police will look. Our people will look." I did not see Mr. Bajwa, although he rarely left a rival adviser alone with Mr. Gupta.

Mr. Gupta patted the space next to him. Since I had begun doling out the money, Mr. Gupta had been showing me more respect. I sat down and tiredness made me sigh. The ceiling fan was turning slowly because only one generator powered the whole house. Both Mr. Gupta and Mr. Tuli were shiny from perspiration.

"It was Ajay's money they found," Mr. Tuli told me. "He'd been collecting money by telling people it was for Mr. Gupta's campaign. Of course, he had never turned over any of the money to us."

"I hope he's dead," Mr. Gupta said, and gave me a half-smile, as if to tell me not to believe him. "He's run away. He might have more money."

"When was the raid?" There were no overturned and slit sofa cushions. The kitchen, which I had passed on my way to the living room, had all its plates and pots on the shelves. One of the latches to a closet had been pried off. Where the latch used to be was a gash that revealed the yellow wood beneath the red varnish.

"Two, three hours ago," Mr. Tuli answered.

"Ajay said Mr. Bajwa had helped him get the money."

This made sense, because Ajay could not know who needed what favors. "From whom?" I asked. I marveled at Mr. Bajwa's talents, that he had been able to raise money without my ever hearing of his efforts.

"I hit him with my shoes. I nearly knocked off an ear. He cried like a woman." I could not understand Mr. Gupta's voice. It was tight with anger, but slow and almost dreamy.

"Ajay probably sold the same thing to two people and one phoned income tax," Mr. Tuli said. "In an election this close, income tax wouldn't raid a candidate unless they expected to find something in particular."

"I hit him in front of his wife. That was stupid."

"What are you going to say about the money?"

"That it was money from land Mr. Gupta sold, and because nobody will believe it, we'll suggest that the money was Ajay's dowry. Nobody cares about not paying taxes, and people understand dowry, especially for an MP candidate's son."

"Mr. Karan, I am relying on you now," Mr. Gupta declared. "You will have to help me." He looked in my eyes when he said this. I think Mr. Gupta hoped to have some jocularity in his voice, but the statement sounded serious and made him appear desperate.

"How much money did they find?"

Mr. Tuli answered, "Eight lakhs. Five in cash. Three in bank-books." Mr. Gupta grimaced at the lost sum. This was vastly more than I had expected. It was equivalent to selling a school. Mr. Gupta's campaign must be so confused that at night people couldn't tell what had happened during the day. I wondered whether the BJP might abandon the campaign. An ordinary candidate, even one who lost, was better than no candidate, but a bad candidate, one that harmed the BJP's reputation, was worse than no candidate.

"How much do you think you can raise?" Mr. Tuli asked. I understood the answer would affect how much effort the BJP was willing to put into the campaign.

"I have enough money already to win this campaign," I said, and thought that if Mr. Gupta was relying on me to save him, it was time to leave Mr. Gupta.

"Bring the money," Mr. Gupta said.

Late morning the next day, I went to the many banks in which I had stored the bribes and withdrew twelve lakhs, about half the money I had accumulated. Anita had confirmed my belief that I should turn over only part of what I had raised. As I carried the bundles of rupees in the rubber briefcase Mr. Mittal had given me, I realized that since last night I had begun thinking of the money as more mine than Mr. Gupta's.

The boy who parked cars jumped up and saluted me from where he was sitting in the dirt eating roti and subji off a leaf plate. Again Mr. Gupta's tall yellow house was silent. The silence made the building appear to be waiting.

Mr. Gupta was busy, I learned. He had spoken at a cow-retirement farm in the morning and was meeting the student-body president of Delhi University in the afternoon.

I held out the money as Mr. Gupta changed into a fresh kurta pajama in a room on the second floor. When they are introduced, vast amounts of money always arrest whatever is going on. Mr. Gupta stopped buttoning his kurta. He put the briefcase on his dresser, opened it, took out several bundles and put them on the dresser, thought better of it, and returned them to the briefcase. He then hugged me tightly, emotionally. In the middle of the hug he asked, "Is this all we have?"

"No."

Mr. Gupta looked at me, as if waiting for me to reveal how much we had, but when I did not, he did not ask. This made me think the situation was even more dire than I had thought. Many of the rooms in his home were used at times as office space, and the room we were in, which had been a bedroom, had several folding tables with pamphlets and papers scattered on them. The interim nature of the room made me sense Mr. Gupta's vulnerability. I had to find a way to buy protection from the BJP and Congress.

The idea of ruining Mr. Gupta did not horrify me, for I was certain he would do the same to me if necessary. But I felt sad at his helplessness. Mr. Gupta started dressing himself again.

"The BJP is robbing me," he said. "All the posters and vans are hired through them. How much should a single poster cost, from printing to up on a wall?"

"Twenty, thirty rupees."

"One hundred and forty, the BJP says. A poster on plain thin paper. And then because I want more posters than the BJP put up, because I can't afford their price, I have to lie and go around them and hire people on my own. I had to buy a minimum of ten thousand posters from the BJP." I wondered whether Mr. Gupta thought that revealing his exploitation would somehow make me be kinder to him. Since the campaign started, perhaps to win people's affection, Mr. Gupta had begun talking about his feelings. Because of the problems that always beset him, this openness made him appear complaining, distracted, and lost. "They were supposed to give me two generators. Why do I have one?" Having finished dressing, Mr. Gupta said, "Come tonight at about eleven and we'll drink tea."

I imagined Mr. Gupta had made the invitation because he wanted to shore up our relationship.

The oddity of tea at such a late hour, however, was so great that Anita said she would stay awake and wait for me to return home and tell her about it. I watched the news before leaving for Model Town; the tax raid was mentioned only briefly.

I arrived at the requested time, but Mr. Gupta was away at a dinner. My headache from yesterday was still periodically clamping my skull. It had enervated me and I fell asleep in a chair waiting for him. I was awakened when he arrived a little after twelve-thirty, and I had tea with him. All I remember from the meeting was that the more he tried charming me, the more anxious I became.

"Something has to be done," Anita said when I described this.

"What?" We were in the common room and I was holding a glass of water.

"You have to take care of us." I wondered if she was encouraging me to find a way to abandon Mr. Gupta. "He's nobody's friend."

"If this scandal dies, then things can go on."

Anita stared in dissatisfaction at my answer. I finished the glass of water and then went to get one more.

When I returned, she asked, "Do you have crops to irrigate that you want so much water?"

I wondered how Anita's anger would get deflected when I had nothing to confess every night.

I did not see Mr. Gupta the next day, because even though I believed it was correct to betray him, the actual misery this would create was too much to imagine and I did not want to see the person I would hurt. At night he phoned, and when I said hello, he said, "You didn't come by."

"I am sorry. I was busy all day."

"Ajay is still not home."

"He's probably ashamed and hiding."

Mr. Gupta was silent for a minute. "He should be hiding from me, but he would have contacted his mother if he was all right."

This made sense, although I didn't say so.

"His mother is having a prayer for him tomorrow morning. Come and bring your family. It'll make his mother feel better if a lot of people are praying."

I asked Anita if she wanted to come and she immediately agreed.

The pockets of the boy who parked cars were bulging with keys. A calf that must have wandered in off the street was being shoved out of Mr. Gupta's courtyard. The eucalyptus trees that had been torn to feed the elephants appeared ravaged.

"This is not such a nice house," Anita said when we arrived in an

autorickshaw. I had forgotten that during her life with Rajinder
Anita had seen many things and people I knew nothing about.
"Maybe that's why he's running for Parliament."

"It's across from a park," I said.

The prayer was held in the large room in the back of the house
where Ajay had tried to get me drunk in order to get the shawl. A
pundit on a thick cotton mat beneath a window was singing, and a
crowd of women and a few men listened seated on bamboo mats. An
air conditioner and a ceiling fan whirred, and I wondered whether
this was the only room that the generator's electricity was being
directed to. Along a wall opposite the pundit were several wooden
chairs, on two of which sat Mrs. Gupta and Pavan. Mrs. Gupta was
short and fat, and this made Pavan's beauty more distinctive.

We had been led to the prayer by a servant. While I stood deciding where on the floor to sit, Mr. Gupta came in through another
door, examined the room for a minute, and left. "Like a mill owner
looking at his workers on the factory floor," Anita said, and moved
to the chairs. She sat down beside Pavan.

"My daughter Anita. The poor girl is a widow and lives with
me." I told them this so that they might treat her with the deference
due to a widow. But at my words, one of Pavan's hands rose into the
air as if warding something off.

After a moment, as the hand sank back into Pavan's lap, Anita
took it between her own hands. "Don't worry yet," she said.

We watched the prayer in silence. Mrs. Gupta cried when, in the
middle of reading from the *Ramayana*, the pundit stood and closed
the curtains of the window behind him so that the room became
dim. An hour after we arrived, a servant whispered in my ear and
brought me to Mr. Gupta.

Over the last two days I had begun to believe that I would have to
split the money I had raised between Congress and the BJP. But I
was waiting for some sign to act. Now, though, as I followed the servant through empty rooms, I felt that an omen was at last going to
be given me.

Mr. Gupta was sitting on a sofa. He wore a suit and tie but was barefoot. Seeing me, he stood and laughed. "You look worried, Mr. Karan." The bare feet reminded me of my mother. Would he be murdered? I wondered.

"No, sir. I've been sick. I've had a headache for three days."

"Good; you shouldn't be worried."

I wondered whether he was aware of how vulnerable he appeared. Whereas before, when I went to see Mr. Gupta, I felt as though I was being granted an appointment, now I had the sense that I was the one whose time was being taken up.

"I talked to Mr. Maurya yesterday and he said that he can win this election for us if we have the money." Mr. Gupta said this eagerly. I knew he was lying. The only way to guarantee victory in a close election was by stealing vote boxes, and this was not possible in the capital. Mr. Maurya would not even imply a guarantee, because he could not swindle a BJP candidate so obviously and hope later to do business with the BJP. When I did not respond, he added, "How much money do we have?"

I did not want to reveal anything to Mr. Gupta but, unable to see where a lie might lead, answered.

"That's good. Twelve is enough," he said.

This encouragement heightened the abjectness of his lie.

"Bring me the money today."

"Yes."

"Are you going to do it, Mr. Karan?" Mr. Gupta smiled as he asked this. I wondered if Mr. Gupta had chosen to ask today instead of during the phone call last night because he thought it would be hard to refuse a grieving father.

I did not think I would give him the money. "Yes, sir." The BJP and Congress would make any promise I asked for in exchange for my giving them the money I had collected. But it was doubtful that they would honor their promise. I looked away from him. "Have you talked to Mr. Bajwa?"

Mr. Gupta stared at me and I wondered whether he was deciding to lie. "Yes, for a minute. He hadn't phoned because he was afraid of my being angry. I told him I wasn't."

The obvious impossibility of this made me think that if Mr. Gupta could say something this ridiculous, he must be lost inside his worries.

"A broken pot can't be made whole by anger."

Mr. Gupta nodded. "Bring me the money today."

I went to see my doctor after leaving Mr. Gupta's house. Anita stayed behind at the prayer. Dr. Aziz's narrow office was next to a bakery in Khan Market. When he saw me, he immediately said, "You are not well."

"No."

"How long have you been feeling this way?" Dr. Aziz was a short, bearded Muslim with a feminine smile. His examination room had a long table to lie on and a large metal desk whose top and sides were covered with plywood. In the nearly one year I had known him, he had never said a thing to make me think he was stupid or unconcerned.

"A few days." I told him about the nosebleeds.

"And when did your weight start to drop?" I now realized that he had not been referring to my concerned face when he suggested I looked bad.

"A month and a half ago, I lost my appetite and it hasn't come back. When I'm hungry I take two bites and I'm full."

Dr. Aziz took my blood pressure, which was low, and collected blood and urine samples. "It could be that you've lost weight and your medicine needs to be readjusted. That might be good." I smiled so broadly that Dr. Aziz immediately said, "We'll see."

The possibility of good health gave me confidence that I would be able to maneuver Congress and the BJP. In the autorickshaw home, I thought of the various people in Congress and the BJP whom I could approach to negotiate my security.

My brother Krishna was drinking tea in the living room. He was sitting on a love seat with his legs folded under him, his saucer in his left hand, and the cup held above it with the right. Anita sat across from him on the sofa, the edges of her lips curving down as they sometimes did in sleep. She was still in her green sari, which meant that Krishna must have arrived immediately after she returned home. They were not talking, and there was an air of offended dignity to Krishna's thin white mustache. As I entered the living room, Asha came in holding a plate full of biscuits. "I bring good news," Krishna said. "Munna is getting married." He sounded relieved to see me.

"Congratulations." For me, Munna remarrying had all the meaning of his changing jobs. Asha put the biscuits on the table and sat beside me on the bed.

"He's young," Krishna said. "It's important that he have a wife." The unnecessary justification suggested that Anita had put Krishna on the defensive. Krishna would take a sip of tea and then press down his mustache with his fingers.

"He's marrying the sister of the one who hanged herself." Anita looked at me as she said this. She looked ready to cry.

"Water?" Asha asked. I nodded yes.

"It's good for Munna and for the girl. Otherwise, who would marry a suicide's sister?" I said.

Anita kept looking at me.

"It's good for everyone," Krishna agreed. "The girl's name is Vineeta." Asha brought a glass of water and sat back on the bed.

Anita opened her mouth but did not speak.

Krishna invited me to the engagement ceremony and started to leave. Politeness required me to ask him to linger, but I did not.

I stood and was about to go change my clothes when Anita said, "No wonder I am angry all the time." I could not tell whether she wanted me to say anything. "The girl says she will only marry Munna if he lives away from home and they live alone."

"That's smart."

"Asha, do you understand what has happened?"

Asha nodded.

"A woman has to fight just to avoid being murdered. What kind of world is this?" Anita asked her.

I waited, and when Anita appeared to want a reaction, I said, "It's a bad one."

"You're stupid." I did not respond, and Anita said, "Do you think I'm being unfair to be angry at you about Munna?"

I shrugged. I did not know if she was. The sadness of Asha watching this made me imagine a world where I had not committed my crimes.

"This is your fault, too, because you are the same as everybody else and everybody else is the same as you. So I might as well hate you as everyone else." Anita laughed. I stayed quiet. "Go change your clothes."

I left for my room. A minute or two later Anita appeared in my doorway. "You know that Pavan and Ajay's marriage was a love marriage."

"Yes." I hung my pants on a hook.

"She loves him." Anita said this with such intensity that I wondered what love meant to her. "Pavan and I ate lunch." She paused. "Why should she love him? He's a fool. He was drunk at his own wedding reception." She stopped after this. Though her voice was angry, the pauses made her sound puzzled.

"A heart is what does not listen."

"I know. I told her she shouldn't blame herself."

"She shouldn't."

"I know. Why are you saying that? I need your permission to tell her not to blame herself?"

I took off my shirt.

That night, a little before eight, one of Mr. Gupta's servants, a boy judging from his voice, phoned and said that Ajay's body had been found and would I please meet Mr. Gupta at the morgue near the ISBT. He gave me the address.

I tried speaking with the man who listened to our phone, but he would not respond when I jiggled the receiver and said, "Hello, hello."

The morgue is ten minutes from the Old Vegetable Market. The sky was darkening, but there was enough light to read shop names from the autorickshaw without effort. I kept thinking of Anita, Asha, Kusum, and Rajesh dying. The thoughts made me keep touching my forehead.

I imagined the building would smell strange, of formaldehyde and chemicals. When I rang the bell, a man in a white lab coat and rubber slippers opened a narrow door next to the wide ones. Mr. Gupta was not there yet. The man took me into the basement, which was a long white hallway with rooms on either side. Walking down it, I smelled flesh fermenting in death. The stench came in sudden eruptions through a sweet orange smell. "What's that orange?" I asked.

"To try covering the stink. It never works, but we have a lot of it to use up." The stench was so strong that my stomach curled and actually hurt. Most of the rooms we passed had curtains but no doors. Some of them were lit and revealed fragile-looking metal tables waist-high and just slightly wider than a kitchen counter. We stopped outside a door that was bolted. The smell was so strong that my throat would take in only sips of air. The technician pulled part of his coat over his mouth and nose and said, "Oh, God," with familiar disgust. He flipped a light switch on the wall outside the room and opened the door.

The creatures on the bare floor did not appear human. There were three and they had swollen limbs and faces. Parts of their skin were gray and other parts black. For a moment shock kept me from seeing Ajay among them. Someone had taken his shirt and shoes. He was wearing white pants. Along his throat were two close-together black cuts, one starting almost above where the other let off. Then I realized that it was not dirt on his throat and his collarbones.

Once when Ajay was a child and visiting our office, he asked me to tie his shoelaces.

"Someone was sitting on his chest when they cut his throat. There were footprints on his shirt, along the ribs. Eight of his ribs are broken. But that could have happened in moving him."

"Put him on a table, for God's sake," I told the technician. And because I knew he would not listen to me, I added, "He's MP Roshan Gupta's son. Are you crazy?" I felt afraid for Mr. Gupta.

"I wasn't told anything," the technician said, lowering the lab coat. He was bald, with a thin face. He looked in my eyes to see if I was lying.

"Wash him, clean him. Or Mr. Gupta will put you in jail."

With me gripping Ajay by his pants and the technician holding him by his armpits, we were able to lift him onto a stretcher. Ajay's body had become rigid and this made him look surprised. We rolled him into a lift and, on the second floor, pushed him into a room where several men were sitting watching television. They had food spread on a long table with two sinks at one end. "Make him look all right. This is MP Roshan Gupta's son." I was not sure whether they believed me, but they set about their work, and I left the room.

I washed my hands with soap in one of the rooms on the second floor. The stink left them only after several washes. I then went outside. It was night now. The streetlights were on. Somewhere nearby dung chips were burning, giving the air a musty sweetness. The idea of Mr. Gupta's seeing Ajay as he was now frightened me, as if the event would add permanently to the weight of the world. While I waited I checked under my fingernails, because I could smell the stink again.

Mr. Mishra was the next person to arrive. I felt such relief at seeing him that I hugged him even before he had paid the autorickshaw driver. "I've been calling Mr. Gupta every day to have him sign something and he hasn't been calling back," Mr. Mishra said. "When I phoned tonight, a servant told me."

I described what I had seen, and we waited outside together. "I am glad my son has no political ambitions," Mr. Mishra said at one point, but mostly we were silent. I wondered why Mr. Gupta was taking so long.

We were about to go in and check on Ajay when, one after the other, perhaps ten cars and police jeeps pulled up before the morgue. The boy who parked for Mr. Gupta popped out of one and began lining the vehicles in a row along the road.

Mr. Gupta came to me and Mr. Mishra and thanked us for coming. He was wearing the suit he had worn at the prayer. We, along with Mr. Mishra, several BJP men, police officers in khaki uniforms, and five or six of Ajay's relatives whose names I did not know, moved together into the morgue.

Ajay was on a table on the second floor. The technicians had tugged a white short-sleeved shirt onto him, and they must have sprayed water inside his mouth and orifices, because drops kept slipping from his nose. The water somehow made Ajay appear more dead.

The stench was undiminished. My eyes teared from it, but perhaps from politeness, of the fourteen or fifteen men there, no one covered his mouth or nose. We stood around Ajay for several minutes. Mr. Gupta and Ajay's father-in-law, a tall Sikh with a loose white beard and a shirt pocket full of pens, stood closest to Ajay. His father-in-law was the only one crying, in slow sobs, like a candle beading as it melts. The BJP men whispered among themselves. A neighbor of Mr. Gupta's, a businessman, had taken off a heavy metal watch and was jiggling it in a loose fist. Two of Ajay's brothers-in-law, boys about seventeen and nineteen, leaned against a wall and looked at everything but him. Mr. Gupta kept turning his head from side to side, as if he was waiting for someone else to take charge.

I had to betray Mr. Gupta soon, I thought, or I would be betrayed. Here was a man who could not scare people away from killing his son. How was he going to win an election?

"He can't be taken home this way," Mr. Gupta finally said calmly, "he should be put in formaldehyde."

"Formaldehyde won't stop the smell," a technician answered. "The only thing that will stop the smell is a special coffin."

The BJP men stopped talking. The brothers-in-law looked at Mr. Gupta. But no one said anything for a while. "Shall we arrange the coffin?" I asked. Mr. Gupta appeared lost again. The only alternative was to take the body directly from the morgue to the crematorium.

Ajay's father-in-law said, "Yes, do it." He had a rich British accent.

For several minutes the crowd stood still as Mr. Gupta watched the body. The doctor was supposed to come and reassure them that Ajay's body would receive the best possible care. I did not want to stay for this. I told Mr. Gupta that I had to return home. He did not acknowledge what I said.

Mr. Mishra left with me, and when we were outside, he hugged me. "Be careful," he whispered, "you are better than these thieves." The road was empty and all the shops had closed. We walked half a kilometer or so to the nearest bus stop. We did not speak. Mr. Mishra hugged me again before he got into his bus and I into an autorickshaw.

At home the tapped telephone made me think of Ajay, and the phone became pregnant with danger. Once Mr. Gupta lost the election, the BJP would not continue to protect him. He had no history with them. His ability to raise money would cease once corruption charges were brought against him. Congress might even have him killed. Because I had raised the Congress money which Mr. Gupta stole and because I had managed the sale of school lands, there was no way his fall would not include me.

I lay on my cot and imagined disappearing with the campaign money. I would be found eventually and, if not, then the BJP's and Congress's anger would focus on Asha and Anita.

Congress was not as dogmatic as the BJP and would be easier to buy protection from.

Mr. Maurya was eating lunch by himself in his office, a small air-conditioned room. From the name printed on the paper napkins on his desk, I could tell that the food had been brought from a restaurant. When I sat down across from him, he said, "My wife is a vegetarian and won't eat with me if I am having meat." I smiled and nodded. "Will you come with me to Mr. Gupta's?" he asked, pulling off the last piece of flesh from a chicken bone and depositing the bone into a polythene bag with other bones. I was dressed in a white kurta pajama, ready to join Ajay's funeral procession.

"It's a tragedy," I said, and then, waiting a beat, "The boy caused so much trouble for his father."

Mr. Maurya considered this. "My leg is bad, so I can only walk a short while with Ajay."

I was encouraged. I again paused for a moment and said, "We are going to lose the election."

Mr. Maurya put the napkins in the bag and knotted it.

"If we are frank, it appears that way."

"What will Congress think of you for having worked with the BJP?"

"Sometimes you make mistakes." His allowing me to question him was promising. "The BJP will take Delhi municipality but will lose the Parliament seat. Congress will be angry for a while, but in time it won't be so bad."

"I want to protect myself." Mr. Maurya watched me. "My daughter just became a widow. I need to take care of her and my granddaughter." He remained silent. "You have friends in Congress who could help me," I said.

Mr. Maurya sighed and moved the bag to one end of his desk. "Friendship is just a word, Mr. Karan."

"I can pay Congress if they promise not to have me jailed or bring corruption charges against me." I did not want promises to be made to me. People either need to have a history together or need to be equals before promises between them count. My hope was that promises would be made to Mr. Maurya.

He could give Congress an enormous donation and claim that he had convinced me to betray Mr. Gupta in exchange for amnesty. Mr. Gupta's money would give Mr. Maurya more clout than the same amount donated from his own pocket.

"My business is local. I can't anger the BJP."

"The BJP knows Mr. Gupta is going to lose. Him against Rajesh Khanna. All they wanted was to put up some candidate against Rajesh Khanna. I'll pay the BJP, too. They'll be happy to get whatever money they can from his campaign and let Mr. Gupta go." Mr. Maurya sat back in his chair. "Friendship is just a word. Nobody expects your heart, Mr. Maurya." He did not say anything. "You've done a good job for Mr. Gupta. Now he is losing. That doesn't mean you haven't done a good job or that you should drown with him."

"How much money can I give Congress?"

"Seven lakhs."

"A nice amount." After a moment Mr. Maurya said, "I can help."

I reached into the plastic bag I had brought with me and pulled out one of the two bundles of bankbooks I had prepared. "Withdraw the money quickly."

Mr. Maurya took the bundle, put it in a drawer, and said, "We have to go separately to the funeral."

I thought Anita would be impressed by how well I was managing Mr. Gupta's betrayal.

Thirty or forty women in white saris were seated on Mr. Gupta's courtyard floor. There were about a dozen men, also in white. A tent roof had been put up for shade. Some of the people looked too poor to be Mr. Gupta's relatives and must have been servants recruited to make the mourning grander. The doors to one of the rooms that bordered the courtyard were open and I could see a gray steel coffin on the floor. The coffin was surrounded by more men and women in white. I did not know many Christians, so this was only the second or third coffin I had ever seen. It was half a meter deep and narrower on one end than the other. It appeared to be such an example of technology that it felt inappropriate. Some of the gathering were crying, but most were quiet and attentive. Servants in white were edging through the veranda pouring water from steel pitchers into glasses. Outside the house poor children stood barefoot and watched, in case food or used clothes might be distributed.

As I waited to see if a servant would direct me, I saw Anita leading Pavan into the room with the coffin. Anita had an arm around Pavan and they were taking small steps together. The crowd parted to let them get to the narrow part of the coffin. Anita eased Pavan down. When one of Ajay's brothers-in-law had called earlier and told me the time of the funeral procession, Anita had been specifically invited.

Mr. Maurya appeared, did not acknowledge me, and went and sat against a courtyard wall.

I entered the room with the coffin. There was no smell. Pavan was sitting hunched down into her knees. Anita saw me and came over. "The doctor gave her an injection," she whispered. "A calf has tried getting into the house the last few days and Pavan began saying it was Ajay reborn. We told her that the calf was at least six months old, but Pavan became crazy."

"What happened to the calf?"

"One of her father's friends has a farm and they've taken it there in case it actually is Ajay."

Mr. Gupta, Ajay's father-in-law, and the two brothers-in-law appeared. Again the crowd parted to let them get beside the coffin. They were all dressed in white kurta pajamas. They stood near the coffin not talking. Anita's face grew still and concentrated. "Ajay must have fought. Who can let his throat be cut?"

I went up to Mr. Gupta, but he did not appear to recognize me.

"Come," Ajay's father-in-law said, and one by one, with Mr. Gupta last, they stooped to pick up the coffin handles along its sides. They lifted it to their shoulders, which made me think that the coffin could not be as heavy as it looked.

As soon as the body was lifted, the women both inside the room and in the courtyard began wailing. Then, together, instantly, they stood. When the men took their first steps, the women mustered in front of them. Some of the women shook their hands while crying as if their fingertips were burnt. Others pressed their temples between their hands. The men attempted to move again, but the women would not budge. Mr. Gupta's and Ajay's father-in-law's faces were blank, but the brothers-in-law looked afraid. A few of the men in the room began moving the women out of the way. The noise was so great that I could hear only a few words of what these men were saying.

In the courtyard the coffin again became completely surrounded by women. They did not budge as they shouted, "What shall we do now?" or "Save us, God!" or "Why are you leaving us?" Mrs. Gupta appeared to be pushing Mr. Gupta so that he would drop the coffin. After a moment of standing in this frenzy, the coffin retreated.

A few minutes later it was again carried into the courtyard. Some men tried opening a path through the women, but the women kept filling whatever gaps were forced. Again the bearers began retreating. As they did, Mr. Gupta's wife shouted at Mr. Gupta, "You're a man. Push us out of the way." Mr. Gupta sobbed and stood still. A man grabbed Mrs. Gupta and shoved her stumbling out of the coffin's path. Others began doing the same to the rest of the women.

The weeping became enormous and inconsolable. I moved into a corner.

The coffin was finally carried out of the house, with its bearers quickly chanting, "God's name is Truth." About twenty-five men followed, also repeating this. It was so hot and bright that everyone was squinting. I was one of the last to join the march. Mr. Maurya was not far from me.

The house we left behind was wailing. Pavan had begun beating her head with her fists. Mrs. Gupta stood behind Pavan, with her arms wrapped around Pavan's stomach. Anita was sobbing.

The farther we got from the house, the quicker we walked. The poor boys trotted along, watching us silently. People came onto the balconies of their houses to look. Mr. Maurya accompanied the procession for a block and then got into a car. There were three groups. Directly behind Ajay's bearers were family and friends. Behind this was a smaller bunch of BJP men. Last was the largest group, neighbors and business acquaintances.

Mr. Tuli was among the BJP men. He had such a quick walk that his white hair seemed an affectation. Mr. Tuli was high up enough in the BJP that he could commit the party to a decision. I moved over to him and after saying "Namaste" did not wait for him to return the greeting. "Ajay brought it on himself," I said. "He must have been taking money and making promises, and maybe the people who gave him the money realized he couldn't keep his promises." I think some irrational part of me just wanted to finish the betrayal and so had set me jabbering.

Mr. Tuli kept repeating, "God's name is Truth," but he looked at me.

I was leaning over slightly, like a pimp whispering, "Girl. Girl." "In India," I said, "it doesn't matter if you were powerful once, or famous once. That's why there are these once-rich businessmen, like the Biscuit King, who get murdered in police custody. You have friends only as long as you are powerful." We had slowed down as I spoke, and now people were bumping into us. We sped up.

"It depends on the kind of friends you make," Mr. Tuli said.

I wondered if he was indicating willingness to offer friendship. "I believe in the BJP." Fear gave my voice more fervency than I had intended.

"Of course you do." We were looking into each other's eyes as we moved at almost a trot.

"I am a poor man who's had to raise three children on a peon's pay. Three daughters. Would you condemn a man for stealing to feed his family or marry his daughter?"

"You have two daughters, not three."

"But my son is stupid and so is dependent like a daughter." Mr. Tuli did not say anything to this. "God's name is Truth," I cried.

"I can't help you."

I knew the disgust in his voice could not last. "Mr. Gupta has lost the election. I have given Congress the money we stole from them. Less than we stole. I will give you the rest of Mr. Gupta's money if you promise no one in the BJP will hurt me or my family."

Mr. Tuli grimaced. "I've been loyal till now. I am only in trouble because I believed in the BJP. You don't want Mr. Gupta representing you. He's dirty all over. I am giving you his money. You can withdraw your support of him, and people will think the BJP is honorable not to back a corrupt candidate. If you don't help me, I'll have to trust in Congress."

"You believe in nothing."

We walked to the B-block bus stop without talking. The silence began making me nervous. Mr. Tuli could choose not to deal with me simply because he did not like me. After all, the money I was offering the BJP was not going into his pocket.

Near the bus stop an ambulance was standing under a neem tree. Several cars, jeeps, and vans were parked beside it. There was a water cart surrounded by funeral goers. The ambulance back was opened and Ajay's coffin was slid onto the floor. The bearers and Mr. Gupta climbed in and sat on the benches which ran along the sides of the ambulance.

"How much money?" Mr. Tuli asked. We were standing next to a white Ambassador sedan. People were within two or three feet of us and I imagined they could hear.

"Five lakhs." Being asked about money increased my confidence.

"Have you no shame or pride?" he asked, looking at me.

"I am afraid." Mr. Tuli's clean white hair, his broad, sturdy shoulders irritated me. "Will you promise me?" He did not say anything. "What use is it hating me now? The election is lost."

"Are you coming to the crematorium?"

"No." When this did not lead to an answer, I hissed, "Mr. Gupta steals from children. He should be hijacking school buses and stealing lunch money." Mr. Tuli emitted a startled giggle. "Do you want to give him the BJP's support?" Car and van doors were shutting. "Promise me no corruption charges. No beatings."

Mr. Tuli and I looked at each other for a minute. "Yes."

I was so relieved I thought for a moment that I had not heard correctly. I gave Mr. Tuli the bank deposit books.

• • •

Other than telling Anita what had happened, I had nothing to do that evening. I went onto the roof and stood watching the sky tilt from blue into red. It was the first time in a month and a half that I did not think I should be accomplishing something. There was a breeze. The day's traffic noises were easing. I thought of my improving health and all the years ahead of me. I had expected to feel guilt, but did not.

We had dinner, lentils and rice, on the roof. I was cheerful. "We're eating in the dark because your mother doesn't want us to see what's in the food," I said to Asha. Anita had been with Pavan most of the day and kept staring at things, the ground, a plate, and blinking slowly.

We watched the Hindi and English news on television. Anita had to be told about my betrayal because Ajay's funeral ceremonies were continuing the next day and she was supposed to attend. By then the BJP would probably have informed Mr. Gupta the party was withdrawing his nomination and he would have learned what I had done. Anita and Pavan's new friendship made me afraid that she would be angry at me instead of glad I had protected us. The television was turned off. I did not tell her what I had done. Anita and Asha went upstairs to their cots.

In the morning we ate breakfast. Asha went to school. Anita dressed for the next part of the funeral.

I was sitting on my cot in my underwear and undershirt. I also had socks on because I kept thinking maybe Mr. Gupta had not learned and I should go. "Why aren't you dressed?" Anita asked from the common room.

"I gave the money to the BJP and Congress." There was no need to identify what money. Anita entered my room and stood before me. Her lips were sunk at the ends. "Seven lakhs to Mr. Maurya for Congress and five to Mr. Tuli, who works for the BJP and is reliable." Anita kept looking at me. "I'm sorry," I said.

Anita turned and left. A little later I heard the living-room fan whirl.

Neither Anita nor I went to Mr. Gupta's.

That evening Mr. Gupta called. I was in my room, and Anita and Asha were on the roof getting laundry. Only after sitting on the sofa did I pick up the phone. I had been planning for this.

The ordinary introductory hellos let me understand that Mr. Gupta was not sure what I had done. "The BJP is not going to sponsor me," he said.

I waited and then said, "I know."

"You know?" Mr. Gupta sounded surprised.

"The BJP came here yesterday and told me. They took all the bankbooks. They said the money had been raised in their name."

"Why didn't you phone me? You should have phoned immediately."

"It was done. What good would phoning you be?"

Mr. Gupta was stunned for a moment by this answer. The oddness of my reply, I believed, might just possibly lead him to believe I had not acted willingly. Mr. Gupta began shouting. "You think I can't count. I know. I understand. You sold me into slavery."

"Several men from the BJP came here last night. They told me."

"I can have you killed."

"They told me I had to give them the books or they'd put me in jail. You are like my older brother," I said. Anita came into the room and I repeated everything for her to hear. "There were four BJP men. They said that you weren't their candidate anymore and if I didn't give them the money, they had a police jeep in the alley to take me away in. They said they would take me, shoot me in the chest, and throw my corpse in a ditch. Anita and my granddaughter were crying."

Anita leaned into the phone. "Guptaji, it's true. That's what happened. What could we do?" I was amazed by her joining me. "One of them grabbed my neck. Asha, my daughter, was crying."

Mr. Gupta hung up. I put the receiver in its cradle. Anita smiled nervously and sat on the bed. My heart was racing. We did not talk for several minutes.

Anita's lips began turning down. "I should go see Pavan. Maybe Mr. Gupta would have a harder time doing something then."

"I'm sorry."

Anita did not respond. Her lips pulled the rest of her face down. "What could you do?" she said.

I could have never gotten involved with Mr. Gupta. I could have withdrawn when Mr. Bajwa appeared. But Anita did not point these things out.

That night excitement and joy roused me out of sleep. Half awake, I did not understand where the pleasure was coming from, but I wanted it to be morning and for me to be drinking tea and hanging my laundry on the balcony ledge. It took several breaths for my thoughts to clear. Then I understood my happiness was from Anita's taking my side. Maybe Ajay's murder had frightened her with how complicated and violent the world was, and perhaps my confessions had made me appear less dangerous and readied her for some sort of reconciliation. Whatever the reasons, things were different.

My room was silent and dark. The flat beyond my door and the city outside the flat were also silent and dark. I lay on the cot and felt the world exhaling with me.

NINE

Two days after Mr. Gupta's nomination was withdrawn, our flat was raided by income tax agents.

The doorbell rang. Asha got up from the common-room floor, where we were eating breakfast. The bell could have been a holy man begging or the man who threw newspapers at our door, but I felt my attention arching. I had asked Krishna to come with his boys and stay with us because I had been worried about violence. They had brought shotguns wrapped in olive duck-cloth that they kept under my cot. Most of the day they spent lying on their sides on the floors of various rooms, playing cards and smoking rolls of bitter-smelling bidis.

"Income tax," a man's voice called from Anita and Asha's bedroom. Immediately five men sped into the common room. Munna and Raju jumped up. All the tax people wore the jackets and ties of office workers. I was frightened even though I was certain there was nothing to find in the flat. "Who is Ram Karan?" someone asked, and I stepped forward. A man passed me several identification cards. The stamps on the cards were accurate, but I showed them to Krishna to flatter him. Even as he was examining them, the income tax people spread through the flat. Munna and Raju followed them to see that no evidence was planted.

"Who are they?" asked the man who had given us the identification cards. He was in his early thirties and had hair only along the sides of his scalp.

"My nephews."

"Guns," somebody shouted.

"They are registered," Munna answered.

Krishna went to join his sons.

We moved into the living room, and I signed a document attesting to my name and residence. "It's all right," I whispered to Anita, who sat beside me on the sofa. I brought out receipts for the television, refrigerator, and some of the furniture. I was once offered a scooter as a bribe. I was glad I am frightened of driving. All my receipts were from local stores, which diminished suspicion.

The tax people went through the flat taking off the covers of pillowcases and poking in the flour and lentil tins. They turned upside down the can in the latrine that we use to flush. We tried to make sure they were never out of sight.

As minutes passed and nothing was discovered, Raju became bolder. "We're so poor, we hope you plant evidence."

"Shut up," said the man who had given me the identification cards.

When the tax people began gathering in the living room as if there was nothing to find, my fright eased enough for me to speak out. "I am a poor man. This is a registered slum," I said.

The raid took a little more than an hour. When they left, Krishna and his sons returned to their breakfast while Anita and I cleaned the flat. Looking around her bedroom, which appeared no different from before, she spoke to herself, "I'll mop today."

I was still uncertain of her tolerance of me. "There's nothing in the flat to find."

We ate our now-cold breakfast.

I went to work. I had been at the office for twenty minutes when Anita phoned. "There's a tax raid," she said. "I told them there was one two hours ago but they don't know about it. They have identification also."

"Should I come home?"

"No. They're just standing and talking in the living room."

"It's Congress and the BJP seeing if there's any more money to be had."

"At least the neighbors will think we're rich," she said.

I went to Asha's school that day because I wanted to comfort her if she was worried about the tax raid. But the way Asha talked of the raid, it appeared that she thought of it as an adventure.

That evening the man who tapped our phone called. "Mr. Karan," he said, "why didn't you come to me with the money you wanted to donate. I could have helped."

I wondered who this man was and whether he could still harm me. "I needed to get things done quickly."

"I wouldn't have been slow."

"I am sorry."

"I'm sorry, too."

The man remained on the line. "I wasn't thinking." He sighed and did not hang up. I thought he might want money. "I'm poor now."

When I did not follow this up, he abruptly said, "Okay. Tata," and clicked off. It was an hour before the dial tone returned, and at first I believed disconnecting my phone line was going to be his revenge.

Krishna and his sons stayed for three weeks. Asha and Raju would play badminton for hours on the roof. After they left, Anita and I began playing badminton with Asha. I played with her only if Anita was also on the roof.

•   •   •

I did not talk to Mr. Gupta again after I told him that all his campaign money was gone. I did not hear from Mr. Bajwa either. I had stopped thinking of Mr. Bajwa when his wife phoned.

The one phone for the junior officers is on a table in a corner. I had been sitting at Mr. Mishra's desk talking and got up to answer the ringing. As soon as Mrs. Bajwa introduced herself, I knew why she must be calling.

"My husband hasn't been home in three weeks," she said. "I haven't seen him." Mrs. Bajwa sounded both angry and afraid.

"He hasn't phoned here."

"I've called Mr. Gupta many times. He hasn't telephoned back." Mr. Gupta had not been to the office since the BJP withdrew its nomination. A corruption investigation had been started against him. As part of this, I had been interviewed and asked to mail in a form. "Perhaps you can help."

I immediately assumed that Mr. Bajwa was dead. I looked at his desk. Its top was bare. Mr. Bajwa was younger than I. "I haven't talked to him."

"Do you know where he could be?"

"You know what happened with the election?" She did not, so I told her of the withdrawal of the nomination and Ajay's death. When I told her about Ajay she began crying.

"My husband was emotional. I'm worried because of that. You know he became religious after he began being investigated? And then he stopped being religious after Mr. Gupta found work for him. His thoughts run around. That's why I'm worried." I wondered if she was suggesting suicide. The idea of killing yourself was so strange to me then that I believed Mrs. Bajwa did not want to imagine her husband assaulted and unprotected during his last moments and so was explaining things through suicide.

"Is there a guru he used to go to?" I suggested.

"I've already talked to him."

"Do you want me to talk with Mr. Gupta for you?"

"Yes."

I phoned Mr. Gupta as soon as we hung up, and left a message.

Mrs. Bajwa never called again.

Several days later Mr. Mishra learned that Mrs. Bajwa had appeared at Mr. Gupta's house and forced him to meet her. When he denied knowing what had happened to Mr. Bajwa, she became hysterical, claiming that Mr. Gupta was lying because he hated Mr. Bajwa and did not want to comfort his wife.

One Sunday afternoon, six or seven weeks after this, Mrs. Gupta and Mr. Maurya came to the flat. I had been asleep on my cot. Anita woke me and I went to the living room. Mrs. Gupta was sitting on the sofa holding her hands together in her lap. "Your friend has been kidnapped." I did not know whom she was referring to. "Your friend's wife has come to ask for help."

I sat across from them. Anita stood near me.

Mr. Maurya explained. There is a small lake in Model Town around which people walk in the morning and after dinner for exercise. In the morning people arrive on scooters and in cars but wearing bathrobes so people might think they live on the lake. Mr. and Mrs. Gupta had just begun their stroll when a police jeep pulled up beside them. Mr. Gupta was handcuffed and hurried into the jeep. When Mrs. Gupta called the police twenty minutes later with the jeep's license plate, she was told there was no such jeep. The kidnappers had phoned and said they wanted ten million rupees.

"I have no money," I told Mr. Maurya.

I knew Congress or whoever he was working for was trying to find out whether I had more money which I hadn't turned over.

"Think of your friend," Mrs. Gupta said. She had a square face and a round body. The brown sari she wore made her appear even smaller than she was.

"She called me," Mr. Maurya said, "because she thought I might be able to help sell her house quickly."

"I swear," I said.

Mrs. Gupta shouted, "The money you have is not yours."

That night Mr. Gupta's body was found in a ditch behind a

school. The kidnappers had spoken with Mrs. Gupta only once, and this convinced me that the murder was not for money but for revenge.

For weeks afterward I had dreams that someone was in my room and was going to kill me. Once, I woke up screaming "Help!" but neither Anita nor Asha came to see what had happened.

Of course, after Mr. Gupta's death, the corruption investigation against him vanished. The form that I had been told to fill out and mail in asked questions such as how I first met Mr. Gupta and whether I had any knowledge of potentially illegal activities in which he might have been involved. After Mr. Gupta's death, I kept the form in my desk for a week, then threw it away. I shivered when I took it out, as if I were picking up a hunk of hair and clotted blood.

Mr. Maurya came to the office one September morning and asked whether I wanted to collect money from Delhi's schools for the BJP Party, which had won Delhi. Without Mr. Gupta, the various groups within the education department, Hindi, English, Science, had begun collecting money separately. Principals were complaining about this. I told him I did not want to collect bribes.

"Why?"

"I'm afraid," I answered, and Mr. Maurya laughed.

When he left, he gave me ten thousand rupees. "A tip," he explained.

Autumn came, short-sleeved shirts during the day and sleeveless sweaters at night and in the early morning. During the summer, you start to think that everything bad comes from the heat and so begin believing that once the weather changes, the dark thorns in your spit will no longer be there. The temperature drops, yet you have only to rub your face at any time of the day and a film of grime rolls up onto your fingertips. Living in Delhi is like residing in a coal miner's lung.

The BJP won Delhi, but Congress formed a coalition majority in Parliament. Narasimha Rao, a seat warmer, a turtle of a man, someone who smacks his lips so much that I am sure he wears dentures, became Prime Minister and somehow held on to power because everyone expected him to die and spent their time preparing for that. And because he was so solidly dull, it took us a while to focus on him and discover that he, too, was a shameless thief. After he began to implement the World Bank's demands, Parliament members got into fistfights but finally agreed to the proposed budget. The day the BJP officially took control of Delhi, there was a swarm of trucks full of yelling loyalists racing around the city. Rajesh Khanna was shown on TV swaddled in geranium necklaces and was never seen or heard from again.

When I stopped seeing Mr. Gupta's posters, I finally felt that whatever could be resolved had been, and with passing time came a sense of having swindled fate.

Life continued as before. I saw Asha at her school several times a week. I paid Anita two thousand rupees at the start of the month. My weeks were so easy that I wondered whether I was not paying attention. At work, I napped and chatted with Mr. Mishra. When I arrived home, I drank tea and, before the weather changed too much, lay on the common-room floor with the radio.

After the nightly news, Asha continued wanting to hear stories. Because I had no more confessions, I began telling her about my past. I told her how when the king of the region that included Beri died, all the men and boys had to have their heads shaved. I told her about the young student who had lived down the alley from Radha and me when we were just married and who was possessed by a German ghost. Anita would be with us in the common room, listening. She appeared bored most days, and I was not sure whether she listened for entertainment or because she didn't want me to be alone with Asha.

Searching my life for interesting events, I began realizing how sprawling my years had been. Recounting the past somehow made it more focused, and this, after months of confusion, felt like one more source of wealth. There was a teacher I knew who went to Canada and returned for a holiday with a white woman. He was too cheap to stay in a hotel and they stayed with Radha and me for a week. The white woman was so afraid of getting sick that the only thing she ate was the chocolates that she had brought with her. Once, while the couple was out of the flat, Kusum opened the woman's suitcase and, along with Rajesh and Anita, swallowed five or six large chocolate bars. When the woman returned and discovered what had happened, she wept as though she had learned her mother was dead.

Asha laughed and talked to the characters in my stories while I recounted them. Anita listened silently.

Sometimes Asha would get angry at Anita's quietness. "Why don't you tell me a story?" she asked once.

"I don't have stories."

"Why?" It was obvious by then that Asha resented the difference between my gregariousness and her mother's reticence.

"I haven't lived as long as your grandfather."

"When do you think you'll be old enough to tell a story?"

Anita shrugged. Now that her anger was gone, she often appeared unguarded, crumpled, an abandoned house dissolving into the ground. I was afraid of openly defending Anita because I was afraid any help from me might appear unfair. In a just world I should be the one needing support. Listening to them, I thought that my good fortune had been intended for Anita but had come to me by mistake. The superstitious part of me shivered.

"What's wrong with you?" Asha demanded.

"Don't you love me?" Anita asked.

Occasionally Asha was kind. "I love you most in the world."

I felt that offering Anita comfort directly would be like a thief offering solace to his victim. But I tried giving Anita distractions. I brought home magazines and books. Anita read them, but she had no real interest. She could put a book down in the middle of reading it and only remember to go back when I asked her to tell me its story.

Before, Anita had been curious about current events. Now she no longer read the newspaper. I asked what she thought of Narasimha Rao and she answered, "We have tried idiots and villains as rulers, now we'll try not having a ruler at all." Her anger, therefore, had not vanished, nor her wit, but something had removed the banks through which they coursed and they appeared still.

There were occasions when Anita appeared engaged and happy with Asha. These were rare, but to encourage attempts at them, I bought playing cards. Anita refused to join us.

Anita loved visitors, though. When Rajesh came home, she was so happy that she followed him around the flat. From the concern she showed him—Do you have a heater? How many blankets do you have?—I realized that she was enormously lonely. Rajesh was too suspicious for such attention, though. He would turn her questions upside down and shake them to see if something dangerous might fall out and scuttle across the floor. Then his answer might be "I have enough blankets."

Anita started a brief correspondence with Kusum. They exchanged several pale blue aerograms with Anita's writing tiny and crammed with information and Kusum's long, easy sentences having such spaces in and between them that it appeared as if the details that give meaning had been sieved away. "You live on a hill? How high is it? Is yours the only house on the hill?" Anita wrote. "Do you come down the hill on a road, or on steps, or on a path? A station wagon? Is that a car or is that a wagon with horses? What do you wear to work?" When Anita told me a letter had arrived, she sounded as if she were boasting.

Kusum took longer and longer before answering and then stopped altogether. I wondered if Anita appeared needy or belligerent to her or whether Kusum just did not want to make the effort.

A few times, Anita took Asha and visited relatives around Delhi. They rented comic books for Asha and somebody was sent to buy sweets, but years of jealousy over Rajinder's success had made them see Anita as arrogant, and there was little Anita could do to win their affection other than beg.

Once, Anita told me a story of how she fell in and out of love with Rajinder over the course of a day. I found it so sad that I felt blamed and remained quiet, and, I think, appeared uninterested. As if I had missed the point of the story, all I could say was "Do you want to get married again?"

Anita began crying at this. It was the first time I had seen her cry in months. I had just returned from work and was taking off my shoes in the common room. I could not understand how such a sad and serious conversation could take place between my removing my shirt and my starting to unlace my shoes. Asha came into the common room then. Anita was in the kitchen. Seeing Asha, Anita turned so that her back was to us.

"What use would that be? I would still be the same person."

"Marriages are difficult. What happened was not your fault."

"It's not as though other men would be any better. I would have to be the one who changes."

"Are you complaining again?" Asha asked. She looked at me out of the corner of her eye, as if to have me admire her bold sarcasm.

Before I had even seen Anita turn and flash out of the kitchen, she was beside Asha.

I grabbed Asha by the neck and shook her so that I would be the one to hit her and she would not blame Anita.

"Cry, cry as much as you make other people cry," Anita said to Asha.

One night early in 1992, I went to Mr. Mishra's house for dinner. He wanted me to meet his son and daughter-in-law, who were in Delhi on a New Year's holiday. It was the first time I had been to his home. I got an autorickshaw right outside the alleyway and it took me quickly to Tilak Nagar. The night was so cold I sat on my hands.

The house was one story, white, and on a quiet side street amid a network of quiet side streets. There were no streetlights in Mr. Mishra's neighborhood and the autorickshaw's lamp did not work.

Parts of the road were excavated for sewer repair, so the autorickshaw had to maneuver cautiously. "This is it," the autorickshaw driver kept saying and stopping.

"This is not it. I want a 2/3."

Mr. Mishra was standing on his lit veranda and he called out, "Mr. Karan?" when the autorickshaw slowed before his house. I had begun thinking I would have to return home.

While Mr. Mishra opened the veranda gate, his wife and son Naveen came out to greet me. Naveen was short with enormously broad shoulders. Like his father, he was wearing a kurta pajama. "These roads are difficult, Uncleji," he said, and put his hands together in namaste.

"If it rains you can fish in the ditches," Mr. Mishra said.

"We think they're building a canal," Mrs. Mishra added. "Any morning we'll wake to a ship's horn. Will you have tea first or are you hungry?" Mrs. Mishra was a physical education teacher and I had once supervised her.

I followed them into a wide room where three sofas in an L surrounded a low table. In the back of the room, near a doorway, was a dining table. Naveen's wife, Lakshmi, sat on one of the sofas with her infant son asleep in her lap. She wore a yellow sari and her hair, which was long and straight, was loose on her shoulders. "Namaste," Lakshmi whispered when I came in. "I'll put him away," she said, and stood. The sofa cushions were shiny from wear, and some of the chairs around the dining table were mismatched. Till then, because Mrs. Mishra worked, and Naveen was an IAS officer, I had always thought of Mr. Mishra as wealthy.

When Lakshmi returned, she went into the kitchen with Mrs. Mishra to prepare tea and samosas before dinner. I asked Naveen if Lakshmi worked in the district where he was stationed and was astonished to learn that she had not studied beyond twelfth standard. "In the beginning my postings changed so much, Uncleji, and I wanted Raul to have the same care that I had as a child. No servant can take care of a baby the way a mother can." Probably Naveen had been asked this question many times before, for he continued, "Lakshmi is very smart. She was first in her standard and she went to a good school. She would have continued to college."

"Naveen's mother never went past higher secondary," Mr. Mishra interrupted, "and I have never thought less of her or imagined she could have been a better mother if she had."

"I did not even finish higher secondary," I offered, to eliminate any possibility that I was being condescending.

"But Lakshmi's grandfather wanted her married before he died and he was quite sick," Naveen finished. Because Mr. Mishra was so proud of him and because Naveen was an IAS officer, I had expected that he would want me to acknowledge his stature, but he never gave me that sense.

Lakshmi came out of the kitchen carrying a tray of samosas and papar. Behind her came Mrs. Mishra with a tray of teacups. The samosas were not very good, perhaps because Mr. Mishra could not afford good oil, but the tea was strong and sweet. The only other IAS officer I had ever met ran the docks of Bombay and was so rich that he had built an enormous house for his parents in Model Town.

Probably because Mr. Mishra and Naveen kept complimenting me by asking my opinion on the IMF negotiations or Narasimha Rao's chances of survival, I had the sense that the entire family was very smart. I was surprised that Lakshmi talked freely in front of her in-laws and that she had opinions on these issues. "Congress will fall after the next elections," she said.

I had known that I, too, was lonely, because of how much I enjoyed talking with Mr. Mishra at work, but only during that dinner, as my face got flushed and I kept smiling and spilling words everywhere, did I feel how extreme my isolation had been.

The snacks and dinner lasted hours. There were always two people watching me and listening or speaking. Through dinner, Lakshmi checked her baby every twenty minutes. There was rice, roti, two dry subjis and two liquid ones. I praised everyone and everything so much that I began wondering if I appeared to be lying.

By ten I was still excited enough to lean forward whenever I spoke. Mrs. Mishra and Naveen periodically put their hands over their mouths to hide yawns. I hoped they would offer another cup of tea even though I knew I should refuse if they did. I went to the bathroom.

The hallway was fifteen feet long, with two doors facing each other at the end. The bathroom was on the left. As I reached the doors, I noticed the one on the right was slightly open.

I saw a partially lit bed, Lakshmi's shoulder, and the side of the baby's head at an angle as if it was feeding. I thought, I can open the door; it might be considered an accident. Lust's mineral taste filled my mouth. I leaned forward to get a better look.

The door swung open without a creak.

Lakshmi looked up. Both her breasts were uncovered. The nipples were black. She stared at me in shock and did not say anything. I thought, Close the door. I made no move to do so. Still holding the baby, Lakshmi reached for a sheet at the foot of the bed. She couldn't get it. Act surprised, I thought. My face remained rigid. One second. Two seconds. Three seconds. Finally, I pulled the door shut as I whispered an apology.

T E N

A month later, I returned from work one evening. It was February and the sun had already set. There was a garbage heap smoldering outside the compound. I walked through the smoke into the courtyard. There were children playing cricket against a wall, with wickets drawn with coal.

My memory dawdles.

Asha was not waiting on the gallery. I did not notice this then. My eyes and nose were burning from the smoke. I entered the flat. I crossed Anita and Asha's bedroom. I walked into the common room.

Anita was on the balcony looking at the sky. She entered the common room, her arms wrapped around herself.

"Where did you go for lunch?"

I had eaten with Asha. Because I had rehearsed explanations for this confrontion many times, I even felt falsely accused. I had never touched Asha. "I've done nothing."

"I know. I looked. I would have taken her to a doctor." Anita was swaying back and forth slightly.

"I went to her school once for work and her principal told me that Asha cries all the time in class. I began going to see her. I wanted to help. I used to cry like that after Ma died." I started feeling fear.

"Be quiet," she shouted, and waved her hand in front of me as if saying goodbye.

"I visit her sometimes during lunch and talk. Only in a restaurant."

"How many times have you done this?"

I hesitated. "Often. There are always people around. Some of Asha's school friends even come with us and I buy them cold drinks." I stepped forward and Anita moved back. She looked ready to run away. All my explanations were coming out as I had practiced them in my head, but the extent of Anita's fear and anger made them unconvincing even to me. "I would never do anything."

"You did it to me. It was impossible then also."

This was the part I found most difficult to explain in the imaginary conversations I had conducted. "If I were still like that, I would have done something with all the chances I've had." I took off my short-sleeved sweater. I sat down on one of the chairs and sighed. I should have begged.

"Here you have raped your daughter till she bled. And then here you are with your granddaughter, rubbing yourself against her like she's a pillow. You wait twenty years between the two as if nothing has happened. People stop smoking for a decade and then start at a party." I had, of course, thought that perhaps Asha was safe with me only because my disease was latent. Anita held up a hand with the palm facing up, and then turned it down. "Who would trust you with a paisa?"

"I could already have done something if I was going to."

"I don't want explanations," she interrupted. "Look at what you've done to me," she said, and touched her throat.

I took off one shoe, as if continuing the daily routine of return-ing from work would make things normal. I was going to say I loved Asha, but stopped. "I am different."

"You were different, weren't you, when after twenty-some years you rubbed against Asha?" There was no answer to this.

"I'll give you more money."

"People don't change."

I had not started visiting prostitutes after going into Lakshmi's room. "People do."

Asha, attracted by our voices, came down the ladder onto the balcony. She looked tired. "What are you doing?" Anita shouted. Asha's face was so still it appeared tiny. "Upstairs!" Asha raced to the roof.

I took off my other shoe. For me bare feet are always about to step on glass or nails. "Anita, watch me. Guard me. I'll be your pris-oner. I won't be able to do a thing."

"I already thought you were my prisoner."

"Ask Asha every day whether I've seen her or talked to her."

"You might get her to lie."

"I don't know what else can be done."

"Neither do I." She was silent and then said, "Why don't you die?" She asked this and slumped. "I hate you. Even if there were no Asha, I would hate you."

We were silent for a long time. The sky lost its blue and became black. There were the noises of the squatters, the crank of a hand pump, and a man complaining loudly about something. Anita's eyes never left me.

Suddenly she said, "I am going to tell everyone. I want everyone to watch you. I am going to tell Mr. Mishra. I am going to tell all our relatives, the neighbors. I want everyone to help me watch you."

I didn't believe she could do it, but I said, "Don't do that."

"What else can I do?"

"You're not angry because of Asha. You're angry because of what I did to you. Nothing can be done about what's happened."

"Ha!" Anita shouted.

We stared at each other. Finally, she left and went up to the roof. Anita and Asha did not come down till the morning.

While Asha bathed, I left my room and came out into the common room. Anita, standing near the kitchen, said, "I am going to tell everyone." Now I believed her. She wore the same sari as last night. Instead of fear I felt sadness. How could my world end like this? We were standing on opposite ends of the room.

"If you do, I won't let you live here. If you do, I won't give you a paisa." My voice quavered.

Anita leaned forward with her shoulders, though she stayed where she was. "I can live somewhere else."

"Where? Who wants you? Who wants Asha? You're stupid if you think they do." I sounded pleading instead of angry and threatening as I wanted to.

A tap which had been splashing in a full bucket now began ringing in an empty one. Because Asha bathed with only one bucket, this meant she would be coming out soon.

Anita left the common room and went into the living room. I followed. "I'll change my will. When I die, which will be soon, you won't get the flat." The windows were closed and the light was slate. Anita went near the windows. I kept several meters away.

"I'll put you in jail."

"The police do nothing without money."

I remembered when she demanded I confess, and I shut the windows to muffle her screams.

"I am going to tell Asha when she comes out of her bath."

"We just left the common room, so Asha wouldn't hear."

"So?"

"Who will take you in? Your mother-in-law? If she learns what I did, she'll think Rajinder was cheated and married a whore."

"I have jewelry."

"You had jewelry before." I knew from this bad answer that Anita must realize her few options. "How much is gold selling for?"

"Enough."

"You'll have to stay here. And you know me. I'm shameless. Once your threat of revealing is gone, then what check will you have over me? As long as you have the threat, I'm stopped. Once the threat is gone . . ." I put my hands in my pockets, because they were trembling, and then I jiggled them to suggest sex.

Anita looked at me with disgust and anger for a moment and then walked past me into the common room. She returned almost immediately with Asha. She was cupping the back of Asha's head with one hand and pulling her forward. "Sit," she said, and moved Asha onto a love seat. Asha was wearing her school uniform. Anita sat down beside her.

"Your grandfather wants to touch you here." Anita put her hand on Asha's crotch over her skirt. Asha had no reaction to this. She turned her head in my direction. "Do you want to show her how you touched me?"

"No," I said. I thought that this was so strange, so unbelievable, that it would not be possible to remember it tomorrow. Then I wanted to sob, because this was the end of my life. "What's the good?"

"I want her to know what happened to me," Anita cried gleefully.

"Because it will make things different?"

"For me it will."

Anita gently pressed Asha back in the love seat. She put her hand under Asha's skirt and repeated, "He wants to touch you here. Then he wants to take out his thing. The thing boys have. A penis." Asha kept staring emotionlessly. "He wants to put his thing in you, from where you pee, even though it will hurt very much if he does. It will make you bleed."

"I don't want to do that at all."

"Don't let him. Don't let him," Anita said, and paused. She stared into Asha's eyes and asked, "You'll let him, won't you? Yes." Anita smiled softly and nodded. "Yes. Yes. It's fine to say 'Yes.' "

Asha nodded back.

"Stupid girl," Anita hissed.

"She'll say yes to anything you ask," I said.

"Don't let him. If you do, I'll kill you and I'll kill myself. Your grandfather is bad. Will you let him?" Asha shook her head no. "You will, won't you?" Asha continued shaking her head no. "You will?"

"No," Asha whispered.

"It will kill you if he does. I'll kill myself if he does. If you let him. Scream if he tries." Anita looked at me. There was nothing on her face.

Anita decided the first person she was going to speak to was Shakuntala, Radha's sister.

"Why make it worse? Asha wouldn't let me now."

Anita did not respond as she pulled a sandal strap around an ankle. She was sitting on her bed. Asha, still in her uniform, was standing beside her. "All this will do is destroy your only weapon."

"And if I don't do it?"

"I won't do anything." Anita watched me for a second and stood. I continued, "Nobody will help. People cry with you one day, two days. Then they say, 'She's always crying. Why does she bring her unlucky face here?' "

Anita left the flat. I had to lock the door, and by the time I caught up with them, they were in the alley. Asha was sobbing. I followed next to them, pleading. I was so confused by what was happening that I could not tell whether I was merely saying things or whether I believed them. "I'll make a deed turning over everything to you in three years. Even if I'm not dead, you'll have everything." People were noticing us, the rapidly walking woman holding the crying girl by the hand and the old, bald man beside them whispering feverishly. "I'll sell you the flat for five rupees if you come back home."

At the bus stop, like a child who does not want to go to school, I felt relief every time a bus approached and it was not for us. By then I had stopped talking. There was nothing to say. It was a hot bright morning. The road was as crowded as always and seven or eight people stood with us. We waited and waited. Sweat leaked down my back. "I've only been kind to Asha."

Anita snorted.

The bus came and we got on.

Anita did not look at me as the bus moved. Asha stood by herself. There were a few people between us. We disembarked in Morris Nagar near the Big Round-About. We walked on the sidewalk along the red-brick wall that encloses University Quarters. The trees that stretch over the wall were leafless. Occasionally a bus or an autorickshaw went by, but most of the sounds were birds chirping. I felt as though we were walking along a beach.

We entered University Quarters through a small gate. There were two rows of single- and double-story red-brick houses separated by fifteen or twenty meters of grass. The brick paths in front of the houses had long since disintegrated into yellow dirt. Shakuntala's husband was an administrator in the registrar's office of Delhi University. At one point I stopped walking and watched them proceed without me. Then, because I did not know what would be said, I followed.

Shakuntala opened the door. She was less than five feet tall, with an enormous wrinkled face. I became so afraid that I felt blood tingling through my hands and face. Shakuntala looked surprised.

"I must tell you something," Anita said, and Shakuntala led us across the courtyard into a room. The room was dark and had a television against one wall and cots along two others. Shakuntala sat on a cot and Anita, Asha, and I on another. Shakuntala had her head covered with a fold of her sari, because even though Radha was dead, I was still her family's son-in-law. I wondered if this was the last time I would have any social status.

"Water?" Shakuntala asked.

"No," Anita answered for us all.

I thought, I have to interrupt this. "You won't be able to keep the house after Sharmaji retires?" I asked.

"Maybe for one year. There are rules we must follow."

"He retires next year?"

"Yes. Why?"

Anita glared at me and then turned back to Shakuntala. "When I was Asha's age, Pitaji raped me. He did this many times." Anita said it so steadily, I was amazed. Shakuntala's mouth opened. She looked at me, and all I could think of was to protest that Anita had been older than Asha. I said nothing, and she turned back to Anita. It was done. I wondered where I would sleep in the new world that had just been formed.

"There used to be blood everywhere after he finished with me."

"Put Asha in another room," Shakuntala said.

"I've told her everything." Shakuntala looked uncertain. "It was like having a knife put in. When I first menstruated, I thought it was an old wound that had broken." Asha lay down on the cot and closed her eyes. "Ma found out, but what could she do? She had two other children. She sent Kusum to be raised by Naniji."

"Yes," Shakuntala said.

I wondered whether the "yes" meant she agreed with Radha's reasonableness or whether it was intended to comfort Anita by saying that the fact of Kusum being sent away was confirmable and Anita was believed.

"But Ma had to stay with him." Anita turned toward me and slapped me. I wanted to become invisible and didn't even touch my cheek. When I didn't respond, Anita hit me again.

"Of course." Shakuntala only cast brief glances at me.

"Last year, in May, I caught him touching Asha. I told him not to do it. Yesterday I learned he's been going to see Asha at school."

"I didn't know people like you existed in real life," Shakuntala said to me. She used the familiar you.

"I haven't done anything to Asha." The more times I repeated this, the more times I felt that this was just an excuse, that if not now then sometime later I would have touched Asha.

"Come here, daughter." Anita went and sat by Shakuntala, who embraced her. "Don't worry, I'll take care of you." Anita whimpered and started crying against Shakuntala's neck. "What unhappinesses God has given you." Anita cried and repeated her story with more details. Shakuntala occasionally rocked Anita back and forth.

In the early afternoon the doorbell rang. "It's him. Coming home for lunch," Shakuntala said, too traditional to use her husband's name. She got up.

"Mausiji, will you tell him for me?" Anita held Shakuntala's hand and looked into her aunt's eyes as she asked this. "I don't want to cry anymore."

Shakuntala gazed at Anita sadly for a moment. "What's the use of telling him, daughter? It will only make it harder to convince him to let you live with us."

When I saw the surprise on Anita's face, I knew she had not believed my warnings. I felt a little relief. Perhaps this confirmation of what I had said would cause Anita to stop. Shakuntala went and let in her husband, Mr. Sharma.

During lunch I talked the most, trying to keep the conversation off why the three of us had suddenly appeared in Morris Nagar. To talk and pretend nothing had happened filled me with energy. The excuse we used was that Asha had been sleeping a lot and we wanted Mr. Sharma to examine her. Mr. Sharma had bought a doctor's certificate a few months earlier as a source of income after retirement and had begun building a practice by writing the first prescription free.

Asha was woken to eat, and after she finished, Mr. Sharma asked a series of questions, most of which Asha answered no to. He wrote Asha a prescription and left for work.

Anita told Shakuntala she wouldn't stay in Morris Nagar. "I only wanted to let you know what he did." Shakuntala answered she was glad to learn and made no further offer of help.

I was amazed to leave the house and see the world still there and hear the birds.

We went to Bittu's house next. Bittu, Radha's brother, lived in Sohan Ganj, a ten-minute walk from our home. He had two rooms in a three-story building which had been built by his grandfather. The house was divided among him and the several sons of his father's brothers. His two rooms were shared with his wife, son, and daughter-in-law.

Bittu was asleep in one room, and in the other, the three members of his family were sitting on a bed drinking tea and playing cards.

Anita interrupted the offers of tea that greeted us with "I have a serious thing to tell."

Bittu's son, Rohit, woke Bittu. He entered the room sneezing. He wore a kurta pajama and carried a string of worry bends in one hand. Vibha, his daughter-in-law, brought him a chair. We also had chairs and were sitting in a row in front of the bed and Bittu's chair.

"I must tell you something," Anita said.

Bittu looked at me, as if to ask what it was about. I gave no response.

"When I was a child, he raped me." Anita turned toward me so that there would be no mistake as to who "he" was.

"Remove the child!" Bittu's wife, Sharmila, shouted. Rohit immediately stood and took Asha out. We all waited in silence. I wondered what would happen if I got up and left. In a day of impossible things, this appeared no more unlikely than anything else.

The story was told again. Sharmila kept interrupting with questions, because she found everything so unbelievable, and Bittu repeatedly told her to hush. Nobody said anything to me, though they watched me with such attention that I began looking at the floor. The floor was made of a yellow stone with green specks in it. I wondered what would happen to Anita. Nobody was going to take her into their home after this rumor spread, and it would spread, because scandal always did.

At some break in the story, which had been going in circles, Sharmila said, "Bring the older people. Something must be decided."

"Yes," Bittu agreed, and went to collect the men of his and my generation and the one person, his father's sister, surviving from the previous one. They gathered, one by one, in Bittu's front room. These were Radha's cousins and they had known me for thirty-five years, during which, just because I was the family's son-in-law, whenever we met in the street they felt compelled to buy me a cup of tea or a cold drink.

Anita told the story again. It was late afternoon. The audience was louder now. "In the old time we could have killed him," a man said. The members of the group egged each other on.

"The police would not care if we did."

"Look up," shouted Koko Naniji, Radha's aunt. I did, and the glares made my head drop again.

Anita looked with great concentration at whoever spoke.

"What were we thinking when Radha was married to him?" someone asked.

"Poor Radha," people periodically said. I wondered whether Anita realized that the loyalty of Radha's family was to Radha, not to her. Sharmila and Vibha made tea and began passing around teacups. I was given one also, which I found comforting.

"Get the girl away from him."

"Who, Asha?"

"Asha also."

"Anita needs a home of her own."

"Homes don't grow on trees."

"Neither do daughters."

"She needs protection."

"We are here."

"She can't live with us forever."

"Why not?"

The decision was made by acclamation. Marry Anita. Then people began murmuring about the dowry. "In this bad world no one will marry a widow, especially one who doesn't work and has a child, without a dowry."

"Will you give her a dowry?" Koko Naniji asked.

It took a moment for me to realize that the question was addressed to me. I looked up to say yes, and this time my head did not fall. If Anita got married, my responsibilities would end.

"I don't want to marry," Anita said.

The voices trailed off.

"What do you want, daughter?"

"I don't know."

"Think of Asha," Sharmila said.

Anita looked at the faces watching her. Evening had come and there were shadows in the room. Soon the lights would be turned on.

"What do you expect from us?" Bittu asked.

Anita did not answer.

"Rahul is a widower," someone offered. For a while names and suggestions were exchanged. It seemed Anita's desires had been ignored.

People began dispersing back to their rooms. No one made Anita an offer to let her stay with them. Koko Naniji was the only one to even acknowledge we were leaving. She did this by giving advice. "Lock him in his room at night. Give him a bucket to piss in."

The stars were out as we walked through the narrow alleys that connect Sohan Ganj to the Old Vegetable Market. A wind carrying dust and bits of gravel coursed around us. The sounds of people leading their lives, cooking, talking, listening to the radio were everywhere. I wondered if Anita's anger had at last eaten everything it could reach.

I opened the flat door and let Anita and Asha enter before following. "Go take a bath and change your school uniform," Anita said. Asha left to do so. I realized with surprise that I would sleep again on my cot tonight.

I sat on the sofa in the living room. Anita went to the phone and, after looking something up in the phone directory, began dialing a number. I did not dare ask whom she was calling. The fluorescent light above me thrummed.

"Hello, this is Anita. I'm Mr. Karan's daughter. Yes. Is Mr. Mishra there?"

ELEVEN

The phone is black, heavy, with a metal bottom. There are brown stains on Pitaji's scalp. I wonder whether they mark where his skull is softest, like bruises on a cantaloupe. The triumph of telling the world faded when I sat in Bittu Mamaji's rooms. I smelled masala roasting, somebody's dinner, and thought, What now? Calling Mr. Mishra is joyless. As I explain to him what Pitaji did, fear for the future clambers into me. Pitaji wheezes while I speak.

"Do you want to talk to Pitaji?" I ask when I am done.

"No," Mr. Mishra says. He stays on, and I have nothing to add. I put the phone down without saying goodbye.

Pitaji stands and, looking at the floor, walks to his room.

Asha is asleep on our bed. The side of her face is pressed into her pillow while one arm stretches ahead as if she were swimming.

After half an hour, I shake Asha's shoulder and say, "The whole world is dying for you and you're asleep." She opens her eyes immediately, as if even in sleep she is waiting. "How old are you that you need this much rest?"

I decide to clean the flat. It is my flat, too. I mop on my knees. Asha dusts. I want to punish Asha for sleeping all day. She had slept while sitting on a chair at Bittu Mamaji's and almost fallen off. I suffer and she cannot even watch.

As I swing the gray rag from side to side and crawl over the floor, I keep thinking, I have nothing to threaten Pitaji with. To be angry without power is to be ridiculous. Asha finishes before me because dusting is easier. She does not thank me for doing the harder labor. She goes to bed again. Kneeling in the common room, I call out, "If it weren't for your school, I would live with Rajesh." The words shame me. I stop working and stand. To be hopeless means believing there is no future different from the present. I leave the bucket and rag where they are and go to Asha.

I lie beside her. I ask Asha to drape herself over me. I used to ask Asha to do this sometimes when Rajinder was alive. I repeat my request until she complies. Asha smells like sugary milk. I smooth the back of the gown she is wearing. "This flat is mine. We are going to live here forever," I say. Her breathing does not change and I realize that I can offer her no safety.

Pitaji stays in his room that night.

I worry over my choices.

I cannot marry. Marriage would mean having to share what little I have with a stranger.

No relatives will keep me in their home for long. I lived with Rajinder's family for a month after he died. Even to think of being homeless, of remembering to put back in your suitcase everything you take out, is exhausting.

In the morning and during the day I think, If Pitaji tries to force us from the flat, I will stand on the gallery yelling his crimes to the compound till he relents. I know this is not a good plan.

Pitaji does not leave his room.

At night I keep a hammer beside me. Several hours after going to bed I hear water splashing in the latrine bucket. It is a hollow sound at first, and then, as it thickens and my mind rouses, I know Pitaji is no longer in his room. I had expected Bittu Mamaji and Shakuntala Mausiji to come during the day and see what was happening. Again I count the money I have taken from Pitaji. If I did not have to pay for housing or Asha's school, we could live on it for a year.

In the morning Asha goes to school. I spend the day waiting for Pitaji. He does not appear. The next day also passes this way. At night the refrigerator door opens and closes and the water bottles clink. I grip the hammer's wooden handle. Pitaji bathes. Like a child afraid of moving in her bed for fear of attracting the ghost that is in the room, I lie still. Once, I squeeze Asha's hand so tightly that she wakes hitting me. A week goes by without my seeing Pitaji. One morning I find his undershirt bunched on a chair in the common room. I become so panicked, I throw it into the squatter colony.

During the day, when I am alone, any unexpected sound can cause my heart to thump. At night I dream regularly that my hammer is being wrested away. I put a knife under the bed. Sometimes I wake to find the light from the common room bleaching the darkness on my face. Another week goes by.

When Asha is at school and Pitaji is behind his blue door, the idea that there is no one to help me makes me so lonely and afraid that I begin boiling sheets or washing all the walls with soap. By working hard I can prove the flat is mine.

With Asha home, I feel better, even though we hardly speak. She often goes to the roof with her schoolbooks. Asha never mentions Pitaji's absence. Once, I ask her what she is thinking. Asha answers, "I didn't say anything."

Waiting distorts time. I sometimes imagine I will get white-haired and Asha will leave home for college and then one day Pitaji will emerge from his room unchanged.

•　　•　　•

But I know Pitaji will reappear soon. To delay this, I begin preparing elaborate meals for Pitaji before going to bed. I hope that if he has good food he will be less likely to reenter the world. Every morning I also slip the newspaper, unfolded till it is thin enough, under his door.

Weeks into this strategy, its purpose changes. I now cook as a bribe, to diminish the anger he will feel when he finally starts living in the day. Perhaps we can return to where we were. We could live together again. The purpose alters, because I realize Pitaji cannot stay in his room forever. When he comes out he might force Asha and me to leave the flat.

One morning, while I am in the kitchen cleaning the breakfast plates, Pitaji's door opens. He is wearing pajamas with an undershirt. His face is gray with beard. My blood fizzes from adrenaline. My hands become numb. Pitaji stares at me. His beard makes him look dangerous. As his mouth twists to speak, I run to the balcony, up the ladder, to the back of the roof.

My fear is so basic that I do not understand it. Until I saw Pitaji, I had been willing to live with him. I take small breaths. Delhi's roofs line all the horizon. Pitaji had said that if I told people, in a year or two he would forget his shame and repeat his crime. This I know will occur. This is his nature.

I come down in an hour. Pitaji is back in his room, his door closed.

Later, I am kneeling on our bed, ironing a sari, when Pitaji reappears. My back is to him as he enters our room. I spin around. I consider leaping to the gallery and then down the stairs. Pitaji has shaved. He stares at me. He has on pants, shirt, and shoes. His lips are parched white. I had wanted to wall him from the world by revealing his crimes. His leaving the flat means I have failed and shame has no power over him.

"I didn't do anything to Asha," Pitaji says.

"Enough. What you did."

Pitaji stands and watches me for minutes. I cannot look away. All the weight he has lost makes his face drape. Pitaji touches a cheek with his fingertips. This is a new mannerism and I wonder if it comes from being alone too long. Pitaji appears to shake before me, like broken film fluttering in a projector.

"You don't have to leave," he offers softly.

"I wouldn't. Even if you tried. The flat is mine."

Pitaji is quiet, as if he is planning. After a while he says, "I'm not so bad a man."

I laugh. In my fear I had forgotten how strange he is. He keeps looking at me. I wonder what he is thinking. Pitaji goes out into the sun.

I continue to press the sari. Pitaji will attack Asha someday. This is as likely as gravity. I must now leave these rooms and live the rest of my life on other people's kindnesses. Maybe Kusum can give me money, but I cringe at the thought of her resentful generosity.

The hot press releases a sweet soap smell from the clothes. I was the first person in our extended family to own a press. Rajinder bought it for me. Rajinder was hard. Once, when we were robbed by a cleaning woman, he demanded the police beat her till she showed us where she had hidden my bracelets and Rajinder's watch. I do not have the courage to go to the police and make up a story that Pitaji tried to rape Asha.

Perhaps an hour later, as I put the clothes in their cupboard, I hear a neighbor outside say, "What are you thinking, Karanji?"

"Nothing," Pitaji answers. I peer into the gallery. He is standing at the very end, near the steps to the compound. His back is against a wall and he is looking straight ahead, with his shoulders hunched and a hand on his cheek.

Pitaji returns. He walks past me without meeting my eyes, goes into his room, closes the door.

Pitaji's room can be bolted from the outside. The bolt makes a scratching noise when I draw it. I do not think about what I am doing till the bolt is at rest. Pitaji must have heard me, but he does not ask me to unbolt the door.

I then take Pitaji's medicines, his diuretics and beta blockers, his brown glass bottles, orange plastic vials, two cardboard boxes, one of pink tablets and another of blue, from the refrigerator and throw them in the dustbin on the balcony. I do this and go to the living room. I stand there shifting from one foot to the other. I enter the common room briefly and see Pitaji's locked door. I go to my room, where I sit on my bed and look at the floor while gripping my knees. Ten minutes later, not certain whether I am hiding my act or keeping Pitaji from saving the medicines, I shake the dustbin into a polythene bag, race from the flat, down into the alley, throw the bag into a garbage woman's wheelbarrow.

Soon after Asha returns from school, Pitaji knocks on his door. Because he did not first try to open it, I know he was aware of being locked in. Asha, still in her uniform, is drinking water near the refrigerator. I unbolt the door and step aside. Without looking at me, Pitaji goes to the latrine. I wait next to the door. I do not acknowledge Asha's gaze. When Pitaji returns, he pulls the door shut behind him.

Asha goes to the roof with her school bag.

I am ashamed of myself and want to love her. From the balcony I call, "Do you want juice?"

Asha comes to the top of the ladder and looks down. "I will forget you. Both of you. When you are dead, no one will ever think of you." I want to grab Asha and beat her till she falls to the ground crying.

I go back into the flat. The refrigerator even looks empty. I smile.

At night, before I go to bed, I unbolt Pitaji's door.

When Pitaji comes and kneels beside where I sleep, the fluorescent arms of the clock are past two. I am not afraid and do not reach for the hammer or the knife. "My medicines. They're not in the fridge."

"I don't know." I pretend to have been woken. I am on my side facing him.

"My medicines?"

"Am I your doctor?"

Pitaji sits on a chair across from the bed. I keep my eyes slitted open. He stays there for nearly an hour. He looks like a dark mound.

Earlier, he looked so weak standing at the edge of the gallery that I know I can fight him.

The next morning Pitaji goes to his doctor. I feel that I must continue my war. A few minutes after the door closes behind him, I phone Dr. Aziz. I tell him who I am and say, "My father raped me when I was twelve." He does not respond to this. I want to tell him all the details but am embarrassed. "I have a daughter who is young. Do you think he might rape her?"

"I don't know anything about that. I have never talked with him about such things." His voice is hesitant and sad.

"Thank you."

"Can I help?"

"No," I answer.

Pitaji returns and, unexpectedly, puts his medicines in the refrigerator again. When he is sitting on his cot undressing, I come and stand in his doorway. Pitaji looks up, frightened. His thinness and fear turn him mysterious.

I ask, "What did Dr. Aziz say?"

"He said I was fine and gave me new prescriptions."

"What do I care about that?" I smile to let him see my hate. "Did he tell you I phoned and told him about you? He kept quiet, so I told him about the newspapers you put under me to catch the blood. He called you a monster."

Pitaji watches me. I glare at him. He stands unsteadily and closes his door in my face. I bolt him in. I then take his new medicines, put them in the paper bag he brought them home in, and slip the bag over the balcony's ledge into the squatter colony.

My revenge begins this way.

I start cooking six rotis for Pitaji instead of four and pouring a spoon of butter on each. I am not responsible for his appetites.

Pitaji is locked in all day. At night, before going to bed, I unbolt him. He so thoroughly eats everything I prepare that I worry he is throwing away the food. I check in the latrine and I check in the squatter colony, but there is no indication of this. We rarely speak. He occasionally comes into my room and wakes me to ask where the laundry soap is or where to find a needle and thread. He does not mention his medicines again.

One Sunday afternoon, while I am in our room, Asha opens Pitaji's door and demands that he come out and watch television. She is saying, "Come here," when I enter the common room. Pitaji is on his cot staring at Asha. I grab her and hurl her away from the door. I lock him in again.

The weeks pile into months. Mrs. Chauduri from work phones. I can tell from her false solicitousness that she is hoping for gossip. "He is sick," I say, and we end the conversation. No one from Ma's side of the family tries to contact us. Krishna calls. "You have the shamelessness to pick up the phone," he says. "Bring my brother." I hang up. I am surprised that the news has taken so long to spread. He calls a minute later and, without any insults, asks for Pitaji. Pitaji says he is fine and that yes he cannot understand the lies I have told about him. Pitaji's stomach has again begun to spill into his lap. I am in the doorway to my room. After Pitaji hangs up the phone, he tells me, "I do everything you want." He appears to wait for me to say something. I do not, and sighing, he stands and leaves for his room. I bolt him in.

Perhaps three months after I first locked Pitaji in his room, Shakuntla Mausiji and Sharmila Mamaji visit one afternoon. I had stopped thinking of the outside world. I hear the doorbell and unbolt him. I often wonder how he spends his day. The only times I see him are when he wants to leave his room. Pitaji is lying on his cot in his underpants looking at the ceiling fan. He must have heard the bell, too.

Mausiji and Mamiji sit on the living-room sofa. Both are small and fat, with nearly white hair. I prepare tea and bring out biscuits.

"How are you?" Mamiji asks when I return from the kitchen.

"Good."

"We worry about you," she says. This cannot be true, for why has it taken them so long to visit?

"Now what, daughter?" Mausiji asks. Shakuntala Mausiji is Ma's older sister, and even though I know not to believe that people of her generation are especially protective or wise, I expect them to be.

"Have you thought of marriage?" Mamiji interprets the question. "There is a man I know who works in a ball-bearing factory. He is good, but was married to a Muslim for two years."

Because I am worried they might discover what I am doing to Pitaji, my voice remains softly polite. "One marriage in one life," I say, trying to appear as traditional as possible.

"Throw yourself on a pyre, then?" Mamiji responds.

"Asha can live with us," Mausiji says. "It'll make getting a husband easier."

Hearing this is a shock. "Asha is the light of the world."

"Daughter, don't cry."

I wipe my face with a fold of my sari.

"Something has to be done," Mamiji says.

"Pitaji is fine to live with."

"It might be safer for Asha to be away," Mausiji adds.

Immediately tears roll down my cheeks. "Don't say that." I cannot imagine what might force me to give up Asha. Without her not a single good thing would have happened in my life.

After a while Mamiji asks, "Should we say hello to your father?"

This frightens me. "He's lying down," I say, hoping they will understand this as his being asleep.

"Is he awake?"

"I don't know."

Together we go into the common room. Pitaji is still lying in his underpants.

"Namaste," Mausiji says.

After a moment Pitaji replies, "Namaste."

"How is your health?"

"All right."

Mausiji and Mamiji exchange glances. They linger. I think they cannot decide whether to mention the man who works in the ball-bearing factory.

"Namaste," Mausiji says. They depart.

This time I do not close Pitaji's door till I have washed the pot the tea was made in and the cups in which it was drunk. Bare and still and so passive, he does not seem dangerous. But I cannot imagine the future with him in it. The need to live is so strong that only a mountain piled on top can stop it. With Pitaji, living is the same as destroying. He was able to wait twenty years and then act exactly the same as he had before. Yet nothing in his soft round face or his swollen stomach demands the death I wish him. When I close his door that afternoon it is not to cage him, as it has been before, but to remove him from sight so I can forget.

"I am a good woman," I say to myself.

"Who can understand what I have suffered?"

"Or how alone I am."

In the weeks and months that come, I forget him, sometimes for several hours. Then something will remind me and I will know exactly when I last thought of him and how I nearly imagined him while mopping the floor, and again when the fan's breeze stirred some newspapers. I talk so little, I begin to envy Asha for being able to go out into the world and speak to other children.

Late one night Pitaji begins to scream. He is so loud that Asha jumps upright on the bed still half-asleep. "What?" I say to her, as if I cannot hear. Pitaji continues. The shrieks are high and desperate. I turn on all the lights and go to the common room. Asha follows. I look at his blue door. It is unbolted and he has not been out that night. "He'll ask if he needs help," I murmur.

"Do something," Asha says angrily.

"He knows what's best for him."

"God!" Pitaji bays.

The fan whirrs. The tube light keeps the dark dammed out of the common room. At times Pitaji's cries drop, becoming moans.

The doorbell rings. I go to answer it. It is the woman from next door, a widow with such a square face she looks almost like a man.

"Pitaji ate onions with yogurt and got a stomachache," I say. Asha is with me.

"When he had his heart attack, my boys kicked open your front door." She is smiling, as if this was an adventure, and then, almost with regret, says, "This time we won't have to." She leaves.

The cries stop an hour or so before dawn. But Pitaji does not appear that morning. Late in the afternoon, when I have begun thinking I should check to see if he is alive, Pitaji enters my bedroom. I am sitting in bed reading the newspaper. He is wearing only his underpants. His stomach pushes their top down.

"I'm not dead," he says quietly. He comes and stands close to me.

I remain silent, because I do not know how he will react to anything I do.

"I cannot die, serpent."

Then he goes back to his room and lies on his cot. He does not close the door. I am too frightened to do so. I stay in the living room. When Asha descends from the roof into the common room a little later, Pitaji calls out to her, "Your mother is murdering me. She throws away my medicine and is feeding me so much I have had another heart attack." I come into the common room. Asha looks at him and then at me. It is strange to have everything described so clearly. Asha climbs back up the ladder. "Murderess," Pitaji tries shouting, but his voice is no louder than a normal person speaking. He falls asleep and I lock his door.

When he wakes, he shakes the door instead of knocking on it as he normally does when he wants to be let out. I bolt him in when he goes back to sleep.

The thing that made him scream also leaves him without energy. Most days he remains on his cot. But he no longer lets me lock the door. As soon as he finds out he is locked in, he begins shaking the door.

One afternoon he comes into my room. I am sitting on a chair lengthening Asha's school skirt. "I don't want to see your unlucky face," he says. His voice is buried and far away. "Keep the door closed. But I am no animal to be locked in."

At first I am half relieved, because it suggests Pitaji will stop me eventually. But he does not go to buy his medicines and he continues to eat the ridiculously rich food I make. I put butter even in his yogurt.

The new compromise works for a while.

I want to celebrate Asha's birthday quietly. I do not know what Pitaji might do if he finds out. I make halva for her before she goes to school. I pray with her in our room.

Asha takes the bowl of halva I have given her to Pitaji's door. "Nanaji, it's my birthday. Do you want some halva?" I am in the kitchen.

Pitaji opens his door. Asha holds the bowl forward with both hands. He looks surprised and then angry. Pitaji takes the bowl and turns it upside down in front of Asha. The spoon in it clinks on the floor.

Pitaji stops lying on his cot except at night. He wanders the flat. Periodically he grabs folds of his stomach, shakes it at us, and speaks in a falsetto, as if it is his stomach talking. "After he dies, will I keep living?" I refuse to answer him when he is in such moods. In front of Asha he has his stomach say, "It's his penis that made problems, not me. Why should I die, too?" Mostly Pitaji makes pronouncements and does not attempt conversations.

Pitaji tries to enter every part of our lives. He plays cards against himself on our bed. He sits beside us during meals and sometimes in the middle of them starts spooning subji from our bowls and breaking off pieces of our rotis. I can't touch my food after he's touched it. He treats Asha the same way he treats me. I ignore him, and Asha begins to follow my example.

Pitaji sometimes comes into our room in the middle of the night and turns on the light and sits at the foot of the bed without saying anything. Sometimes his anguish stirs my own and I wish to comfort him. In these moments I look away.

But one day I notice Pitaji's ankles are dirty. Then I understand that patches of his skin have turned black from the absence of blood. I start to cry. When unhappiness is so great, how can one separate mine and yours?

Pitaji looks down at his ankles and murmurs, "My life."

There is a period when Pitaji takes to leaving the flat. He goes down the gallery to the flat next to ours and tells the widow who lives there and her two sons that I am killing him for money I believe he has.

The widow tells me this. "If we had money, wouldn't we spend some?" I tell her. I am afraid of being robbed and murdered if rumors of wealth spread.

Then Pitaji goes down into the compound and tells them what he has done to me but claims that these are all lies. I learn from the widow that he cries as he tells the story. Then he always tells his audience that he is being slowly poisoned for money.

I do not care that he is telling them what happened or claiming that this was a lie. But I worry about crime. One evening, when he is wandering around the compound with his story, I go down and shout, "Senile fool, leave these people in peace." Then I address the two old women he had been talking to: "Come upstairs. Look in my home and see what we have that's worth stealing." They follow eagerly while Pitaji stays downstairs. I show them how dull my knives are. I point out that I've been thinking of buying a deodorant for the latrine but don't want to get caught up in unnecessary expenses.

One day Pitaji comes into my room and announces, "I am taking the flat back." He is wearing pants and shoes. Going down the gallery, he moves with his feet splayed out and carefully, as if he is afraid to slip. I wonder how the clouds and blue sky look to him.

When he returns from his lawyer, he again lies down on his cot. It is the last time he leaves the flat.

Once, I find Asha standing beside Pitaji's cot.

"Come here," I demand, and she does. Pitaji looks at the ceiling.

His face is wet as it almost always is. "What were you talking about?"

"I asked why he cries all the time."

Asha looks at me. She has the face of someone so much older that I am afraid. "What did he say?"

"He said he doesn't want to die."

TWELVE

K usum worried as she watched the low white buildings of Indira Gandhi International Airport drift by the window. The flight had been delayed in London, and it was early morning. To Kusum the slow confusion of the trucks and vans guiding the plane seemed the result of fatigue. Ben, Kusum's husband, was asleep in the aisle seat, and their six-year-old daughter, Carolyn, her bare feet hovering midway between seat and floor, lay dozing in the center. Kusum and her family had arrived in Delhi to meet Asha and decide whether or not to adopt her.

Waiting in line to go through customs, Kusum slipped two fingers through a belt loop of Ben's jeans, and he, automatically, caressed the back of her neck. Several times since Pitaji died they had discussed taking in Asha. Because all the neighborhood knew of Pitaji's rape of Anita, Asha was considered naturally inclined toward depravity. Grown men sometimes surprised her when she was walking alone and shoved her into walls and then pressed themselves against her. Now that Asha was fourteen and developing breasts, the molestations were more frequent and violent. Also, she was nearing the age when the U.S. government would make immigration difficult. "I won't let Anita force us into anything," Kusum said, looking up at Ben. She released Carolyn's hand and put both arms around her husband's waist. Ben was slender, with thinning curly hair. Beneath the airplane odor on his shirt, she found his smell of clean laundry and apples and wondered why she was so distrustful of people.

Outside, the light reminded Kusum of how little she had slept. The morning smell, thinly herbaceous, with whiffs of diesel and sweat, meant India to her. Everything was so much the same, she could have left yesterday. Kusum's stomach clenched. A crowd waited along the terminal windows. Terrorism in the early eighties had forced people to greet returning relatives on the airport's wide sidewalks.

Even after ten years, Anita was immediately recognizable. She had some wrinkles and her hair was almost white. She stood slightly at an angle, as if to keep a greater area under surveillance. Rajesh was near her. He had gotten so enormously fat that his head seemed supported by his chins.

"Say namaste to Kusum Mausiji," Anita said in English, and that's how Kusum realized that the tall, broad-shouldered girl standing a few feet away was Asha. Asha was wearing a long olive army raincoat and eating a sugar cube. Kusum's image of Asha was from a decade-old photograph in which she sat tiny between her parents on a sofa. Asha still had a child's moon face, round and soft, and this was the only part that looked her age. Kusum had expected someone less distinct.

"Namaste. Can I go to America with you?"

Laughing politely, Kusum replied, "If you want."

"I do. When?" Asha stared at Kusum.

"Quiet. They're too tired for your jokes," Anita said, again in English.

"We slept on the plane," Ben said, smiling in a puzzled and slightly conciliatory manner.

"Shall we take a bus?" Rajesh asked. Etiquette should have required that he, as the man from Kusum's side of the family, pay for a taxi. Rajesh owned two Pizza King restaurants and could afford the taxi.

"Shame, Rajesh," Anita said in Hindi. "We should pay." Rajesh grimaced and did not answer. Kusum knew Anita had little money. Inflation had destroyed the value of what little Pitaji had left her. She was planning to sell the flat she and Rajesh had inherited and either move in with Rajesh or rent a single room.

"You don't want the presents I brought?" Kusum said to Rajesh in Hindi, smiling as if she was teasing.

"Teach him a lesson," Asha said, and laughed.

A bed dominated the front room of the flat. Rajesh sat beside Ben on two chairs and showed him a five-hundred-rupee bill. "Three, four years ago, you almost never saw these. Soon they'll have bills as large as an undershirt." Kusum sat cross-legged next to Anita on the bed and looked at Asha's report cards. Everyone but Carolyn was drinking tea. The report cards were from first standard through ninth. In the last two years, Asha's marks had improved enormously.

The report cards, Kusum understood, were marketing materials for Asha, but she did not feel put upon. Kusum looked at Carolyn sitting near her and thought how difficult it was to be a good mother. Carolyn was staring anxiously at the twirling ceiling fan.

"It won't fall on you," Rajesh said to Carolyn.

Carolyn looked at him and then at the fan, which not only spun but shuddered, as if its speed was about to wrench the bolts out.

"God is kind," Asha added, "they tend to fall when their owners are asleep." She was sitting cross-legged on the floor. Carolyn's face tensed. Kusum noted the teasing. "Don't worry, every flat in India has one," Asha said.

Carolyn kept looking at the fan.

Ben laughed. He was sitting on a chair against a wall. "Tell Asha you're going to sleep on the side of the bed and make her sleep right beneath the fan," he said.

Carolyn looked shyly at her father and, unable to muster up the meanness to tease, said, "I'm going to sleep on the side," and giggled.

Asha laughed as well.

"Asha would be number one in her class, but the father of the student who is first is a doctor and gives free medicine to the principal," Anita complained.

Ben laughed.

"It's true," she said. "This is India."

"Does the principal take whatever medicine is given or does he ask for specific ones?" Ben asked.

Rajesh chuckled, and Anita began protesting.

"Mummy says the secret to success is working hard and cheating," Asha said. As everyone stopped in surprise, she grinned.

"You don't cheat, do you?" Ben asked.

"Asha, what's wrong with your head?" Anita asked. "Do you think a stick would fix it?"

"Take me to America." Asha addressed Kusum. "Here the answer to everything is 'stick.' "

Now Kusum worried whether Asha cheated. One more complication she would have to deal with if they adopted Asha. "Why did your marks go up so much the last two years?" Kusum asked.

"She began going to an all-girl school," Anita said.

"I found a friend with a VCR and I started watching movies and understood I would never have any of what I saw unless I worked," Asha added.

"What about wanting to make me happy?" Anita asked.

"You'll never be happy."

"I'm making more tea," Anita said, and stood. From the kitchen she called for Asha.

Asha hissed, "Stick," and left.

In the aisle, between the chairs along the wall and the bed, Kusum began unpacking the suitcases. To make space for her, Rajesh moved from beside Ben to the bed. She was glad to be able to talk with Rajesh without Anita present.

The sound of Asha's and Anita's voices arguing came from the kitchen.

Kusum took an electronic thermometer out of a suitcase and placed it on the bed. "Is that the one I asked for?" Rajesh inquired.

"Yes."

He took the thermometer from its box and, after spending several minutes discovering how to use it, put it in his ear. "Did Anita write crazy letters?" he asked Ben, because Ben was the husband.

"No," Ben said. Another reason Kusum loved him was that he was discreet, even on behalf of those who were not discreet themselves.

Rajesh appeared offended at being rebuffed so directly. A moment later he spoke in the patient voice of a friend delivering a warning. "Anita's crazy. Whether she acts it or not." Rajesh had written Kusum once in ten years, and then only to ask for the thermometer and a Walkman because he had learned she was coming to India. Listening to him, Kusum wondered why being away for so many years did not make things feel more unexpected.

"She must be unhappy," Ben said.

"What does that explain? I'm unhappy, too. What she says Pitaji did happened how many years ago? After all those years she suddenly had to tell people?"

Ben's face froze the way it did when he was offended and was waiting so that he would not speak from automatic disgust.

"Pitaji threatened Asha," Kusum said. She was thrilled to hear evidence that she need not adopt Asha and wanted to confirm the evidence.

"I don't believe that. Ask Asha what Pitaji was like and she'll only say good things."

"Why do you think Anita's crazy?" Kusum asked.

Rajesh took the thermometer from his ear and looked at his temperature. When he spoke, he sounded embarrassed. "After she told everyone about Pitaji—who knows whether everything she said was true—the family said she should get married and she wouldn't.".

"You want to use the bathroom, Carolyn?" Kusum said. This was the excuse she and Ben had developed to tell her to leave a room. Carolyn departed. "That's not crazy."

"But she kept telling everyone about Pitaji—who knows whether it was true—even when it would do no good. After he was dead. She told everyone in the compound. Did she expect them to be kind to her? Did she expect them to admire her bravery? Asha walks down the street now and boys grab their buttocks and show her their tongues."

"Is that true?" Ben asked.

"Asha keeps a razor blade with her in case she's attacked. Once, in her old school, she was suspended because she used it on a boy who attacked her."

"No," Ben exhaled. Kusum knew this story. When the first of Anita's letters arrived telling of Pitaji, Kusum had felt accused, as if she had stolen something. This sense had not faded over the years, and when she translated Anita's letters for Ben, she left out the details that most revealed the abjectness of Anita's and Asha's lives.

"Yes! Yes! This is what Anita's done."

"How is this Anita's fault?" Kusum asked, avoiding Ben's surprised, inquisitive glance.

"Everything had been quiet for twenty years when she started this."

"How have you helped?" Ben asked softly.

"You don't know my worries," Rajesh said. "Everybody thinks I have plenty of money, but I don't."

Ben waited a moment. "I ask only because it seems Anita and Asha have so little."

Rajesh looked out at the gallery and the blue sky. "I might let her live with me."

Kusum felt relieved that Ben had not asked her how she had helped her sister. She too stared out the door.

"Did you ever get Ma's saris?" Rajesh asked.

"No." She had never even thought of inheriting anything from her mother.

"Pitaji told Anita to divide up Ma's saris between you and her."

She knew Rajesh wanted her to be angry at Anita. Kusum wondered if she would have felt guilt without years of Ben's steady goodness as an example. What would Ben think if he could read her thoughts?

She said to Ben, "I'll go help Anita with the tea. She works hard."

The next morning Kusum kept trying to wake, but her eyes would only open a minute or two and then sleep reclaimed her. In her dreams she heard a whapping sound, and it was this sound that woke her at last and drew her to the door of the living room. Carolyn and Asha were beating the sofa with broom handles. First one hit; the sofa puffed dust several feet high; they laughed; then the other lashed. They were covered in sweat and grime. Carolyn was wearing the dress that she was supposed to have on when they went to see the relatives who had raised Kusum. Kusum felt her hand curving to grab Asha. Asha should have noticed Carolyn's dress and not let her play this ridiculous violent game.

When angry, Kusum tried to be especially sweet. "Baby, come here and kiss me." Saying this was enough to calm her. Carolyn walked to her and kissed the chin Kusum thrust forward and then the nose she tilted down. Asha briefly regarded the kissing and returned to thrashing the sofa. "You might tear the cover," Kusum said to her.

"Why should I care," Asha answered, looking over her shoulder. "I am going to America."

Kusum wondered if Asha was crazy. Even a child knows to hide the most blatantly selfish parts of herself. "You might not go," Kusum said, and struggling, forcing herself, continued, "I don't know if I want to bring you."

Asha did not turn around. She kept beating the sofa. She raised her arms far behind her back and whirred down as long a portion of the broom's handle as possible. "I'll begin shouting at the airport that I'm your daughter and you're leaving me behind. I can cry any time I want. You want to see me cry?"

"I'm joking, Mausiji," Asha said as Kusum left the living room.

In the kitchen Kusum found Ben photographing Anita. Anita was frying chiwra and Ben kept making her move back and forth because of the sunlight and the waves of heat from the oil. It was probably years since Anita was last photographed, and she followed his directions eagerly.

Kusum bathed quickly, and soon they were out of the flat and on their way to Bittu Mamaji's house, where Kusum had grown up.

The houses are taller in Sohan Ganj than in the Old Vegetable Market, and this makes the alleys shadowy, so that they seem narrower. The side streets were noisy and crowded in a way Kusum's memory had left out. Some of her memories had even been addled. The shop whose owner she used to defeat regularly at cards was nowhere near the bottom of a sloping alley. And there were things she had completely forgotten. Badly maimed cows were everywhere. They passed a calf that had had one of its hooves pulped, so that a leg ended in a long dark flap of skin. The calf was hobbling toward a pile of garbage in such stunned fly-specked misery that Ben picked up Carolyn to keep her from the vision.

Kusum and Ben carried plastic bags full of gifts. They had wrapped the presents, although most were specifically requested.

"Where did you play?" Carolyn asked.

"All over. We were told to stay in one or two alleys, but, of course, we didn't. I knew every building."

"Did you play with Aunt Anita?"

"We lived apart. I didn't see her much."

"Did she live far away?"

"No." It was only a ten-minute walk from where Anita had grown up and where she had. At this idea Kusum thought, I am no worse than most people. I am good for even coming to India and thinking of adopting Asha.

They came to Bittu Mamaji's house. It was so narrow that a scooter parked in front covered half its length. There was a water pump across the street. "I remember when we got running water. Till then I used to be the one who carried the buckets for the entire house. That pump is where I got my bad back." Kusum laughed then, because she did not want to sound self-pitying. The stone steps up to the first story where Bittu Mamaji lived had grown beveled over generations. "My buckets did that," she said, and laughed again.

Rohit was the first to see them. "Hello," he shouted, and led them into Bittu Mamaji's rooms. Vibha came out of a back room at his shout. "Kusum, sister," he said, and shook Ben's hand. Then he lifted Carolyn and said, "You're the one in the photos." They moved into Bittu Mamaji's rooms.

Bittu Mamaji appeared, putting on a shirt. He had sandalwood paste smeared on his forehead and was a round head on a round body. Sharmila followed him. Soon they were all sitting in the main room drinking tea. The bags of gifts were placed in a line against a wall and nobody mentioned them for a while.

The talk first scratched across the details of life in America. Was Morris Plains near enough to Jersey City for Kusum to deliver a rose to a friend of Bittu Mamaji's. "I could, if you wanted, Mamaji. But it's not nearby." Kusum had never liked Bittu. She had thought he was lazy and so had no right to the condescending voice he had always used. But for some reason she now wanted to please him. She wanted Bittu Mamaji to admire her.

"Have you seen an Indian rose?" Bittu Mamaji asked Carolyn.

No, she shook her head.

"We'll show you that. Yes, Rohit?"

"Yes."

"Come sit beside me," Bittu said to Carolyn, and she joined him on the bed. "We'll show you Indian clouds. We'll show you some Indian birds."

"So now you are a full believer in the BJP," Kusum said.

"I love my country. Yes," he replied quickly. "I would never leave where I was born."

"Why is Sonia Gandhi running for Parliament?" Ben asked.

"Some files about her husband's bribery are about to be released and she wants to stop that," Bittu Mamaji answered, his voice soft and polite before the family's son-in-law. "And this way she keeps enough power to let her daughter run for office later if Priyanka wants to."

Relatives began arriving. Among them was Koko Naniji, Kusum's grandfather's sister, the woman in the family Kusum liked most. Koko Naniji was well past eighty, with a deeply pockmarked face. "Namaste, daughter," she said, and squatted easily in one corner. She believed chairs made you sick.

"Namaste," Kusum answered. "Carolyn, go touch Koko Naniji's feet." Koko Naniji's smile broadened. Because Koko Naniji was so old, as far back as Kusum could remember she had always been more of the bully than the victim. She occupied a large room on the ground floor of the house Bittu Mamaji lived in. Periodically family members tried taking over the room. Once, when she was away on a pilgrimage, a nephew and his wife had been moved into her room. Upon returning and discovering this and finding that her demands that the room be returned to her were being ignored, she took a stick and broke everything that could be shattered in the room. Then she went out on the street and began shouting that her family was making her homeless and that she needed a place to sleep. All those years of authority had made Koko Naniji's craziness seem amiable.

Everyone was nervous around Ben's whiteness, and so the conversation remained at the level of facts. Ben explained his work.

Someone asked him if he knew that Indians had invented the airplane. He said it didn't surprise him, and there was a pleased murmur in the room. People spoke one at a time.

When enough of a crowd had gathered, Kusum began handing out gifts. Everyone was impressed by the wrapping and the little taped cards with their names on them. Somehow when the gift wrap was carefully eased off and the requested portable phone or the iron with the automatic off was discovered, there was a sense of surprise. A blood-pressure measurer was passed around. "Thank you, Mr. Ben," said people who felt uncomfortable applying the *ji* to a white man's name. A few acknowledged Kusum, but quietly, so as not to offend him. Koko Naniji received an elegantly thin shortwave radio, and she was so pleased that she clapped her hands and refused to let anyone touch it, even to put in batteries. "This is a good gift," she said to Ben, "but not enough for an educated girl who can go out and earn money."

Someone translated for Ben and he joked, "You haven't been getting my checks?" He acted so shocked that when this was translated back, Koko Naniji was convinced that somebody had been taking the envelopes in which the checks arrived.

Kusum had known that the vast majority of the compliments would go to Ben just because he was a man. But the meagerness of the praise she received left her impatient.

The gift-giving had released some of the tension in the room, so that multiple conversations, conversations over people's shoulders and between talking faces, started. Women came up to Kusum and offered her information about the vast extended network of relatives. But the girls she had grown up with had long since married and left the house. Those who spoke to her were either women so much older than she, or women who were introduced as the mother of some child or as capable of making an incredibly thin cauliflower paratha, that politeness kept Kusum from saying much.

Eventually lunch was served. Kusum sat on the floor next to Koko Naniji. The joy of the radio was still with her, and after the batteries were put in, Koko Naniji was delighted enough to tell a lie: "I dream of you all the time."

"What do you dream?" Kusum asked, puzzled.

"Things," Koko Naniji answered, looking at the radio in her hands and flipping through its stations. Kusum was disappointed despite herself at this halfhearted flattery. "Will you have one or two more children, daughter?"

"He doesn't want to," Kusum said, and then, deciding she should not act as needy as she felt, changed her answer to "We don't want to."

"A daughter is other people's wealth. If I had had sons, I would own my own house."

"I earn more than he does."

Urgently Koko Naniji said, "Don't tell people that. They gossip."

Kusum had not hoped to find much satisfaction from Koko Naniji and so did not continue asserting herself. "Anita wants me to adopt Asha and take her to America."

"The way we took you."

This suggestion of *quid pro quo* angered Kusum, and without thinking she said, "I was a servant in this house." Immediately regretting her words, she tried to distract Koko Naniji from the topic. "Rajesh says not to trust Anita."

"That wretch will say anything. He's gotten rich with his restaurants and so he acts better than everyone."

"Asha is strange."

"You're not running an orphanage. Make her work." Koko Naniji smiled slyly as she said this. Kusum was so hurt she felt lonely.

Anita's shrieks were jabbing in and out of Rajesh's shouts. Asha stood on the gallery in front of the flat. When Kusum and her family stopped just inside the compound's main gate, Asha called, "Carolyn, you want to see two monkeys dance?" A few of the compound's denizens were standing in the courtyard, talking to one another and regarding Asha. Now they turned their gazes on Kusum.

"The reason I wanted to be a grown-up," Ben said with a sigh, "was so I wouldn't have to listen to people fighting."

"I am going to stop them," Kusum replied. The rage she had not felt at Koko Naniji now made her light-headed.

"Let's go to a hotel," Ben said.

"You stay here."

Kusum hurried up the stairs to the gallery.

Anita was sitting on the sofa in the living room and Rajesh was standing near the common-room door. On the low table between the sofa and the love seats were two teacups and a plate of biscuits. "Fatso. How much more will you eat, fatso?" Anita was screeching.

Kusum came into the living room. "The whole world can hear."

"Let them die," Anita answered in a scream.

"Rajesh," Kusum said.

"I keep quiet while she goes on."

"I'm not stopping."

"What happened?"

"He wants me to pay for the food when we live together. I have to cook his food, of course, but I can't eat what I cook unless I pay."

"I want her to pay half the electricity and water, but she won't, so I say, pay for something, pay for the food."

"You're forcing me out of my home," Anita shrieked.

"This flat is mine also."

"What did you pay for it? What I have done and suffered."

"What did the will say?" Kusum asked.

"You. You," Anita hissed, shaking her finger at Kusum. "I don't have to follow that dead animal's will. This is not your business."

Kusum could feel the blood pulsing behind her eyeballs. "Where are the saris?"

"What saris?"

"Ma's."

"That was seven years ago. They were cheap cotton. Were you going to spend your days starching them?"

"They are fighting about saris," Asha called to the audience listening in the courtyard. "Saris that Ma left." Then she translated this into English for Carolyn and Ben.

Kusum looked at Asha standing in the sun on the gallery. Kusum hissed, "All the saris were bad?"

"Now they are whispering," Asha cried. "Unfair."

"Come in here," Kusum said.

"Neighbors, they want to keep secrets."

Kusum turned away from the gallery. "All the saris were bad?"

"They were mine."

"No, they weren't," Rajesh interceded.

"Ma wanted us to share."

"Why should I care about Ma?"

"You hate Ma, too?" Kusum was astonished at this, because she had never given Ma enough thought to imagine her capable of being disliked.

Before Anita could say anything, Rajesh spoke: "Ma was a saint. Ma loved all of us."

"Ma loved nobody."

"All you are is anger and unhappiness," Rajesh spat.

"What do you know about my life?" Kusum said.

"Who's talking about you?" Anita asked.

"What I've done? What people have done to me?" Kusum continued. Asha summarized this for the crowd. "Show me some kindness for even thinking about taking Asha. That lunatic who's shouting everything to the neighbors." Asha translated this as well, and Kusum felt her own cruelty.

"You want thank yous. Thank you. Thank you. Those saris were mine, but if you take Asha to America, I will say thank you all my life."

Ben entered the room. His whiteness brought instant silence. He sat on the bed. The silence continued. Carolyn remained on the gallery with Asha. Rajesh sat down on one of the love seats. Kusum settled beside Ben.

"Kusum." Ben rarely used her name, almost always preferring an endearment. "You don't wear saris. What would you have done with them, tear them and make bandages?" At first Kusum thought she had not heard him. The joke felt like an insult, like being called a fool before people who were trying to swindle her.

He opened his mouth, but the look on her face must have stopped him.

Anita laughed.

"The world you live in," Kusum said slowly to Ben. "What's a joke there, in your world—that's the only reality in this world. It's the only reality one can think about, that one can imagine." Then she turned back to Anita and, wanting to cry, hissed, "My saris."

"I don't have them anymore." Anita waved a hand in the air.

"None of them?"

"Thank you. Thank you," Anita said, and laughed. "I want some thank yous also. At least twelve. I want thank yous for living this life while you lived yours."

Kusum watched Anita and wondered why she had believed kindness could matter to Anita.

"You're whining, Kusum," Ben said.

"Whining," Kusum repeated.

"Whining like a baby," Anita said.

"You don't care about saris," Ben added. Kusum looked at Ben and thought he did not love her. She wanted to cry but decided she would not.

B en was packing a nylon duffel bag with what they might need for the trip to the Taj Mahal. They were going to stay overnight in Agra and then return to a hotel in Delhi. Kusum was sitting on a chair in the front bedroom watching Ben.

Anita hurried between them down the aisle to the gallery. She had a plastic bag full of trash in one hand. She went down the gallery to the courtyard.

"I love you," Kusum said, wanting him to tell her he loved her and wondering whether she would believe him if he did.

"We have so many years to lean against. A fight doesn't matter," Ben said.

"We're rich so we can waste."

"I love you." He smiled and kept packing.

The words were not enough. Her world was a joke to him.

A few minutes later Anita returned, closed the door, and went to the kitchen.

"Am I wonderful?" Kusum asked.

"Perfect."

"I need specifics." Kusum looked at Ben and wondered how long it would take for the fear she was feeling to dissipate.

"Your shoulders are especially nice."

"So I can carry heavy things. I need more."

"No matter how much love you need, I can love you more."

Kusum did not believe him. Her world was ridiculous and abject, and if he could love anyone, why love someone like her?

The doorbell rang, and Kusum stood and opened the door. The garbage woman was standing there. She looked surprised to see Ben. "You live here?" she asked Kusum.

"I'm visiting."

The garbage woman, tiny, with hands so rough they appeared yellow, stinking of rot, regarded them suspiciously. "Who lives here?"

"Why?"

"First, you answer my question."

"Anita," Kusum shouted, and Anita instantly appeared.

The garbage woman opened her fist and a ShopRite plastic bag dangled forth. "This is yours?" she asked Anita, using the informal you.

"No."

"Whitey didn't bring it?"

"No."

"Whore." The garbage woman turned to Ben and held up the ShopRite bag. She pointed at him and then at the bag.

Ben asked Kusum to explain what was happening. The garbage

woman must have guessed the meaning of the exchange, because she said, "This woman doesn't want to pay me to take out the garbage and so throws it in my wheelbarrow when I'm not looking."

"Every two months she raises the prices," Anita said. "This is extortion."

Kusum explained the accusations to Ben, and he started laughing. He laughed so much he sat down on the bed.

The garbage woman appeared amazed at the sight of a white man laughing.

Ben picked up his camera from the bed and said, "Let's take a photo of her hitting Anita."

The garbage woman had straightened her back as soon as the camera was lifted.

"Ask her," Ben said.

Kusum did, and the garbage woman smiled and held up a fist. Ben took a picture of her shaking the ShopRite bag. Kusum was astonished. Anita laughed.

Carolyn and Asha wandered in from the roof, where they had been watching kites being flown. Ben introduced Carolyn to the garbage woman. "You look alike," the garbage woman said politely, though all she probably meant, Kusum knew, was that both Carolyn and he were fair-skinned. Carolyn leaned against her father's leg and his hand dropped to her head.

Kusum watched this and thought that she would like Carolyn to have Ben's capacity to move through worlds, carrying jokes and kindness and possibility with her. Then she felt Ben's love. She felt this and then, for the first time, felt the sharp shape of her guilt at having lived her life while Anita lived hers.

A sha stared out the airplane window. Kusum sat beside her. Kusum and her family had flown back to America after agreeing to adopt Asha. Kusum had returned to India a week ago to finish the adoption paperwork.

Asha had known for four months that she was leaving India. But in the last few weeks she had been inconsolable, had begun to walk and talk in her sleep. At the Indira Gandhi Airport, she kept saying, "I was lying. I don't want to go." When the plane rose over the dust of Delhi, Asha pulled the red airplane blanket over her head and wept till they were over the ocean, at which point she fell asleep.

Now the Air India flight had just left Heathrow.

"Are we over a park?" Asha asked, turning to look at Kusum.

Kusum leaned over Asha's shoulder. The land was a perfect green, carefully divided by broad black lines. "Those are paths?"

"Highways." Kusum stared past Asha at the landscape tilting beneath them until it righted itself and disappeared from view.